0 00 30 0436099 0

THE PERILS OF
PURSUING A PRINCE

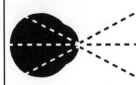

This Large Print Book carries the
Seal of Approval of N.A.V.H.

THE PERILS OF
PURSUING A PRINCE

JULIA LONDON

WHEELER PUBLISHING

An imprint of Thomson Gale, a part of The Thomson Corporation

THOMSON

GALE

Detroit • New York • San Francisco • New Haven, Conn. • Waterville, Maine • London

LIBRARY OF CONGRESS CATALOGING-IN-PUBLICATION DATA

London, Julia.
  The perils of pursuing a prince / by Julia London.
    p. cm. — (The desperate debutantes) (Wheeler Publishing large print romance)
  ISBN-13: 978-1-59722-620-2 (alk. paper)
  ISBN-10: 1-59722-620-3 (alk. paper)
  1. Wales — Fiction. 2. Large type books. I. Title.
PS3562.O78745P47 2007
813'.54—dc22   2007027352

Published in 2007 by arrangement with Pocket Books,
a division of Simon & Schuster, Inc.

Printed in the United States of America on permanent paper
10 9 8 7 6 5 4 3 2 1

For Klo, Nagno, and Sanman.
I could not make up
better siblings than you.

Wrth gicio a brathu,
mae cariad yn magu.

— a Welsh proverb

(Whilst kicking and biting, love develops.)

ONE

For some inexplicable reason, the first thing that occurred to Greer Fairchild when three men — robbers, for all she knew — stopped the coach in which she and Mr. Percy were traveling was that the death of Mrs. Smithington, to whom Greer was a traveling companion, was not only tragic, but extremely inconvenient.

They had almost reached the foreboding Llanmair, having lumbered up a rutted road for the better part of an afternoon, yet the day's gloomy light had not faded so much that Greer couldn't distinguish the ancient gray castle from the crag on which it sat, rising high above the woods and mountains that surrounded it.

It was an imposing structure, four stories high, built with gray stone, and anchored by four turrets in each corner. They were so close to the castle! They were so close to ending Greer's ordeal, and now this!

"Stay here," Mr. Percy said, looking quite grim when the coach rattled and groaned to a halt at the approach of the three riders. "I shall speak with them." He climbed out of the carriage, shut the door soundly, and strode forward to the three men who now stood between Greer and the man in the castle who held her inheritance.

"This is not to be borne," she muttered under her breath. Not after all she'd endured in the last year. Not after her guardian aunt's death and the endless hours she'd spent with Mrs. Smithington in public coaches with people who thought nothing of bringing their chickens and dogs along with them. Not after all the bouncing she'd endured along every pit and rut as they'd traversed empty moors, or losing sight of the sun in forests so thick with trees that no light could filter through. She'd come within a quarter of a mile of the gates to what she hoped was her final destination, only to be stopped.

It was *extremely* vexing.

Greer peered out the window to where Mr. Percy had confronted the three men with his legs braced wide and his arms akimbo. She groaned with exasperation and laid her head against a torn squab. She supposed she ought to feel frightened of the men, being as far from civilization as she was, but she felt nothing but exhaustion and the grime of hard travel on her body. Not to mention the disgust of having traveled three days in the same gown, for it was bloody cold in Wales and the poor gown was the warmest garment she possessed.

"*Astoundingly* inconvenient," she said aloud.

Really, if Mrs. Smithington hadn't died when and where she did, poor thing, Greer might have made this trip to Wales in the summer, when the sun was bright and warm. Not now, in late autumn, when the weather was dreadfully cold and damp. She might have reached Llanmair, where the Prince of Thieves — as she'd come to think of him — supposedly lived in half the time it had taken them over these ridiculously muddy and pitted roads.

But then poor Mrs. Smithington had lain down for a nap on the very day Greer reached her uncle's dilapidated and long-sought estate. The elderly woman had just lain down and never awoke. It was a horrible way to die — alone, with no relatives save one distant nephew, her heir, in London. While it was true Mrs. Smithington could be entirely too vexing, Greer had developed a certain exasperated fondness for her, and would not have wished such a lonely death on her.

Mrs. Smithington's tragic death, on top of everything else, made Greer wish she'd never come back to Wales. If it weren't for good Mr. Percy, she surely would have turned back for London along with Mrs. Smithington's effects. But Mr. Percy had encouraged her to continue on her journey.

The journey had begun a year ago, when Greer's legal guardian, Aunt Cassandra, Lady Downey, had died unexpectedly. Aunt Cassandra's second husband, Lord Downey, had no desire to support Greer or her cousins, Ava and Phoebe, and had firmly and eagerly stated he was prepared to give them to whoever asked for their hand, regardless of social standing or fortune, or *their* wishes in the matter.

That was intolerable enough, but as Greer was merely the ward of Lady Downey, she was at the greatest disadvantage. She had no family or fortune left with which to entice a proper suitor, even if Lord Downey were inclined to see her married well. All she had of her past was an old letter, a few minor possessions that had belonged to her mother, whom she could scarcely remember, and fragments of memories that included an elderly uncle, a distant father, and no siblings.

Desperate to keep herself and her cousins from the fate Lord Downey would condemn them to, and knowing that her father had died several years ago without siring an heir, Greer had embarked on this wretched journey to find her uncle and ask after an inheritance she wasn't even certain existed. She had no knowledge of her father's fortune, or if he even had one, but she thought certainly there must have been *something* left of the man's life. And if there was something left, it surely would have been left to her father's brother.

It was a fragile hope, but a hope nonetheless.

Unfortunately, the only way she could possibly afford to travel to Wales was as the companion of the ancient and constantly complaining Mrs. Smithington, who wanted to see the "wild bits of England."

After traveling for *months* in the company of Mrs. Smithington, Greer had finally reached Bredwardine, an English village on the border of Wales, where she found her uncle's estate shockingly dilapidated. The vague memory she held of a grand home with lush lawns and fountains was a fantasy. The house was little more than a manor, not a mansion, and there was no lawn sur-rounding it, just a small yard with an old pig wandering aimlessly about.

The only inhabitants of the house were an aging caretaker and his wife. Moreover, most of the rooms had been emptied of furniture long ago — there was no place to sit, no place to rest, save two rooms at the very top of the stairs, which, for reasons Greer did not want to contemplate, still boasted two old and lumpy featherbeds. And as Greer had wandered about that afternoon pondering what on earth she would do now, Mrs. Smithington had begun to complain of feeling poorly.

Greer thought nothing of it at the time. Mrs. Smithington had complained endlessly since they'd left London. They'd no sooner left the outer limits of the city when she'd begun to carp about the weather (too rainy), the condition of the roads (too rutted), and the fact that there really wasn't very much to see once one traveled through so many miles of rolling countryside (too many trees and too far from London).

At first, Greer had found the woman's complaining amusing in an odd sort of way, but it quickly grew tiresome, especially when Greer was the one forced to hold hat-boxes or small trunks in her lap while they traveled in tight public coaches.

But then Mr. Percy had boarded their coach in Ledbury and had proceeded to compliment Mrs. Smithington's youthful smile and claimed to be shocked by her advanced age. Dear Mr. Percy, tall and handsome with brown locks and shining hazel eyes, could have charmed the gray right from Mrs. Smithington's head if he'd so desired.

By the time they reached Herefordshire, Mrs. Smithington had persuaded Mr. Percy to accompany them to Wales with the excuse that "in the company of a gentleman, no one will prey on two poor unmarried females."

Greer imagined that even the most depraved of villains would be deterred by Mrs. Smithington's constant complaining, but Mr. Percy's attention to Mrs. Smithington had been a welcome relief for her. Not only was he exceedingly charming, he was also a very good escort. He was very solicitous of their needs.

Actually, it was in the course of Mr. Percy's particular attention to *her* that Greer learned what had happened to her uncle. On occasion, when Mrs. Smithington would retire early, Greer and Mr. Percy would sit by the fire in whatever inn they happened to be residing in and chat. He would invariably compliment her — her eyes as blue as the deep sea, her hair as black as India ink. Greer found his compliments lovely, but having been out two Seasons in London, she was hardly diverted by such talk.

Eventually, he felt comfortable enough to explain how a gentleman of his obvious standing had come to be riding the public coach. As it happened, he was returning to Wales to try and reason with a ruthless relative who had stolen his rightful inheritance and cast him out of his family home, all for the crime of having an English father. It was a sinister tale, and while Mr. Percy put a very brave face on it, Greer thought his relative criminally deplorable.

The story was so deplorable that she felt compelled to likewise confess that she was looking for her paternal uncle, the last known male relative on her father's side, who had hailed from Bredwardine. But when she mentioned her uncle's name to Mr. Percy, a strange look came over his face. "Randolph Vaughan?" he'd repeated incredulously, and suddenly leaned forward, took Greer's hand in his, looked at her with eyes full of sympathy, and said, "Miss Fairchild, it is my sad duty to inform you that Mr. Randolph Vaughan has . . . *died.*"

Greer gasped. *"Died?"*

"Kicked by a horse he was gelding. The poor man lingered for days but never recovered."

"Oh," Greer had said, quite at a loss upon hearing the unexpected news. "Oh my."

"Ah, but you mustn't fret," Mr. Percy had said with a confident squeeze of his hand. "I know there are more of your kin in Wales."

"More?" she'd asked, confused. "But I thought my Uncle Vaughan was the last one."

"Of *your* family, perhaps. But his wife's family was rather prominent."

Greer had felt quite confused, and remembered asking, "If I may, sir . . . how do you know so much about the Vaughan family?"

"Oh, that's quite simple, really," he'd said with a charming smile that instantly put her at ease. "Wales is rather like a small village — Welshmen are well known to one another."

Welshmen.

Greer turned her attention outside the carriage and saw one of the men suddenly swing off his horse and put a hand on his waist, revealing a gun. She gasped as Mr. Percy swept off his hat and pushed a hand through his thick brown hair, then replaced his hat. He did not seem to be terribly frightened of the gun.

But then again, Mr. Percy was not the sort to be easily rattled. The day Greer had found Mrs. Smithington cold and stiff in that bed on the upper floor at Bredwardine, she'd given in to despair. After the shock of finding her companion dead, Greer had realized she had very little money, was far from any semblance of proper civilization, and was no closer to having what she'd come for than when she'd left London. But Mr. Percy was instantly at her side, soothing her and helping her to decide what must be done, and thankfully, making all the proper arrangements.

And when Mrs. Smithington was buried in the church cemetery, and arrangements had been made to have her effects sent back to London, Mr. Percy had asked, "You mean to go on, don't you?"

"Go *on?*" Greer had cried. "Where might I go? My companion is dead, my uncle is dead, and his estate is falling down. I have no place to go but back to London, and I've scarcely the money for that."

"I shall of course escort you wherever you choose," Mr. Percy had said at once. "I am at your service, Miss Fairchild."

"I couldn't possibly impose." Nor could

she possibly risk the scandal of traveling with a man who was not her kin. She was walking on precarious ground as it was with Lord Downey, and besides, Ava and Phoebe would be positively apoplectic if they knew Mrs. Smithington had died and that she was traveling with a man she scarcely knew.

But once again, Mr. Percy had been very persuasive. "It is no imposition, I assure you! I've no fixed schedule. Furthermore, I know of a solicitor who might be able to direct you to the person who has taken over your uncle's affairs." At Greer's curious look, he said, "Your uncle has died, but you may yet be entitled to an inheritance."

When Greer demurred, he'd said with great authority, "Here now, Miss Fairchild! You've come all this way on your quest. You cannot abandon it without at least *speaking* to the gentleman. If he has no news for you, then I shall help you catch the first coach for London. There is little harm in asking, is there?"

She couldn't argue that point.

The solicitor, Mr. Davies, was an elderly man whose office was in a very old building with sagging wood floors. After Mr. Percy had gallantly used his kerchief to dust off a chair for her, Greer explained her situation to the diminutive man: that she suspected

19

she was her father's only heir, but wasn't certain, given her estrangement from her father at an early age.

Mr. Davies said nothing as she spoke. When she finished, he donned a pair of spectacles, ran his hands through a shock of stiff gray hair, then searched through a stack of papers and binders. He finally found a large leather binder, from which he pulled a sheaf of papers. He laid them out on his crowded desk and proceeded to study them, muttering to himself while Greer sat impatiently across the desk from him, Mr. Percy standing attentively behind her.

After a time, Mr. Davies removed his spectacles and peered closely at Greer. "Indeed, you are your father's only living heir," he said flatly.

Greer gasped with surprise and elation; Mr. Percy put a steadying hand on her shoulder.

"Unfortunately, as no provision was made to find you, and your whereabouts were unknown, the estate of your father, Mr. Yorath Vaughan, passed to his brother, Mr. Randolph Vaughan, who is your late uncle. Mr. Randolph Vaughan likewise had no surviving heirs, and upon his death, the whole of *his* estate — which included your father's portion, naturally — was passed to the husband of his deceased wife's deceased sister, his lordship Rhodrick Glendower."

Greer blinked, trying to follow. Mr. Davies returned his spectacles to his face and folded his hands on top of his desk. "He is known in England, indeed in Bredwardine, as the Earl of Radnor. But not three miles from here, in Wales, he is known by another name."

Mr. Percy's hand tightened on Greer's shoulder. "I beg your pardon, but you can hardly mean —"

"I do indeed, Mr. Percy!" the solicitor said grandly, obviously quite pleased with himself. "Miss Fairchild's inheritance — if indeed it does exist — has passed along with your uncle's estate to none other than the prince of Powys!"

"Who?" Greer asked as Mr. Percy's hand slid away from her shoulder.

"The *Prince of Powys,*" Mr. Davies articulated carefully. "A hereditary title in the eyes of the English, perhaps, but in *Wales,* madam, he is known simply as 'The Prince.' He is not a man to be trifled with."

Honestly, she didn't care if he was the bloody king of England — he had her inheritance. "How do I find him?"

Mr. Davies slammed shut the leather binder, from which arose a cloud of dust so

21

thick that Greer had to wave it from her face. "At Llanmair, of course, where all the princes of Powys have resided before him and shall continue to reside long after he is gone."

"And where, precisely, is Llanmair?" she pressed.

The solicitor chuckled low, pointed at the small dingy window. "West. At the base of the Cambrians, in a wood thick with game."

Greer squinted at the old man. He held her gaze, daring her to challenge his poetic yet impractical directions. As he seemed the intractable sort, Greer stood, fished in her reticule for a crown, and held it out to Mr. Davies. "Thank you, sir. You've been very helpful."

Mr. Davies extended his bony hand and snatched the coin. "Good luck, Miss Fairchild," he'd said, chuckling in a manner that sent a shiver down Greer's spine.

Naturally, Mr. Percy persuaded her to continue on and to hire a private coach. Greer was rather reluctant to do so, given her dwindling funds, but Mr. Percy thought it absolutely necessary for traveling so deeply into Wales, which, naturally, he convinced her she must do. "There was something left of your father's estate, Miss Fairchild, just as you've hoped! Of course you must go on! But it is a hard journey, and in the privacy of a hired coach, I should think there would be less speculation as to who you are."

That was his very polite way of reminding her there was a way to avoid scandal. Still, she debated it — she had just enough money to go back to London, or, with a little luck, to claim her inheritance. At the time, she believed Mr. Percy was right. She had come a long way and she might as well finish her journey. So against her better judgment, her sense of propriety, and every blessed thing she had learned at Aunt Cassandra's knee, Greer set out with Mr. Percy in the direction of Llanmair.

In a private coach.

That *she* had hired.

It wasn't until they were far from any village or sign of civilization that Mr. Percy confessed that the prince of Powys was none other than his wretched uncle, the man who had ruined him.

"You can't mean it!" Greer had cried, shocked.

"You shouldn't be surprised, really," he'd said cavalierly. "The man wields considerable influence in these parts. How else could he have . . . ?" His voice trailed off, and with a sidelong glance at Greer, he clenched his jaw and shifted his gaze out the window.

"I beg your pardon — how could he have *what?*"

"I cannot say, Miss Fairchild. You are too . . . too pure to hear of the *vile* nature of that man."

Greer had snorted at that. As she was traveling into Wales with a man who was not her husband or otherwise related to her, she rather thought goodness was no longer a consideration. "I have made my decision and I am quite determined, sir. You must tell me what you know of this man, for now he has *my* inheritance as well as yours."

"Yes, of course, you must stand up for what is rightfully yours," he'd agreed instantly. "You are to be commended for your bravery, Miss Fairchild."

She wasn't the least bit brave, she was desperate. "Then please do tell me what I must know."

With a sigh, he'd looked at the broad palms of his hand. "In addition to seizing my lands, the details of which you are well aware, the blackguard also compromised the daughter of a solicitor in Rhayader, and then steadfastly refused to do the honorable thing by her."

Greer blinked; Mr. Percy suddenly surged forward, put his hand on her knee, and said

24

low, "But that was not the worst of it. Soon after his refusal, the young woman went missing. The entire county looked for her high and low . . . but she was nowhere to be found."

"Oh dear God," Greer exclaimed, her mind racing with all the horrible things that could befall a woman in a land as remote as Wales.

"But then, by some miracle, in the middle of a vast forest comprising thousands of acres, *he* found her." He leaned back, removed his hand from her knee. "She was dead, of course. Broken neck."

"Oh God, *no!*"

"He alone led the authorities to her body, *miles* from Llanmair."

"How tragic!"

But Mr. Percy narrowed his gaze and suddenly surged forward again. "I think you do not fully take my meaning, Miss Fairchild. Twenty-five thousand acres of virgin land and forest surround Llanmair. It is impossible to traverse them all. Yet somehow, *he* managed to find her in a very remote ravine."

His implication sank in, and Greer blinked. "You mean . . . *murder?*" she whispered.

Mr. Percy shrugged and sat back again.

"There are many who believe it is so. There is no end to the man's depravity."

Now, several days later, as Greer looked out the coach's window at that huge foreboding castle and the three mysterious men, a shiver ran down her spine. Suddenly, she needed to be near Mr. Percy and opened the coach door and stepped out just as she caught sight of a rider coming toward them. Mr. Percy saw him, too, for he instantly turned and held up a hand. "Stay in the coach, Miss Fairchild!"

But Greer did not move — she was transfixed by the approaching rider.

He was thundering toward them at a dangerous speed. His greatcoat billowed out behind him like the wings of an enormous bird and he leaned tightly over the neck of a large black steed that sent up thick clods of earth from his hooves. It seemed almost as if the man didn't see them standing there, as if he intended to ride right through them. Greer cried out, darting behind Mr. Percy just as the rider reined to a hard stop, causing the horse to rear. The steed's enormous legs churned the air as he came down, and the man reined the horse again, hard to the right, away from the other horses.

With a tight hold on the agitated horse, he glared at them all, and as Greer stepped out from behind Mr. Percy, he turned his glacial green eyes to her.

She'd never felt such a shiver in all her life.

The rider was older than she, perhaps by ten years or more. A scar traversed one side of his face, from the corner of his eye to the middle of his cheek, disappearing into the shadow of his beard. His jaw was clenched tightly shut, and beneath his hat, she glimpsed the distinctive black hair of the Welsh with a bit of gray at the temples. He was not a handsome man and not even the least bit agreeable — in fact, he looked quite fierce.

And angry.

Mr. Percy instantly stepped in front of Greer and spoke in Welsh. Whatever he said, the man spurred his horse forward a few steps so that he could look at Greer again with those frightfully cold green eyes.

At the same moment, a fat raindrop hit the top of Greer's bonnet, startling her. It was followed by another, and then several more, and she impulsively said to the man, from whom she had not been able to take her gaze, "If you please, we should like to pass. We mean to reach —"

Mr. Percy clamped down on her forearm and spoke in Welsh, and again the man did not respond, but looked at Greer.

"I beg your pardon," she whispered to Mr. Percy, "but I think we should explain who we are."

"What do you think I have been attempting to do this last quarter of an hour?" he responded curtly under his breath. "If you will just allow me —"

"But it is beginning to rain," Greer said, noting the hint of despair in her own voice, and looked at the man in black again. "I don't mean to be untoward, sir, but I fear we shall be caught in the rain."

The man said nothing. Greer was getting wetter by the moment and stepped forward. "We have important business with the earl of Radnor . . . the, ah . . . the *prince* . . . so please do kindly allow us to pass."

Once again, her plea was met with cold silence. Greer glanced anxiously at Mr. Percy. "Do you think he understands me?" she whispered.

"Oh . . . I am quite certain that he does," Mr. Percy said assuredly.

If the man did or did not, he refused to make any indication, and her fear began to melt into anger at his rudeness. She lifted her chin as she stared at his rugged face, her eyes steady on his.

He surprised her by saying something in

Welsh to the three men who stood between them. He then reined his horse about and rode off just as quickly as he'd arrived.

"What did he say?" Greer asked, surprised by his abrupt departure.

Mr. Percy sighed and gestured for her to step into the carriage. "He gave us leave to pass," he muttered, and taking her arm firmly, handed her up to the coach. He glanced up at the driver. "Carry on," he barked, and followed Greer inside.

When the coach began to move, Greer wearily brushed rainwater from her cloak and said, "His lordship may very well be a murderer, but I intend to let him know how unbearably rude his man is."

Mr. Percy sighed irritably. "Miss Fairchild, that unbearably rude man *was* the prince of Powys!"

Oh dear *God.*

TWO

The three horsemen escorted the coach the remainder of the short drive to the castle gates. Once the coach passed through, it came to a halt in a courtyard large enough to host more than a dozen carriages at once.

Llanmair was an enormous structure, a palace more than a castle, its size deceptive from a distance. The boughs of ancient trees reached across a large round of lawn. It was an incongruous sight. After traveling through the wild forests, Greer had expected peasants and barnyard animals, not a civilized setting. But as she climbed down from the coach, she looked up and noticed birds' nests on various nooks and crannies in the castle's walls. In those nests were enormous birds. Some were black, others were red, some of them preened while others rested, and some of them simply watched.

Greer was instantly reminded of a line from *Macbeth: "The raven himself is hoarse,*

That croaks the fatal entrance of Duncan. . . ."

A shiver ran down her spine as two foot-men, dressed in black livery, appeared in the main doors to the castle and hurried forward to the carriage. Behind them, another man, dressed in the black and gray uniform of a butler, walked toward them. When he reached them, he bowed low and said, *"Bonjour."*

"Bonjour," Greer said politely, but Percy responded in Welsh.

The butler answered in kind, and Percy, nodding to whatever he said, offered his arm to Greer. "We are to be shown inside."

A small finger of fear warned her against it — she was uncomfortable in her inability to understand the language, and was walk-ing into the home of a murderer where predatory birds nested — but Percy squeezed her hand reassuringly and per-suaded her once more.

Stepping into the castle was almost like stepping into another century. It seemed medieval — the interior was dark and close, the stone walls damp. They passed through a small entry into a large foyer, where a stunning array of swords and armor was displayed on the walls — an entire ancient regiment might have been outfitted from those walls. There were also several banners

31

and standards bearing Welsh words and the symbol of a flying red dragon that Greer vaguely recollected from her childhood, and an enormous mirror to reflect what little light there was.

The butler continued on, as did Greer and Percy, down a dark corridor, through one of the turrets, and yet another corridor lined with dark paintings and more accoutrements of war.

At the end of that long corridor, the butler opened a pair of oak doors and said something in Welsh.

Percy led her through.

The room might have been quite grand had it been properly furnished. It was painted a warm shade of yellow, the draperies were made of floral chintz, and the ceiling was painted with a scene of someone being lifted up to heaven on the wings of angels. At the far end of the large room was a small grouping of overstuffed furniture situated around a carved marble hearth that stood at least six feet tall. That was all. There were no other chairs, no console, no commodes, and no great pieces of art.

Greer tilted her head back to look at the ceiling while Percy spoke briefly with the butler. When the butler had quit the room, Percy joined her looking up at the ceiling.

"Sir Thomas Lawrence is the artist," he said, and walked to a window and looked out. "He has painted several of the portraits within these walls."

Sir Thomas Lawrence! He was a famous British artist, and the name delighted Greer. She was a great admirer of fine works of art, and with her bonnet dangling from her hand she turned in a circle twice, examining the intricate details of the painting. It was magnificent, far more impressive than anything she'd seen in London.

When she lowered her gaze, she walked to where Percy stood and looked down, exclaiming with delight at the gardens laid out below her. Even though dusk was descending, she could see how extensive they were — row upon row of shrubbery, expertly shaped into circles and arcs and figure eights, and surrounding stands of roses, arbors, and elaborate fountains throughout. The foliage was planted down a gentle slope that ended at the forest's edge, an enchanting and stark contrast to the cold entrance to Llanmair. "I've rarely seen such beauty," Greer said, awed.

"The prince is quite well known for his gardens," Percy said. "Rather remarkable, isn't it, given his nature?"

Indeed, it was hard to understand how a

thief and murderer could take such care with a garden. She rather expected him to spend his time torturing small animals and frightening children.

Percy must have sensed her apprehension because he turned a smile to her and said, "You mustn't worry, Miss Fairchild. Upon my honor, I will protect you — he can do you no harm, I assure you."

"Thank you," she said gratefully, not relishing a meeting with the ogre of Powys under any circumstance, and putting aside the question of how, exactly, Percy would stop a determined ogre from anything. "But the sooner we demand that he return to us what is rightfully ours, the sooner we may quit this place," she added.

"Yes," he said thoughtfully. He glanced out the window, then abruptly put his back to the vista. "If I may," he said, taking her hand in his. He averted his eyes for a moment, then turned a very tender gaze on her. "If I may be so bold, Miss Fairchild. I have given our rather unique situation some thought, and I would like you to know that I —"

The door suddenly swung open with such force that Percy started, dropping Greer's hand and stepping away from her as the ogre swept into the room, still wearing his riding cloak and flanked by two enormous wolfhounds. His face was dark; his black hair with the hint of gray swept back and to his shoulders. He strode into the room with an almost indiscernible limp, halting in the middle, his legs braced apart. He glared coldly at the two of them with a pair of vivid green eyes that slanted slightly and said something softly in Welsh. The two hounds instantly moved and simultaneously sat on either side of him.

Those eyes made Greer shiver for a second time today.

He did not, however, spare Greer a glance, but spoke Welsh to Percy in a deep, low voice. Greer had the impression that he never raised his voice because there was no need — she believed he could send long tentacles of fear into a person's heart by speaking with the utmost calm.

Whatever he said, it caused Mr. Percy to color slightly. Mr. Percy held out his hand to Greer, which she took, for lack of certainty what else to do. "May I present Miss Greer Fairchild," he said.

Greer reflexively sank into a curtsy.

The man eyed her boldly, his icy gaze sweeping over the top of her head, down her body to the tips of her boots, and back up again.

She couldn't move, as transfixed by him as he was curious about her. His presence seemed too large for the room somehow, too much man for so delicate a space. It occurred to her that she was looking at one who wielded such power that no one dared to question him, and her knees began to feel a little weak at the thought of having to ask him for her inheritance.

But she had to ask. She couldn't succumb to cowardice now, not in the eleventh hour. She desperately wanted to be done with this ugly business as soon as possible so that she might flee this wretched place and never look back. With a vision of her being safely inside the coach she'd hired and being whisked away, she forced herself to speak. "Your highness," she said.

He raised a brow. He gave the distinct impression that he did not speak a word that wasn't carefully chosen. "I am an earl, Miss Fairchild. Not a king."

Greer didn't know which startled her more — the perfectly spoken English or the way his eyes seemed to bore right through her. "M-my lord," she said. "Please do forgive our intrusion . . . but it was necessary that we come all this way."

He nodded curtly and turned away — much like a cat would turn away from some trifling bit of prey — and strode to a console with that slight limp in his gait. He poured a whiskey from one of several crystal decanters there, then glanced at Percy from the corner of his eye. "Whiskey?"

"Please," Percy said. Radnor — Powys — whatever his name, gestured lamely to the contents of the console and moved away, leaving Percy to serve himself.

How ill-mannered! What was the point of such abominable behavior, other than to humiliate Percy?

But the man was looking at Greer now, his eyes brashly raking over her body as he tossed the whiskey down his throat. "You are Welsh," he said as he put the tot aside.

She hardly knew if it was a question or an observation. "I am." She clasped her hands anxiously behind her back. "My parents were Welsh but resided in the English village of Bredwardine. Vaughan was their name."

"Then how have you come to be known by the very English name of Fairchild?"

She was reminded of the suffering Percy was forced to endure at this man's hands merely because he was half English. "My mother died when I was very young, my lord. My father, Yorath Vaughan, had no wish to raise a daughter alone, so he consented to allow my mother's half sister, Lady Bingley, to take me in. She lived in England, and when my father died, Lord Bingley gave me his surname of Fairchild."

The prince nodded thoughtfully as he brazenly studied her figure, his gaze lingering on her décolletage as he scratched behind the ears of one of the hounds. "And what business," he asked in that soft, cold voice, "have you with me?"

Greer could not say what happened to her at that moment — perhaps it was nothing more than the overwhelming exhaustion that had been building in her for so many days, or perhaps it was the way he spoke to her, as if she had no right to seek him out at all. Whatever happened, it vanquished her fear, forced aside the fatigue and frustration, and filled her with weary indignation. "My business is very simple," she said, her voice calmer and stronger than she had expected. "You have what is rightfully mine."

He seemed to almost smile, but Percy quickly said something in Welsh. The ogre did not look at Percy, but kept his gaze on Greer, his darkly stoic expression working to goad her into a fury greater than all of his alleged crimes stacked together.

When Percy had finished, the ogre's eyes

narrowed on Greer and he asked, "What could I *possibly* have of yours?"

Again Percy intervened in Welsh, but the prince threw up his hand to stop him and peered closely at Greer, awaiting her answer.

"You have —"

"Miss Fairchild!"

Percy's strong voice startled her; she jerked her gaze to him, and he began to address the prince in Welsh, his voice sounding almost frantic. Whatever he said seemed to perturb the prince; his expression was one of superior disdain. And when he spoke to Percy, he spoke in such a way that Greer knew his words dripped with rancor.

Percy responded with equal rancor, and the two men continued to speak in that awful language, Percy's voice growing louder, the prince's colder.

But then Percy said something that obviously struck a chord, for the devil prince pinned her with a very fierce look.

Greer took a small step backward.

"The hour has grown too late for you to safely return to Rhayader. We shall make accommodation for you here."

"Here?" she echoed, glancing anxiously at Percy. "Surely we can return to Rhayader — it is not yet dark, and the rain —"

"It is impossible," the prince said

brusquely. "As for your . . . *business* . . . I shall entertain it on the morrow." He snapped his fingers; the two beasts were instantly at his side. He strode out the door with them trotting behind him before Greer could say what she had come for, before she could utter another word.

As the door closed resoundingly behind him, robbing her of the opportunity to demand what was hers for the time being, she whirled around to Percy. "What . . . what *happened?*"

"I explained to him that we have come for our inheritances," he said, moving toward her. "Of course he will not give in without a fight."

Greer groaned. She was too angry and exhausted for this, really. She had wanted to ask him herself, had wanted to claim what was hers from that vile man in her own words, and she hadn't even understood that her case was being presented at all. "Mr. Percy, I really must *insist* —"

"Miss Fairchild . . . *Greer,*" he said, interrupting her. "You don't know him as I do. He's frightfully unscrupulous — he will have no mercy for a defenseless young woman."

At her skeptical look, he quickly closed the distance between them and took her hands in his. "I yearn to help you, to *protect* you. Miss Fairchild — *Greer* — what I have to say will seem indecorous, I fear, but . . . but I have contemplated it for some time."

The intensity in his eyes and the gravity in his voice sparked her feminine intuition — she suspected instantly what he meant to say and panicked. He meant to do this *now?* "Mr. Percy!" she cried, trying to yank her hands free. "I beg you, please do *not* —"

"Surely you know that I have come to hold you in the highest regard," he continued doggedly. "I would have preferred a proper courtship — you deserve no less — but as we have been thrown together by fate, I can no longer defer the honest and true declaration of my feelings. It is important that I speak up now, for I believe we will be far more successful together than we possibly can be apart."

She tried to absorb this sudden admission. Of course she'd noted his attention to her, but she'd never suspected a depth of feeling such as *this.* And while she found him charming and was somewhat fond of him — after all, he'd been a tremendous help along the way — she had not thought of him in any capacity that even remotely resembled a husband.

And really, what an awful moment to of-

41

fer for her hand! She could scarcely think of anything but that wretched prince! It was so absurd that it seemed almost a dream — she was standing in the middle of a medieval castle in Wales of all places, the guest of a murderer and a thief, receiving an offer of marriage she neither wanted nor had anticipated. "Mr. Percy, I could not *possibly* —"

"Don't answer yet," he said, and earnestly kissed her hand. "But please do me the honor of at least considering my offer. And as you do, be assured of the depth of my esteem for you. I have been captivated and bewitched by you, Greer, and I pray that you will return my good opinion of you by consenting to be my wife."

"Mr. Percy, please!" she cried, pulling her hand from his grip. "This is a very ill-timed proposal!"

"I know it must seem that way, but given his nature, this may be the very *best* time. Just think of what this could mean, Greer! Together, with our inheritances, we will have a comfortable living, you and I. We might settle in a manor house in the country and rear our children —"

"You presume too much, sir!"

He smiled sweetly and touched his knuckle to her temple. "Consider it — that is all I ask."

Oh God, it was too much to be borne. If only Ava and Phoebe were with her now! Surely one of them would have suspected Percy's intentions, would have at least *warned* her, but Greer hadn't seen it coming. She'd been too single-minded of purpose, too intent on retrieving her inheritance and returning to London to even *consider* —

"I have obviously distressed you," Percy said. "But surely you cannot be so very surprised. Surely you *knew* —"

The door opened behind him, and Percy whirled about like a guilty boy caught peeking up his mistress's skirts.

It was the butler, who spoke to Percy. When he had finished, Percy sighed, put a hand to his waist, and looked at Greer. "He's readied a room for you," he said irritably, then quickly smiled. "Promise me you will consider what I have said."

"I will consider it," she said, and escaped his probing gaze by stepping around him and hurrying forward to put herself in the hands of the butler, who had yet to speak a word of English.

THREE

The butler led Greer through a darkened corridor to a small, austere room with a bed, a rug, and a table that doubled as a vanity. There was a single window, which looked out on the sheep pens. The butler — a small, dark-haired, and stoic little man — told her in French that an evening meal would be served in her rooms.

"Merci," she said, and because her French was not very good she pleaded for someone who spoke English. *"Y a-t-il quelqu'un qui parle anglais ici?"*

"I speak English," he responded solemnly.

This place seemed odder and odder by the hour. "Thank you," she said, looking at him curiously. "Might I have a fire made?"

"A footman will attend you shortly." He bowed and stepped out of her room.

With a sigh, Greer tossed her bonnet onto the bed and walked to the window, where she stared out at the muddied pens and the sheep who, in spite of the cold and wet weather, chewed contentedly on their cuds. She wished she could be as content as they, have nothing to worry over except when she might be let out to pasture again. Unfortunately, her burden seemed insurmountable at the moment. She'd gotten herself into quite a mess.

Greer stood at the window hugging herself tightly, contemplating what she should do, until a knock at the door roused her. It was a footman, come to build a fire. As he filled the hearth with wood, she asked, "I beg your pardon, but is Mr. Percy close by?"

The footman looked at her strangely. "*Saesneg* no good," he said.

"Oh." She smiled weakly and turned back to the window.

The day was fading into black, and the wind was picking up, making strange groaning sounds in the castle. When the footman left, she noticed that the wind sounded like keening cries at a distance. It made her nervous. She almost expected the witches from *Macbeth* to jump out from behind the single drape and chant:

When shall we three meet again
In thunder, lightning, or in rain?
When the hurlyburly's done,

45

When the battle's lost or won.

She stepped away from the window, and moved to the hearth, hoping that the crackle and hiss of burning wood would drown out the awful groans of the wind.

She thought of Ava and Phoebe, of their house in London, of the soirées and balls they'd attended since they'd come out, their carefree lives in which their greatest concern had been which of the many young gentlemen they might marry one day. She missed them terribly, missed their counsel and confiding in them. She thought of her aunt Cassandra, who always laughed, always promised them great things.

She thought of Bingley Hall, where they had lived when they were children, and the balls her aunt and uncle had held. On those special nights, Aunt Cassandra would visit them in the nursery, dressed in her finery. She always looked like a queen to Greer.

On one such occasion, Phoebe had grown petulant. "I want to attend, Mamma," she'd insisted.

"Not tonight, darling, but one day you will attend all the balls," Aunt Cassandra had said reassuringly, and took Phoebe by one hand, Greer by the other, and nodded at Ava to take their hands, too, so that they formed a circle. "You remember the reel I taught you?" she asked as she moved them in a circle. "One day, you shall all dance as many reels and minuets and waltzes as you like."

"Where?" Phoebe had asked suspiciously.

"Where!" Aunt Cassandra had playfully scoffed. "At Ava's house, of course, for Ava will be mistress of a very fine house, and she will host balls and soirées and elegant supper parties that will be the envy of everyone in London."

"Who will I marry, Mamma?" Ava, older than Greer by a year, asked.

"A *lord*. A very handsome and wealthy lord, darling, and he will adore you completely."

"What about me?" Phoebe, the youngest of the three asked, frowning.

"You are my very special child, Phoebe," Aunt Cassandra had said with a warm smile as they slowly moved in their circle. "When you are grown, your beauty will be so great that every man in Britain will desire you for his wife. But you will be quiet and very careful in settling your affections on one of them, for you will have an important secret. It will take a very special man to see your secret and its importance to you."

"What is the secret?" Phoebe cried, happy

to be the one to have an important secret.

"Why, how could I know, darling?" Aunt Cassandra asked gaily. "It is *your* secret. But it will be a precious secret, and you will share it with the one man who loves you above all else."

"What of Greer?" Ava asked.

"Greer!" Aunt Cassandra laughed and squeezed Greer's hand affectionately. "That's quite easy. Greer is clever and witty and will be in great demand at all the most important social events because she is the life of any good party. All the gentlemen will esteem her greatly, but our Greer is so clever, she will prefer to play with the gentlemen as if they were mice and she the cat."

"Won't I marry?" Greer asked, daunted by the prospect of toying with grown men.

"Of course, darling! But you won't marry just any man — he will be at least as clever as you and will recognize instantly what a jewel you are."

The circle slowed as the three of them had looked at each other, trying with all their might to imagine themselves as grown women.

"I don't want to marry," Phoebe said at last. "I want to stay with Ava and Greer."

Aunt Cassandra laughed and leaned down

to kiss Phoebe's blond head. "Men shall flit in and out of your lives, my lovelies, but the three of you will be together always and forever. You will be like a great brotherhood of knights, defending and protecting one another throughout your lives. You will share your sorrows and your hopes with one another, you will share in your joy and tragedy, and you will raise your children together. Never forget that while you will love your husbands and your children, no one will ever be closer to you than your sisters."

"Greer isn't our sister, Mamma. She is our cousin," Phoebe had clarified.

"Thank you, darling, I am aware she is your cousin in name. But she is your sister in heart."

She had kissed them all good night then and left them in the company of their nurse, sweeping out of the room in a gown that sparkled when she moved.

Greer never forgot that night. Aunt Cassandra had been right in many ways — she was invited to all the social events and sought after as a partner in games and dancing and at supper tables. Gentlemen always seemed to like her, but she had yet to meet one in London that held her interest for very long. It saddened her, for she wanted the life Aunt Cassandra had painted for her that night. She wanted children, and to live near Ava and Phoebe in London in the midst of the social whirl. And she did very much want to marry a man who was clever and kind and not the least bit intimidated that she knew the latest news of Parliament, as some of her suitors seemed to be.

Greer missed Aunt Cassandra desperately, especially now. Her aunt would know what to do about everything — about Greer's inheritance, about Percy, about this awful castle.

And of course Greer thought of her mother, a woman whose face was frozen for all time in the tiny personal portrait Greer carried with her. She did not have a portrait of her father, and could not remember what he looked like. She couldn't remember him at all, really. But her mother — Aunt Cassandra's half sister — she remembered in vivid snatches.

But she was chasing a ghost, she thought morosely. Scattered bits of memory, a tiny little portrait, and nothing more than the recurring dream she'd had of her mother in the last few years. In the dream, her mother stood at the door of a white mansion, bathed in sunlight, beckoning Greer inside. And Greer would run to her mother, trying to reach her before her mother disappeared inside. She could never do it.

It was hardly enough of a dream to have brought her here, to a remote and gloomy castle, as far from the Wales of her memory as she could possibly be.

It was ironic, really — she'd always been so very practical. She excelled in her studies and yearned to know more of math and science and literature. She was not the sort to follow a flight of fancy, no matter how dire the situation. So how was it that she'd allowed herself to risk her life and her virtue on a wild-goose chase?

The room was growing colder in spite of the fire in the hearth. Fortunately, another footman appeared with Greer's trunk. She lit a candle and opened the trunk, found a serviceable evening gown and a Kashmir shawl that she donned for warmth, and performed her toilette with the ice-cold water in the basin. Sometime later a third footman appeared with her meal. As he stoked her fire, she removed the silver dome and looked at the food. Fish stew, from the look of it. She replaced the silver dome; she had no appetite.

When the footman left, she tried to occupy her thoughts and hands by taking her hair down and brushing it. The wind grew fiercer still, and rain lashed at the small-paned glass window as if someone hurled pebbles at it. It was too nerve-racking to endure, so Greer tied her hair at her nape and began to pace.

The light of her candle flickered with the strength of a draft, and Greer was suddenly reminded of a novel Phoebe had read to them aloud one long winter night of a girl trapped in a castle with a ghost. The story had caused the three young girls to sleep in the same bed for several nights.

Another gust of wind rattled the window, and Greer's anxiety increased to the point she felt she might very well crawl out of her skin.

She could scarcely bear it, felt an almost desperate need to leave that wretched room before a witch or a ghost appeared. She glanced at the small watch she wore pinned to her breast. It was a quarter to ten. Surely she might move about the corridors of the castle without disturbing anyone at this hour — the place seemed so large and devoid of human life. Just a quick walk-about to find Mr. Percy, who would un-doubtedly keep her company until the storm passed.

A clap of thunder sent her to the door. She opened it carefully and peeked out.

There was one light at the far end of the corridor that was flickering so badly it looked in danger of being extinguished. But it was light, and where there was light there might be a person — a living, breathing, person.

She picked up her candelabra and stepped out into the corridor, retracing the path the butler had taken to bring her to her room. At the end of the corridor, however, she could not remember if they had come from the left or the right.

She went right.

After walking for several minutes with her heart pounding loudly in her ears, she reached another corridor that was long and narrow and lit by beeswax candles in wall sconces. It was an extravagance that few people could afford, but Greer was glad for it. She blew out her light and put down her candelabra, then moved quietly down the corridor, looking at the paintings as she went.

She found it quite interesting that the devil prince, for all his sins, had quite an impressive art collection in this hall, but really little else in the castle.

As she neared the end of the corridor, she came upon a painting of a woman seated beneath the boughs of a tree. Greer recog-

nized the distinctive work of Thomas Gains-
borough, and paused to admire it. The
woman was wearing a white dress over pan-
niers with a blue sash. On her head was a
wide-brimmed summer bonnet and her
bejeweled slippers peeked out from beneath
her hem. A little black dog was lying at her
feet, looking up at his mistress. Greer
stepped closer to admire the painting,
squinting up at it, when she heard the creak
of a floorboard behind her.

She jerked around with a cry of alarm,
which caused the two dogs behind her to
start barking ferociously, their bared teeth
gleaming in the candlelight.

Just behind them, a man appeared in a
doorway, filling the frame, and Greer's heart
stopped beating. He spoke sharply to the
dogs, who instantly went down on their bel-
lies.

Terrified, Greer gasped for breath, her
hand on her throat, and tried to focus on
the prince. He had divested himself of his
cloak, and for that matter, his coat and
waistcoat and neckcloth, too. In fact, he
wore nothing but a pair of trousers and a
lawn shirt with the tails hanging midthigh.
The shirt hung open at the neck; she could
glimpse the dark hair that covered a muscular chest. His dark hair was mussed, his feet

bare, and he leaned against the door frame, holding a bottle in one hand. He looked hardly civilized, and he was scowling at her.

"I beg your pardon," she said instantly, and moved to flee.

"I ble rydych chi'n mynd?" he said, his voice sharp.

Greer suppressed a shudder and swallowed hard before glancing warily at him from the corner of her eye.

He spoke again to the dogs, who moved instantly at his command and disappeared through the door into the room behind him. Still, the prince did not move, but squinted at her, taking in her gown and the shawl that had fallen from one shoulder to her arm, her slippers, and her hair as he drank. When he lowered the bottle, he met her gaze. "I know who you are, you know," he said. "What are you about?"

"I was . . ." She thought twice before telling him she was restless and fearful and had to quit that small room before she went mad. "I am lost," she lied.

"Lost," he repeated, his gaze lazily skimming her body. "You've never been *lost.*"

His response confused her. "I, ah . . ." She glanced down the corridor she had just walked. "I wanted some water," she said, seizing on a random thought — any thought

— to explain herself. "I was looking for the butler. I must have taken a wrong turn."

The prince pushed off the doorjamb, his gaze steady on her bosom, his legs less steady. "Didn't you think to use your *magic?*" he asked, wiggling his fingers at her. "Or at least the bellpull?"

The bellpull. She hadn't even looked to see if one hung in her room. She did not respond, just watched him move toward her in his uneven gait. The man had obviously fallen deep into his cups, and God only knew what he was capable of under the influence of drink. A jolt of panic overwhelmed her; Greer glanced frantically down the corridor again and contemplated running from him.

But he was upon her, and Greer swallowed down her fear and instinctively stepped back and away from him, bumping up against the wainscoting.

Any number of things went through her mind as he looked at her, his gaze hard and ravenous. She could smell whiskey mixed with a spicy cologne, could see the dusting of a beard on his square jaw.

He stared down at her, his gaze dipping to her lips. *"Beth ydy'ch enw chi?"*

Greer blinked and held her breath.

He lifted his gaze. "Are you not Welsh?"

56

She did not dare respond.

The prince dropped his gaze to her bosom again, and a heat fired deep inside Greer, creeping out to her limbs.

He cocked his head slightly and sighed. "What is your name?" he asked. "Your *given* name," he added, lifting his gaze to her eyes once more. She was startled — she hadn't noticed how vividly green were his eyes, the very color of spring. But those eyes were scrutinizing her every move, almost seeing through her, and her heart began to pound with fear. What did he see? What did he think to do with her?

He lifted a thick brow, waiting for her answer.

"Greer," she said, her voice damnably weak.

"Greer," he repeated softly, and continued his perusal of her — the top of her head, the hair tied at her nape and hanging over her shoulder. He lifted his hand as if he meant to stroke her hair, and Greer instinctively closed her eyes and turned her head.

But the prince didn't touch her hair, as she expected — he touched *her.* He brazenly touched her, his fingers skating across the flesh of her bosom. Her eyes flew open. *"My lord!"* she gasped loudly.

He ignored her. He was holding the charm

she wore around her neck, studying it intently. It was the one Aunt Cassandra had given her years ago, a cross embedded in three circles. Greer tried to move away from him by pressing her back against the wall, but he shook his head, silently warning her against it. He held the cross in his big hand, his fingers thick and dark against the smooth pale skin of her bosom.

Her breathing was coming in gulps now; a fountain of panic had welled in her and was threatening to erupt into hysteria. She madly debated striking him, pushing him away, screaming for help — but she felt paralyzed, unable to scream, unable to find her voice. She couldn't seem to do anything but stand there with her fists clenched at her sides, her head turned to one side as he studied the cross.

"It is Welsh," he said. "An amulet." He dropped it; his fingers brushed against her skin like the lick of fire. Greer covered the necklace with her hand. "I hardly think so," she said hoarsely. "It was purchased in London, I am certain."

"It is Welsh," he repeated. "I *know* you. I know you seek to haunt me," he breathed, his eyes almost blazing. She could not look at those eyes and not be drawn in, and she turned her head again, but he put his hand to her jaw, ignoring her whimper of fear, and forced her to look at him.

They stood almost toe to toe, their gazes locked, her face turned up to his, her breathing harsh, his calm. "I know what you want . . . but you will not succeed," he murmured, and then, to her horror, he kissed her. His lips were warm and wet, moving seductively over hers. His hand touched her neck and she had the sensation that he could strangle her with one large hand if he so desired. His hand then slid to her shoulder, and to the swell of flesh above her décolletage, his light touch unnervingly arousing.

He was, incongruently, gentle and demanding in that kiss, tasting her, nibbling at her, and extraordinarily erotic. Her body was reacting in a way that surprised her, heating beneath his touch, resonating with desire.

Just when she believed she might faint, he suddenly broke away and staggered back. His mouth curved into a dangerous smile and he raised his bottle, took another drink, then pointed the bottle's neck at her. "You will not win," he said. His gaze raked over her once more. He took another healthy swig from his bottle, then turned unsteadily and limped back to the room from which he'd come.

When he disappeared inside, Greer gasped for the breath she had not dared to draw, put her hand to her mouth, and slid down the wall to her haunches, completely spent. It was several moments before she could stand. She grabbed up her shawl in one hand and strode back the way she had come, swiping up the candelabra she had left at the end of the corridor, lighting only one candle so that she might retreat as quickly as possible from the mad prince in the middle of absolutely nowhere.

In his study, the prince took another swig from his bottle, emptying it, and resumed his place on the settee. He tossed the bottle aside, scratched the head of the one dog that had raised his head from slumber, and then put his hand on his knee. He began to rub vainly against the pain, giving up quickly and falling back against the arm of the settee. He slung one arm over his eyes and waited for sleep to relieve his agony, knowing it would not be enough.

FOUR

Greer hardly slept at all, waking with every sound and the storm's every hurly-burly, fearing the prince would appear at her door with that wildly savage look about him. And she feared her reaction to him if he did. She'd been so shocked, so frightened, and so astoundingly aroused — and *that* disturbed her more than anything that had happened to her thus far.

And so she awoke with a start the next morning when someone tweaked her toes. She bolted upright, pushed her hair from her face, and gaped at the girl standing at the foot of her bed.

"Wh-who are you?" she asked.

The girl, a slight thing, stared back at her with dark eyes as big as marbles. "I am Lucy, mu'um. But most call me Lulu. I've been sent to tend you."

The girl's plain English surprised Greer and she eyed her suspiciously, jerking her feet away from the girl's fingers and encircling her arms around her legs. "Where did you come from? You don't sound Welsh."

"Oh no, I'm not, mu'um. I'm from Shrewsbury."

Shrewsbury was at least on the right side of the border, and Greer let down her guard a bit as she swung her legs off the side of the bed. "And how did you find your way to Llanmair?" she asked wryly. "Hired coach?"

"Oh no, miss. My father brung me so I might work." She gestured toward the basin. "I've brung you water. His lordship bids you breakfast in the main dining room, then come to his study when you've finished."

Greer colored slightly at the reference to the prince; she avoided the girl's gaze by standing up and walking to the basin. She splashed ice-cold water on her face to help her wake. When she turned around, Lulu had opened the drapes and sunlight was pouring in through the window.

"The rain has stopped," Greer muttered, more to herself than to Lulu.

"Aye, it has indeed," Lulu said with a cheerfulness that seemed out of place in the dreary little room. "It's a bonny day, to be sure. Shall I help you dress?" she asked, picking up a soft amber morning gown

Phoebe had fashioned for Greer from one of Aunt Cassandra's discarded gowns.

"Thank you . . . but I will need a traveling gown," Greer said. "I'll be leaving Llanmair today."

Lulu nodded and returned to the trunk. She found a rose-colored gown, the fabric of which was far too light for this country, but it was all Greer had. Lulu carefully laid it across the arm of a chair, admiring it.

Greer sat at the little table and began to brush her hair. She watched Lulu as she went about tidying the room, wondering how a girl so slight could possibly live at Llanmair. Frankly, the more she thought of it, the more Greer could not curb her curiosity, and she put down her brush. "You say your father brought you to work here?"

"Yes, mu'um. It will be two years at the end of November."

How could her father have done it? Perhaps he did not know of the prince's reputation. Poor thing — Lulu must have been very fearful, abandoned to the household of a man whose character was as black as night. "You are a brave girl, Lulu. I am sure you were frightened."

Lulu laughed with surprise. "*Frightened?* Oh, Lord, no, mu'um! If you must work for your bread, there is no better place to be than Llanmair. I considered myself quite lucky to have got on."

The opportunities to work for one's bread, as Lulu put it, must be quite meager indeed in this part of the world, if being sentenced to Llanmair and that wretched devil of a man was considered lucky. But Greer said nothing more and completed her toilette. Lulu helped her dress, but she had trouble putting Greer's hair up. In the end, the girl braided it and tied it with a ribbon. "I'm sure it's not as fancy as the hairdressings in London, mu'um, but it's quite nice for Wales."

Greer smiled and refrained from replying. She wondered — as she had several times since crossing the border into Wales — how she could possibly be Welsh. Everything here seemed so foreign to her. Granted, she'd just turned eight when she'd left — fourteen years ago in all — but still, she'd thought *something* would seem familiar.

Lulu showed her to the main dining room, where Greer was heartened to see Percy. He stood as she entered and held out his hand to her. "How did you sleep?" he asked as she slipped her hand into his. "Oh dear, by the look of it, not very well. You look quite tired."

"As bad as that?" Greer asked with a wry

smile. She *was* tired and cross, and the day had only just begun. "I didn't sleep well at all, in truth," she said. *Considering the prince had kissed her so intimately.* "The storm, and *noises* —"

"Ghosts," Percy said solemnly.

"What?" Greer cried.

He laughed and kissed the back of her hand. "I apologize. I was teasing you. I hardly noticed the storm at all — I slept like a child," he added with a wink. "Here — sit, sit," Percy said sternly. "I'll fetch you a bit of breakfast."

Greer sat. Having forgone the fish stew last night, she was ravenous. Percy served her porridge, eggs, toast points, and coffee. As Greer ate, he sat across from her, watching her. When she gave him a questioning look, he smiled thinly. "We are to see the prince after breakfast."

She nodded.

Percy abruptly looked around as if he expected someone to be listening, even though he and Greer were the only two in the room. He said low, "I must warn you that this is a man who knows how to get what he wants, and generally by any means imaginable. I have every expectation that he will attempt to turn you against me by accusing me of terrible acts. But they are all lies, Greer, designed to influence your good opinion of me. He will seek to divide us in order to deny our claims, mark me."

"I don't see how he could possibly accuse *you* of a terrible act after all he's done."

"It's simple, really — he thinks himself above the law. I've seen him do it before, to others," he continued softly. "He will stop at nothing to put you off course from seeking what is rightfully yours. He will attempt to intimidate you."

Greer glanced at her half-eaten porridge and thought about last night, the prince's broad hand against her skin, his gaze hot and intense, and could not imagine how he might possibly be more intimidating than he had been then. But to try and say something against Percy was ludicrous! How could he think she would believe his slander? How could he think her ignorant of Mr. Percy's good character, having come all this way with him?

"You needn't worry, Mr. Percy," she said firmly. "He cannot convince me that you are anything other than what you are — a good, decent, and honorable man."

Mr. Percy smiled warmly. "Dear Greer, how I cherish your good opinion of me — you must know it. Dare I ask . . . have you considered my offer?"

She instantly lost interest in breakfast. "Of course I owe you a response," she said, her mind racing for a polite rebuff. "One that I have duly considered. But . . . but I confess that so much has happened that I've not —"

"Of course you haven't," he said instantly. "I am wrong to press you before you've had the opportunity to conclude your business here." He reached across the table for her hand, taking it before she could politely remove it. "Yet I cannot let pass an opportunity to tell you how ardently I wish for your affirmative answer." He brought her hand to his lips and kissed her knuckles passionately, then let her go.

He was charming, she'd give him that. But she could scarcely think of his offer, not now, not with the devil's pall hanging over her head and lingering on her lips.

Fortunately, the butler entered the room and prevented any further talk. He said something in Welsh, to which Percy's smile faded to a frown, and he looked at Greer. "He is waiting. Shall we have this ugly business over and done with?"

Greer fingered the cross that hung around her neck and nodded. "I am ready."

Rhodrick Glendower, the earl of Radnor,

felt much improved this morning in spite of a slight headache from all the whiskey he'd drunk. But the pain in his knee — the result, along with the scar on his face, of a fall from a horse years ago and as familiar to him these many years as his old dogs — had passed with the rain.

The pain was a dull and constant struggle, particularly in the wet months, for he refused his physician's advice to ease the pain with laudanum — he despised the sluggish feeling the drug gave him, the sort that lingered into the next day. Whiskey was hardly a better choice, but the effects of it were usually gone by the next morning.

This morning, however, he felt more rested than he had in several days, and wanted to get on with his business, of which he had quite a lot to attend to. Unfortunately, he first had the distasteful task of an interview with Owen Percy.

A knock on the door drew him away from the bank of windows through which he could see the forest that surrounded much of his castle. He clasped his hands behind his back and unthinkingly turned his head as he'd learned to do long ago to hide his scar, and watched as his two unwanted guests entered behind his butler, Ifan.

Percy entered first, sweeping in with all

the swagger of a peacock. Rhodrick was impressed with his suit of clothing — he himself did not possess such fine clothing and had only recently received two new suits of clothing from a tailor in Aberystwyth.

Percy's coat was made from superfine cloth, the cut of it exact. His shirt and striped waistcoat were made of silk. It was obvious to Rhodrick that in the years he'd been banished, Percy had found a benefactress, undoubtedly an older and wealthy woman who would, with a bit of flattery, hand over her purse to the blackguard.

Behind Percy came the woman, and Rhodrick was once again a bit staggered by her appearance. He wasn't entirely certain why — she was beautiful, but not stunningly so. In the gown she wore today — red or orange, he thought, although he couldn't say with certainty — her blue eyes were the color of a morning sky before sunrise, dark and moist with the promise of vivid light behind them. Blue was one of the few colors he could see, and the blue of her eyes was so intense that it was a shock in the midst of the dull, faded colors that he saw around the room.

Her shiny, thick, ink black hair — *Welsh* hair — hung like a rope down her back. Her lips were full and darkly red and curved into dimples in her cheeks, and he was jolted by the memory of those lips beneath his.

Yes, she was beguiling.

An opinion that was, he told himself, the result of having gone far too long without the company of women, save a few good friends whom he viewed more as sisters. It had been long enough now that he'd forgotten how delicate a woman could be, and how a man's body responded to such delicate beauty and the taste of a woman's lips.

This one's elegance was the sort to inspire paintings, and under other circumstances, he might have felt a wee bit anxious around her, for he'd never felt very comfortable in the company of beautiful women. He self-consciously turned his face away a little more, embarrassed by his jagged scar.

Fortunately, she'd be gone soon — her presence here was insupportable.

"Good morning, my lord," Percy said, bowing low. Behind him, the woman curtsied, but she kept those rich blue eyes on him, watching him warily, as if she expected him to do something heinous. Kiss her, for example.

"Percy," he said, shifting his gaze to his cousin's son, his eyes narrowing with disgust. "What in God's name has brought you to my door?"

"Your lordship," Percy responded with insincere decorum, "I think you know very well why I have come."

Oh, he knew all right. The scoundrel had come to bilk money if he could. "Suppose you tell me, so that we are both quite clear."

Percy glanced briefly at the woman, but then turned his attention to Rhodrick and said in Welsh, "I have come to help Miss Fairchild regain the inheritance you have stolen from her, and to inform you that my inheritance will soon be due to me."

Rhodrick raised a brow, amused by Percy's switch to a language the woman obviously did not understand. He almost laughed — the villain was intent on defrauding the villainess, he was certain of it. "What is this, Percy?" he responded in Welsh. "Hasn't your partner in crime guessed that your intent is to fleece her as well as me?"

"You cannot bait me," Percy said with an easy smile. "It is obviously your pleasure to make false accusations against me, but they are nothing to me. Miss Fairchild will soon be my partner in more than name. She is my fiancée."

At the mention of her name, Miss Fairchild looked questioningly at Percy, her winged brows knit in a pretty frown.

"Aha," Rhodrick said with a nod. "Of course. That explains it. Your inheritance reverts to you at the age of thirty, or at the time of your marriage, whichever comes first. And as you are not yet eight and twenty, you have found someone with whom to share the spoils, have you?"

Percy kept the smile pasted to his face.

Rhodrick looked again at the woman. "Pray tell, how did I come into possession of *her* inheritance?"

"She is the daughter of Yorath Vaughan, who was the brother of Randolph Vaughan, a man well known to you, I am quite certain."

Randolph Vaughan was indeed known to Rhodrick, but not well. Once, a very long time ago, when Rhodrick had been married, his young wife, Eira, had a sister, Mary, who was married to Randolph Vaughan. After both women had died in childbirth, Rhodrick had lost touch with that Vaughan altogether.

He did not volunteer this to Percy, however, but remained silent, calmly waiting for him to speak, for a man who could not bear silence usually filled the silence with more information than he ought.

Percy did not disappoint him. "Yorath Vaughan died without male issue, and the whole of his estate was left to his brother, Randolph," he continued in Welsh. "That was, in turn, left to you when Randolph Vaughan died without any living heir."

That much was also true — the man's estate had been bequeathed to Rhodrick, who was the best relation that could be established. "And?" he prompted Percy, impatient to arrive at the scheme the pair of swindlers had devised.

"Yorath Vaughan died without *male* issue. But he left behind a daughter, who stands before you now."

Rhodrick glanced at the woman from beneath a swath of his hair that had fallen over his eye. She looked at him, then at Percy, and at Rhodrick again.

It was clear to him now — the two swindlers had concocted an arrangement by which Percy would marry and gain his inheritance. In the course of it, they had added a fictional tale with the hope it would gain them another, unclaimed inheritance. Rhodrick further supposed that such machinations meant Percy had lost his benefactress, whoever she might have been. He said, "How convenient for you to have found an heiress to wed."

Percy smirked. "You have what is rightfully hers, just as you have what is rightfully mine. The law will force you to return them both once we are married."

Rhodrick shifted his gaze to Miss Fairchild and wondered how a woman as youthful and pretty could have reached such a desperate point in her life to join Percy in this abominable act.

His gaze drifted to the amulet around her neck, and he recalled the warmth of her silken skin last night.

Ah yes, that indiscretion. He had nothing to say for himself, other than he'd been drinking whiskey heavily, and the small amulet had caught his eye. In his inebriation he'd thought she was *her,* of course, the amulet making him believe it. It was only further evidence to his mind that he was, perhaps, mad.

He felt his body heating in such close proximity to her now and turned away, so that his back was partially to her, and said in Welsh, "If I have what is rightfully hers, she will not need the law to obtain it. I will gladly give it to her. As for your inheritance," he said, looking at Percy again, "you are entitled to receive it when you reach your thirtieth year or you marry. Not a moment sooner."

Percy's smile began to sag. "Then at least relieve Miss Fairchild's suffering and return her inheritance."

Rhodrick chuckled. "Before you so happily enter into this conspiracy, you might ask your . . . *fiancée* . . . what she was about when she was roaming the castle last evening."

Percy's lids fluttered faintly, and he looked at Miss Fairchild.

"Ask her," Rhodrick said again, glancing at her sidelong.

Percy cleared his throat and said in English, "His lordship remarked that you were wandering about the castle last night."

Miss Fairchild colored slightly. "Yes. I was lost." She glanced nervously at Rhodrick, then asked Percy, "I beg your pardon, what did he say?" When neither man responded, her color deepened. "I was thirsty," she said, perhaps a little too adamantly. "I was seeking the butler to ask for water to be brought to my room."

"A pity that your fiancé was not available to tend to your needs," Rhodrick muttered as he moved to sit at his desk.

"I beg your *pardon?*" she exclaimed, her eyes widening with shock.

Ho there, this was an interesting turn. "Your fiancé," Rhodrick responded before Percy could answer. "You don't mind, do you, that Percy has given me your happy news?"

But mind Miss Fairchild did, and Rhodrick was glad he was not on the receiving end of the heated glare she bestowed on Percy. He almost laughed, imagining the two of them devising some diabolical plot, and all the while, Percy was scheming behind her back to keep whatever money they could manage to bilk. Clearly, that was precisely what he intended, for in marrying her, any money they gained was, by law, his.

"I beg your pardon, my lord, but he is not my fiancé," Miss Fairchild said quickly.

She was careless, he thought. Speaking without thinking. He shrugged. "I should think that if you did not begin your journey as an engaged couple, or preferably, a *married* couple, you most certainly should end it that way — unless, of course, he has no care for your reputation."

Miss Fairchild turned quite red — he had the distinct impression that she would have kicked him in the shins if she were standing close enough to him. Instead, she pressed her lips tightly together and looked at the floor for a moment. "Mr. Percy has offered, sir, but I have not yet given him my response," she said quietly. "The blame for my conduct is entirely mine."

"I did not mean to suggest otherwise."

Her eyes narrowed slightly, but whatever she might have said was lost when Percy suddenly demanded in Welsh, "Leave her be! Our particular situation is none of your affair! Just return our inheritances as quickly as possible so that we might leave Llanmair and never return!"

"I wish I could take you at your word," Rhodrick drawled in Welsh. "But it sounds to me an empty promise. Frankly, I should have seen you hanged when I had the opportunity."

Percy paled. "Just give us our due and we shall leave," he said tightly.

"*Our* due? Tsk-tsk, Owen. You count on her money and you've not yet even had her in your bed."

Percy's face now flooded with the heat of his fury, but Rhodrick merely shifted his gaze to Miss Fairchild again and said in English, "I have what was left of the Vaughan estate in its entirety, Miss Fairchild. The whole of your uncle's and father's estates combined comes to approximately four thousand pounds. If you can prove to me that you are who you claim to be, it is yours to take."

She gasped and looked at Percy, the surprise evident on her face.

"Before you allow the excitement of that sum to make you ill with delight, understand this — I must have *proof* that you are who you say you are. By that I mean someone other than this . . . *man,*" he managed to say in spite of what he was thinking, "must vouch for you."

"I have a letter," she said instantly, and opened the little beaded bag that hung around her wrist. She unfolded the yellowing vellum and strode across the room to deposit it on his desk.

Rhodrick took it, glanced at the date. It had been written some twenty years ago. He quickly scanned the letter — it was written to Mrs. Randolph Vaughan from Mrs. Yorath Vaughan, who wrote at length about her darling daughter, Greer, making several references to her recent visit with her aunt and uncle, Randolph and Mary.

When he had finished reading it, he pushed the letter across the desk to her and turned his head. "Quite poignant, but hardly the proof I require."

Miss Fairchild seemed confused; she picked up the letter and frowned at it. "But . . . but this was written by my mother."

"You could have come by this letter in any number of ways. You might have written it with your own hand for all I know. I will need something more definitive than that — a letter addressed to me should suffice."

Still frowning, Miss Fairchild carefully folded the letter and tucked it safely into her reticule. She lifted her gaze to him, her blue eyes filled with loathing. "I should very much like to have my mother write a letter directly to you, my lord, but as she has been dead these fourteen years, I can hardly ask it of her."

Her fear of him seemed to have taken a most decided turn into white-hot fury. "No, I don't suppose you can," he said coolly, "but surely there is someone on this earth who knows who you are."

"Lord Middleton," Percy muttered behind her.

Middleton? How intriguing. Rhodrick knew Middleton was a powerful marquis, heir to a very important duchy. Surely she wouldn't be so foolish as to claim *that* connection. What a careless wench she was. "Are you some relation to Lord Middleton?"

"He has recently married my cousin, Lady Ava Fairchild. Ava is the daughter of Lady Bingley, my late aunt."

"Then by all means," he said, feeling somewhat amused by her overreach, "you may entice Lord Middleton to vouch for your identity or you may bring me the evidence of your identity from the parish rolls. Either way, I shall give you the four thousand pounds that were left to me from the combined Vaughan estates."

"But . . . but that could take *weeks*," she started to say, only to be silenced by Percy's hand to her arm.

"We shall give you the proof you need, my lord."

"But —" Miss Fairchild started again, but Percy's grip tightened on her arm and he gave her a pointed look that silenced her.

"May we have a few moments to confer?" he asked politely.

Rhodrick had grown weary of Percy's game and this meeting and abruptly stood. "Have as many moments as you'd like," he said curtly, and walked to the door, opened it, and turned back to Percy. "But have them somewhere other than my home."

Percy's eyes narrowed. "We will be gone as soon as possible, do not doubt it, my lord. But first, I should like a word alone with Miss Fairchild."

"As you wish," Rhodrick said, holding the door open for them.

Percy fairly pushed Miss Fairchild out of the room ahead of him. As they passed,

Miss Fairchild looked at Rhodrick and he could see the memory of his kiss in her eyes. But she quickly looked away — revolted, no doubt — and walked through the doorway. He shut the door behind them and started back to his desk, but spotted something white on the carpet. He walked over to it.

It was a handkerchief. It must have fallen out of her reticule when she retrieved her silly letter. He picked it up. It looked to be fine Irish linen and lace, expertly embroidered with green vines that wound their way around the letter *V,* with a smaller *A* and *B* on either side of the *V.*

Rhodrick stared at the handkerchief for a long moment, then slowly lifted it to his nose and breathed in the scent. It smelled of lilacs and . . . and *woman.* Sweet, soft, woman.

It was a scent he'd not had the pleasure of knowing for many years. He breathed in again, then tucked the lacy handkerchief into his pocket and continued on to his desk and his work.

FIVE

Owen marched Greer to a small waiting room near the main entrance. Once inside, he shut the door and leaned against it, trying to contain his racing pulse. His efforts, however, were in vain, and he glared at Greer. "What in God's name were you doing roaming about last night?" he demanded.

"I beg your pardon?" she shot back, appearing damnably guilty.

"Did you try and see him without me?" he asked her bluntly.

She made a sound of effrontery. "I did no such thing!" she exclaimed hotly. "I told you, I was lost." Her gaze hardened, and she folded her arms. "And what exactly are you implying, sir?"

Owen checked himself. "Nothing at all," he said quickly. "But I don't understand —"

"There is nothing to understand," she said

sharply. "And may I ask why you told him we were engaged?"

"Is it not obvious? I was trying to protect your reputation."

That seemed to take her aback.

"You must not forget that I *know* him, Greer. The man has no respect for anyone, particularly not for women. Surely, after all that I've told you and what you've seen, you believe that much is true."

The slight shudder that went through her body confirmed that she did, and Owen quickly closed the distance between them, put his hands on her shoulders. "Dearest, if you want to see the four thousand pounds that rightfully belong to you, you must at least *appear* to be engaged to me. He will never hand that sort of money to a mere female."

"But he said —"

"I know what he said," he interrupted her. "But it's as I have told you — the prince is not an honorable man. He will say whatever he thinks you want to hear with no intention of honoring his word."

She gaped at him; myriad thoughts clouded her blue eyes. But then she firmly shook her head. "Perhaps that is true, Mr. Percy, but I do not say what one would like to hear, and I *do* honor my word. I cannot lie and say that we are engaged when it is not true."

Dear God, the chit made this difficult. "Greer. Darling," he said, forcing a sympathetic smile. "I cannot begin to imagine how very trying this ordeal has been for you. I have only said what I must to *protect* you."

She looked at him skeptically; Owen put a hand to her cheek and smiled again. Her lids fluttered a moment, and then she returned his smile with a tentative one of her own.

"I confess," he said, "that perhaps I spoke out of a sincere hope that you will agree to marry me."

Her smile deepened, and she tried to look away, but he moved closer, held her face with his hand, and looked deeply into her eyes. "Will you tell me that you haven't thought of it, if only a little?"

"I have," she said softly.

He could feel her resolve weakening. "Imagine a manor house," he whispered, and kissed the bridge of her nose. "And children," he added as he kissed her smooth cheek. "A strapping lad to carry on my name," he said, moving to kiss the other cheek, "and a girl with her mother's beauty."

He kissed her on the lips then, carefully, tenderly, and without any demands. Greer did not resist him, just lifted her head and allowed him to kiss her. She was not, however, very good at it — something he would be delighted to remedy.

He lifted his head and smiled down at her. "Forgive me," he uttered earnestly, "but I cannot resist you."

She smiled a little and stepped back, and put her hand to her cheek.

"In the future," he said gently, "I suggest you allow me to deal with the prince while you imagine our life together in a country manor."

She nodded uncertainly, then frowned. "But . . . but I can't possibly afford to hire a room for the weeks it will take to send a letter to Ava and receive her response," she said, and glanced up at him. "We must find the parish rolls."

"Searching the parish rolls could take weeks as well." With the pad of his thumb, he caressed her bottom lip. "Don't fret. I will speak with him. Rest easy and know that I do this for you."

"Mr. Percy, you really mustn't —"

"I would do anything for you," he said, interrupting her again, and slipped his arm around her waist and drew her in to kiss her. Only this time, he kissed her much more ardently.

It seemed to work. She seemed to forget all about the bloody prince for a moment.

Greer did not, however, forget the prince for very long — how could she, holed up in some dreadful receiving room, waiting for Percy to return from his private discussion with him? She paced restlessly, crossing frequently to the window and staring out at the castle's gardens and the bright blue sky.

When Percy did at last return, she could tell by his grim expression that things had not gone well. "He's unmoved," he said simply as he led her to a settee and sat beside her.

She tried very hard not to look as panicked as she felt. "What are we to do?"

Percy shrugged. "He has given us leave to stay another night. In the morning, I shall inform the prince that I see no alternative than to include the authorities in our discussion. At that point, I think we should proceed to Rhayader and speak with a solicitor."

Dear God. She should never have come here, should never have let Percy talk her into this. "But . . . but I have no money to retain a solicitor," she anxiously reminded him. After Percy's insistence that they stay at public inns and eat more than once a day, she had a little less than four pounds to her name. She was effectively stranded here without help.

"And what of the coach?" she continued. "The driver will expect to be paid to wait —"

"Oh," Percy said casually, "I took the liberty of dismissing him."

Greer's heart sank to her toes. How would she ever leave this place now? "You . . . you *dismissed* him?"

"We'll hire another one in Rhayader," he said, smiling.

But Greer didn't return his smile. She was troubled by a dark sense of foreboding. She said nothing to Percy of it, however, but allowed him to talk about contacting the appropriate authorities in Rhayader, as well as taking rooms there. He suggested perhaps they find a little house, forgetting, she thought, that they were not even engaged, much less married.

She let him speak, but she was hardly listening — she was thinking of how she might speak to the prince herself. It seemed foolish to allow Percy to make her case in Welsh when she did not speak the language. Perhaps something was lost in translation. Perhaps the prince did not fully understand what Percy was telling him. In fact, she wouldn't rest until she spoke to him, for it was impossible for her to remain in Wales indefinitely. Not like this. Not with Percy. Not with less than four pounds — a situation that left her at the mercy of such a dark man.

That evening, Percy and Greer were served dinner in a small dining room that seemed as far from the front of the castle as one could be. With a fire blazing and old tapestries hanging on the walls, it was quite warm and stuffy, and it seemed to add to Percy's ill humor.

"He has put us away like servants," he said sourly as they waited to be served. "He treats us no better than animals." When a scullery maid arrived, she very unceremoniously placed a bowl in front of each of them and lifted the domes that covered the food.

Percy wrinkled his nose with disgust. *"Cawl,"* he spat. "He dines like a king and serves us *cawl* as if we were peasants!"

Greer was not insulted in the least, for the moment she caught scent of the traditional Welsh stew, a flood of memories came rushing back to her. She remembered sitting on a stool at a long wooden table in a large kitchen, her feet swinging above the floor. And she remembered her grandmother, a lovely old woman with thick gray hair wrapped in a bun and a bosom as warm and soft as a cat, sopping her bread in Greer's *cawl.*

As Percy rattled on about how detestably they were being treated, as well as all the things he expected the prince would say of him at one point or another — primarily that Percy was a roué and a blackguard — Greer feasted on what she thought was the most delicious stew she'd ever eaten in her life.

After supper, they were shown to a library. Greer began to inspect the shelves as Percy lay on a settee in high dudgeon.

She was impressed by the array of subjects. From history to agricultural techniques to great works of literature in both English and French, and of course, an entire section of Welsh titles.

"He is well educated, it would seem," she remarked.

"He should like for you to believe that is true," Percy scoffed, and flung his arm over his eyes, sighing with exasperation.

Greer picked up a book by Theophilus Evans, *A Collection of Welsh Travels and Memoirs of Wales,* sat across from Percy, and began to read. After a half hour, the sound of Percy's breathing had grown deeper; Greer glanced up from her reading and watched the rise and fall of his chest. He was asleep.

She debated the opportunity that confronted her. On the one hand, she did not relish another incident like the one she'd endured last night. On the other, she didn't know when she'd get the chance to speak to the prince again without Percy present. She carefully laid the book aside, rose from her chair, and quietly quit the room.

Greer took a deep breath and began walking purposefully down the lit corridor.

She ignored the portraits this time, her thoughts focused on the task at hand, and with every step she attempted to gather the courage she needed to face him. When she reached the doors leading to his study, she stood there debating with herself, her pulse racing, her hands trembling.

After several steadying breaths, she found the courage to lift her hand and rap on the door. Her rap was immediately met with a ferocious round of barking, and with a squeal of surprise, she reared back from the door. She heard him sharply command the dogs into silence. A moment passed, and the door was yanked open.

He filled the width of the doorway. But unlike last night, when he'd been scarcely dressed, tonight he was wearing black tails and a waistcoat and a neckcloth of white silk. His hair was combed back from his brow and tamed in a queue and his face seemed to be freshly shaven. She noticed that he instantly turned his head so that his scar was away from her.

It was obvious that the prince of darkness was going out for the evening, and that rattled Greer even more. Where did he go? What sort of people consorted with him? Men? Women?

"Yes?" he asked curtly, his scowl an indication of his displeasure.

"I, ah . . ." *Speak!* "If it is not inconvenient, my lord, I should like a word, if you please."

"It is inconvenient."

"I will only take a moment of your time," she quickly assured him.

He sighed — or growled, she wasn't quite certain — and withdrew his pocket watch and glanced at it. He glanced up, his green eyes narrowed on her. "A *moment.*" With that, he turned and disappeared inside his study.

Greer hesitated before stepping across the threshold. She was instantly met by the two enormous wolfhounds, who went about the business of sniffing her until they were satisfied, and then trotted back to the hearth.

She remained standing just inside the

room, her hands clasped before her. She had not noticed earlier today how plainly this room was arranged. There was a large ornate desk and a single leather chair before the hearth. He was obviously a solitary man who did not have need for a second chair. No one sat with him here, only his dogs.

The prince stood in the middle of the room, his weight on one hip, a hand on his waist, clearly impatient and a far cry from the wild, disheveled man he'd been last night. His dogs, she noticed, had lain down before the fire and seemed perfectly relaxed.

"Well, then?" he demanded.

"My lord . . . I shall not waste your time —"

"You already are."

Affronted by his lack of civility, she lost her nerve.

"You were saying?" he said, gesturing impatiently for her to continue as he turned away from her.

He was truly the rudest man she'd ever met. "I was saying," she said deliberately, "that I understand your need to have verification that I am who I say I am . . . but I cannot stay in Wales indefinitely. Not only am I needed in London, I have no place to stay."

"That, Miss Fairchild, is something you

might have considered before imposing on my hospitality."

Ooh she despised him, *reviled* him. "You are right, of course," she managed to bite out. "I apologize for having imposed. But I came here with the belief that an honorable man would return what is rightfully mine with utmost haste."

"An honorable woman would have brought proof that she is who she claims to be so that a man might do precisely that. For all I know, you are a charlatan. You are certainly in the company of a charlatan, Miss Fairchild, and as they say, birds of a feather . . ."

The last remnants of her fear were eclipsed by her fury. She tried to keep her breathing steady, tried not to gasp in shock at every word he uttered. "I am *not* a charlatan, sir, and neither is Mr. Percy."

He responded with a disdainful snort. "What do you know of Mr. Percy?" he spat, and looked at the carpet for a moment. "You present me with a dilemma, Miss Fairchild. I cannot determine if you are in cahoots with him or merely the most naïve young woman I have ever met."

"I have no idea what you mean."

"That would point to naïve."

"I cannot claim to know of your dealings

with Mr. Percy, my lord, but what I know of him is good. He has been very kind to me and my late traveling companion, Mrs. Smithington."

"By the bye," the prince asked with a pointed look, "was your traveling companion an elderly and wealthy woman?"

"What?" she asked, the question taking her by surprise.

"Your companion. Old? Rich? Quite alone in the world?"

"Yes," she said uncertainly.

He smirked and looked away again. "That is because your Mr. Percy is very fond of elderly rich women. He preys on them. And, I rather suspect, so do you."

She bristled at the accusation, and this time, her fury took hold of her tongue. "How can you *possibly* be so vile?"

"Do you think me stupid, Miss Fairchild?"

"I think you are cruel," she said. "You have stolen an inheritance from a good man for the crime of being half English and *you —*"

"Allow me to tell you a bit about your *good* Mr. Percy," he said dismissively, cutting her off. "I have been sweeping up his wreckage for years."

Greer rolled her eyes heavenward and folded her arms across her middle before

94

returning a very hot gaze to him. "It is just as Mr. Percy said it would be — he warned me you would attempt to assassinate his character."

"Did he, indeed?" he asked, raising a brow as he casually straightened the cuffs of his shirt. "And did he also tell you that he fathered a bastard child and left his lover to suffer the scandal and censure? Or that he gambled himself into such a large hole that he all but obliterated the fortune my cousin — his father — had left to him, thereby necessitating that it be taken away from him so that he wouldn't squander it *all* before he reached his thirtieth year? Or did he, perchance, relate to you that he was almost killed by the cuckolded husband of yet another, *married* lover, costing me five hundred pounds to save his bloody neck?"

"I don't believe you!"

"Now he preys on older women who worship his false flattery. But I do not understand who *you* are, Miss Fairchild. I must assume that you are a conspirator of his, one out to defraud me of the small fortune a man left to no one."

"How dare you insult me, sir!" she said hotly. "I am not a thief!"

He looked at her with such disgust that she felt it to the tips of her toes. And then he suddenly crossed the room to her, bearing down on her like a bull, causing her to cry out and stagger backward, away from him and his hard eyes. "What should I believe, with your silly letter and your claim, Miss Fairchild?" he demanded hotly. "How can I *possibly* believe you are a child of Wales? You don't even speak Welsh!"

"I was raised in England!"

"I don't care if you were raised in China. You were born to Welsh parents who lived but three miles from Wales!"

She gaped at him. "You clearly do not believe me, and for that there is nothing I can do until I have provided the proof you need. But I cannot afford to stay in Wales to see it done! I had hoped we might find some middle ground on which to bargain."

"No," he said, shaking his head firmly. "No. There is no middle ground, Miss Fairchild. I suggest you write your letter to your alleged *connection.*"

Lord God, how she despised him! "All right," she snapped. "Very well. Please do me the courtesy of giving me pen and paper."

He frowned. *"Now?"*

"Now!" she insisted.

He studied her a moment before stalking to his desk. He opened a drawer and withdrew a piece of vellum, which he slapped down on top of the desk so hard that his dogs lifted their heads. He gestured to the seat and the inkwell, then stepped back and bowed low.

This time, Greer did not hesitate — she marched across the room, sweeping past him and taking a seat at his desk. She angrily dipped the pen in the ink. "By all that is holy, you are a *boorish* man! I have never been treated in such an infamous and ungentlemanly manner!"

"Spare me your cries of impropriety, Miss Fairchild. You have sought *me* out three times now."

"Ah!" she cried, glaring up at him. "I did *not* seek you out! I was lost! And *you,* a man who is obviously not a stranger to whiskey, took advantage of me!"

"Indeed?" he asked, leaning over her, his arm brushing hers as he righted the inkwell she had all but managed to tip over. "You didn't seem to mind it, as I recall. Now do please write your letter, Miss Fairchild. You are keeping me from a prior engagement."

"Your behavior is *unconscionable.*"

"You deserve no less."

She angrily dipped the pen in ink, gritted her teeth, and began her letter.

Dearest Ava and Phoebe,
I hope this letter finds you well.

She paused and glanced up at the prince. He was staring at her, his eyes as hard as jade, his jaw clenched. For once, he seemed heedless of his scar.

Greer dipped the pen again.

I have unfortunate news! I have found the man who holds my inheritance, and as it happens, he is the most <u>egregiously</u> odious and <u>disagreeable</u> man I have ever had the misfortune to meet! I had hoped for better from Wales, but he is <u>quite</u> wretched in his appearance and his comportment, and I shall look forward to the day I shall have not the least to do with him. Unfortunately, he refuses to release my inheritance without proof that I am who I say. My mother's letter has not been met with any satisfaction on his part, and this wretched <u>beast</u> of a man, this <u>ogre</u>, demands a letter be written to him from Lord Middleton vouching for my identity.

Dear Ava, I know this is asking far too much of your new husband, particularly as he has only met me once. But if you could prevail on him to please write so that I might return home as soon as possible? I fear what shall become of me if you do not act with some haste! Please direct your letter to The Right Honorable Earl of Radnor, Prince of Powys, at Llanmair. And pray you do not fret overmuch for me, as Mr. Percy is most brave in the face of this monster and protects me against his churlishness.

Yours, G.

She looked up at the prince, who was waiting impatiently, judging by the way he kept glancing at his watch. She picked up a blotter and blotted the excess ink, then carefully folded the vellum and dashed off the names of her cousins and the directions to Downey House in London, where she knew Phoebe would be. For all she knew — and feared — Ava could be in the country now.

She picked it up, waving it violently around to dry it quickly, then sealed it with a bit of wax. When she was done, she stood up, held the vellum out to him.

He took it and tossed it into a wooden tray.

"Might I at least know when the post is to come?" she asked pertly.

"Day after tomorrow." He impatiently

gestured for her to quit the room.

"Dear God," she muttered.

"Do not despair, Miss Fairchild. You may think me uncivilized, but I shall not toss you out into the forest. You and Percy may reside here at Llanmair. I wouldn't wish him on the rest of Wales."

That did not relieve her in the slightest. She tossed her head and began striding for the door.

"When are you to be married?" he asked.

She stopped midstride and glared at him. "I am *not* engaged to him."

He snorted. "I hope, for your sake, that you do not lie to me, Miss Fairchild. For if you are *truly* Greer Vaughan, the moment you have said your vows, your inheritance, by law, becomes his. Mark me — the scoundrel will leave you quite destitute."

"Once again you have proven he is true to his word," she said coldly. "He told me you'd say reprehensible things about him, in spite of all the unspeakable things *you* have done."

For a moment, the prince looked as if he might explode with rage. But he clenched his jaw tightly, which had the effect of making him look meaner. He pointed to the door. "If you are *quite* finished, Miss Fairchild."

"Oh, but I am," she said angrily, and strode out the door.

Six

Margaret Awbrey, Rhodrick's oldest and closest friend, looked at her dinner guest, then shifted her gaze to her husband and sent him a silent but pleading look. Thomas shrugged.

Rhodrick was not very good company tonight. He had little to say. Although Margaret was accustomed to that, he usually could be depended upon to follow the conversation.

Tonight, however, he kept his eyes on his plate, and his grip on the stem of his wineglass was so tight that Margaret feared it would snap. He was deeply troubled about something.

"I cannot bear it a moment longer," Margaret said when the fruitcake, *bara brith,* was served on gold-rimmed china. "You really must confess what occupies your thoughts, Rhodi. Your mind seems to be in another place entirely."

"I beg your pardon," he said. "I should not have come, for I am wretched company this evening."

"Nonsense," Margaret said with a reassuring smile. "You are always the very best of company. But really, what has you so preoccupied?"

He lifted a gaze glittering with ire. "Owen Percy has returned to Llanmair to claim his inheritance."

Shocked, Margaret gasped.

"The devil you say," Thomas exclaimed, his bushy brows meeting in a frown. "I thought we'd seen the last of him for a time."

"Wishful thinking, it would seem," Rhodrick said angrily. "He appeared at my door just yesterday. He's obviously fallen out of favor with whomever he'd managed to dupe and is in need of funds."

"Good Lord," Thomas said, and as he asked Rhodi about Owen's arrival, Margaret could scarcely hear the conversation.

Her heart went out to her old friend — he'd suffered enough through the years. When he was a child, there had been constant teasing because he was big and gangly and not nearly as handsome of visage as his sister or his parents. His father, a big, strapping man himself, laughingly called his son

103

Goliath at every turn. Before long, all the parish children called him that, too, and Rhodi grew into a brooding, dark youth with a terrible temper. He was always fighting, always striking out.

Margaret had never thought him ugly as many people did, but a horrible fall from a horse, right before he reached the age of nineteen, had broken his leg and scarred his face, had only made matters worse, giving him a sinister look.

That opinion was held by several, apparently, for when he'd reached the inevitable age when it became time to make a match and produce heirs, as required any male of the aristocracy, no one would have him. His fortune notwithstanding, more than one young debutante feared his looks and dark mien.

Then his father had found Eira, whose father agreed to a match with Rhodi before the poor girl had an opportunity to meet him. But Eira never seemed to mind Rhodi's looks. Perhaps she, like Margaret, found him far more charming than ugly. Whatever she thought of him, the dear had managed to soothe the beast in Rhodi. In the few short years of their marriage, Rhodi grew tamer, his dark moods all but banished. He became one of the kindest, most thoughtful and considerate men Margaret had ever known.

Oh, but he'd loved Eira dearly. Her death had devastated him completely, sending him into black moods again. He retreated into himself, staying away from society by sequestering himself at Llanmair. And then Owen Percy had come into his life, bringing tragedy with him at every turn.

Since then, Margaret had tried desperately to bring light to Rhodi's world again. She had introduced him to several female acquaintances, but he would have none of it. He was never impolite with her, but was quite firm in his desire to be left alone. And he remained a solitary figure, riding about the forest on his enormous black horse, a lone, almost sinister figure in the minds of the very superstitious Welsh people.

And now, to be forced to endure Owen Percy *again*.

"I am right sorry to hear it," Margaret said sympathetically when he had said all he would about Percy's arrival. "Is there anything we might do to help?"

He shook his head. "I shall gladly be rid of him soon enough."

Margaret graciously let it go at that, but she fervently hoped he would be rid of the reprobate quickly, for his sake.

But Owen Percy was obviously weighing heavily on his mind — he did not seem to be in the mood to converse and said little else the rest of the evening. Margaret felt compelled to review her recent journey to the seaside resort of Aberystwyth, which had begun on a brilliantly sunny day, but had ended with a raging rainstorm, as often happened in Wales.

As she spoke, however, she couldn't help noticing the tight clench of Rhodrick's jaw and the hard look in his eyes. She fretted that the deep-seated anger was coming back to him, and that concerned her. No one knew as well as she how quickly and completely that blackness could descend on him.

Aware that he was poor company, Rhodrick left the Awbreys early. He was up at dawn the next morning, off to settle a dispute between two of his tenants. It took longer than he anticipated — the two men were related by marriage and their dispute seemed to have more to do with the wife of one man than the grazing land in question.

He pretended to listen attentively, nodding at all the right places, but in truth, he could not seem to think of anything but Miss Fairchild's blustery blue eyes, or the way her hip curved into her waist, or the elegance of her long fingers and the slender column of her neck.

That wasn't all. He was having awful, decadent thoughts of Miss Fairchild; he imagined her naked, her lithe body bent over his desk, her back arched in ecstasy as he took her.

It was she who troubled him, of course, she who brought more than a shock of blue into his faded world. At a stream, where he had stopped to water his horse, he took her handkerchief from his pocket and held it to his nose for a moment, then put it back in his pocket and closed his eyes, his head filled with the scent of woman.

Such thoughts disturbed him greatly — he was a grown man, not a boy — but he couldn't seem to stop them from coming. She had kindled something in him. At first, he'd believed it was fury, rage, but now he was beginning to realize that it was something deeper and baser than that. That kiss had awakened a beast that had lain dormant in him for years, a man's desire.

The turn of her fear of him into defiance had prodded the beast, too — she didn't look at him with pity or revulsion. She looked at him with impertinent scrutiny, unafraid to assess him openly.

That had aroused an uncommon curiosity

in him, had diverted his mind from life's more practical side, and, in fact, had obsessed him.

It was afternoon before Rhodrick returned to the castle, at which point he was asked by his gardener to examine a weakness in a retaining wall.

Rhodrick had built many of the terraces in his vast gardens over the last twenty years with his own hands. He was quite proud of the gardens and the fact that they were renowned throughout Wales. He could not see the full beauty of them, really, as he was unable to distinguish so many of the colors. But he knew them to be impressive.

He and the head gardener determined that the wall could be shored up, and as he often did, Rhodrick unthinkingly removed his coat and waistcoat, rolled up his sleeves, took a shovel from one of the workers, and began to dig a trench where they would leverage posts to support the wall.

He was knee high in mud when he paused to drag the back of his hand across his damp brow and happened to catch sight of Owen Percy and Miss Fairchild above him at the terrace wall. They were leaning over to see what the work was about.

The sight of them caught him off guard; Percy was smirking — but that wasn't what made him feel so absurd. It was the expression on Miss Fairchild's face. She looked at him not with animosity, but surprised wonder, as if her mind could not quite grasp how a gentleman could be enticed to such hard labor.

For an uncertain moment, Rhodrick wondered that himself, and all at once he felt egregiously pedestrian. He passed the shovel to a boy and stepped out of the hole they had dug — his bad knee buckling slightly as he did so — and unrolled his sleeves. He stole a glance up at the terrace again and noted Percy's mouth was near her ear.

Miss Fairchild's gaze was still on Rhodrick, and for her, he could only scowl. Yet she did not turn her gaze from him until Percy put his hand on her elbow and turned her about. Even then, she glanced over her shoulder as if she was awed by some grotesque thing she was seeing.

Rhodrick picked up his coat and waistcoat, slung them over his shoulder, and strode away, leaving his men to finish the work. He walked into the ground floor of the castle and through the storerooms, hoping to avoid his unwelcome guests. The path took him up to the main floor and through the formal entry, where he was met by a very large gilded mirror.

He had never once paused to look at himself in that large mirror, but he did now, quite unable to keep from doing so. He was repulsed by the sight of himself — it was little wonder that Miss Fairchild had looked at him as if he were a beast. He was covered in mud, and his hair, which had been properly combed this morning, was in terrible disarray. His shirt, open at the collar, revealed hair matted with sweat.

Miss Fairchild surely thought him no better than a common gravedigger.

What incensed him was that he should care one whit what she thought of him.

He angrily yanked on a bellpull, then tossed his coat and waistcoat aside. Ifan appeared almost instantly; Rhodrick ordered water to be drawn and heated for a bath at once. He ascended the stairs two at a time, oblivious to any pain, his thoughts as far from his bloody knee as they could possibly be.

Seven

After their tour about the gardens — which were indeed stunning, and surprisingly so given that the approach to the castle was so stark and cold — Percy led Greer back to the drawing room in which they had been practically confined during their short stay here.

"You see how he is," Percy said as Greer took a seat on a divan. "Very ignoble," he added with the same smirk he'd worn all day. "Digging about like a common laborer."

Greer didn't know if the prince was particularly ignoble, but she did know that she'd never seen a gentleman quite so . . . *potent.* It surprised her, really, to see a prince covered in mud, unafraid of work — she'd never seen a gentleman exert himself so. She had no idea that it could be so . . . stirring. She could not forget the sight of the muscles in his thick arms and his broad back, clearly evident through his lawn shirt, pasted to his body with the sweat of his exertion. He had removed each shovel of mud effortlessly, had worked as quickly and stoically as men who had been born to do it.

Oh yes, the sight of him had indeed aroused her on some level, had awakened what seemed to be an innate knowledge of men, and had made her feel strangely and wildly feminine.

"He has never understood the boundaries of propriety," Percy continued as he walked to the window, not a hair out of place, and braced his arm against the frame of it in a manner that did not stretch his coat.

It occurred to Greer that perhaps Percy had never known the boundaries of honest work, for which she immediately chastised herself. Percy was her *protector.* The prince was her enemy.

He glanced over his shoulder at her when she did not respond. "You look quite fatigued, darling. This ordeal must be so very tiresome for you. We really must consider going to Rhayader to hire the services of a solicitor so that we might bring this matter to the proper justices. I fear that your health will be affected if we do not."

That was patently ridiculous. Why did he

always assume she was wilting like a fragile flower? "I am perfectly fine," she assured him. "And as I have told you, I cannot afford the services of a solicitor." She had told him that more than once, actually, yet he stubbornly continued to press the point. Of course she understood that, like her, Percy was anxious to be on his way, to be out of this awful castle with the strange sounds and the cold, and the awful musty smell that seemed to permeate certain rooms. But surely he could understand that without even a five pound note between them, hiring a lawyer or taking a suite of rooms in the nearest village was out of the question.

"Then I shall speak to him again," Percy said authoritatively, and pushed away from the window. He strolled to where Greer was sitting, and with a flip of his coattails, he sat beside her, his arm stretched along the divan behind her. "I admire your bravery, you know," he said soothingly, and leaned over to kiss her. His arms around her felt warm, his lips soft, and while Greer knew it was wrong to encourage him in the slightest, she allowed it. She felt a certain comfort in his arms, and she desperately needed to be comforted.

More cold rain fell that night, making

Greer's room feel even drearier, if that was possible. To make matters worse, the fire in the hearth died at some point in the night. Greer drew the bedcovers up over her head and tried to sleep, but she was shivering too hard to relax.

She was miserable, floating between sleep and wakefulness. It seemed as if she had barely slept at all when a sound awoke her. Greer thought it was Lulu come to rouse her, but when she pushed the bedcovers from her face, she was shocked to see her mother standing in the doorway, her long black hair wound up at her nape, wearing a red gown that seemed out of fashion. But she was smiling, too, her smile as warm and inviting as Greer remembered it, almost as if she'd never left.

A sound at the window startled her, and Greer jerked around. It was wind, she realized, and turned back to the door, but her mother was gone. The door was gone. In its place was the white mansion nestled in the trees, and standing at the entrance was the prince, half his face in shadows. His eyes were so hard and green and cold that she couldn't help but shiver uncontrollably.

She woke with a start and bolted upright. She was shivering with cold, not fear. There was no one about — not her mother, not the prince — and in fact, morning had come. The first thin shafts of light were filtering in through the window.

Nevertheless, it had seemed so real, as if she could reach out and touch him. "Sweet heaven," Greer muttered, still trying to catch her breath. She wrapped a blanket around her shoulders, winced at the cold when she put her feet to the floor, and scurried to the hearth to attempt to revive the fire.

Her efforts were not working, however, and she was still at it a quarter of an hour later when she heard a knock at the door and a gray-haired woman entered Greer's room. She took one look at Greer, then at the hearth, and said, "Oh dear. You must be quite cold." She smiled and moved to help Greer revive the hot coals into fire.

"Thank you," Greer said, and looked at the woman curiously.

"I am Mrs. Bowen, the housekeeper," she said in response to Greer's look. "Lulu is working in another part of the castle this morning, so I came to tend you."

"Ah," Greer said, thankful that she spoke English, albeit with a heavy accent. She watched as Mrs. Bowen used a hand bellows to fan the flames, grunting with the exertion of pressing it over and over. But when she had the fire going, she stood up, dusted her hands on her gray gown, and smiled at Greer. "I pray you weren't too uncomfortable . . . or that any ghosts paid you a nocturnal visit."

Greer stilled. *"Ghosts?"* she asked, suddenly feeling very ill at ease.

"Oh, 'tis an old Welsh tale," Mrs. Bowen said as she moved to the bed to make it. "They say spirits douse the fires so they cannot be seen, you know, so that they may move freely among us. That is why it is best never to speak ill of the dead."

"But I didn't," Greer said, feeling even more uncomfortable.

"Oh, of course not, miss!" Mrs. Bowen said with a warm smile. "I meant *generally* speaking. 'Tis an old folk tale. Naught more."

An old folk tale, perhaps, but it prompted Greer to dress quickly.

She joined Percy in the breakfast room, and even he claimed to have spent a sleepless night. He once again pressed Greer to seek help in Rhayader. But Greer was adamant she could not. Of the thirty pounds with which she had left London, she had less than four pounds remaining. It wasn't even enough to see her back to London, what with the cost of a hired coach and inns along the way. She didn't want to stay here, but at the moment, it seemed the lesser of two evils — the spirits and dreams and sounds notwithstanding.

She and Percy spent the remainder of the morning walking the grounds — her hand in his, for he could not seem to leave her hand be — and when they tired of that, they repaired to the drawing room to wait for what Greer assumed would be another interminable day.

She stood at the window that overlooked the gardens, calculating how long it would take her letter to reach Phoebe and Ava in London. She determined it would be three weeks at the very least due to the rainy weather and rural roads. Once the letter arrived, it might be as much as a week before they could arrange everything and send for her. If they replied straightaway, the reply might take another three weeks to return to her. That was assuming that Ava was even *in* London. She might be in the country, with the marquis.

Seven weeks in all, if luck was on her side.

Seven weeks and very little money. Greer was determined she could find a small room and manage to live on her paltry three or four pounds over seven weeks. But she could not support Mr. Percy as well.

It struck her as odd that she should be thinking of Mr. Percy's support at all, particularly given her dire circumstances. Certainly he had not asked it of her, but she had a strange feeling that it was somehow expected, as if they had struck a tacit agreement.

But they had not . . . had they? Had she given him any indication that they would continue on together, once the issue of her inheritance was solved? She was mulling that over when Mr. Percy surprised her by catching her shoulders in his hands.

"Ah!" Greer cried out. He chuckled, put his arms around her, rested his chin on her shoulder, and hugged her as they looked out the window. "And what do you see out that window to fascinate you so, Miss Fairchild?"

She focused on the garden below her, saw the men working on the terrace wall again today, and was greeted with the memory of the prince, glistening with the sweat of his efforts. "Gardens," she said.

He laughed low in her ear, his breath warm, and a slight shiver trickled down her body. "Nothing more?" he asked.

"Is there something more?"

"There is the horizon — do you see it?" he asked. "And nestled within that horizon

118

is Rhayader. If I were a gambling man, I'd wager that perhaps one more day of this bleak house and you will agree that we must get to the village before we quite lose our minds."

She wasn't certain they hadn't already. "And if I were to say yes . . . how would you suggest we pay for our keep, sir?"

She could feel him shrug at her back. "Have you nothing of value, darling? A trinket you might sell, perhaps?"

"Have you?"

Mr. Percy said nothing at first, but then took her firmly by the shoulders and forced her around to face him. His hazel eyes shone brightly, which only reminded her of the prince. The two men shared the same thick dark lashes, the same piercing gaze.

Percy smiled sympathetically at her. "Greer, dearest. When we've settled this wretched business with the prince, I shall replace your trinket with a thousand. You must have faith — we *will* settle this business, for the law is most decidedly on our side." He dipped down, so that he was eye level with her. "You trust me, do you not?"

"Of course."

"And you realize, don't you, that were you to accept my offer, he could not possibly refuse your claim?"

119

"He couldn't?" she asked, uncertain how an engagement to Percy would change the prince's feelings about her inheritance.

"He could not."

"But I . . . I don't . . ."

"And I won't be able to bear it if you refuse me," he continued. With a kiss to her forehead, he rose up. "I cannot bear to be away from you for even a day, much less a lifetime," he added, and kissed her on the lips.

It occurred to Greer that she ought to tell him she'd not decided anything — not even where she would be for a *day*, much less a lifetime — but the touch of Percy's lips silenced her. The feel of a man was so . . . comforting. It made her feel a little fluttery inside, and frankly, she felt safe. Much safer than when she was shivering under the covers in that dreadful room.

When Percy's hand boldly found her breast, she gasped, surprised by the sensuous thrill of it.

She could not honestly say how they ended up on the divan, her arms around his neck, his hand on her breast, and his mouth on her neck. She just remembered a bit of moving about and then the feeling of sinking with a man's hard body pressed against hers. That was not an entirely new sensation to her — after all, she had been out for two years among London's best bachelors — but rarely had anything in which she'd been engaged progressed to such shameless fondling.

Her thoughts vacillated between an awareness of her lack of decorum and nothing but a desire to continue on with the physical pleasure she was experiencing. Perhaps it was the diversion from the sheer tedium she had suffered the last two days that propelled her, but whatever it was, she quite forgot herself and was, therefore, humiliated beyond repair when Percy suddenly lifted his head, grinned at her, and turned that grin to something or someone on the other side of the divan.

Greer dreamily turned her head and glanced around to see the prince standing just inside the room, his arms folded implacably across his chest, his expression full of fury.

The sight of him snatched her breath clean from her lungs, and for one terrifying moment, she could not breathe or move. But then the heat of shame flooded her face, and she pushed hard at Percy, who was still wearing an impertinent smile and was much slower to stand.

"Get *off!*" she cried, pushing hard, forcing

him to stand. She half rolled, half leapt off the divan and with her back to the prince, hastily shook out her skirts and adjusted her bodice. Never in her life had she felt as vile as she did in that moment — she was no better than a common strumpet, carrying on wantonly on the man's divan, and it mortified her to her very core.

But then the prince walked into the room, and Greer made the mistake of stealing a look at him. His expression of disgust made her sink even lower.

He shifted that look of revulsion to Percy. "You both *revolt* me," he said, his voice dripping with it. "Had I not arrived when I did, you would have tarnished my house with your fornication!"

That remark nearly sent Greer to her knees.

But Percy merely snorted. "Don't be absurd." Yet the censure in his voice was incongruent with his expression. For some inexplicable reason, Percy looked almost *pleased* that they had been caught in such a compromising position.

It confounded Greer, but at the moment, the look of utter rebuke the prince was directing at her distressed her to the point that she thought she could be ill. She turned away and somehow managed to stumble to the window, where she braced her hands on the casing and tried to compose herself with great gulps of air.

"I think all the absurdity and depravity in this room lies with you," the prince said with great rancor. "It is obvious to me that if you seduce Miss Fairchild in such a public manner, she will have no choice but to marry you, and that, sir, is a rather convenient path to her money, as well as yours."

The implication stunned Greer; she pivoted about. "That's preposterous!"

"Pay him no mind," Percy said acidly. "If a true gentleman happens upon two lovers, he will look the other way. But a scarred and lonely man will act with jealousy."

Percy's remark caused the prince's eyes to fill with murderous rage. His body, large and fierce, tensed as though he was restraining himself from leaping on Percy, and Greer expected him to lash out, to strike Percy. But he did not — he turned that rage to her. His unfettered scrutiny shamed her terribly; she pressed her hands to her cheeks and said shakily, "I beg your pardon, my lord."

"You owe him no apology!" Percy snapped.

But she *did* owe him an apology, they *both* owed him one, and she was appalled that

Percy would consider their conduct above the reproach of *any* man.

"You don't," Percy reiterated defiantly. "He is not our conscience and he is certainly the last person who should judge us!"

"Mr. Percy!" she exclaimed, mortified.

The prince said something in Welsh to which Percy returned a violent stream of what Greer was certain was the worst vitriol.

It must have been, for whatever Percy said changed the prince's mien — he suddenly looked very dangerous. *Lethal.* She believed he could snap Percy's neck with only one of his large paws. But he surprised her — with a scathing look at the two of them, he pivoted about and strode out of the room.

When the door closed behind him, Percy swiped angrily at an oil lamp and sent it crashing to the floor. "A *cretin!*"

"Mr. Percy!" Greer cried. "He saw us in a most unflattering light! How can you be so cavalier?"

"For God's sake, do not come unhinged now!" he snapped at her.

The admonition chafed. "Have you quite lost your mind? My reputation has just been irrevocably ruined, and you caution me against becoming *unhinged?*"

"This is hardly the time for theatrics, Greer!"

124

"Theatrics!" It seemed as if she didn't know the man standing so angrily before her at all. "Are you not alarmed, Mr. Percy?"

"Alarmed?" he scoffed. "I couldn't possibly care what Radnor thinks, for I know —"

Whatever he knew was lost, for the door was suddenly thrown open with such force that it hit the wall. Through it swept the prince with three footmen at his back. Two of them instantly started toward them, and Mr. Percy quickly pushed Greer behind him.

"Would you kill an unarmed man?" he demanded of the prince as the footmen advanced.

"God in heaven," the prince spat. *"Get him out of my sight!"* he roared.

"If you want to settle this like gentlemen —" Percy tried, but the footmen grabbed him. He began to struggle, ranting in Welsh at the prince, his face red with anger. Greer screamed as Percy fought mightily against them. One of the men managed to twist Percy's arms behind his back, which effectively entrapped him.

And yet the prince stood by, watching him through narrowed eyes, his massive legs braced apart, his thick arms folded. When the man had tied Percy's hands, the prince nodded curtly, and they began to drag Percy from the room.

"Mr. Percy!" Greer shouted, terrified. *"Owen!"*

Her protector did not hear her, as he was cursing his host and the three men who dragged him away. When they had left the room, and she could hear Percy's shouts moving away from her, the prince slowly turned his head and looked at her so coldly that Greer panicked; she instantly shoved up against the wall and frantically searched the room for an escape.

"Stop acting so fearful, Miss Fairchild. You will come to no harm under my roof — I am not like your *lover.*"

He said the word in a way that made her feel dirty. "He is *not* —" She quickly thought better of debating that now, given what the prince had seen, and thought about her own neck. "What do you intend to do with me?"

"I don't know," he drawled, his eyes hungrily raking over her as he casually moved forward. "What do men typically do with whores?"

Greer gasped and eyed the door. But the prince shook his head. "You cannot escape. I will not allow Percy to ruin you and take your inheritance, no matter how much you obviously would enjoy the ruining."

"You are a wretched, *vile* man!" she snapped.

"How easily you toss such words about, given your own reprehensible behavior, Miss Fairchild," he said, and moved again.

So did Greer.

He paused and sighed, muttered something in Welsh, then pushed a hand through his hair before settling both hands on his waist. He peered at her, assessing her. "Will you come of your own volition, or will you force me to take you?"

Take her? Terror choked her. "Take me *where?*" she cried.

"I intend to keep you apart from Mr. Percy for a time so that you are not tempted any deeper into ruin. Will you come willingly?"

"I will not go *willingly* with you."

He smiled dangerously. "Frankly, I think a poor, stranded woman of low morals is not in a position to choose," he said, and suddenly lunged at her.

Greer screamed as she made a mad dash for the door, but he easily caught her and overpowered her. She struggled, but he held her tightly, his arms like iron bands around her. Her breasts were mashed against the wall of his chest, her body pressed against the hard length of his.

He smiled meanly as she struggled, his gaze dropping to her lips. "Whose kiss do you prefer, Miss Fairchild? Or are they all the same to you?"

She cried out and turned her head.

He caught her face in his big hand and roughly forced her to look at him, his gaze on her lips again. "One would think you'd be more selective with whom you lie. But I suppose a pound is a pound —"

With a cry of fury and fear she kicked him hard in the shins. If the man felt it, he gave no indication. He stood there, holding her as if she were nothing, his heated gaze drifting to her bosom. Greer continued to struggle breathlessly, but he seemed not the least bit winded, restraining her until she was spent.

She stopped struggling and the tears began to well.

"Stop that," he said gruffly. "There is no need for crocodile tears."

"Please don't kill me," she said weakly.

He snorted, let his hand drift to her throat. "*Killing* you is not the first thing that comes to mind, Miss Fairchild," he drawled.

She thought he would kiss her, thought he would force himself on her right there, but he suddenly picked her up. Greer shrieked and tried to free herself, but he tightened his hold so easily that she was completely helpless.

He carried her out the door and down the corridor to a stairwell she had not seen before. He put her on her feet there, but held her in his unbreakable grip before him as he forced her up the stairs.

"I am not what you think I am!" she insisted, dreading their destination, dreading what he intended to do to her, and frantic to bargain her way out of this. "What you intend to do is criminal! Be forewarned that I will bring it to the attention of the highest authority!"

The prince snorted and pushed her up the stairs, his body pressed against her back, his anger and strength propelling her.

"You are despicable!" she said as he shoved her up the stairs. "You have nothing to say for yourself because you *know* what you intend to do is despicable!" She believed it — as they climbed that spiraling staircase, the many things Percy had told Greer about the prince of Powys began to percolate like a bad brew in her mind. He was a murderer, a thief, and she feared for her virtue *and* her life. She caught a second wind and began to struggle again, trying to kick him and scratch him, but he merely caught her by the waist and hauled her up the stairs as if she were a small child.

They reached the top of the stairs and went up another, narrower set, and finally arrived at the topmost landing. There was a single door. He held her with one arm around her waist as she tried to claw free, her back to his chest, her legs against one powerful thigh that tensed as he used the other leg to kick the door in.

He pushed Greer inside. She stumbled across the room, catching her balance against a chair as the prince calmly walked in behind her and stood just over the threshold.

She was panting. Tears over which she had no control were sliding down her cheeks. She took in her surroundings as she caught her breath. They were at the top of a turret, in a round room with three windows. There was a bed, a single chair, and a writing desk. Greer assumed that behind a privacy screen was a water closet and a basin.

She believed she was in a bedchamber and turned a look of pure abhorrence to him.

"You shall be comfortable here for a time," he said as his gaze slowly traced the length of her body, making her feel exposed. "You will not be harmed, Miss Fairchild. Whatever you might think of me, your fears are for naught — I do not consort with whores."

The word sickened her, but not as much as the thought that suddenly occurred to her. *He was going to leave her here.* She would be forgotten and eventually disappear, just like a fairy-tale princess in a tower. She panicked again and made a lunge for the door, trying desperately to pass him and escape, but he caught her in his arm and held her with infuriating ease.

"Unhand me!" she screamed, her fury unleashed, clawing at him, kicking him, attempting to bite him. He tried to subdue her, but she bit his hand at the same moment she kicked his shin.

"Stop!" he roared, and with a grunt of effort, he whirled around with her in his arms and shoved her up against the wall, holding her there with both arms. *"Calm yourself,"* he said through gritted teeth.

Exhausted, Greer gave in with a whimper. Her eyes searched his face — the jagged scar, the ever-present shadow of his beard, and the hard, cold glint of his eyes. It was useless. Whatever he would do with her, he would do — she was powerless to stop it. More hot tears slid down her face.

He frowned darkly and pushed away from her, let her go. Greer closed her eyes and hugged herself tightly for a moment, thankful for the small reprieve. When she opened her eyes, he was standing at the door, his hand on the knob. He held her gaze for a long, heated moment, then stepped out, pulling the door shut.

As the door began to close Greer's panic swelled again. With a screech, she launched herself at the door the same moment he shut it, fearing that when the door shut, she would be locked in this room until she died. She fell against the door, heard the tumble of the lock, and the panic rose like bile in her throat.

She screamed and pounded her fists against the door. "Mr. Percy!" she shrieked. *"Mr. Percy!"*

She heard nothing but the sound of receding footfalls.

She screamed again, flailing at the door with her fists, using both hands to try and force the handle.

When it became clear she could not escape through that door, she looked frantically about, and ran to one of the windows. She was high above the ground, fifty feet or more, with no way down.

It was hopeless. She was locked in, destined to die here. Greer leaned against the wall, her cheek pressed to it, as sobs racked her body — sobs so great that she could scarcely hold herself up and fell to her hands and knees, desperately trying to drag air into her lungs before her fear choked the life from her.

Eight

When Greer had cried herself dry — there was not another tear in her body, she was certain — she took a big gulp of air and picked herself up off the floor. Given the paucity of furniture in the room, she opted for the bed. She lay on her back, stared up at the bare ceiling, and had a rather stern talk with herself.

Behaving like a madwoman would not solve her predicament. She had to clear her mind and *think*. So she forced herself up, walked behind the screen to the basin and water closet, washed her face, straightened her gown, and tried to repair her hair, which had come undone from its coif. It could not be salvaged, so she combed it with her fingers, letting it hang down her back, and began to pace the floor.

She walked round and round that room that afternoon, studying her situation from every conceivable angle. She ran through a gamut of emotions — a sharp fear about what would happen to her, fury that she'd been taken prisoner, and creeping doubts about Percy. She was beginning to think of things that did not make sense — such as his lack of funds and his sudden desire to marry her.

Oh God, how she wished for Phoebe and Ava! She needed someone to talk to, someone who would tell her if she was right or wrong about him. She reached no conclusions other than the most obvious: she had to escape this place *at once.*

But she had no idea how to go about escaping, and had paced herself almost into exhaustion thinking about it when she heard a commotion on the stairs outside her door. The sound alarmed her, and she looked around for something with which to protect herself. Thank God, the bloody fools had left a fire poker. She snatched it up, brandishing it in both hands, her legs braced apart, ready to strike.

"Greer!"

It was Percy. *Percy!* His voice was so unexpected that a wave of relief nearly buckled her knees. She dropped the poker and rushed to the door, grabbing the handle, knowing it was locked, having tried a dozen times or more, but hoping nonetheless.

She couldn't open it. "Owen, I am here!" she cried, pounding on the door. "I am here, I am *here!* Open the door, please open the door!"

"Greer, please listen carefully," he said on the other side of the door.

"Open the door!" she shrieked.

"I am going for help," he continued, his voice earnest. "I shall ride to London and your cousin and ask that she bring all the force she can bear down on this place!"

"I'm going with you!" Greer shouted, banging her fists against the door. "Please open the door!"

There was a pause, and in that moment, Greer felt her heart sink. Her gut instinct told her she'd been deceived.

"I cannot," he said, his voice much quieter.

"Percy! Open the door!"

"I shall return as soon as I am able, you must trust me! You *must* be strong, darling! The prince will not harm you; he has given me his word. But you must be strong!"

"No!" she screamed, beating the door again with her fists. "Don't you *dare* leave me here!"

"I shall return as soon as possible, I swear it to you!"

"Percy! Don't leave me!" she screeched.

But it was too late — she could hear him running down the steps, and her only hope running down the steps with him.

"Percy!" she screamed again, but she knew he was not coming back. Not now, not ever. After a moment, there was nothing but silence, and Greer dissolved into despair, flinging herself facedown on the bed, as disconsolate as she had ever been in her life.

Ifan reported to Rhodrick that Miss Fairchild had refused supper, and had, in fact, kicked the contents down the steps when Griffith, a footman, had divested her of the fire poker she had wielded with the intent of braining him.

Rhodrick believed she'd be ravenous this morning, and carried the tray up himself. He knocked on the door, but heard nothing. He adjusted the tray he held, fished in his pocket for the key, and fit it into the lock, fully expecting to be attacked the moment he entered the room.

But Miss Fairchild surprised him. She was sitting cross-legged on the bed, her legs tucked up under her gown, her hair unbound and spilling wildly about her shoulders, watching him warily with the stormiest blue eyes he'd ever seen.

"*Bore da.* Good morning," he said quietly. She did not respond.

He deposited the tray on the writing table. "You must be hungry."

Her response was a look so full of loathing that it made Rhodrick feel a wee bit off-kilter. He turned his face away, looking at the tray, and from the corner of his eye, saw Miss Fairchild rise and calmly walk to the table. She gave him an icy glare, and with one swipe of her hand, she sent the tray flying to the floor. With another withering look, she impudently passed so close to him on her way to the bed that her skirt and arm brushed against his body.

He looked at the spilled food and the broken porcelain on the carpet. "That was not very smart," he opined.

"I don't want your opinion," she said as she resumed her seat on the edge of the bed.

"You might need your strength."

"Why? It looks as if I shall be locked up here until Percy returns, and if that is true, I would rather die." She fell to her back on the bed, her gaze fixed on the ceiling.

"Percy will not return," he said. "He agreed to leave my house for one hundred pounds. He had the opportunity to take you with him, but he did not believe one hundred pounds was enough for two."

Her eyes narrowed menacingly at that news. "You are a liar," she said, her voice surprisingly hoarse. "Mr. Percy has gone for help."

As he suspected, the woman was uncommonly stubborn. How could she possibly believe that Owen had gone for help? Was she truly so naïve? "He has gone, Miss Fairchild," he said impatiently. "But not for help. He won't come back, for he has what he wants for the time being — one hundred pounds and his freedom."

Miss Fairchild suddenly sat up. "Suppose that is true. Then what do you intend to do with me?" she demanded. "Keep me locked away in this godforsaken place until the world has forgotten me? Or do you intend to use me for your base desires?"

The question made him feel a bit guilty; he had indeed thought of taking her into his bed. It didn't ease his thoughts in the least to find her so wildly alluring this morning, her blue eyes crystal and bright, her hair bearing the look of having had a lover's hands run through it. Her gown, he noticed, was wrinkled. If he hadn't known she was locked inside this room while they escorted Percy out of Powys, he might have believed she'd just come from her lover's bed.

Frankly, the image of her beneath Percy, as he had found them yesterday, had not left him all night. He could think of nothing but her body, Percy's hand on her breast. *Of himself, buried deep inside her.*

He unthinkingly clenched and unclenched his right hand. "You are a young woman, Miss Fairchild," he said quietly. "You cannot possibly understand the strength of a man's desire or his true intentions. Yet I trust that with time, one day you will realize what I am telling you today is true: Mr. Percy was only moments from having your virtue and your fortune, and you were only moments away from handing it to him."

She colored, but lifted her chin defiantly. "And what if I were, my lord? What business is it of yours?"

"None. Your life is yours to waste as you see fit, your body yours to give to whomever you please. Once I have proof of your identity, you may yet throw your life away on the likes of Owen Percy — I cannot stop you. But without proof of your identity, I will not hand you four thousand pounds that I know will end up in *his* hands."

"You are a monster," she breathed angrily, "the most despicable creature I have ever met."

He flinched inwardly, but shrugged indifferently.

"It will take *weeks* for proof to arrive from London, especially now with winter upon us. And I suppose you think to keep me prisoner here?"

"I prefer to think of you as my reluctant guest, and I your reluctant host. You may stay . . . or you may go. I care not which."

She snorted indelicately. "I am hardly *free*," she said disbelievingly. "I can't even walk out that door if I choose."

He glanced at the door and stepped back, gesturing toward it. "You are free."

"Ha," she said. "What if I were to walk out that door, and the gates, and keep walking until I reached Rhayader? Then what would you do, my lord?"

"It is quite far. And there are clouds coming in. But you are free to attempt it."

She looked warily at the door, then at him. She slowly came to her feet, her eyes on him. She moved haltingly at first, as if she meant to test him — then slowly walked around the bed, watching him closely.

When she passed him, she ran.

Rhodrick did not try to stop her, but stood and listened to the sound of her shoes on the stone steps, running as hard and as fast as she could from the monster in the room.

He shoved his hands in his pockets,

gripped the handkerchief she had dropped in his study, and waited until he could hear her no more. Then he began the painful descent to the main floors.

After finding Mrs. Bowen — "There was a bit of a spill above," he said — he returned to his study, intent on working while Miss Fairchild foolishly wandered the hills, searching for her lover for all Rhodrick knew.

Miss Fairchild might look for him all she liked, but Rhodrick felt certain she would return when she was cold and hungry.

An hour or so later, however, when he happened to glance up, he noticed a bank of black clouds had engulfed the peaks of the Cambrians. Storms that rode in from the west like this were often quite dangerous. As much as he would like to leave her to her own devices, he couldn't. He groaned; Cain and Abel began to thump their tails in anticipation of something exciting happening.

"Bloody *chit*," he muttered angrily as he stood and glanced at his dogs. "Out," he said, and the two hounds were instantly on their feet and at the door. The three of them made their way to the foyer, where Rhodrick was met by Ifan, who held out his hat and his gloves.

"Did you see the girl's direction?" he asked in Welsh.

"The main road, my lord," Ifan responded, and bowed so low that Rhodrick could almost see his reflection in the bald pate of his head.

"Had she anything with her? A cloak? A bonnet?"

"A red cloak, milord. And a small beaded bag."

He nodded, took the hat and gloves, and stepped outside. Cain and Abel bounded forth ahead of him, their noses taking in the day's events in the courtyard.

The dark bank of clouds was moving steadily forward like an invading army from which there was no escape, so Rhodrick hastened his step to the stables, had his mount saddled and another horse fitted with a ladies' saddle. Holding the reins of the second horse, with his dogs running alongside, he rode out through the castle gates.

NINE

Greer stopped running when her lungs burned and began to walk, striding purposefully down the rutted road, wincing each time she stepped on a rock. Would that she had taken a moment to change into her sturdier boots, for her shoes were all wrong for this sort of terrain. She'd paused only to grab her cloak and the reticule in which she kept the things most dear to her.

She paused to catch her breath and sat on a rock at the side of the road, thought again how she would personally like to string the prince up and beat him like a carpet. Envisioning him being dragged behind a team of oxen appealed as well. It was remarkable, she thought, that she was not frightened any longer, but simply exhausted and incredibly frustrated.

She looked back the way she had come — she had walked far enough that she could see nothing but the road and the thick forest whose towering firs rose up on either side of the road.

Greer shifted her gaze to the direction in which she was headed. She could see nothing but the road and the firs in that direction, too. The only difference was that in the direction she was walking, low black rain clouds had formed and were moving toward her.

Honestly, she believed she might walk for hours and hours before reaching anything even *resembling* civilization. That is, if she wasn't left for dead by highwaymen or some sort of forest creature that wanted to feast on human flesh.

The sting of tears in her eyes caught her by surprise — she opened her reticule and looked for her mother's handkerchief, which she always carried, realizing that she had managed to lose it in that wretched place. So she removed her glove to dry her eyes.

What a *fool* she'd been! She'd trusted Mr. Percy with her life, had believed his esteem of her was real. How could he possibly have left her here for one hundred pounds? *Bloody bastard. Rotten blackguard.* She realized that he'd enticed her into all sorts of trouble with his charming manner at every step of the way.

The sound of an approaching rider startled her, and she vaulted to her feet, looking about frantically before crashing into the dense foliage of the forest and hiding behind a tree, one hand to her pounding heart, the other over her mouth to keep her gasp from being heard.

She heard the rider — *riders?* — pass by. She removed her hand from her mouth and tried to see through the foliage as she quickly fit her hand in her glove. The riders slowed, then stopped. And then started back toward her. Greer froze; her heart almost leapt out of her chest. She did not move — she *dared* not move. But her pulse was pounding in her ears and she did not hear the dogs until they were almost upon her. A tiny shriek of surprise escaped her, and she instantly clamped a hand over her mouth. *He'd come to take her back!* The bloody scoundrel had lied — she wasn't free! He was toying with her!

The dogs, realizing she was known to them, trotted on. Greer did not move, but stayed behind the tree, holding her breath. She heard a horse neigh, then the sound of hooves again, coming toward her. She pressed her back to the tree, closed her eyes, and prayed.

He stopped again, near enough that she

believed he could reach out and touch her. Several silent moments passed in which Greer's heart beat so hard and her fear grew so suffocating that she suddenly fled. She just ran into the forest, holding her hands before her to push the bushes and tree branches from her face.

She heard him bellow her name and veered left, sliding recklessly down a slope. She could hear him coming for her like a wild boar crashing through the trees, drawing closer and terrifying her.

She screamed when he caught her, tackling her legs and knocking her to the ground, the two of them landing in a shower of leaves. Greer kicked out and clawed the earth, trying to drag herself from his grip, but he scrambled up her body, flipped her onto her back, and pinned her arms to the ground with his hands, her body with his legs.

His eyes narrowed angrily on her; they were both panting. Greer screamed again, and he winced at the sound. "God in heaven, there is no one to hear you, so you may as well save your breath!"

"You are a *liar!*" she shouted. "You said I was free!"

"You *are* free, you foolish chit!"

"Then why are you following me?" she

demanded, valiantly attempting to free her arms.

"I have asked myself that very question and could arrive at no satisfactory answer," he said, and clamped his legs around hers in a viselike grip when she tried to buck him. "Inexplicably, I feel the need to protect you. *Again,*" he added with a dark frown at her breasts, which were dangerously close to spilling out of her gown.

Their closeness and his gaze on her bosom made her feel terribly exposed; she could feel the heat of her discomfort bleeding into her face and neck, and bucked harder.

"If you are foolish enough to believe you are in some sort of danger and insist on fleeing on foot, so be it," he snapped, his grip on her arms tightening. "But you cannot possibly make it to Rhayader with a storm imminent!"

As if the heavens wished to prove his point, a few drops of rain began to fall. Greer ignored them and twisted beneath him. "If I didn't have to run through the forest to escape your *protection,* I'd be quite capable of walking to Rhayader."

"And if you weren't so bloody stubborn, we'd be sheltered now. And for your consideration, I will tell you that you have walked only three miles thus far. Rhayader is yet another *six*."

Greer stopped struggling and glared up at him. "As far as *that?*" she cried. Several more fat drops of rain fell. "What sort of place *is* this where there is no civilization!"

"I have no patience or time for your foolishness." He got up and leaned down, slipped his hands under her arms and jerked her to her feet. "If you insist on running into the forest to hide behind trees, I will not stop you. You may find the journey to Rhayader easier if you avail yourself of one of my carriages on the morrow," he said, clamping his hand around her wrist. "But at the moment, you will return to Llanmair!" He began to march her along behind him, pulling her when she lagged, holding her up when she slipped.

It was almost as if he were perturbed that she had interrupted the course of his day by escaping. Then again, Greer imagined murderers, profligates, and imprisoners of unmarried women were quite often impatient.

Nevertheless, a return to Llanmair was really more than she could endure. "If I am to believe you, then why can't I have a carriage now?" Greer demanded.

"Because a storm is coming."

"A storm! That is naught but an excuse!"

she argued. "I believe you fear that if I reach Rhayader, I shall tell them all how abominably I have been treated, and the authorities shall come for you straightaway."

The prince paused, and for the first time, he smiled. Actually, it was scarcely a smile, rather a flash of amusement that had skirted the features of his face. "To whom do you think the good citizens of Rhayader owe their allegiance, Miss Fairchild? A silly young woman from London who, by all indications, has no more sense than a woodchuck? Or to me?"

"The good citizens of Rhayader will not stand for false imprisonment!"

"Indeed not. But I would suggest that as you will arrive under your own free will, free to come or to go as you please, the residents there might question whether or not you have indeed been falsely imprisoned, or if you're not simply a bit barmy!"

She gasped with indignation.

"I am returning to the castle," he said firmly, "and so are you. I would suggest you steel yourself to soldier through another night at Llanmair."

As if she could possibly soldier through another night! But his grip was ironclad, it was beginning to rain more heavily, and thunder rumbled closer to them. She was stuck, the realization of which made her feel even more exhausted and ravenous and *furious* with the world at large. "How do you expect me to 'soldier on' in either of the horrible rooms I have been given at your castle?" she asked petulantly. "I will not go back to that locked room or I shall go mad!"

"You may return to the room where you first slept if you like."

"That is even worse!"

He paused again, looking surprised. "I beg your pardon?"

"The bedchambers to which you subject your *guests,* reluctant or otherwise, are horrible!" she exclaimed. "They are very cold, and there are quite a lot of mysterious creaks and moans to keep a body awake at night, and all the rooms seem to lock from the outside. It is a very unaccommodating castle!"

"Forgive me, Miss Fairchild, if my house is 'unaccommodating.' I was not aware that one required a bit of luxury to better swindle her host! If it is another room you require, you need only ask," he said, and jerked her forward again, marching at a remarkable clip, given his uneven gait. The rain was cold and hard against her skin, and Greer wished she'd brought a bonnet. How had she ever thought to escape wearing nothing but the clothes on her back and one ridiculously thin cloak?

"Do you know how to ride?" he asked gruffly as they reached the road.

"Yes, of course I know how to ride," she snapped.

He pushed her toward the horse bearing the ladies' saddle and moved to lift her, but Greer threw up a hand. "I am perfectly capable of mounting a horse! I don't need or require your assistance."

With a smug smile, the ogre stood back. She tried to get her foot in the stirrup, but it was too high, and her skirt was not full enough to allow her to lift her leg without revealing too much of it to her observer.

With one failed attempt, she stood back, studying the saddle. "Oh for God's sake," the prince said irritably, and roughly grabbed her about the waist.

"I beg your pardon!" Greer exclaimed hotly, but he ignored her, lifting her up and seating her squarely on the saddle. He looked up at her face; his hands slid to her hips. She could feel the heat in his gaze and his hands, could feel her body responding to it, and shifted in her seat. "I will thank you not to do such a thing again."

"You have my word," he snapped, dropping his hands. He remounted his horse, then turned back to Greer and reached for the reins of her horse, but she promptly snatched them up. "At least do me the favor of allowing me to *ride* the horse, my lord."

His gaze fell to her lips for a brief moment before he turned and spurred his horse forward. Greer's horse, apparently not wanting to be left behind, broke into a trot before Greer had even situated herself. She grabbed tight hold of the reins, brushed her wet hair from her face, dislodging several leaves in the process, and with her back straight and stiff, she rode along, pretending she was the one in command.

They had ridden just a few minutes when thunder cracked directly overhead, causing Greer to shriek in fright. Ahead of her, the prince suddenly veered off the road onto a path through the forest. So, of course, did her mare — she may as well have been riding a mule, the horse was so stubborn, refusing to obey any command she attempted to give it. In fact, the stupid little mare broke into a gallop in her haste to reach her companion and the dogs. Once again, Greer was helpless. She looked straight ahead as the little mare caught up to the big black hunter and trotted alongside him.

Greer did not deign to look at the prince,

catching only a glimpse of him with his hat pulled low over his eyes. He shouted above the rain, "If you pull up and back, she will heed you."

"I *know* that," Greer shouted back, and lifted her chin as if she intended to be trotting alongside him.

He shook his head and said something in Welsh that she did not believe sounded very flattering, and she shot a heated look at him. "I beg your pardon? I do not *speak* Welsh —"

"You should."

"But I *don't.* So if you were speaking to *me,* I did not understand you."

"I wasn't speaking to you!"

"Then to whom where you speaking? Your horse?"

"Yes! My horse!" he snapped. "I was remarking to my *horse* that you are uncommonly *mulish.*"

"Argh!" she cried, incensed.

The prince raised his brows, daring her to disagree.

Greer snapped her gaze to the path ahead of them. "I prefer we not speak at all. *Ever.*"

"That would suit me exceedingly well," he agreed, and spurred his horse just ahead as another loud clap of thunder exploded over them.

The trail they were riding was steep, and they crested a ridge as the storm seemed to intensify. Below them, Greer could see the huge castle that was Llanmair. By leaving the road, he had taken a more direct route home, she realized.

He kept on, looking back often to assure himself she was there, as if she had any choice with such a stubborn little mare. Greer turned away and looked to the west, into the valley. And in the valley, not but a few miles from Llanmair, was a grand white mansion.

She scarcely had time to see it before a bolt of lightning struck a tree not twenty yards from her. The mare made a sound unlike anything Greer had ever heard from a horse and reared, clawing the sky in fear. Greer grappled for the pommel, but the leather was wet, and she couldn't hold on. She tumbled off the side of the horse, landing hard, the wind knocked from her lungs.

She tried to roll over, to get up, but could not seem to move. In the next moment, the prince was leaning over her, scooping her up in his arms and then diving with her, tumbling just as a horrifying cracking sound rent the air. Greer twisted about and saw that a tree had fallen exactly where she'd been lying.

She gasped and clung to the prince, her heart beating erratically as she realized how close she had come to death. It had all happened so fast! How had he known? But he had her, one arm around her waist, holding her with her back pressed against his chest, one large hand on the crown of her head. The wind had picked up as the storm moved over them, bending trees and kicking up leaves into their faces.

"Are you hurt?" he shouted above the roar of the storm.

"No . . . I — perhaps my ankle," she said uncertainly.

He moved instantly, letting go her waist, and felt her legs through her cloak and gown, then her arms.

"The horse!" Greer cried, realizing the mare was nowhere. "She's gone!"

"She'll find her way home," he said, and picked her up, carrying her to his horse and depositing her just ahead of the pommel before swinging up behind her. He swept his hat off his head and put it on her — the thing fell down to her brows, but she was grateful for it. The prince anchored her once more with his arm around her waist, pulling her into the safety of his broad chest.

As he spurred his horse forward, Greer realized with an incredulous gulp that the ogre had just saved her life. He could have left her and no one ever would have known — but he'd *saved* her.

She twisted in his arms, pushed the hat back, and looked at him, almost expecting to see someone else. An angel, perhaps.

It was no angel behind her. He looked down, frowning. "What?"

"You *saved* me," she said. "You saved my life!"

He instantly looked away, turning his head slightly. "I saved my horse," he said. "You happened to be in the way."

By the saints, he was undoubtedly the most discourteous man she had ever encountered! She could hardly wait to tell Ava and Phoebe all about him — assuming she ever saw them again — but if she did, she would tell them all the horrible things he'd said about her character, the medieval accommodations in his little kingdom, and his locking her up, for God's sake! And now, treating her as if she were a horrible bother, when *he* had kept her here against her will!

Really, she was so incensed that she began to imagine she would write a book about her perils: *My Journey to Wales,* by Greer Fairchild. *The Perils of Pursuing an Inheritance.*

She had written the entire first chapter in

157

her head by the time they rode through the back gates of Llanmair.

Fortunately, the prince did not attempt to help her down, but allowed a footman to do it. She returned his hat, and as she pushed wet hair from her eyes, he took it and said, with all the finesse and warmth of a rock, "You will dine with me this evening."

She glared at him. "Thank you, but *no.*"

He nodded curtly and strode into the castle so fast and hard that his cloak billowed out behind him.

Shivering from the cold and her close brush with death, Greer hoped she had not just been so foolish as to refuse any supper at all — she was absolutely faint with hunger.

TEN

Rhodrick strode through the foyer, tossing his gloves and hat at a footman before bounding up the stairs, taking them two at a time with the dogs on his heels. When he reached his study, he slammed the door behind him, walked to the hearth, and stood there, his hands on his hips, his aching knee forgotten as he glared into the flames.

He absently clenched his hand and then slowly unclenched it, stretching the fingers long and wide. Miss Greer Vaughan Fairchild, if that was truly her name, was the most exasperatingly stubborn, *willful* woman he'd ever met. He'd be very glad when she was gone — she had brought enough trouble into his life as it was without adding insolence and ingratitude to the list.

As he mentally reviewed that *annoying* incident in the forest, he could only seem to see her blue eyes and the dark circles under them. He would have lost his temper altogether if she hadn't looked so worn down. And it certainly didn't help matters that she smelled quite as nice as she did, like lilacs in bloom, or how her body had felt so exquisitely soft beneath his. It had taken an uncommon strength to prevent his arousal.

Intolerable.

He thrust his hand in his pocket and withdrew her handkerchief and looked at the delicate embroidery. Such regard for her fair looks and feminine ways was absurd and ill-advised, to say the least. But he couldn't seem to help himself, to stop thinking of her . . . or imagining her in various stages of undress, or posed in various acts of love-making.

As a result, he was glad she hated him so. Let her eat in her suite and never come out for all he cared. He hardly needed the aggravation.

Rhodrick stuffed the handkerchief in his pocket, stalked to his desk, and sat heavily. He stared out at the storm for a time, his mind's eye filled with how close she'd come to serious injury, if not death, when the lightning had splintered that tree. Only by the grace of God did it sway in the wind long enough for him to dismount and grab her up before it fell.

He thought about her long black hair

blowing wildly about her shoulders, the soiled hem of her cloak — her ruined shoes and her garments, soaked completely through so that he could see the curving outline of her body.

It was a while before Rhodrick could shake such images from his thoughts and force himself to concentrate on some correspondence. But he did concede one small thing to Miss Fairchild: he instructed Ifan to prepare a suite of rooms on the west side of the castle. He had no idea what a woman's sensitivities might require in a set of rooms — one would think a bed, a basin, and a fireplace were sufficient — but he thought the suite that had once been his late wife's would be the closest thing to pleasing a woman that Llanmair might possess.

The rooms likewise had the advantage of being agreeably situated on the other side of the castle, far away from the master suite and study.

That night he dined alone. The two footmen who always attended him stood silently by the sideboard, moving stealthily to remove a course and replace it with the next. Rhodrick had dined in this manner for the last ten years, and he'd never once given thought to his surroundings or his solitude. Yet tonight he couldn't help but look about the dining room and wonder how a woman might find it. It seemed perfectly fine to him, but as he had been told that his castle was "unaccommodating," he was mildly curious.

Perhaps the room was a bit austere, as there was nothing on the walls save a large painting of a hunt scene. And the color of the walls — he wasn't quite certain of it, but thought them brown.

He would ask Meg Awbrey. She would tell him truthfully what needed to be done.

As he sat contemplating the décor of his dining room, a most extraordinary thing happened — he heard the faint strains of music. Rhodrick stilled, uncertain what he was hearing at first, until the melancholy chords, beautifully played, registered. Haydn, perhaps? No, Handel — he'd heard this particular piece in London several years ago. And now it was bringing a touch of civility to his home, a beautiful sound, richly melodic, calming and tranquil.

Intent on the music, he picked up his brandy and stood, oblivious to the footman who hurried to pull back his chair, and quit the room without a word.

As he neared the music room, he noticed the door was ajar and slowed his step, moving carefully, so as not to disturb her. As he reached the door, she stopped playing, and he froze, thinking she'd heard him, expecting her to retreat. But a scant moment later, the chords of a lugubrious song, masterfully played, rose up and filled the hall.

Through the sliver of the open door, he could see her back. She had pinned up her hair, twisting it in a way that defied description. The gown she wore — green or gray — fit so tightly across her back that he could see her small shoulder blades moving elegantly as she played, as well as the graceful curve of her arms as her hands performed their dance on the keys of the pianoforte. She swayed forward with the crescendo, then slowly sank back again with the diminuendo.

Rhodrick was quite moved by it. Music had always spoken to him, but this went far beyond that. This transported him. He closed his eyes and let the music swell around him. He stood in the middle of the corridor where the candlelight flickered in the constant draft, his snifter held carelessly between his fingers, his weight cocked on one hip and off his bad knee, the music filling a hole in him he had not known existed.

It had been years since he'd heard anything that remotely sounded like life in his home, and he'd not even realized that he relished it as much as he did until this moment.

But then the music suddenly stopped.

Rhodrick reluctantly opened his eyes and started.

Miss Fairchild had twisted on the bench at the pianoforte and was staring at him wide-eyed through the sliver of the open door, as if she had seen the devil's shadow.

He felt a fool — how she had sensed him, he had no idea, but it had caught him quite unawares and made him feel uncharacteristically vulnerable. He was walking before he realized it, trying to disguise a limp that had worsened with the cold rain.

Greer braced herself against the pianoforte, closed her eyes, and drew a deep, steadying breath. She waited until she could no longer hear his uneven gait in the corridor before she relaxed and removed her hands from the keyboard.

Her mind whirled around the improbable. *Had she imagined it?* Had she imagined the warmth that had come over her like a draft of heat from the hearth, in a room where the hearth was cold? *Something* had made her turn around and see him.

Whatever it was had startled her, and she

had abruptly jerked around to see him standing there, his head tossed back and his eyes closed, seemingly lost in the music she was playing. The wave of empathy that had filled her at the sight of him had alarmed her. She'd gaped at him, wondering how long he'd been standing there, mystified by how she could possibly feel anything for a man like him.

Yet to see how her music moved him also moved something in her, nudging her a bit, casting a weak shadow of doubt across her thoughts.

What nonsense! Such sentiment was absurd — *all* beasts were soothed by music and he was certainly no exception. Perhaps . . . but this beast had also saved her life today.

Such strange thoughts were disturbing, and Greer was much relieved when, a few moments later, Mrs. Bowen appeared in the doorway jangling the keys she wore at her waist. "We've readied a suite for you, Miss Fairchild."

"Thank you," Greer said gratefully, and followed Mrs. Bowen in the opposite direction the prince had gone.

The path to her new suite of rooms was rather long. It seemed to Greer that they'd wound around to the farthest reaches of the castle so that she might serve out her imprisonment away from all human contact.

But when Mrs. Bowen opened the door, she was pleasantly surprised. The furniture looked old and out of fashion, but it was of excellent quality. The furnishings were a little bare, but it was easily the most comfortable room she'd seen in the entire castle.

They entered through a sitting room that boasted two overstuffed chintz-covered armchairs that matched a settee, a small dining or writing table, and a pair of upholstered footstools.

The walls were painted a sunny yellow, although the paint had begun to fade, leaving squares of brighter yellow where paintings had once hung. Greer followed Mrs. Bowen through the sitting room into a smaller but similarly appointed dressing room, then into the bedchamber. She was ridiculously pleased with the accommodations.

The bedchamber was built in a turret, but was warmed with bright green and gold floor coverings that matched the bed's canopy and coverlets. A fire crackled at the hearth and two small windows had been trimmed with gold velvet draperies, which gave the illusion of sunshine.

"You'll find your toilette in the dressing

room," Mrs. Bowen said over her shoulder. "And there is a bath. Just use the bellpull when you are of a mind." She glanced appraisingly around the room, then at Greer. "Does the suite meet with your satisfaction?"

Greer smiled for the first time in days. "Very much indeed. Whose rooms are these, if I may inquire?"

"They were the late mistress's rooms."

She assumed Mrs. Bowen meant the prince's mother until she clarified, "The late princess."

She could not have surprised Greer more — she had not once thought of the prince as married, and in fact she could not picture him married. "How long?" she asked, perhaps a bit too forcefully, since Mrs. Bowen looked at her with some surprise. "How . . . how long has it been since she occupied this suite?"

"Oh, it's been many years," Mrs. Bowen said reassuringly. "No one has used the suite since it happened. And the room was thoroughly cleaned afterward. Mrs. Jernigan — she's a healer in these parts — made a potion that we put around the bed to drive the spirits away."

"*Spirits?*" Greer asked.

"A precaution many of the Welsh like to

take," Mrs. Bowen said with a motherly smile.

She said it so matter-of-factly, as if the spirits were real and as if Greer knew what had happened here. But she *didn't* know, and she was afraid to even imagine how the princess might have died. *Poisoned? Hanged? Stabbed to death in her sleep?*

She meant to ask, but a strong gust of wind rattled the shutters and sent a draft through the bedchamber that startled both women. "The weather has taken quite a turn," Mrs. Bowen said, and hurried to close the drapes. Greer hugged her arms tightly to her as she glanced around the room, seeing it through different eyes now, trying to imagine the woman who would marry such a dark man and then meet her ultimate demise here.

The initial charm of the suite faded with the suspicions that began to mushroom in Greer's head. By the time she retired, she fell into a restless sleep and dreamed the prince was trying to kill her. When dawn broke, Greer was a mass of frayed nerves.

She felt all at sixes and sevens, uncertain as to what to do now, unsettled by her conflicting thoughts about the prince and this place. Her situation was becoming much more complex than she ever could have imagined.

She wished desperately that Ava and Phoebe were within reach. How she needed their counsel and their strength just now!

Lulu's arrival eased her somewhat, for when she was bustling about with a cheery countenance, things didn't seem quite so peculiar.

Greer tried to smile from her seat at the vanity. "It seems I shall be at Llanmair for a time with little to keep me occupied, Lulu."

"Oh! His lordship has the finest library in all of Wales. He's quite well known for his support of law and literature. Perhaps you might find something there."

Greer looked at Lulu's reflection in the mirror. "The *prince?*" she asked, incredulous. "He is known to support the law and literature?"

"Oh yes, miss. He's got a fine collection of literature. And he's a judge. He's high in demand, for he's earned a reputation for being very fair."

A *judge? Fair?* What fairy tale was this? All right, then, she would take Lulu's advice. She would like to see what literature the ogre read, and moreover, she had to accept that she would be at Llanmair for a time, apparently, but she could not accept that she'd be confined to these rooms every day of every week that it would take for her letter to reach London. She would *not* spend her days dreaming of being murdered and jumping at every strange noise — and there were quite a lot of them.

Perhaps, she thought, as she mulled over her options, if she were to explore the castle and become familiar with the dark corners and strange twisting corridors from which eerie groans arose, she would not feel quite as uncomfortable as she did now. And as she was not yet chained in the dungeon, she refused to be held like a sheep in her pen.

In a moment of decisiveness, Greer strode out of her suite, determined to make the best of a wretched situation.

She wound her way around through hallway after hallway, through peculiar twists and turns, past artwork, austere furnishings, and gold-plated consoles, and over thick carpets that seemed ancient but luxuriant. She had no idea how she did it, but she managed to end up in the foyer, where two footmen, under Ifan's watchful eye, were busily lowering the massive candelabra to light them.

Greer paused to watch them. Ifan looked at her curiously. "Do you require anything, miss?" he asked.

"No, thank you." She smiled. "That looks

quite hard," she said, nodding to the candelabra. "It must be very heavy."

The two footmen glanced curiously at Ifan. "No," Ifan said, clasping his hands behind his back. "It is lowered by a pulley. It is no trouble." He added a bow, as if he expected her to continue on her way.

But Greer had had enough of solitude. "We have gas lighting on the streets in London," she said.

Ifan nodded. One footman looked at her strangely.

"Have you ever been to London?" she asked.

Ifan looked startled. "Me?" he asked. "Of course. In the company of his lordship."

"Oh, yes, of course." She smiled. Ifan smiled thinly. Greer turned her smile to the footmen. "What of your men?"

"Not I, miss," one responded, and got a look from Ifan for it. "But Mr. Salisbury, he's been."

"Who is Mr. Salisbury?" Greer asked.

With a look that seemed a tad bit perturbed, Ifan said, "He is the groundskeeper."

"He kept a rather large house in London, I've heard tell," the footman offered helpfully.

"Not in London!" Ifan snapped. *Corn-*

wall! He's not the sort wanted in *London.*"

"Ah . . . excuse me," Greer said, and walked away as the footman said, "I am quite certain it was London, sir."

She made her way through another series of turns and stairs that seemed to lead nowhere, poking her head into rooms that were empty or seldom used, examining the furnishings. When she somehow ended up back at her room — and in time for luncheon, she was pleased to note — she was feeling a bit more comfortable with her surroundings.

Later that afternoon, she was actually eager to be on her rounds again. She met two chambermaids she had not seen before, and tried to help them move a brass cart from one end of a salon to another. But in her eagerness to help, she managed to catch her hem in the wheel of the cart, which had both of the young women up in arms. It took Mrs. Bowen to free the train of her gown.

She found the very large kitchen and introduced herself to Mrs. Ruby, the cook, who preferred to be addressed as Cook. The kitchen was filled with the smells of baking bread and burning peat, scents which carried Greer back some years. She had a memory of her mother in a kitchen dancing around with one of the servants before settling in to help Greer make a cake. The smell was so inviting and warmly familiar that Greer did not want to leave. She stood in the middle of the kitchen, fiddling absently with a basket of herbs, explaining to Cook how much she missed gathering her own herbs in London.

"We had only a small garden," she said as she put some sweet basil to her nose and inhaled. "There's not nearly as much space to grow them as there is here."

"Ah," Cook said, and almost collided with the scullery maid as they tried to step around Greer.

"Oh, I do beg your pardon. Shall I stand over there?" she asked, pointing to a table. She didn't wait for Cook to answer, but picked up the basket and walked around to the small table and continued to sort through the herbs, trying to identify each one by smell. She was quite oblivious to the spat that had developed between Cook and the maid until Cook asked hesitantly, "Beg your pardon, miss . . . but have you the herb basket?"

"Yes!" Greer said cheerfully. "Would you like it?"

Cook and the scullery maid exchanged a quick glance as Greer handed the basket to them and then settled herself on a stool and began to tell them about Ava and Phoebe. "They are my cousins," she said, "but they are really more like sisters. Ava is beautiful, and kind," she said with a smile. "But she can be very headstrong. Stubborn, you might say. Really rather pigheaded when she wants to be. And Phoebe, oh my . . . she is so very creative and talented with a needle. She embroidered this gown," she said, and stood up, twirling around for them to see. "But Phoebe has a tendency to give her thoughts over to fantasy," she said, and continued to reminisce until Mrs. Bowen arrived.

Cook, she noticed, seemed very relieved as she spoke in Welsh to the housekeeper. Mrs. Bowen blinked, then looked at Greer. "Miss Fairchild, will you come with me?"

"Yes, of course. Where are we going?" Greer asked.

"To the, ah . . . the salon," she said. "I should like your opinion about the décor."

The opinion Mrs. Bowen sought, however, was nothing more than what flowers should be put in a vase. When Greer said, rather thoughtfully, "Irises," Mrs. Bowen thanked her profusely and hurried out. It wasn't until a few moments later that Greer realized she had been tactfully removed from the kitchen.

Now being careful to stay clear of the servants, who did not seem to appreciate her company, Greer found yet another corridor. This one was very wide with an arched ceiling and stone floor. The slight indentation in the stone down the middle of the floor indicated that centuries of persons had walked this way before her.

Along the walls were more armaments and more paintings — one would think there were not enough people in all of Wales to populate the dozens upon dozens of paintings that hung on the castle walls.

In the middle of the corridor was a set of double oak doors standing open, and as Greer neared them, she could hear the sounds of people within. She paused and listened closely. The voices sounded far away, and she guessed she was at the entrance to a large room, perhaps a ballroom.

With a quick, furtive look around to ensure no one was watching her, Greer carefully stepped up to the door. But instead of people, she saw sculptures. More than a dozen of them. It was, apparently, a small sculpture gallery on a balcony above a larger room. And though she could hear voices below her, she couldn't resist investigating this enthralling find. She slipped inside to peruse the alabaster figures.

The Welsh voices below her were those of men, and she recognized one low, magnetic voice as belonging to the prince. Fortunately, there was no light in the balcony, save what filtered in through a pair of windows above her head, but it was sufficient light to see the sculptures of various size and subjects. As the men below seemed to be in a rather intense conversation, judging by all the guttural sounds that were tossed about, Greer moved guardedly to stand behind a life-sized sculpture of Cupid.

The craftsmanship was exquisite. She guessed that it was Italian marble, and admiring the work, she brazenly trailed her fingers along the young man's hips, then up, tracing each curl of the lad's head.

But soon she was distracted by the sound of swords being crossed, and curious, she peeked out from around Cupid, following the line of his arrow, which happened to be pointed directly at the prince below her.

He was wearing a lawn shirt tucked into his buckskins, his collar missing, his sleeves billowing as he fenced with a man she had not seen before. To the side stood two footmen, flanking a table where several foils had been laid.

The sight of him stirred something deep

and disquieting in Greer. She could not take her eyes from him for even a moment. He fenced like a beast, strong and with powerful grace, and as he thrust forward, she could see the power of his hips and thighs outlined in the buckskins he wore. His back, broad and muscular across the shoulders, tapered into a trim waist. His dark hair was tied at the nape with a black ribbon, and he moved with the agility of a man half his age.

The man on the receiving end of his foil was lumbering backward, forced back by the speed with which the prince fenced. Fascinated by the display, Greer leaned farther out from behind Cupid, watching him.

In a matter of only minutes, the prince effortlessly forced his opponent against a column and struck the foil from his hand. His opponent's chest heaved with the exertion of having defended himself and slowly the man raised his hands in defeat, saying something in Welsh that made the prince laugh. He lowered his blade and walked out of Greer's sight as his opponent slid down the column to his haunches, picked up his sword, and gained his feet again. He spoke again in Welsh, and then suddenly lunged.

The abrupt movement prompted a tiny squeal of surprise from Greer — she darted behind another sculpture closer to the balcony's edge to better view what was happening.

The man had put the prince back on his heels, thrusting wildly at his head, chest and flank, forcing the prince to retreat. She thought surely the prince would be defeated now, but he moved casually, almost as if he didn't realize he was in danger of losing. And then, as suddenly as it had begun, the momentum changed, and the prince was moving forward, his foil slicing across his opponent's blade with incredible speed, fencing the man into a wall once again. He swept the man's foil aside and pressed the tip of his foil to the man's throat.

Greer held her breath, expecting him to thrust the point into the soft hollow of the man's throat. But the prince suddenly grinned — a very winsome, endearing grin that she would have thought impossible had she not seen it with her own eyes — and lowered his blade.

The other man laughed with relief as the prince stooped a little crookedly to pick up his foil. The man bowed as he accepted the foil, said something more, to which the prince responded with a flick of his wrist. His opponent laughed again, and with a nod of his head, he walked away, under the balcony, so that Greer could no longer see him.

The prince took a cloth that was tucked inside his belt and cleaned the handle of his foil while the two servants gathered the other foils. When they were done, the prince said something, and the footmen walked in the same direction as the opponent, leaving the prince alone in the ballroom.

Greer remained frozen, behind the sculpture, watching him. It occurred to her that she ought to retreat, that there was something very wrong in watching a man who thought he was alone. Yet she was fascinated by him, by the way he seemed to appear so fearless and vulnerable at once.

He mopped his brow with the cloth he'd used to clean the foil, then tossed it onto the table before walking back to the middle of the ballroom. He paused, leaned down, and rubbed his knee with the palms of his hands, then straightened again, put his fists to his hips, and looked up.

Directly at Greer.

She caught her breath and held it, uncertain if he could actually see her.

"Are you spying, Miss Fairchild?"

Good God, how had he seen her? How could he *possibly* have seen her in the darkly lit gallery, behind the sculpture? She was mortified — young girls were caught spying on men, not sophisticated women, as she liked to fancy herself. But she had no excuse for having invaded his privacy in such an appalling manner, so she reluctantly stepped out from the sculpture and said, "I am not *spying.*"

Of course she had indeed been spying, but she was not fool enough to admit it. "I was admiring your sculptures. You happened to be fencing at the same time."

"What a coincidence," he drawled. "And how did you find the fencing?"

How did she find it? Astounding. Masterful. "Fair," she said pertly.

One of his dark brows rose above the other. "*Fair?* How interesting. I am actually renowned for my skill."

"That does not surprise me," she said flippantly. "You are the prince. People often say to the prince what he would like to hear."

A slow smile tipped up one corner of his mouth. "You are to be commended, Miss Fairchild, for I do not care for false flattery — and you have taken care not to flatter me in the least. I thought that perhaps you watched me so intently as to learn a thing or two about the art of defense, as you seem to fancy yourself in constant danger."

Oh, how damnably embarrassing — he'd known she was up here all along. "Oh no," she said airily. "I am not so foolish as to believe that I could ever best you in a game of physical strength, my lord. I shall defend myself more artfully than with brute force."

"Ah. I should very much like to experience your artful defense."

For some reason, the way he said it made Greer feel quite naked. So naked, in fact, that she could not think of a proper retort.

He stood below her, taking her in. After a moment, he put his hand to his nape, looked at the ground, and said — reluctantly, she thought — "Miss Fairchild . . ."

His voice trailed off; he glanced up at her again, his expression surprisingly distressed.

What was the matter with him? "Yes?" she prompted him.

Again he looked down, but at his hand, and spread his fingers wide as he studied them, and said quietly, "I must ask you to stop bothering my staff."

"Beg your pardon?"

"There have been a few complaints —"

"Complaints?" she exclaimed. What awful traitors filled this house!

"It would seem that you are constantly underfoot. . . ." He glanced up and smiled devilishly. "When you are not spying, that is. Please do have a care that you leave the servants to their tasks, will you? While I am certain they appreciate your surprising willingness to help them . . . please don't."

"Rest assured I will not!"

"Thank you." And with that, he strode out of her sight.

Greer heard a door open and shut, and then nothing. "By the saints!" she exclaimed. "He is the *most* exasperatingly peculiar man I have *ever* encountered. Bothering the servants indeed," she muttered as she left the sculpture gallery.

ELEVEN

Holding his coat and his neckcloth, Rhodrick strode across the lower promenade with no destination in mind other than to get as far from Greer Fairchild as possible within his own home. He could not imagine what he'd done to earn God's wrath, to have deserved a woman who appeared unexpectedly in places she should not and then smiled with the force of a thousand candles.

He had spotted her on the balcony as he had waited for his friend and fencing partner, Hugh Pryce, to compose himself after being foiled by Rhodrick's sword the first time. He'd been so startled to see her peeking out from behind the sculpture that Hugh had managed to catch him off guard and had nearly won the bout.

It was not her spying that aggravated him so completely, although he did not care for it. It was just . . . *her.* He was a man, wasn't he, and he could not help his nature, or the fact that he enjoyed a pretty woman's smile. But a woman's smile did not generally cause him to be so damnably tongue-tied in her presence, and *that* vexed him no end.

His whole demeanor was insupportable — he was a powerful man in this small corner of the world, responsible for the welfare of hundreds of people. He was a respected arbiter and judge, a man accustomed to resolving other men's disputes in which he could be counted to reason and rule fairly.

To discover then, on the eve of his thirty-ninth year that a young woman — who was, for all he knew, a cunning swindler — could unbalance him so completely with a mere smile was humiliating.

He marched on, his temper turning more foul. He wound his way up the stairwell and into the main foyer, past the goddamn mirror he was coming to despise. And up again, to the first floor, on his way to his study, his retreat, the one place where he might forget she was even in his house.

Except that he encountered her *again.*

As he entered the corridor, he was forced to stop, for she was there, her hands clasped behind her and her lovely face tilted up as she examined a painting. She seemed as surprised as he was, and for a moment, she looked as if she might flee. But then again, she *always* looked as if she wanted to flee when she laid eyes on his ugly face.

She did not run, however. This time, she turned and faced him fully.

His mind was racing almost as madly as his heart. Standing this close to her, he could not help noticing the fit of her gown, the way the velvet hugged every curve, the intricate embroidery on the bodice and sleeves. For a thief, the woman certainly wore some very fine clothing.

"Ahem."

He lifted his gaze, saw the devilish sparkle in the eye of a woman who knew she was being physically admired. But then she suddenly squinted and peered closely at his face.

Rhodrick unconsciously reared back. What did she see? Did his face offend her?

"I beg your pardon, but you are bleeding."

"What?" He touched his face and remembered now — he and Hugh rarely wore masks, and the tip of Hugh's foil had caught his cheek, near his scar. He swiped at the dried blood, embarrassed. "It is nothing."

She nodded. Her gaze began to burn him; he felt extraordinarily self-conscious, unimaginably ugly, and moved to step around her at the same moment she attempted to move out of his way. As a result, they almost collided.

They were standing so close he could smell lilac. He glanced down, to the twin mounds of creamy flesh that seemed to spill out of her bodice. He lifted his gaze, looked directly into her sea blue eyes. Neither of them spoke, but Rhodrick could feel something treacherous swirling around inside him.

Their awkward maneuvering seemed to amuse Miss Fairchild, however. She smiled as his gaze drifted to her luscious lips, revealing pearl white teeth.

The treachery in his body intensified.

"I do beg your pardon," she said, and stepped out of his way.

Rhodrick hastily walked on, continuing on to the sanctuary of his study. As he strode inside, he felt a wave of relief, and tossed his coat and neckcloth onto a chair as his dogs padded over to greet him, their tails wagging. Distracted, he patted them both on the head before moving to his desk.

"You seem to prefer this study to all the other rooms in this very large castle."

Much to his amazement and vexation, Miss Fairchild had followed him. He turned sharply to stare at her in disbelief. To add to his surprise, his dogs had now seen Miss Fairchild often enough as to be quite accustomed to her. She was absently petting them both as she watched Rhodrick.

"I . . . I have noticed it," she added tentatively.

What was she doing here, in his sanctuary, petting his dogs? *What was she doing here?* She had made it very well known that she abhorred him — why did she not leave him be?

"It's just that it's such a large castle," she continued, as if he had inquired. "And there are so many rooms."

He blinked. "Yes," he said. Was there some reason he should not prefer this room? With a furtive, uneasy glance around, he tried to see it through her eyes. A bit austere, perhaps, save all the books.

"I suppose it belonged to a Welsh king at one time."

He had no idea what she was talking about and looked at her again. She had moved deeper into the room, and again, he couldn't help admiring the fit of her gown.

"The castle," she clarified.

His dog Abel nudged her hand, and she smiled warmly down at him, scratching him behind the ears. *Bloody dog. Did he not understand who fed him?* "Isn't there someplace you should be?" Rhodrick demanded.

"No," she said pertly. "I am a prisoner here, remember?"

"You are *not* a prisoner."

One sculpted brow rose above the other. "Oh, that's right, I do beg your pardon. I am a *reluctant guest.*" She took a deep breath. "I wanted to thank you for saving my life," she said, and then quickly turned her attention to the shelves that lined three of the four walls. "You have a *lot* of books."

"Yes," he said, taken aback by her expression of thanks, curt though it had been. "In addition to the books in here and in the library, there are more in the drawing room. Perhaps you'd be more comfortable admiring books there."

She looked impressed and easily ignored his suggestion. "That is quite a *lot* of books. I can't imagine the king of England has as many as this. I am rather astounded you would enjoy reading as much as you obviously do."

"Astounded?" he echoed, surreptitiously glimpsing the curve of her hip and imagining it very bare. "Why?"

"I don't think of tyrants as being terribly disposed to improving their minds, I suppose. Would you mind if I were to borrow one or two?" she asked. "To pass the time," she added quickly. "It's really very . . . *quiet* . . . here."

Tiresome, she meant. There was nothing at Llanmair to entice a woman like Greer Fairchild. "A book? I am likewise astounded that *you* would enjoy reading."

"Why is that?"

"I suppose I don't think silly young women who go chasing about the Welsh countryside with men they scarcely know as being terribly disposed to improving their minds," he quipped. "But you may borrow as many books as you like. Just . . . *do* it. Please," he said, gesturing to the door.

With a wry smile, she looked at the shelves. "I shouldn't expect you to understand my reasons for coming here, my lord. They are too pure to be relevant to a man with your purported moral character."

He snorted at that and took a seat behind his desk, determined to concentrate on his work and *not her.* "You speak very elegantly of morals, Miss Fairchild. One might think you were actually in possession of one or two."

She muttered something under her breath he could not quite hear. "May I start here?" she asked coolly.

With a wave of his hand, he said, "Anywhere you like."

"*Thank* you." She cast a smile over her shoulder that swept down his spine.

Rhodrick looked at the papers before him and tried to concentrate, but he could not. He was conscious that he was not dressed properly, and glanced ruefully at his coat and neckcloth tossed so carelessly onto the chair. Just beyond the chair, Greer Fairchild reached for a book on the highest shelf, and her gown stretched tightly across her back. He couldn't help noticing her trim figure, her long and graceful arms. Her hair was swept up into curls and affixed with small ribbons to the back of her head. He could smell her, could recall the feel of her body against his, and could feel his own rusty body beginning to turn like the cogs of an old wheel as he imagined taking her in his bed.

She withdrew a book and opened it, turning slightly as she read so that her profile was presented to him. She had a slender column of a neck, and a dimple that creased her cheek as she smiled to herself at something she read. Her lashes, long and dark, flickered, and she lifted a hand, toying mindlessly with the earring dangling from her ear.

She wore her Welsh amulet around her neck. He recalled that amulet, the warmth and smoothness of her skin. The memory made him uncomfortably warm, and he was suddenly overwhelmed by the desire to touch her again.

This was absurd — Rhodrick forced his gaze to his desk. He was not some randy lad with no control over his sex. He'd gone too long without the company of a woman, that was all. He was allowing her scent to invade his thoughts, the image of her body to crawl under his skin. He squinted at the paper before him and read a sentence or two, but a moment later, Miss Fairchild exclaimed softly.

He glanced up.

"I have longed to see India," she said, and glanced at him from the corner of her eye. "Have you been?"

It was a desire they shared, for he'd long been fascinated by India.

"This is a book about India," she continued blithely. "It bears an inscription in Welsh."

"Are you certain?" he drawled. "Having no recollection of the language, how might you determine if you are looking at Welsh or Greek?"

She colored slightly and shrugged a little. "I am certain it is Welsh, for it is in your house."

He clucked his tongue and stood from his chair. She kept her gaze on him as he walked around the desk to her. When he held his hand out for the book, she placed it in his hands, her eyes on his as he attempted to take it from her. His fingers grazed hers, and that whisper of a touch singed him.

Miss Fairchild seemed to sense the heat, for her eyes glittered above a soft smile that brought a single dimple to her cheek.

He could feel the treachery stirring in him again, could feel his body awakening, the furnace deep inside him firing from a cold stone hearth.

Her smile widened, as if she sensed what she was doing to him and understood the power of her femininity. Yet he could not look away, nor seem to remove the book entirely from her hands. He could not seem to do anything but gaze into those eyes and feel his arousal warm his body.

Miss Fairchild's gaze flickered to the page of the open book and to his eyes again. "You do *read* Welsh as well as speak it, do you not?"

He dragged his gaze from her face as he took the book from her hand and glanced at the inscription.

It took a moment for his mind to register

what he was reading, for him to remember the book, and he felt as if he'd been kicked in the gut. It had been years since he'd received it as a gift, years since he'd even laid eyes on it.

"What does it say?" Miss Fairchild asked.

He shut the book and handed it to her. " '*Rwy'n dy garu di,* Eira.' "

She took the book and opened it again, looked at the inscription, running her elegant fingers over it. "What does it mean?"

"It means . . . 'I love you, Eira.' " He turned away, walked back to his desk.

"Oh," she said behind him. "Do you know who Eira was?"

Rhodrick took his seat and looked out the windows at the rain that refused to stop falling, before shifting his gaze to Miss Fairchild. "She was my wife."

Miss Fairchild's eyes widened, but she did not speak. The playful look of amusement was gone from her face, replaced by something else entirely, something he could not and did not want to identify. "Perhaps you might enjoy the book in your suite," he suggested.

She lowered her gaze, closed the book, and laid her hand on the cover a moment before returning it to the shelf. "I think I should prefer another one, if I may," she said, and returned the book on India to its place on the shelf before taking another one nearby. "This is entitled *A History of Wales and Her Peoples*."

Rhodrick did not recall that book, but it scarcely mattered. He looked at his desk, his mind racing for something to say, something to remove Eira's presence from the room.

"Thank you," Miss Fairchild said, the spark gone from her voice. "Good evening, my lord."

He nodded helplessly, heard the rustle of her skirts, heard her walk through the open door, her footstep light on the carpet beyond the door.

When he could hear her no more, he muttered, *"Nos da."* Good night. He leaned back in his chair and closed his eyes, thinking of a wife he had not thought of in years.

Twelve

In her suite of rooms, Greer's dinner sat before her untouched, the book open on her lap.

She could see the words, but she could not comprehend them. She could smell the delicious aroma of beef but could not eat it. She knew the rain pattered against the window, but all she could hear was his voice, the low swell of hoarseness as he spoke. *She was my wife.*

The man was such an enigma! He hardly spoke at all, seemed to chafe at her presence, yet she had seen glimpses of raw human emotion shining through that gruff exterior, the hint of a man the world could not see. And she could not forget how fearlessly he'd saved her from harm.

Having been at Llanmair a full week now, Greer was beginning to appreciate that things were not as they seemed, and that discovery — or perhaps the questions it raised — intrigued her.

She looked at the open book in her lap, *The History of Wales and Her Peoples,* and began to read.

When Mrs. Bowen came to straighten her room the next morning, Greer had reached the point in Welsh history where Owain Glyndwr had led a revolt against England. As that would seem to require her studious concentration, she put the book aside. At present, she was more interested in Mrs. Bowen . . . or rather, the information Mrs. Bowen could give her.

She followed the housekeeper into the sitting room, where Mrs. Bowen was arranging a bouquet of hothouse flowers. They were very beautiful; they made the room seem less old somehow.

"They are stunning," Greer said, leaning over to inhale their scent.

Mrs. Bowen smiled. "His lordship will be right pleased to hear it."

Greer glanced at Mrs. Bowen. "Did . . . did *he* send them here?" she asked, astounded and appalled by the tiny surge of hope that accompanied her inquiry.

"Oh no, miss, I brought them up. But his lordship is very proud of his hothouse and the gardens. He's known all over Wales for the gardens."

The tiny bit of hope retreated to its proper place — deep and buried, thank you — and Greer walked around the table, running her hand over a porcelain figurine. "I'd wager that Lady Radnor had the hothouse built, expressly for the flowers . . . do you suppose?"

"The hothouse was here for many years before Lady Radnor was mistress."

"Ah," Greer said, and pretended to study the porcelain figurine. "How, ah . . . how did you say Lady Radnor died?"

"Childbirth," Mrs. Bowen said as she picked up a pillow from the settee and plumped it. "Quite tragic, really. She bore him a girl, but bled something awful and never recovered. She passed two days afterward. And the infant, just two days after that."

"How very *awful*," Greer said. She had imagined a more sinister death — murder, suicide — not the tragedy of a childbirth gone awry.

"Oh yes," Mrs. Bowen said, nodding. "It was devastating to his lordship." She looked up from her pillow and glanced to the door before shifting her gaze to Greer and saying low, "He did not move from his study for days. He did not eat, nor did he speak. There were some who feared for his sanity."

A sliver of trepidation snaked up Greer's spine. "Was it very long ago?"

"Nigh on thirteen years," Mrs. Bowen said, and picked up another pillow. "He's all right now, of course. It's all in the past, may she rest in peace." She finished fluffing the pillows and smiled at Greer. "Is there anything you require, miss?"

"Yes," she said quickly. "If you please, I should very much like some paper and ink so that I might write."

"Of course."

"My cousins and I write frequently," Greer added with a bit of a laugh. "There are three of us, and Ava, now that she is married, is often in the country, and Phoebe — well, Phoebe hasn't determined exactly where she will reside —"

"I shall be happy to arrange for pen and paper," Mrs. Bowen said from the door. Greer hadn't even seen her move.

"Just a few sheets of vellum," Greer said after her. "I shan't waste them. And . . . and two pens, if you please, for sometimes when I am writing, I wear out the quill."

"*Yes*, miss."

"Thank you!" Greer called after her as the housekeeper quit the room.

She walked back into the bedchamber and looked at the bed, picturing a young woman

198

struggling to give birth and dying from the exertion. The image made her shudder, and she turned her chair around so that she couldn't see the bed.

With a look at the windows — *Still* raining, she noted with some despair — she picked up her book and began to read about the warrior Owain Glyndwr.

Greer read through midmorning until her eyes were bleary. Fortunately, she was saved by the arrival of Lulu, who had come to gather her clothes for laundering. She watched the girl as she gathered the gowns Greer had worn this week, clearly admiring them as she folded them carefully.

"My cousin Phoebe made most of them," Greer said.

Lulu quickly put the gowns down, embarrassed to have been caught admiring them.

"Oh no," Greer said, rising to her feet. "You really *must* admire them. Phoebe is very talented." She reached around Lulu and picked up the gown she had worn the first night she was at Llanmair and held it up to Lulu. "It suits you well," she said, nodding thoughtfully. "A little large, but nonetheless."

Lulu blushed. "Thank you, mu'um."

"You must try it on," Greer said authoritatively.

"Oh no, mu'um! I *cannot!*"

"Of course you can!" Greer said with a grin. "It will divert us!"

"Mrs. Bowen will have my head!"

"Ah, but Mrs. Bowen isn't here," Greer said with a wink, and a quarter of an hour later, Lulu held the extra fabric of the gown tight at her back and twisted one way and then the other, admiring herself in the mirror, as Greer sorted through her jewelry to enhance Lulu's new appearance.

Lulu was delighted and exclaimed more than once she'd never felt so fine. But eventually, Lulu reluctantly put the gowns away and went about her work, leaving Greer to her book. As riveted as Greer was by the history she was reading, she desperately needed some air and decided to take yet another tour of the castle.

This time, she headed for the west wing, where she had not yet been.

Apparently, scarcely a soul had set foot in the west wing. The corridors were quite empty and cold and distinguished by the number of bedchambers — she counted a dozen — and sitting rooms it housed, as well as a salon that would, she thought, take the afternoon sun if it ever stopped raining.

What little furniture there was had been covered, and almost every room had a dank smell to it. It hardly surprised Greer — she could not imagine that a man like the prince had the sort of friends who would linger over a long weekend. Especially in a place as remote as Llanmair.

On the main floor of the west wing, she saw Lulu and another chambermaid polishing a pair of end tables. She dared not chat with them as she would have liked for fear of being rebuked for it, and slipped into a room nearby.

It was a formal dining room. It was furnished with a long table that would accommodate forty persons — Greer counted the number of upholstered chairs set around it. One wall was actually a long bank of windows overlooking the gardens; its opposing wall was lined with two enormous buffets and a massive hutch that held china marked with a seal. Three large gold chandeliers hung above the table, and on the far wall was a hearth so large that a child could play inside it.

It was very impressive, but like so many other rooms in the castle, it looked as if it were seldom used. Greer pulled the door shut and idly walked to the door across the hall as she tried to picture the prince at the head of such a large table. She wondered if he managed to converse, or if he treated all his guests, reluctant or otherwise, to a lot of *yeses* and *nos.*

That's what she was thinking when she opened the door across the hall. Until she saw the footman, she didn't realize that she hadn't even knocked. Her heart thudded with surprise and embarrassment, and she quickly shut the door and backed away from it. Before she could make an escape, however, the footman opened the door wide, bowed low, and stepped to one side so that she could see the prince.

The room was a smaller, more intimate dining room, and he was seated at the head of the table having a solitary luncheon. His intense eyes were coolly watching her — he was leaning back in a thronelike chair, one arm draped across the arm of it, one hand wrapped around the stem of a wineglass. His hair brushed the tops of his shoulders, and his clothes were impeccable — he wore a black coat, a striped silk waistcoat, and a neatly tied neckcloth.

Greer realized she was gaping at him and summoned a smile. "Good afternoon."

The prince picked up a piece of meat from his plate as his gaze took her in. He sucked the meat from a small bone as he casually perused her, then tossed it onto his plate, picked up a linen cloth, and wiped his mouth. "Does one enter rooms without knocking in the fine homes of London?" he asked as he neatly folded the linen cloth and laid it beside his plate.

A bit of heat spread across Greer's scalp. "I do beg your pardon, my lord, but I thought this wing of the castle was as empty as the rest of it."

"Were you looking for something . . . or perhaps someone? What am I to think, when you are forever appearing in places you've not been invited?"

Surprisingly, Greer thought she detected the barest hint of a smile on the prince's rugged face and gave him a withering look. "You are to think your reluctant guest is quite bored. I was just having a look about," she said, and glanced self-consciously at the two footmen attending him. "You may have noted that it is still raining, and I have grown rather restless."

"I can only imagine your restlessness, as this is not high society."

She folded her arms and leaned against the door frame. "No," she said wryly. "Far from it."

He smiled a little before sipping from his wine goblet. "Have you eaten?"

She nodded.

"Then is there something else I might do

for you?"

"No. Thank you." She thought to leave him to his luncheon, but couldn't quite bring herself to do it. His gaze flicked over her, eyeing her so intently that she began to feel as if she were standing there not clad in the blue day gown she wore, but in her chemise. Or perhaps even less. "Well . . . ," she said, and pushed away from the door. "I shall leave you —"

"Mrs. Bowen informs me that you would like to write," he said.

"I . . . yes. Yes, if that is not too much to ask."

He took another sip of wine, then pushed the goblet away. "Perhaps you would like to write in the conservatory. It is built into the gardens."

"The conservatory?" she asked, her brow wrinkling.

"Have you not discovered it during your examination of this empty house?" he asked as he rose from his seat. A footman darted to his chair, moving it out of his way. The prince hardly seemed to notice him at all as he began walking toward Greer. "And I thought you'd left no stone unturned."

"I have indeed," she said jauntily. "I have endeavored to draw out my exploration of the castle as long as I possibly can in order to avoid having nothing to do."

He laughed. *Laughed.* And she saw again that rare but lovely, endearing smile.

He paused directly before her and clasped his hands behind his back. He was a good six inches taller than she, and much broader. His green gaze, framed with thick black lashes — which she had found so hard and cold — seemed quite blistering now. She could feel the trickle of warmth that had begun in her scalp begin to seep down her spine and spread to her limbs.

"A good plan, all in all. The longer you are occupied in snooping about the castle, the longer you are not causing any particular trouble to me. Shall I show you the conservatory?" he asked in that damnably low voice of his, and gestured to his left.

Greer nodded and walked beside him. Or marched, as it were.

Neither of them spoke as they strode purposefully down that long, wide corridor, yet Greer was acutely aware of his powerful presence beside her, exuding masculine energy that caught her up in its wake and dragged her along. He walked quickly, his gait sure and strong, and she had the sense that he was endeavoring to contain himself to keep from leaving her behind.

They rounded first one corner and then

another. The silence that surrounded them began to feel suffocating — *Why didn't he speak?* Did he truly find her reprehensible, did he distrust her so much?

At the end of the next corridor, the prince suddenly took hold of Greer's elbow and turned her to the right, into a small, narrow passageway. At the end of it was a door. He opened it and gently prodded her through.

She gasped with delight as she walked into the conservatory, forgetting the awkward silence that had accompanied them here. The conservatory was built onto a castle wall so that at her back was a stone wall. But the remaining three walls were made of windows, framed in stone. The ceiling above her was a glass dome, so that she could see the gray rain clouds scudding across the sky and, all around, the gardens.

"Oh my," she said as she walked deeper into the room. "This is *beautiful.*" She moved to the rain-streaked windows and peered out. Grinning with delight, she turned around to the prince, who was watching her with hooded eyes, his hands still clasped behind his back, his expression unreadable. "It is truly lovely, my lord."

One dark brow rose above the other. "Not too cold? Or 'unaccommodating'?"

With a sheepish smile, Greer shook her

head. "Quite the contrary. With a few pieces of furniture — a writing desk, of course, and a divan, perhaps, this could very well be the most inviting room in the entire castle."

"Then I shall have it readied so that you may write to your heart's content."

"That . . . that is very kind," she said, surprised, and walked to one of the glass walls to look out. Through the condensation, she could see what she thought was a water well, and impulsively lifted the handle that held the windows latched, opening one. But a cold blast of damp wind hit her squarely in the face, and she immediately moved to close the window — but the window would not budge. She wrapped both hands around the edge of it and pulled hard, but it would not move.

Blast it all. She dropped her hands, looked over her shoulder, feeling ridiculous. "*Ahem.* It would seem the window is stuck."

He sighed; she turned and tried again. But then she felt him at her back, felt that huge presence closing around her, his essence pushing her against the window. He reached around her and wrapped thick fingers around the edge of the window.

He may as well have put a torch to her back, she was so very conscious of him. She could feel the strength and heat from his body, could feel it thrumming in that narrow space between their bodies. Her entire being seemed to come alive with it; as if some beast inside her were raising its head and sniffing the hot air around her. She shivered with the delicious provocation and wrapped her arms around her body.

With a good yank, the prince pulled the window to and latched it shut. But he did not move his hand. It remained there, on the latch, his fingers gripping the handle, his arm outstretched by her head. He was standing so close that she could have leaned back against him if she so desired.

In a warm fog, Greer turned partially toward him and looked up. He was staring down at her with eyes as soft as moss, his gaze skating down her body to her bosom, and lower still, to where she held her arms wrapped around her middle, then slowly up again. "I will have the hearth lit," he muttered.

She nodded, unable to speak, unable to stop her heart from racing or her skin from heating. She could not help but recall her first night at Llanmair, when he had handled the charm at her neck, when his fingers had skimmed across her skin, spurring the first storm in her.

Yet this was different. Even though he had not touched her, she felt his desire more acutely somehow. Perhaps because he was not full of drink. Perhaps because this time, he knew precisely what he was doing.

He let his gaze linger on her lips, through which Greer was trying to breathe. If he continued to look at her like that, if he remained silent and continued to gaze at her with those eyes, she thought she might very well explode. She could not allow that — she'd already let go of too much.

"Do you know," she said breathlessly, her eyes on his lips, "I have been reading the book you lent me." Greer had no idea what she was saying, but she was desperate to find her sanity, some solid ground.

He didn't seem to hear her as his gaze drifted to her bosom again.

"I found the story of Owain Glyndwr most exciting."

He said nothing; his eyes continued to hungrily roam her body.

"You have some connection to him, do you not?"

"I do," he muttered, contemplating her mouth again.

"He was very inspiring. The story of his rebellion reminded me of a poem I once knew: *'Beware of Wales, Christ Jesus must* us keep . . .'" Her voice trailed off, and she frowned slightly, unable to remember the words while he looked at her mouth like that.

"'That it make not our child's child to weep,'" he murmured silkily.

Those words nudged something deep inside Greer, something that played on the fringe of her memory, just beyond her reach. "You *know* it."

He seemed to shift closer; she could feel his leg against her gown. "I know it well, as does any child of Wales. You were taught it along with your letters."

Greer drew an unsteady breath and unconsciously lifted her chin, half expecting to be kissed, half fearing that he would and half fearing that he would not.

But he did not kiss her. He removed his hand from the window and idly touched a curl at her temple with the back of his hand. "I confess, Miss Fairchild, I cannot help but wonder if you have truly forgotten all you ever knew about Wales," he said as his hand drifted to her collarbone, caressing it, "or if you were rather lazy in your task of extorting money from me by failing to learn those things that would best bolster your claim and have now resorted to seduction."

She caught her breath — the sudden

change in him threw her off balance. "I beg your pardon?"

"You heard me quite clearly, I think."

"How *dare* you!" she cried, stepping to the side and away from him. "I do not *seduce* you! How can you not take me at my word? I have given you no cause to disbelieve what I say. I have not eloped with Mr. Percy as you suggested I would —"

"Only because I prevented it."

Her cheeks flamed with shame at the memory of it. "You are mistaken. Whatever you might believe, I would *not* have eloped with Mr. Percy."

"That is what you say. But you are naïve if you think I don't know what you're about in your sudden tenderness toward me."

"It is *not* tenderness!" she protested.

"Lust?" he asked easily.

"You are a vile man," she said low, and certainly, the tender feelings she was experiencing a moment ago evaporated. "Just as your claim to have *helped* Percy is what *you* say."

He frowned, walked to the hearth, and kicked hard at the grate to dislodge a clump of ashes. "I am speaking the truth. One day, you will wake up from this ridiculous infatuation you hold for Mr. Percy and realize that I helped *you.*"

To think that just moments ago she had teetered on the brink of desiring him!

"The only thing I am guilty of," she said, her voice trembling now, "is allowing myself to believe you are something more than a beast." She swept past him and out of the conservatory, angry with herself.

She had lost her mind! Having been locked in this godforsaken castle had made her feeble and had compromised her good judgment! Well, it would not happen again. Oh no. If she had to confine herself to the rooms in which his wife had died, so be it — she would not put herself in a situation that would prompt her to feel *any* sort of tenderness for that beast again!

She turned the corner, striding furiously away and down another corridor she had not yet seen, one that looked to be a portrait gallery.

Her step slowed as she noticed a six-foot-high painting depicting a man who resembled the prince. He was dressed in the ancient Greek costume and riding a chariot. He looked ridiculous. Greer paused below it and looked up. It was his father or his grandfather, she thought, judging by the date engraved on the gold plate at the bottom of the frame. And the man in the portrait had the same slant to his eyes as the prince and Percy, the same unsmiling countenance as the prince.

She rolled her eyes, looked to her right — and saw a painting of a young girl, dressed in current fashion. She was standing beside a tree, a furry little dog at her feet.

Curiosity won out over her anger, and Greer moved to her right to admire the painting. The girl was a doe-eyed, golden-haired, timid little beauty, perhaps five years of age. Who was she? And why did the Prince of Thieves include her portrait in this gallery of thieves? One would think mothers would keep their daughters quite far from this place.

She started to walk again, but the portrait on the other side of the young girl stopped her cold.

She'd never be certain what caught her eye, but as she stood in front of the painting, something absolutely took her breath away. It was a portrait of a country picnic. There were several people gathered — a man with a violin, ladies on blankets, and children running with puppies. There was a man standing in the forefront who vaguely resembled the prince, and two young girls standing beside him, under a tree, one whispering to the other, who gazed out at the artist.

But most startling was the house in the distance. It was a grand white house, a mansion, surrounded by a lush lawn and grazing cattle.

It was the house from her dreams, the very house in the dream in which her mother had appeared. It was a house she vaguely remembered, but she was confused if she had actually been to it at one point in her life or merely believed that she had because she had dreamt of it so often.

How was it possible that a painting of *that* house was at Llanmair?

She stared at the painting, taking in every detail of it as she fingered the charm at her throat. It looked to be in a valley . . . *in a valley!* She had seen a white house in a valley just as the lightning had struck!

A noise at the far end of the gallery jerked her attention away, and a moment later, the prince strode into the gallery, halting at once when he saw her.

She felt as if she couldn't breathe and could do nothing but point at the painting.

With a frown, he looked at the canvas. "What is it, Miss Fairchild?"

"That house —"

"Is closed," he said instantly.

His response confused her. "What? But it can't be! I saw it, in the valley just as the lightning hit!" she insisted.

His gaze turned hard. "What you saw is an empty shell. That house is *closed.*"

"No," she said, shaking her head as she turned frantically to the painting. "I must see it. My —"

"Miss Fairchild, heed me. You are *forbidden* to go near that house. Do you quite understand me?"

"But I —"

"Miss Fairchild!" he snapped. "I don't know what you might believe or have heard about that house, but it belongs to me, and I have forbidden you and everyone else in this county from going there! So if there is nothing else?"

She gaped at him. Then her eyes narrowed with ire. "No, my lord. There is certainly nothing else." She turned away from him and strode from the portrait gallery.

When she had gone, Rhodrick looked at the painting and the portrait of the girl beside it and grimaced. He could never explain to Greer Fairchild, or anyone else for that matter, that the woman who came to him in his dreams, the woman he had believed Greer to be in his inebriation several nights ago, had led him to discover unspeakable tragedy in that house. As long as he lived, Kendrick would remain closed.

He walked on, unwilling to think of it now.

Unable to think of anything but how dangerously close he'd come to kissing her.

THIRTEEN

When Ifan sought Rhodrick out with an urgent message from the groundskeeper, Rhodrick was grateful for the diversion. The retaining wall they had worked so hard to repair was failing, and it was precisely the sort of task he needed after that encounter with Greer Fairchild, the sort of task that would erase his voracious desire to kiss her, a desire to which he had come precariously close to succumbing. If he had, it would have made him an even bigger fool than he feared he was already.

Greer Fairchild did not want *him.* She wanted his money.

But standing next to her in the conservatory, with the torrid image of her nearing the throes of passion in Percy's arms, he had almost done it, had almost given in to his baser male instincts.

He thought a bit of hard work would mend that deplorable lack of control, and that is how he came to be standing up to his knees in mud, his clothing soaked through, his shoulders aching from the swing of the sledgehammer he used to pound stone into place, wedging it between the others so the mortar could be applied.

It felt good, but it felt futile. The push of earth against the retaining wall was a far greater force than he was capable of containing. But it held for the time being.

When Rhodrick returned to the master suite and the hot bath Ifan had waiting for him, he felt himself again, fully in control of his emotions and his male instincts. It had been a momentary weakness, brought on by the sight of her ankle as she had gone up on her tiptoes to open the window. Or perhaps the shape of her derriere as she'd leaned over to see out the window. Or the brightness of her angry eyes in the portrait gallery.

Never mind — he felt so recovered, in fact, that he decreed if Miss Fairchild wished to be fed that evening, she would dine with him, for he saw no reason his staff should be burdened with serving two suppers at different times and locations.

"As you wish, milord," Ifan said, but it was clear to Rhodrick that his longtime butler did not believe the serving of two suppers to be quite the problem that Rhodrick suddenly deemed it.

Nevertheless, he thought it wise to keep his eye on Miss Fairchild. He refused to acknowledge, even to himself, that he might actually enjoy her effervescent company. She was stubborn and far too sure of herself, and moreover, deceitful. He was merely protecting his property, nothing more.

Rhodrick dressed carefully, donning a waistcoat and suit just delivered from his tailor in Aberystwyth. The tailor, who knew of his affliction with color, sent coats and waistcoats that were meant to be worn together. He knew that the coat and trousers of this new suit of clothing were black, and he thought that the striped waistcoat was a shade of green. Or red.

Whatever the color, it was well made.

He combed his hair back, and wondered about the style of it. He'd not been to London in years — he hadn't the slightest notion of what was fashionable any longer. So he tied it in a queue with a ribbon, stood back, and looked at himself in the mirror.

He was tall, at least two inches over six feet. He was an active man, so he had not developed a paunch around his middle as so many of his peers had seemed to acquire in the last few years. No one could find fault with his form, he thought, but his face always gave him pause. He wasn't hideous, not like a man he'd seen as a boy whose face had been eaten away by leprosy.

But he was not, by any definition, a handsome man. His sister was considered very handsome, as were his parents. He looked like none of them. His eyes were too close together, someone had once told him, and his nose crooked from having been broken more than once. The scar across his right cheek crossed the corner of his eye, the result of a fall from a horse that also had broken his arm and his leg, as well as his nose for the third time. The wound on his face had not healed properly, and though it had been years since the accident, it was still noticeable and quite ugly.

Rhodrick was angry with himself for caring. She was a thief. An attractive thief, but a thief nonetheless. Still, he studied himself critically, noting the crow's-feet deeply embedded in the corners of his eyes, the constant shadow of his beard, and the gray that was beginning to appear in his hair.

His father used to say that he possessed a face that would frighten the ghosts from the attic. He used to tease him that he looked like Goliath depicted in the biblical painting that hung in the grand salon. When he and his sister, Nell, had come of age, the family decamped to London to immerse Nell in the social whirl of the Season. Rhodrick's entry into society had been an afterthought, and his mean looks had prevented him from pursuing debutantes. His mother had tried to soothe him, saying more than once, "Someone will come along who cares not a whit for looks, my darling."

No one had come along, and Rhodrick had discovered carnal pleasure in darkened rooms with whores.

After Nell married, his family struggled to make him a match, but it seemed that none of the young ladies deemed suitable to marry heirs and lords found *him* particularly suitable. As there had been several unmarried heirs at the time, his father had had a devil of a time scaring up a woman who would have him. A match was finally arranged with Eira, but the poor girl, who had the misfortune of hailing from the Marches, and therefore did not know of his less-than-desirable features, saw him only once before they took their vows. His father had seen to it that she had no time to reconsider.

But if Eira found him repugnant, she never said so. She was a dutiful wife, as accepting of him as anyone could possibly have been. She had been good to him, and

Rhodrick had loved her. He hoped he had been a good husband to her — he had certainly tried, harder than he had ever tried to do anything in his life.

His wife had brought a softness to his life he'd never known. He'd spent most of his life living up to the Goliath moniker, and as a youth, he'd had a fierce temper, was quick to fight and prove his physical strength where his looks had let him down. Eira had helped him overcome that need, had taught him to be a gentle man.

Yes, he had loved Eira dearly, but he'd not thought of her in years. He'd trained himself not to think of her — it was too painful to remember his loss. And the baby . . . Lord God, he couldn't think of her, that tiny little thing who'd fought so valiantly to live without her mother, without feeling the wrench in his gut to this day.

On occasion, he would see something in his house that reminded him of Eira, but as time marched on, his memories had faded and he'd learned to be content with his own company. It was too difficult for him to even contemplate starting again with another woman. Lord knew, his friend Meg had tried, but her acquaintances wanted someone more dashing than he and to live closer to society than his close ties to Llanmair would allow. He understood the main consequence of his choice to be alone — he would leave no heir — but he consoled himself with the notion that Nell had two healthy sons who would one day inherit.

But then Miss Greer Fairchild had appeared on his doorstep and turned his world upside down, awakening desires he'd thought he'd long since buried.

Rhodrick brushed a bit of lint from his shoulder, straightened his neckcloth once more, and quit his suite, destined for the dining room and the woman who had occupied more of his thoughts in the last week than Eira had in the last several years.

His reluctant guest swept into the small dining room an hour later looking quite perturbed. Rhodrick rose from his seat instantly; she paused dramatically at the door, her long, elegant fingers on the jamb, her face flushed from her trek. The gown she wore — dark and shiny — hugged her bodice so tightly that he harbored an irrational hope her breasts would escape it completely. It was beautifully made, as exquisite as she was. "I am given to understand that if I am to be allowed food, I must take it with *you*," she said, and glided into the room with the train of her gown drifting out behind her like a wisp of a cloud.

The only color he could see with all clarity was her blue eyes, and they were flashing like rare gems with her ire.

Rhodrick moved to her seat to the right of his place at the head of the table, pulling it out for her. "Supper is served in the west dining room."

She glared at him.

He gestured for her to sit. "Are you hungry?"

Miss Fairchild folded her arms across her middle and looked at him suspiciously. "What are you about, sir?"

"Nothing at all. One supper is less onerous for my staff."

"Less onerous," she said with a snort.

He put his hands on the back of the chair. "Please do be seated, Miss Fairchild. When you are sitting here, I know you are not meddling where you ought not to be meddling."

"I don't believe you for a moment, you know," she said with a sniff as she took the seat he offered. "And I don't trust you in the *least*."

Rhodrick leaned over her shoulder. "The feeling is entirely mutual, which is why I would prefer to have you in my sights rather than prowling about."

She turned her head away from him so that he could only see the smooth line of her jaw and delicate ear. But he was certain that on that porcelain skin he saw the dimple at the end of a smile.

He took his seat and placed a linen napkin on his lap. He nodded to Ifan, and a pair of footmen were suddenly moving, placing crystal wine goblets before him and Miss Fairchild, pouring wine. "I suggest we call a truce, you and I," he said amicably.

That certainly caught her attention. "A truce?" she asked, eyeing him suspiciously.

"We are, for better or worse, trapped in this situation until a letter arrives. If you will agree to stop meddling, I will agree to feed you." He smiled.

Miss Fairchild returned it with an impertinent smile. "I will agree to stop *meddling,* as you put it, if you will agree to be less disdainful."

"Disdainful, am I?"

"And proud. You are proud and disdainful."

He considered that. If he was guilty, he had no idea how to stop being either, but nodded all the same. "Done."

She smiled the way he imagined she would smile if she were just shown an entire trunk of new shoes. "Well then," she said cheerfully. "Now that we've dispensed with that . . . do you always dine alone in such a big room?"

Where was he supposed to dine if not in a dining room? "Yes."

"Hmm," she said, as if that meant something.

"Pray tell, Miss Fairchild, have you finished your examination of my home?"

"Oh, I couldn't rightly say," she said breezily. "There are so many strange twists and turns and corridors that it is difficult to know. It seems as if there is a surprise at every turn in this castle." She gave him a very pointed look. "Such as the portrait gallery. I was quite impressed with the number of portraits and the vast array of subjects. It seems as if you have commissioned a painting of every Welsh man and woman."

"Not all of them," he said casually. "Only the prettier ones."

She actually smiled at that. "Where do you suppose so many subjects were found?"

"I don't know that they were *found,* precisely, but they are gathered like any collection — ancestors, family, and other notable personages."

"And some very lonely manors," she said, and lifted her goblet. "And a stately white mansion that attracts the eye." She smiled and sipped her wine. Her smile widened with pleasure as she lowered the goblet. "Oh my — that is a most *excellent* wine, sir."

At the mention of Kendrick, he eyed her suspiciously, but she seemed to be interested only in the wine. "Thank you," he said. "We do manage to bring good wine to Wales."

"I had given up hope of it. I daresay I've not tasted better since I left London."

"Speaking of London," he said, watching her sip again, "when did you leave it?"

"Seven long months ago. Late in March."

"Seven months is quite a long time for an unmarried young woman to be away from her family," he remarked. "I wonder, why would a distinguished family such as yours allow you to be away from home for so long? One would think they'd want you home so that they might make a match for you."

Miss Fairchild glanced at him sidelong. "They are just as keen to allow me to broaden my horizons, my lord. Nevertheless, I certainly never expected to be gone for so long. Would that I could return *now*."

"I daresay nothing would make either of us happier."

Her eyes narrowed. "And I daresay that all the brooding looks in the world won't hide your true meaning behind such a remark."

"I have stated my true meaning quite plainly. Seven months is quite a long time for a woman to be away from her home . . . and prestigious family."

"Aha!" she said triumphantly. "You said *unmarried* woman."

Rhodrick put down his wine goblet and looked at her. "Do you think I meant to impugn your honor?"

She snorted again. "I don't see how you could *possibly* impugn it any more than apparently I have done quite on my own. My reputation was ruined the day I left Bredwardine in the company of Mr. Percy."

That he could not argue.

The sparkle in her eye dimmed a little, and she glanced at her empty plate as her fingers drummed idly on the stem of the wineglass. "Do you know that I intended to be gone for only one month? *One month,* I said. One month to Wales and back. *Ha.*" She shook her head. "I was a bigger fool than even you clearly believe."

"I do not think you a fool," he said quietly, and it was true. He could not vouch for her moral character, but he thought her very clever on the whole — well spoken, capable of thinking beyond the weather. If she knew how truly intrigued he was by her, she would be appalled.

Miss Fairchild smiled wryly, the dimples in her cheeks appearing once again. "Ah, but life has a rather grand way of intervening in the best-laid plans, does it not? Look at me — a full six months later, and here I am as you see me — ruined, impoverished, and rather well stranded."

Oh, but he saw her, he saw every inch of her. He smelled her, remembered the feel of her skin, the texture of the small curl of her hair he'd touched this afternoon in his moment of madness. But he looked away as a footman served a leek and cheese soufflé.

"In London, I'd be partaking of the Little Season's festivities, attending balls and soirées and assemblies. On the other hand, if events had not brought me here, I never would have had the opportunity to view your many fine portraits, would I?"

The lady was, apparently, quite fond of art. "I suppose not," he said simply, and took a bite of the soufflé. He glanced at his guest — her fork was poised above the soufflé, but she was watching him closely. Rhodrick swallowed.

"Isn't there *anything* you would say of your portrait gallery?" she demanded.

"Such as?"

"Such as 'I wonder, Miss Fairchild, if you had opportunity to view them all,' or 'Perchance you viewed the painting of my father or grandfather, or whoever he is, and was diverted by all his Greek glory.' Perhaps you might inquire as to which paintings I enjoyed the most, or which ones I found curious."

"Which, then?" he asked.

"Which what?"

"Which did you find curious? Which did you enjoy?"

She opened her mouth to speak, but thought the better of it and dropped her gaze to her plate. "*All* of them, but most particularly the white house. I should very much like to visit it —"

"Miss Fairchild —"

"But I am certain I have been there!" she said quickly, before he could forbid her again.

She confounded him. "Why would you ever have had cause to be at Kendrick?"

"It is called Kendrick?" she asked excitedly.

"Miss Fairchild, your family hails from Bredwardine, do they not?"

"I did not lie to you, my lord," she said, reading his thoughts. "And I don't know precisely when I was at Kendrick, but I believe I was there with my mother."

"I think not," he scoffed. "There has been

only one tenant in twenty years, and that was Percy."

That silenced her, but her brow furrowed in thought. After a moment, she looked at him again. "But if I might *see* it."

"Miss Fairchild, please," he said as politely as he could, "as I have told you, Kendrick is *closed.* It is not safe and you are expressly forbidden to go there."

She frowned. "Very *well,*" she said, and stabbed irritably at her soufflé. "Yet one cannot help but wonder what is the great harm as there is nothing to occupy a person's time here," she continued crossly. "Really, sir, Llanmair is so *ghastly* uninhabited."

"It is not so *'ghastly uninhabited,'*" he said. "Just because you have not been presented to any society here does not mean it does not exist."

"Oh?" she said, perking up at the notion of there being any society. "And where is the good society? I should think Rhayader, as there were really quite a lot of people milling about the day we drove through. I suppose you mean there, do you not?"

Rhodrick had no idea where he meant, and frankly, only the Awbreys and Lord and Lady Pool came to mind. "There, and other parts."

For some reason, that response seemed to irk Miss Fairchild further. If there was one thing Rhodrick had learned in his thirty-eight years, it was that women could, at times, be very difficult to fathom. He'd also learned long ago that there was really no point in trying to make sense of them, for a man was quite incapable of it, and he did not attempt to do so now.

"Don't you enjoy society, my lord?" she inquired.

"Not particularly."

"Oh? I adore it. I can't think of anything more enjoyable than an excellent meal consumed in the presence of excellent company. Can you?"

He looked at her beautiful face. "I can think of at least one thing that is more enjoyable."

Miss Fairchild shrugged and ate another bite of soufflé, put her fork down, and looked up at the ceiling as she chewed.

"Now what has you displeased?" he asked idly.

She turned her gaze to him. "I should like to know if you are always so taciturn, or is it just me who makes you quite opposed to conversing."

He put down his fork. "I suppose I might ask if you are always so verbose, or if I make you quite opposed to silence."

"I am not verbose, I am polite! I will have you know that I am quite renowned for my conversation in London. I am wanted as a partner at all the parlor games because I can be counted upon to be *conversant*."

"I am hardly surprised you are renowned for your conversation," he said dryly. "One can hardly escape it."

"Perhaps I erred in my desire to fill this room with something other than cold silence, as you would have it."

"Your conversation is most welcome. But you might allow yourself a bite of food now and again between all the conversing." He motioned toward her food. "Please do eat, Miss Fairchild. Cook has gone to a great deal of trouble."

She picked up her fork, took two more bites, put the fork down, and looked at him again. "Are you *ever* to London, or do you remain here, all alone, dining in solitary splendor with only paintings of closed estates to keep you company?"

Rhodrick glanced at Ifan, who instantly moved to remove his dish. "I was once a frequent visitor to London," he said, and paused to pick up his wine. "But I have not been in a few years."

"Oh!" she said, clearly surprised. "Did you

not enjoy the society there?"

"My work keeps me here. I am a judge and I have a great number of tenants who require my attention. I haven't the time to be off in London practicing clever conversation over a parlor game."

"Clearly, *that* is true," she said wryly, and picking up her fork, popped a bite of soufflé into her mouth.

Rhodrick could not help but smile. "Perhaps you will astound me with your talent for conversation over a game of chess after we dine." He glanced at her from the corner of his eye. "You do know chess, do you not?"

She laughed, the sound of it melodic and sweet. "I do," she said, and smiled again as Ifan removed her plate. "And I predict you will be very sorry to have issued a challenge. My cousins stayed very annoyed with me for besting them time and again."

As she launched into a tale of how she had so handily defeated her cousins — which included one rather infamous row, apparently, with Cousin Ava — Rhodrick looked at Ifan and nodded, indicating he should prepare the red salon for the two of them upon the conclusion of supper.

As he ate and listened to Miss Fairchild talk of her cousins, he realized it had been years since he'd looked forward to anything as much as he looked forward to their game of chess.

FOURTEEN

Perhaps, Greer thought, she should have left the wine well enough alone — it weakened her resolve to be firm and aloof, and she put the blame squarely on the shoulders of an excellent vintage for her being in the red salon at all. Which was, she desperately wanted to point out, not red as the prince had suggested, but the color of ripe peaches.

Earlier this evening, when Lulu had informed her she must dine with the prince if she was to eat at all, Greer had been determined to starve to death before she spent as much as a moment in his presence. But when the hunger pangs began, she had decided that perhaps when one's back is against the proverbial wall, the best way to confront the enemy is head-on and without flinching.

She was not flinching, but she'd hardly expected to end up seated cozily before a fire and across a chessboard from him, admiring hanging tapestries that did nothing to keep the cold drafts at bay.

With her chin propped lazily on her fist, she watched him move a knight. When she glanced up, his dark eyes, which reminded her of a wet forest at the moment, were on her, and he raised a brow in silent question.

"Are you certain of your play, my lord?"

One corner of his mouth tipped up. "I am always certain of my play."

His expression suggested he meant something other than chess.

As Greer studied the board, she wondered about his life and his loves — and his style of play in bed. Was he as rough and gentle as he had been with her the night he had kissed her in the corridor? A little shiver ran down her spine. Such thoughts were clouding her vision of the game, and with a sigh, she shook her head, moved a pawn, and settled back to watch him lose.

He frowned lightly as he studied the board, his fingers drumming on the arm of the chair in which he sat. Cain and Abel, his ever-loyal dogs, lay on either side of his chair, their heads resting on their outstretched paws.

The prince looked, Greer thought, rather broodingly handsome and virile tonight. His thick hair was brushed back and tied in a queue. His clothing was of the highest quality, cut to perfection to enhance his muscular build. Indeed, he possessed naturally the sort of dashing figure that men in London could only achieve with padding and corsets.

She looked at the scar on his cheek and imagined the ugly brawl from which she was certain he had earned it. She could imagine him fighting off two or three ruffians at once.

At present, he was studying the board, his every move made to give her access to victory. But she had secretly countered his gentlemanly intention in *her* every move, making him work to lose, giving her more opportunity to study the room.

"Why do you call this room the red salon?" she asked after a moment.

He glanced up. "It is a salon."

She chuckled. "I recognize that it is a *salon,* my lord, but it is not a *red* salon."

"It has always been known as the red salon."

"Perhaps you should rename it to reflect the color to which it has faded."

He frowned slightly and glanced around the room. "What color would you name it?"

"Peach."

"Peach," he repeated, and returned his

gaze to the board. "That does not seem to be the sort of hearty color worthy of a salon."

"There is a room at Downey House, where I live in London, that was painted peach," she idly mentioned. "My stepfather, Lord Downey, was very fond of the color and had every inch of that room painted peach. The ceiling, the walls, the wainscot, the doors. Even the mantel was painted peach. Aunt Cassandra demanded he have it redone, and vowed she could not rest easy in a room in which she was the pit."

The prince smiled.

"Yet he refused," Greer continued as the prince moved a bishop. He sat back, apparently satisfied with his play. "He is a very stubborn man," she added absently. "And by the bye, *that* was not very well done at all," she said with a cluck of her tongue, frowning at his move.

"I beg your pardon?"

"You are clearing a path to your queen so that I might win, and now you leave me no choice but to take it."

He smiled a little, crinkling the corners of his eyes in a way that made him look rather charming. "Why in God's name would I do that?"

"I don't know, really," she said thoughtfully, assessing him. "I suppose there is a bit of a good gentleman rumbling around in you after all."

His smiled broadened, and the effect was unexpectedly mesmerizing. When he smiled fully, his teeth nicely white and even, he was really *quite* charming. And attractive in a ferocious sort of way. "Are you accusing me of handing you the win?"

"Not only do I accuse you of it, I accuse you of doing it very badly," she said, and moved her bishop. "Check, sir."

He glanced at the board and chuckled low. "My, my, Miss Fairchild. You show me no mercy."

"Of course not. Why in God's name would I do that?"

He grinned and nodded at the lone footman who attended them, who came forward to remove the game as the prince picked up his brandy and absently swirled the amber liquid in his glass. "In some quarters, it is considered unwise to call a man on his motives of play unless you are prepared and willing to defend your own. I should have thought your aunt might have mentioned as much."

Greer laughed at that. "My aunt warned me that gentlemen, in general, were not to be trusted. At cards or with debutantes."

His eyes glittered over the top of his snifter and he drawled, "That definitely depends on the debutante."

A flush of heat swept through her. "And the gentleman," she added softly.

His gaze was scorching now. He regarded her openly. "It sounds as if your aunt and uncle were happy."

"Happy?" She shook her head. "They were compatible, I suppose, but I should not call them happy. I think there is so much more that must be present in a marriage for there to be *true* happiness."

He seemed surprised by her answer. "Such as?"

"Love," she said without hesitation. "Desire and passion. Respect." She eyed the prince curiously. For whatever else he was, he'd once been a married man. "What is your opinion?"

"Mine?" He seemed surprised by the question. "I . . . I couldn't say."

"You were married, my lord — surely you must have *some* opinion."

His expression changed instantly; the glitter gone from his eyes and in its place a hardness. "That was quite a long time ago, Miss Fairchild. My wife died at a very young age."

There was something in the way he responded that kept Greer from asking more. "I am sorry to hear it," she said.

"Your aunt and uncle?" he coolly reminded her.

"Well . . . I am certain that my aunt loved my uncle Bingley, her first husband," she said. "Life was very gay for us all at Bingley Hall, and Lord and Lady Bingley were the perfect picture of marital bliss."

He said nothing; he had retreated behind his aloof demeanor.

"But then Lord Bingley died," she continued. "And Aunt Cassandra married Lord Downey, and Ava and Phoebe and I —"

Dear God, what was this? Just the mention of their names, and suddenly there were bloody tears in her eyes! "I miss them," she blurted, surprising herself by the sudden burst of sentiment and feeling quite unable to stop it. "We have been inseparable since we were children, and I miss them *terribly*." Good heavens, even *more* tears flowed behind the first batch and she could feel her face turning red. "Oh dear God, please do forgive me," she said as one fat tear slid down her cheek. "I am not usually so slushy."

He reached in his breast pocket and withdrew a handkerchief, which he handed to her.

"Thank you," she said gratefully. "I seem to have lost mine." She blew into it and daintily dabbed at her eyes. "I apologize for turning so wretchedly sentimental, but I *do* miss them, very much. I miss their counsel and their companionship . . . and Ava's imperious ways, and Phoebe's fashionable sartorial creations." Another tear slipped out from the corner of her eye and ran down her cheek. "Oh *Lord,*" she said, appalled, swiping at the tear on her cheek.

The prince was silent and his expression, as always, very stoic. He surely thought her ridiculous, or worse, weak. And as much as she didn't give a fig *what* he thought of her, for some reason, she could hardly bear him to think her *weak.* She glanced uncomfortably at her lap. "You must find these tears very tiresome."

"No," he said, so softly that she barely heard him at all, and she hesitantly lifted her gaze. "Quite the contrary. I find that you are quite possibly the most . . . *delicate* creature I have ever seen."

The remark astonished her, unbalanced her. A flurry of emotions erupted within her, none of which were appropriate or wise. The prince had not moved, and his expression remained impenetrable — with the exception of his eyes. A shock of sexual desire instantly swept through Greer and she flinched at the intensity of it.

He was gazing at her now as if he'd not really *looked* at her before this moment. "And quite the actress," he added calmly. "Are you a theatrical performer, Miss Fairchild?"

A sound of fury escaped her. "You are the most *ill*-mannered, *un*civilized man I have ever had the displeasure to meet! Here!" she said, thrusting the handkerchief at him.

He reached for it, but instead of taking it from her hand, his fingers curved over hers, holding them tightly, and a current as strong as that of the Thames flowed between them.

He rose to his feet, pulling her up with him. They stood quite close, so close that Greer had to tilt her head back to see his face, so close that she could see the tiny flecks of gold in his green eyes and the dark red edges of his scar.

"Unhand me," she breathed angrily.

He made no move to do so.

"You are the *worst* of scoundrels!"

"And how many scoundrels have you known?" he asked, his voice caressing and low.

Greer's breathing quickened; she could feel a cauldron of apprehension and yearning deep inside her, weighing her down, keeping her from moving. "How *dare* you speak to me in such an ungentlemanly manner."

"What irks you? Do you find the question offensive . . . or merely too personal?"

She gasped and tried to jerk her hand from his, but he held her firm. His gaze dropped to her lips; his black lashes formed tiny little crescents across his cheeks. He lifted his free hand, and carefully touched two fingers to her lips, as if he meant to see if they were real.

It was such a simple gesture, but it was the most sensual thing a man had ever done to her.

Greer found herself in a desperate moment — she had no idea how she had come to this point of desiring him. She was acutely aware that she was courting danger from which no good could possibly come, but her will to act sensibly had deserted her. Completely drawn in by a powerful craving, she locked her gaze on his, parted her lips, and drew the tip of his finger into her mouth, caressing it with her tongue.

"Too personal, it would seem," he drawled.

She bit down on his finger.

The prince only laughed and shifted so that his lips were only a moment from her temple. She could feel his breath warm on her skin, skimming over her eyelids, down her cheek. He had not actually touched her, yet his nearness was blistering. "Surely you know the best way to entice a man is to provoke him," he murmured as he removed his finger from her mouth and slipped his arm around her waist, drawing her into him, pressing her into his body, which was as hard as rock.

"Don't touch me," she said.

"I already am," he reminded her. "But you can stop it, Miss Fairchild, if you so desire. Just a word — *no* — and I shall take my hand from your body."

The word was on the tip of her tongue, but Greer was spellbound by the smoldering look in his eyes, the powerful feel of his body against hers, the silky caress of his hand against her arm.

She tried to summon the word, but could make no sound.

"One word," he said again, his gaze on her mouth. "The very word you would not say to Percy."

She gasped indignantly as he pulled her closer. "Envious?" she breathed.

He suddenly grinned. "*Desperately* so," he said, and lowered his head, painting her lips with the tip of his tongue before pressing his mouth to hers and slipping his tongue between her willing lips.

Greer felt herself go weak and the strength of conviction leave her body. She had never experienced such seduction or anything as wholly irresistible as this man's passionate kiss. She could feel herself sliding into an invisible trap, a pool of desire.

His kiss was remarkably demanding and tender all at once. There was potency behind it, a sense that he could crush her with his male appetite but that he worked to restrain himself, to touch her with care.

But he did not refrain from touching her. His hand began to move on the curve of her hip, then up to her waist, and to her breast. He caressed the flesh of her bosom, plunged his fingers into her cleavage, cupped her breast in his palm, leaving her skin burning with sensations she'd never felt.

His caresses grew more urgent, his kiss deeper, his struggle for restraint reverberating throughout his body and into hers.

A storm of prurient longing rocked Greer toward oblivion — she could feel every sinewy muscle of the prince everywhere they touched, every hard edge, every passionate caress of his big hands. He'd moved her backward, so that she was pressed against the high back of one of the chairs, and buried his face in her neck as he slipped his hand under her thigh, lifting her leg to his waist.

Greer leaned her head to one side, giving him better access to her neck, bracing herself against the back of the chair so that she didn't fall when her knees finally buckled, which she was sure they would do at any moment.

With his other hand, the prince gathered the skirt of her gown, pushing it up and moving his body between her legs, brushing the hardest part of his body against the most vulnerable part of hers. He pressed against her, moving suggestively against her as his mouth found hers again.

An extraordinary pleasure was building in Greer, filling her up to the point of bursting. But when his hand slipped between their bodies, into the slit of her drawers, his fingers grazing hot, wet, skin, she somehow realized in that lustful haze what she was doing, what she was *feeling,* and panicked. It was impossible to feel the strength of his embrace or the yearning in his body without losing every last shred of propriety she had left to her, and in an alarmed moment, she tore her mouth from his, gasping for air and sobbing her dismay at once.

She pushed him and dropped her leg from his waist. "Oh my God," she gasped.

Yet the prince would not let her go so easily. He wrapped his arms around her, put his hand beneath her chin and lifted her face to him, kissing her ardently again, nipping at her bottom lip. When Greer turned her head, he asked roughly, "Why so shy? You were enjoying my attentions."

Greer shoved again, but he was relentless — this time he weakened her with a very tender kiss.

"No," she moaned, twisting away. "I cannot, not with you."

He stilled. "Do you find me so objectionable?" he asked low, and palmed her breast. "Your body betrays you, Miss Fairchild. Your skin is warmed by my attention. I feel your breast swell in my hand . . . my touch arouses you."

"Only my fury is aroused," she said low.

His hand still on her breast, he smiled knowingly. "There is scarcely anything more satisfying than a woman's fury in a man's bed."

She shoved hard at him now; her heart racing dangerously at the mention of his bed. "You are *obscene.*"

"Nor is anything more satisfying than an obscene man in a woman's bed."

She dared not imagine what he meant by that, and struggled to draw a steady breath. When he casually pushed a strand of her hair behind her ear, she slapped his hand away. *"Stop,"* she said harshly.

"Stop?" he echoed, moving the pad of his thumb over her bottom lip. "But it is no less than what you gave Percy."

The remark wounded her — whether it was because of his audacity or because it was so distressingly close to the truth, she could not say.

Lord God, what had happened to her these last months? She hardly knew who she was any longer! In London, she had known her place, had known her personal limits of propriety. But here — she could not remember a time in her life she had been so unguarded or had allowed her emotions to rule as they had in the last two weeks.

She still held his handkerchief and tossed it, badly crumpled, onto the chair, and turned a cold glare to him. "Have you finished humiliating me?"

He dropped his hands from her body and shrugged as he studied her face. "I did not seek to humiliate you, if that is what you think."

"Liar," she said, shaking now.

He shook his head and then turned partially away from her, so that she could not see his face. "I am many things, Miss Fairchild, but a liar is not one of them."

"I don't know *what* you are," she said angrily, and turned and walked out of the room, hoping desperately he would stop her with a single word or an apology; hoping just as desperately that he did not, for she could not trust her response.

She walked into the corridor, her hands balled into fists at her sides, and she had to blink to keep tears from clouding her vision when he did not call her back.

FIFTEEN

"I've been at Llanmair these forty years, and I still find myself turning this way instead of that. This way, if you please, miss," said Mrs. Bowen, who was leading Greer through the labyrinthine corridors of the castle to the conservatory.

As they passed the prince's study, Greer noticed that the door stood open and the hearth was cold.

A wave of relief rushed over her. She couldn't bear facing him yet, not while she was still reeling from the effects of their torrid kiss the night before.

They walked along another corridor and Mrs. Bowen pointed out the various rooms: the linen closet, the china room, and another set of doors that were the dry goods stores.

They climbed up a narrow staircase, and Mrs. Bowen's steps grew leaden and her breath heavy as she told Greer how the stairs had once been used by the English to invade Llanmair.

Greer had read about it in the book she had borrowed from the prince. In the year 1283, Edward I had invaded Llanmair as he sought to quell the Welsh rebellion.

The walls still bore the nicks and marks of sword fighting.

When they emerged from the stairwell, Mrs. Bowen put a hand to her ample breast as she drew a deep breath and pointed to her right. "Just through there, miss, on the other side of the portrait gallery."

"Thank you . . . but if you would, Mrs. Bowen, will you not take a moment more and tell me who are depicted in some of the portraits?" Mrs. Bowen glanced at the watch pinned to her breast. "I won't keep you but a moment," Greer assured her, and with her hand on Mrs. Bowen's elbow, she didn't give the housekeeper an opportunity to decline, and steered her into the gallery, stopping directly before the painting of a man in the ridiculous ancient Greek dress.

The two women tilted their heads back as far as they could to see the top of the man's head.

"Ah yes," Mrs. Bowen said, nodding. "His lordship's grandfather. He's been gone thirty years or more, but I've heard told he was quite fond of the Greek classics."

And himself, Greer thought.

"He built the orangery in the Greek style. You might have seen it."

"I have not, but I shall make it a point to do so. He resembles the prince, does he not?"

"Oh aye, he does," Mrs. Bowen agreed, smiling proudly.

"And who is this?" Greer asked, pointing to a pair of children who looked to be from the sixteenth century.

Mrs. Bowen squinted at them. "I couldn't rightly say."

"Oh," Greer said absently, and pointed to the young girl in the current dress next to the painting of the white house. "Who is this girl?"

Mrs. Bowen's reaction was so flustered that it startled Greer. She pressed her lips together, cast a furtive look down the hall, almost as if she expected someone to come around. "I don't know," she said shortly.

"The portrait seems to have been done quite recently."

Mrs. Bowen's cheeks were turning red. "Perhaps it was. Beg your pardon, but I really must be about my work."

The normally affable housekeeper's agitation mystified Greer. "Of course," she said, and glanced hastily at the house the prince had called Kendrick, fearful that Mrs. Bowen would escape before she could ask about it. "But just one more, Mrs. Bowen, please. Do you know this place?" she asked, pointing to the painting of the white house.

Mrs. Bowen reluctantly looked at the painting, and the hardness in her expression softened. "That is Kendrick, miss. Not six miles from here. But it is closed."

"Do you know if anyone by the name of Vaughan ever resided there?"

"Vaughan?" Mrs. Bowen thought for a moment, then shook her head. "No, miss. Bronwyn was their name."

Greer's world seemed to shift a little. She had not expected Mrs. Bowen to say her mother's maiden name. *"Bronwyn?"* she repeated in a near whisper.

"Many years ago, but aye, the Bronwyns. I was a chambermaid to the family before Mr. Bronwyn died. His cousin took it for a time after that, but when he passed, I believe it sat empty."

Bronwyn! This couldn't be right — Greer was almost certain that her mother was from Bredwardine! "Are you quite certain, Mrs. Bowen?" she asked. "I thought the Bronwyns hailed from Bredwardine."

"Bredwardine!" Mrs. Bowen frowned

thoughtfully. "I don't think so. And look miss, there they are, the Bronwyns," she said, pointing to the canvas and the people attending the picnic. "Mr. and Mrs. Bronwyn," she said, pointing to a couple lounging on a blanket. "And that is Alis, their oldest daughter, and her sister, Fiona. Poor Fiona died of the same fever that took Mr. Bronwyn."

Greer gasped softly and peered at the girl Mrs. Bowen had pointed to, the girl who stared out at the painter while her sister whispered in her ear. It seemed impossible, but that child was her mother. *Her mother!* Now she could see the resemblance to the small hand portrait of her mother that she possessed. And as Greer peered at the girl, she noticed something else — her mother was wearing the charm that Greer now wore around her neck. She gasped again, put her hand to her neck. "Oh *Lord!*"

"What's wrong, miss?" Mrs. Bowen asked, alarmed.

"That is my mother!" Greer said excitedly. "It's *her!*"

"Your mother?" Mrs. Bowen asked skeptically, peering at the portrait, too.

"It is her," Greer said excitedly. "Her maiden name was Bronwyn, Alis Bronwyn, and after she married, Alis Vaughan. *Look,*

256

Mrs. Bowen, she and I wear the same necklace!"

Mrs. Bowen peered closely. "Aye, so it is! But that is a common symbol in Wales. Many girls and women wear it."

"It is *her*," Greer said, touching the painting where her mother stood. "Did . . . did you *know* her?" she asked, her heart racing.

"Oh no, only the sight of her really. She was in the nursery. And then her father and sister died with that wretched fever." Mrs. Bowen shook her head. "A dozen servants were brought to Jesus by that fever, too."

"What happened then?"

"Mrs. Bronwyn married some English fellow and moved away. Mr. Bronwyn's cousin took it, as I said, for another ten years or so, I believe. But then Kendrick was closed shortly thereafter and sat for years until Mr. Percy . . ." Her face darkened again; she looked very uncomfortable and cleared her throat.

"But I have *been* there, I am certain of it," Greer said excitedly. "I remember the door and the way it looks inside —"

"Perhaps when you were very young?" Mrs. Bowen suggested. "It could only have been, for after Mr. Bronwyn's cousin died, it remained closed, except for the *very* short time Mr. Percy was there, several years later.

But it has been closed since . . ." Her voice trailed off.

Greer had the distinct impression she meant to say more. "Since what?" she pressed.

Mrs. Bowen looked at her watch again.

"Kendrick has been closed for several years since . . . what?" she pressed.

Mrs. Bowen stepped back. "Since it was abandoned again, that's all." But she still looked as if she meant something else and was afraid to say it aloud. "I'm sorry, Miss Fairchild, but I am certain the Bronwyns have all died off."

"Is it possible to reach Kendrick?" Greer asked quickly as the housekeeper began to move away.

"What?" Mrs. Bowen cried, her eyes going wide. "Oh *no,* miss! You'd not want to go there, mark me. It's naught but an empty shell now."

"Is there a path, is it possible to walk there?"

"No!" Mrs. Bowen exclaimed. "Put such thoughts out of your mind, miss! The roads are overgrown and the place is nearly deserted! His lordship has forbidden *anyone* to go there. It is closed."

Mrs. Bowen seemed truly alarmed and it occurred to Greer that the housekeeper might mention her questions about the house to the prince. She thought better of pressing the woman, for the prince had forbidden her from Kendrick, and she preferred he not know she intended to go. And she had every intention of going — if it *ever* stopped raining.

She glanced at her mother's young face again, her smiling face and eyes, *Greer's* eyes. "Oh heavens, Mrs. Bowen, I do not intend to *walk* there." She laughed. "I was only curious."

"Well," Mrs. Bowen said as she brushed her skirts. "It's not a suitable place for a young woman."

"Indeed?" Greer asked lightly. "What makes it unsuitable? Did something happen there?"

Mrs. Bowen's silence was her answer, but Greer peered at the housekeeper nonetheless. Mrs. Bowen frowned, pressed her lips tightly together, then shook her head. "Some things are better left unspoken, Miss Fairchild. But heed me." She paused to lean forward and whispered, "The spirits walk among us every day. Some are good and some are bad. And you do *not* want to provoke the bad." She straightened again. "Please do excuse me now . . . I really must be about my work."

259

Surprised by the warning, Greer nodded. "I beg your pardon. I did not mean to keep you as long as this."

"Thank you," Mrs. Bowen said, and with a nod, she bustled off.

Greer stood a moment longer looking at her mother, her mind whirling in shock and confusion at the things she was learning. Aunt Cassandra had never mentioned Kendrick — but then again, there had been ten years separating Greer's mother from her younger half sister, Cassandra, who was the first child of Alis Bronwyn's mother and new stepfather, if Greer's memory served. She supposed it was possible that Aunt Cassandra had not even known of Kendrick. But why did Mrs. Bowen say it had been closed *since* something and mention spirits? Greer put no stock in spirits, but she was certain *something* had happened there.

Pondering those questions, she walked onto the conservatory. To her surprise, the room had been completely done up. It was an astonishing change — it was warm and inviting. A pair of overstuffed chairs and a settee covered in yellow-and-green-striped chintz were now clustered around a blazing hearth.

Behind the settee stood a beautiful writing desk. Greer sighed with pleasure as she ran her fingers along the highly polished finish. A high-backed chair at the desk allowed the writer to look out over the gardens. The rain had stopped, and while the day was still very gray, she could see the lush greenery just beyond the conservatory. She would walk in the garden today, as she was desperate to be outside after so many days of dreary, wet weather.

But first . . . On the desk was a stack of high-quality vellum, two inches thick, as well as three porcelain and silver inkwells and a set of pens. A blotter and a square of wax for sealing were beside the pens. A smile lit up her face and she twirled around, noting for the first time the small brass cart with a variety of decanters. "It's *marvelous*," she said aloud. "Perfectly divine!"

As she sat at the writing desk, a thought occurred to her: Had *he* done this? Had he instructed the staff to make the room so inviting?

No, surely it had been Mrs. Bowen. After last night, she would be quite surprised if the prince even spoke to her, much less had appointed this room so pleasingly. She would have to thank Mrs. Bowen for her efforts, but at the moment, she was anxious to write her cousins. She'd been at Llanmair more than a week now; it would be at least another week before her first letter reached London, and she suspected that was an optimistic assessment.

And then there was her other fear — what if something happened to the post and it never reached London at all?

She vowed then and there to write her cousins every day until someone came for her. She took paper and pen, dipped the pen in ink, and began to write.

SIXTEEN

Several days passed before the rain let up enough to allow the roads to dry, and at the first opportunity, Rhodrick rode to Rhayader.

As he returned home later that afternoon, he pushed his horse hard as he tried in vain to outride the absurdly tender thoughts about Greer Fairchild that had attached themselves to him like a bunch of leeches. He'd begun to dream of her rather prolifically of late. Of himself, too — only in his dreams he had no scar and Miss Fairchild desired him.

Neither of them had spoken of the intimate and scalding encounter they had shared after their chess game, but she'd avoided him for a few days afterward. Eventually, she came around again — when he decreed she would dine with him or go hungry — and he'd had the privilege of watching her at his dinner table, listening to her ebullient accounts of her walks about the grounds before being chased in by rain, or her chance meetings with some of the more colorful characters that worked on his estate.

He listened to her reminisce about the Season in London, and learned that when one debutante had as many as four silk ball gowns, that was quite remarkable. He heard all about the Ladies' Beneficent Society, and how Miss Fairchild, in the course of her work with that charitable endeavor, found it more rewarding than she'd anticipated.

When she tired of talking about London, she amused herself by accusing him of any number of transgressions. He did not feed Cain and Abel enough, they were too thin. There were parts of the garden that were in desperate need of repair. She thought Lulu, a housemaid, needed more time away to visit her family.

Rhodrick rarely spoke — there was no need. Miss Fairchild seemed intent on filling each supper hour with her bright chatter while he admired her lovely face and her elegant, expressive hands, while idle thoughts of the many ways he would like to make love to her flitted through his mind.

But as soon as the supper hour was done, Miss Fairchild would disappear, leaving him alone once again.

Rhodrick spurred his horse faster still, reining him sharply right and recklessly leading him to jump a rotted stone fence, determined to take the fields instead of the road. It was harder riding, but with every jarring step, every jolt, he hoped to dislodge the feeling of useless desire implanted in him — or at the very least, batter it into bloody submission.

But if he could not defeat the monster in him alone, then he would seek safety in numbers. Therefore, he had invited the Awbreys, and their guests, Lord and Lady Pool, visiting from Aberystwyth, to dine at Llanmair this evening.

In the courtyard at Llanmair, a groomsman ran out to greet him, and was startled by the winded horse. When Rhodrick climbed down, the lad turned a wide-eyed look at his mud-caked back and boots.

"Double his oats after you've rubbed him down," Rhodrick said in Welsh, and strode into the foyer, passing the gilded mirror he had come to despise.

By the time Ifan reached Rhodrick, he'd tossed his cloak aside and handed his hat to the butler. "There will be six for supper. Please inform Miss Fairchild that we shall have guests this evening," he said, and whistling for his dogs, he walked on, his knee aching.

The pain in his leg subsided with the help of a hot bath, and by the dinner hour, Rhodrick had recovered somewhat. When Ifan told him his guests had arrived, he was feeling rather jovial, looking forward to an entertaining evening.

"Splendid," he said as he straightened the cuffs of his shirt. "You've asked our house-guest to join us, have you not?"

"I have, my lord, but regrettably, she has declined," Ifan said as he picked up the neckcloth Rhodrick was to wear and held it out to him.

"Declined?" Rhodrick echoed irritably as he took the neckcloth and draped it around his collar. He was surprisingly disappointed by her refusal. After all her expressed discontent about the lack of society at Llanmair, and her overwhelming curiosity, he would have thought she'd be delirious with joy at the prospect of other people. "Did she say why?"

"She did not, my lord."

Rhodrick turned and looked at Ifan. "Did she say anything?"

Ifan looked rather uncomfortable.

"Well?" Rhodrick pressed.

"She said she would not, under any circumstance, join you." He glanced up at Rhodrick. "She said it rather adamantly, my lord."

"*Did* she," he muttered as he quickly wrapped the ends of the neckcloth around before tying them off in an artful knot. "I don't suppose it occurred to Miss Fairchild that she is really not at liberty to *decline?*" he snapped as he straightened his collar and stood back to view the effect.

"I do not believe it did, my lord," Ifan said carefully, and bowed low.

"Thank you," Rhodrick muttered, and walked out of the room, his stride long and determined, his irritation growing with each step.

Wasn't it enough that he had to suffer her presence in his house? Wasn't it enough that he had arranged this supper *expressly* so that he could be *near* her and not touch her? She could, therefore, do him the courtesy of attending!

He marched on, past chambermaids who disappeared into the walls as he strode forward, past footmen who bowed low as he approached, up the stairs, and down another corridor until he arrived at a threshold he had not crossed since a warm summer's night some thirteen years ago, when his wife, and then his child, had died.

He rapped hard on the door of the master suite before pushing it open and startling Miss Fairchild, who happened to be just inside. With a shriek of surprise, she jumped up from her chair before the hearth. In one hand she held a book. The other hand she pressed against her heart as she gaped at him.

She was, he quickly noted, dressed for the evening. Her thick black hair was swept up and fastened with pearls; her gown — he could not detect the color — was perfectly cut, hugging every curve and framing her bosom, and seemed to shimmer in the firelight. All he could think of was the scarcely contained intimacy they'd shared that night in the red salon, and of all the places on her body he would like to kiss her now. Her neck. Behind her knee. The smooth plane of her belly. Her —

"I beg your pardon, sir!" Miss Fairchild exclaimed breathlessly.

Walking deeper into the room, he demanded, "Is there a reason you have *declined* to join me for supper tonight?"

"Must I have a reason?"

"Miss Fairchild, if you are not on your deathbed or otherwise impaired, you will meet my guests and dine with the rest of the household."

She snapped shut the book she was holding. "I am not on my deathbed or otherwise impaired, but I did not realize that an appearance at supper was a *requirement*."

"What objection could you possibly have to meeting my guests?"

"What reason could I possibly have to meet them? For all I know, this is your idea of a Welsh inquisition."

"You seem to keep forgetting that *you* are supposedly Welsh. Is your disguise beginning to wear a little thin, do you suppose?"

"Oh!" she exclaimed, and angrily tossed the book onto the chair behind her. "At least as thin as the disguise of a kindly, law-abiding country earl, for I am certain no man could ever be more vexing to a body than *you,* my lord."

"Coming from you, I believe that is a compliment. Now do come along, Miss Fairchild. The guests are waiting."

She folded her arms across her middle, glaring at him. "I am not going. I refuse to be ridiculed and humiliated by your friends!"

He suddenly realized the root of her anger. *Of course!* He should have understood. Her reputation — what was left of it — was at stake. It was one thing to go about the servants at Llanmair with her reputation in tatters, but quite another to go about in society.

"You have nothing to fear," he said, his voice softer. "My guests have not heard your name before tonight. There are no expectations or impressions of you other than what you may create." He extended his hand, palm up. "Come."

She considered his hand warily. "Very well," she said after a moment with a sniff. "I will meet your *guests*. Perhaps they will see that you have quite lost your mind and will come to my rescue," she added before turning and marching to the dressing room.

Rhodrick clasped his hands behind his back, bowed his head, and waited impatiently. One minute passed, then another. He could not imagine what she could possibly be doing in there. "Perhaps I was unclear," he called out to her. "I meant that the supper would be served *this* evening."

"Ha! You are never unclear, my lord!" she shot back, and reappeared a moment later, her mouth and cheeks rouged. She paused in front of a mirror and played with a curl at her neck before sailing past him with a glare, the small train of her gown wafting behind her.

Rhodrick reached the door ahead of her and opened it, then gestured for her to precede him. She did just that. As they moved into the corridor, Rhodrick caught her elbow and forced her to slow down. "It is unseemly for young ladies from London to run."

"What *really* concerns you, sir?" she asked airily. "Do you fear that I will reach your friends first and that they will believe what I have to say before you've had the chance to tarnish their opinion of me?"

"I am far more concerned that you will inadvertently harm someone in your desperation to walk ahead of me."

She gave him a pert toss of her head. "And precisely who are these *guests,* if I may ask?"

"Old friends."

"Mmm," she said, staring straight ahead. "How interesting. I was of the firm opinion you had no friends. Then again, I undoubtedly have not accounted for the power of a locked tower to persuade one into friendship."

Rhodrick chuckled softly. "I should think a woman as clever as you would view this as a prime opportunity to employ your woeful tale of being orphaned to fleece someone less suspicious of you than am I."

She snorted at that as they hurried down the staircase. "It is not a *tale,* sir, it is the truth, and at last, I may have the pleasure of speaking to someone who will listen to reason."

"I predict that without Mr. Percy to sully the occasion, my friends will find you quite charming."

"Oh!" she exclaimed, and jerked her elbow from his grasp as they moved down the main corridor to the grand salon. "Kindly allow me the pleasure of at least *appearing* to be free."

"Not only will I allow you the pleasure, I will make certain that you are not bound at Llanmair by any possible means, and if you should be charming enough as to secure passage to London tonight, I urge you to *take* it," he said as they came to a halt before the double doors of the grand salon.

She lifted her face to him, her deep blue eyes sparkling with ire. "You may rest assured I *will.*"

"Excellent," he snapped, and opened the door, stepping back. "After you, Miss Fairchild."

She shifted her gaze to the interior of the grand salon and smiled as brilliantly as he'd ever seen — so brilliantly, in fact, that Rhodrick was momentarily distracted by it. He watched her walk across the threshold with the grace of a bloody queen, instantly lighting up the room.

He followed behind her, noting that his good friends were not only surprised, they looked absolutely dumbfounded.

Perhaps he might have mentioned Greer Fairchild before now. He hadn't intended to be coy, but in truth, he hadn't known exactly *how* to explain her.

Margaret was the first to come to her senses. She walked across the room and curtsied deeply before rising up to kiss him on the cheek. "Rhodi," she said, peering closely at him. "How *are* you this evening?"

"Never better," he said, and put his hand on Miss Fairchild's elbow. "I would like to introduce you to Miss Greer Fairchild." To her, he said, "My good friends, Mr. and Mrs. Awbrey. And Lord and Lady Pool."

Margaret, as fair-haired as Miss Fairchild was dark, smiled warmly. "It is indeed a pleasure to make your acquaintance," she said sincerely. "You must forgive my surprise, but Rhodi had not mentioned his houseguest before this very moment," she said, casting a brief but accusing look at Rhodrick.

Rhodrick smiled, but Miss Fairchild laughed. "Oh, I am hardly surprised he hadn't mentioned it!" she said gaily. "It has only recently been established that I would even *be* his guest. Unfortunately, I had a

273

wretched experience with a coach that necessitated my stay."

"Oh?" Margaret asked as Thomas shook Rhodrick's hand.

"Oh yes. The part that connects the wheels broke in half," she said, making a sort of circular motion with her hand, and looked at Rhodrick. "What is it called?"

"Axle."

"The *axle*," she repeated with a devilish smile for him. "It will take much longer than I anticipated to repair it. Naturally I insisted on taking rooms in Rhayader until my business in Wales could be completed, but his lordship is too generous." She cast a brilliant smile on Rhodrick. "He was *quite* insistent that I remain his reluctant guest."

"Oh," Margaret said, glancing curiously at Rhodrick again.

"And from where did you say you had arrived?" Lady Pool was older and seemed more suspicious than Margaret.

"I did not say, but I am from London."

"London!" Lady Pool exclaimed. "That is quite a long way, particularly at this time of year, is it not? What brings you all the way to Llanmair?"

"I shan't bother you with all the dreadful details," Miss Fairchild said charmingly. "It's rather complicated."

274

Lady Pool, however, was not so easily put off. She slipped her arm through Miss Fairchild's and nodded at Margaret. "It's hardly a bother. Do come and sit with us, dear, and tell us how you came to be at Llanmair."

"Well sir," Thomas said to Rhodrick as the ladies situated themselves on a settee, Miss Fairchild sandwiched between them, "you are full of surprises."

Rhodrick smiled wryly, watched Miss Fairchild take the champagne Ifan offered her with a pretty smile, and speak with great animation to the two ladies.

"Indeed you are," Lord Pool agreed. "Most men would boast of having such a treasure under their roof."

Rhodrick shrugged and took a glass of champagne from Ifan's tray.

Thomas exchanged a look with Lord Pool and said carefully, "She is . . . quite appealing. An unmarried man might be tempted by her good looks."

"Or a married man, for that matter," Lord Pool muttered.

A bit of heat slipped under Rhodrick's collar, but he hid his expression behind a sip of champagne. When he lowered the flute, his two friends were looking at him with amused curiosity.

"Well?" Thomas asked, nudging him.

With a rueful smile, Rhodrick said, "A woman as handsome as Miss Fairchild would naturally expect to be wooed by a handsome man. She would not be tempted by the likes of me, and undoubtedly, she will be gone soon enough."

Lord Pool laughed, but Thomas looked at him with an expression that was uncomfortably studious. Rhodrick did manage to steer the conversation for a time, but when supper was announced, they all stood and politely assembled for the promenade into the dining room, four pairs of eyes shifting expectantly to Miss Fairchild.

She smiled charmingly and glided forth to put her hand on the arm Rhodrick proffered as if she had done it a thousand times before. He smiled at the ire flashing in her eyes, covered her hand with his, and began to walk. "I couldn't help noticing that you regaled the ladies with colorful tales of London," he remarked low as they led the way to the dining room.

"And I couldn't help noticing that you knitted two entire sentences together," she whispered in response.

"The broken axle on the carriage was nicely done, I must admit," he said.

Miss Fairchild smiled a little. "I rather

thought so myself."

"You seem to be practiced at inventing tales," he said as Ifan opened the doors to the formal dining room ahead of them.

"I am practiced at being polite. It would not do to tell your guests you hold me prisoner here, for they would be shocked and would flee, and Cook's gone to a lot of trouble to make an excellent supper."

Rhodrick couldn't help himself; he smiled, and his smile broadened as she gasped with delight upon seeing the room. Rhodrick was always impressed with the way Ifan managed to set a table, and this one looked as if it had come straight out of Windsor. Four gold candelabrum were centered down the table. Each place setting was laid with gold-rimmed china, fine crystal, and silver cutlery. Tiny crystal vases at each place setting held pristine Welsh hothouse roses, freshly cut. Four footmen — two on each side of the table — stood in perfect formation, awaiting their charges.

Rhodrick seated a notably silent Miss Fairchild and waited until all his guests had been seated before taking his place at the head of the table. The moment he did, the footmen began to serve wine, Ifan personally tending to Rhodrick's glass.

As the first course of Welsh cakes was

served, the conversation covered the usual subjects: the weather, the latest parish news, Parliament's desire to levy a new agricultural tariff that had Lord Pool particularly irate.

Rhodrick scarcely heard the exchange because he could not take his eyes from Miss Fairchild. His imagination swirled around his doubts about her, but it was impossible to look at her now, so lovely and vivacious, and think of her in Owen Percy's arms. That image forever shadowed his thoughts — he could not seem to put aside his suspicions completely because of her association with that bastard.

"Rhodi, you are so quiet!" Margaret said, pulling him back into the moment.

"What?" he asked, startled.

"Lord Pool was just commenting on Parliament's desire to tax even Lady Pool's nerves," she explained.

"Ah." He smiled and lifted his wineglass in silent toast to Lady Pool.

"I daresay his lordship has no humor when it comes to a lady's nerves," Miss Fairchild said with a sly smile. "To *that* I can attest."

That was met with laughter from the ladies and indulgent smiles from the gentlemen.

"Rhodi, you must endeavor to be good-humored." Thomas laughed.

"Miss Fairchild compares my good humor to that of the many young dandies with whom she is acquainted in London." He smiled. "I am clearly at a disadvantage."

"Perhaps," she said, and smiled, he thought, a little devilishly. "But indeed, my lord, you have scarcely smiled since I arrived."

"I am certain that I have."

"I do not recall it."

"Do you not? I smiled Wednesday night."

Everyone laughed, including Greer, whose eyes, he noticed, could cast a brilliant gleam the length of a table when she did.

"And when *did* you arrive, Miss Fairchild?" Lady Pool asked. "It all seems quite a mystery."

"No mystery," she said easily. "I arrived a little more than a fortnight ago."

"Now *that*," Lord Pool said as he squinted at the contents of the bowl the footman sat before him, "is quite a long time in the company of an unsmiling man." He glanced up at Miss Fairchild. "Your carriage was harmed in some way, did you say?"

"Oh," she said with a dismissive flick of her wrist. "A rock or stick or some such thing. I confess I did not understand everything the coachman told me."

"Did you arrive alone, Miss Fairchild?" Lady Pool asked.

"No, madam. I left London in the company of Mrs. Smithington."

"And where are you hiding Mrs. Smithington, my lord?" Lady Pool asked Rhodrick.

He glanced at Greer. Her cheeks colored slightly and she said, "Ah . . . well." She cleared her throat. "Unfortunately, Mrs. Smithington . . . *died.*"

All eyes suddenly jerked to Miss Fairchild, and Rhodrick could not possibly have been more entertained.

"She *died?*" Margaret echoed incredulously.

"Ah . . ." Miss Fairchild colored slightly and studied the dish before her for a moment. "It was the most tragic thing," she said, frowning a bit, as if trying to work out a tale. "We were to call upon my uncle, and the poor dear was in excellent health until we reached Bredwardine —"

"Bredwardine?" Lady Pool interrupted. "But that is almost to Wales. What is your uncle's name, Miss Fairchild? Perhaps I know him."

"Vaughan."

"Vaughan!" Lady Pool echoed, and tapped

her finger against the tabletop a moment before turning to her husband. "Do we know a Vaughan, Lord Pool?"

"We know scores of them," Lord Pool said gruffly. "There are Vaughans in every nook and cranny —"

"If he is your uncle," Lady Pool said, turning back to Miss Fairchild before her husband could finish, "then are *you* Welsh? You *must* be with a name like Vaughan."

"My parents were Welsh. But I was raised in England."

"And why, then, did your uncle not accompany you here?" Lady Pool asked, eyeing her skeptically.

Miss Fairchild shifted in her seat. "The answer to that question," she said, "involves another unfortunate tale."

She paused; it seemed to Rhodrick as if his guests all leaned forward, as if they were afraid they would miss her answer.

"M-my uncle had, ah . . . well, as it turns out, my uncle had . . . he'd died as well."

"A remarkable coincidence and a tragedy," Rhodrick said, enjoying her discomfiture. "Particularly since Miss Fairchild and her uncle were so very close."

Miss Fairchild shot him a murderous look.

"Oh," Margaret said, peering closely at Miss Fairchild, too.

"Yes," Miss Fairchild said, nodding as if she could scarcely bear to speak of it. "I was very saddened by his loss and it was the news of his demise that ailed Mrs. Smithington. When she heard he'd passed on, she felt the need to lie down, and regrettably, she never awoke."

"How . . . *tragic,*" Margaret said, looking and sounding confused.

"Yes, yes, that is all very sad . . . but Miss Fairchild," Lady Pool said, tapping her finger on the table to gain her attention. "Do you mean that you came all the way from Bredwardine to Llanmair *alone?*"

Miss Fairchild nervously cleared her throat; her fingers fluttered on the stem of her wineglass. "Not . . . not exactly," she said. "I was accompanied by Mr. Owen Percy."

Margaret gasped. Thomas jerked a startled gaze to Rhodrick. Lord Pool dropped his fork and fished about for it in his dish, and Lady Pool's eyes narrowed on Miss Fairchild.

"What?" Miss Fairchild asked, looking around at the other guests.

Rhodrick was so amused that he leaned back, eagerly waiting to hear how she would ever extract herself from this debacle.

"Well," Lady Pool said. "It is certainly

none of *my* affair, Miss Fairchild, but *that* might have been worse than coming here alone. Perhaps that is the way of things in *London,* but —"

"But it is none of our concern, Lady Pool," Lord Pool reminded her.

Lady Pool pressed her lips together so tightly that they disappeared as Lord Pool chewed. "Delicious," he said of the stew.

"But . . . but I thought Mr. Percy had departed Llanmair," Margaret said, more to Rhodrick than to Miss Fairchild.

"He has," Rhodrick added.

"Then . . ."

"The carriage defect has made it impossible for Miss Fairchild to return home just yet," he said. "Please, everyone," he added, picking up his fork, "enjoy your meal."

His guests slowly but dutifully turned their attention to their meals. Rhodrick glanced down the table at Miss Fairchild. If a gaze could actually spark fire, the whole dining room would have been ablaze at that moment.

Seventeen

When the ladies retired to the salon so that the men could enjoy the American cheroots Lord Pool had brought, Margaret smiled and chatted and did her best to maintain her composure, but it was very difficult to do, given her growing uncertainties about Miss Fairchild.

She'd been so pleased to have made her acquaintance, so pleased for Rhodi . . . until the young woman had mentioned Owen Percy.

Fortunately, Lady Pool asked the burning question for her. "How is it, Miss Fairchild, that you came all this way with Mr. Percy? Were you previously acquainted with him?"

"Oh," Miss Fairchild said, averting her gaze as her fingers flitted around a charm she wore about her neck. "We are cousins, actually."

Lady Pool seemed satisfied with that answer, but Margaret was not. She knew it was not true. "Cousins?" she repeated skeptically.

"Once removed," Miss Fairchild added hastily, then raised a brow, challenging Margaret's scrutiny of her.

"How remarkable," Margaret said, forcing a smile. "Mr. Percy and *I* are second cousins, and I am quite certain he never mentioned another cousin. And Rhodi and I have been friends since we were children, and certainly *he* never mentioned —"

"Perhaps our relation is more than once removed," Miss Fairchild said, and glanced at her lap as she nervously cleared her throat. "You . . . you seem surprised by our acquaintance, but Mr. Percy has been gone from Wales a long time —"

"Not long enough," Lady Pool said curtly.

Miss Fairchild looked shocked by Lady Pool's response.

"I am sure he was a perfect gentleman in England, Miss Fairchild," Margaret said politely, "for he is very good at pretending. But around here, he is very unwelcome."

"Margaret!" Lady Pool said. "You are speaking of her cousin!"

"Oh," Margaret said airily, looking at Miss Fairchild. "If Miss Fairchild is acquainted with Mr. Percy, she cannot be surprised, I am certain."

Miss Fairchild blushed. "How long did you say you'd been acquainted with the prince?" she asked, changing the subject.

"All my life," Margaret said. "Our fathers served in the Royal Navy together. We've known one another from the nursery."

"Then you must have known his late wife."

"Of course," Margaret said. "Very well, in fact."

"You've been such a very good friend to him, Margaret," Lady Pool said. "You were so dear to him when Eira passed."

Margaret smiled thinly. "I did what any friend would have done."

But Lady Pool looked at Greer and said, "The prince's wife died in childbirth, you see." She sighed and shook her head. "He was devoted to her. I daresay it broke his heart."

Margaret added, "It is the reason, I think, he has never remarried. He could never bring himself to consider another."

"If I may . . . how long were they married?" Miss Fairchild asked.

"Three years — that is all," Margaret said sadly.

"And he never remarried?"

"Oh no," Margaret said, thinking back to the time Rhodrick had sequestered himself here, alone with his grief.

"What of Lady Freemont?" Lady Pool asked. "She is newly widowed and living in that huge old house in Llandrindod Wells."

"He will not consider it," Margaret said firmly. "Lord knows I have tried, and so has his sister, Nell."

"Oh, she is so bright and lovely," Lady Pool said with an admiring smile.

"And she has tried very hard to make a match for her brother, as have I, but he cannot bear to go through it all again."

"I beg your pardon, Miss Fairchild," Lady Pool said. "We were speaking of your *extraordinary* journey from London to Llanmair in the company of Mr. Percy."

"We were?" she asked weakly. "I didn't think there was anything more to say of it."

"How long do you intend to be at Llanmair?" Lady Pool asked.

Miss Fairchild smiled and folded her hands in her lap, then moved them to her knees. "Actually . . . I mean to be at Llanmair only until I've had the opportunity to visit Kendrick."

Margaret all but came out of her chair. *"Kendrick!"* she cried.

"Yes," Miss Fairchild said, nodding. "It is very near here, you know, and is quite a grand estate. I should like to see it."

"Oh dear," Margaret said. "Oh *no*. Kendrick is merely a poor remnant of what was once a grand old home. There is really nothing to see."

"Are you certain?" she asked. "I saw it from the road and I —"

"I am *quite* certain," Margaret insisted. "There is simply nothing there." She glanced anxiously at the door. If Rhodi heard them speaking of Kendrick — "Do please take me at my word. Nothing good has ever happened at Kendrick. It is best that it remain empty and left alone."

Miss Fairchild looked on the verge of arguing, but the door opened and the men rejoined them. Rhodrick's eyes, Margaret couldn't help noticing, sought Miss Fairchild the moment he entered the room. Lord Pool was speaking to him, and while he seemed to be engaged in the conversation, he was looking at Miss Fairchild.

And he *smiled.*

After a moment, Rhodrick said, "Miss Fairchild, would you do us the honor of playing the pianoforte?"

Miss Fairchild blanched. "Oh my lord, I play very poorly."

"I beg your pardon, but I must disagree. I have heard you and you play beautifully. You must play for us. I had the pianoforte moved into the salon with the hope that you would."

"Yes, please, Miss Fairchild," Lady Pool said.

The young woman glanced warily at the pianoforte, stood hesitantly, and with a smile that seemed forced to Margaret, she made her way to the instrument and sat.

So did the men.

And as she began to play — Rhodi was right, she played beautifully — Margaret could not take her eyes from Rhodi. He sat very still, his gaze intent on Miss Fairchild. He was, Margaret realized, completely captivated.

Greer, however, was playing by rote, her thoughts miles away, at Kendrick. As her fingers moved through a piece by Handel she had played dozens of times, she could think of nothing other than how she might manage to go there, to see the place where her mother had been born. She felt strongly that she had to go there, as if an invisible tether was pulling her toward the place. The more she was told not to go, the more she felt she *must* go.

Tomorrow, then, if the sun held. She would walk if necessary, now that the roads were dry, but she had to see it.

It was another hour or more before the

Awbreys and the Pools took their leave. Greer followed along behind them as they made their way to the foyer and trilled good night as they donned their cloaks. When the doors opened and the party stepped into the courtyard, Greer stepped back, intent on making her escape, but the prince caught her elbow and held it firmly. "Not yet," he muttered.

With a sigh, she let him lead her out into the courtyard. She smiled and waved as boys with big lanterns ran ahead of the carriage to light its way to the road. And it wasn't until the carriage had bounced out of the courtyard and the giant gates had swung shut behind it that the prince let go of her arm.

Greer instantly turned and strode back inside, the prince on her heels. As they walked inside, two footmen shut the thick plank of a door behind them, bolting it shut. Greer paused — the foyer was so dark that she would never be able to navigate her way to her rooms without a candle. The prince obviously had the same thought, for he picked up a flint box and struck a light, then lit the three candles of a candelabrum on an entry console and handed it to Greer.

"Thank you," she said, and took it from his hand. But as she did, her fingers grazed his, and her body reacted — badly. She couldn't help herself — she glanced up at his dark eyes and the scar that coursed his cheek. She was struck with the image of him holding her and kissing her. *Why* that image continued to plague her she could hardly guess.

He turned slightly, so that his scar was in the shadows.

"Are you satisfied?" she asked suddenly. "I am most decidedly ruined — there is no pretending otherwise." Indeed, she could feel the heat of her shame flood her cheeks as she recalled the way Mrs. Awbrey and Lady Pool had looked at her, the censure in their eyes when she'd so foolishly tried to claim a relation to Percy. Ava was right — she was a wretched liar.

"I can only imagine what your friends must think of me — the circumstances of my travel sounded absurd even to my own ears," Greer said bitterly. "You have succeeded in making me the laughingstock of Wales."

"That was not my intent," he said quietly.

Not his intent? "Then why, in God's name, did you force me to attend?" she cried. "What did you suppose might happen? Did you think no one would wonder how an unmarried woman came to be living in your

291

house? I know your opinion of me, sir, but I cannot understand *why* you insisted —"

"Because I have lost my mind!" he snapped. "Because I can no longer rely on my good judgment to tell me if you are lying, if you deceive me, if you mean to defraud me of four thousand pounds, or if you are the most naïve woman I've ever met and deserve my pity. *That* is why."

She laughed derisively. "I don't want your pity or your four thousand pounds, my lord. If the price of having what is rightfully mine is my complete ruin, then you may have the money, for in the end, it hardly matters if a woman can feed herself or put a roof over her head — the only thing that matters is her *virtue*," she said angrily, and moved to walk past him.

But the prince caught her arm, forcing her to stop and turn around. "I did not ruin your virtue, Miss Fairchild," he said coldly. "You managed to do that on your own, the moment you put yourself in a carriage with Owen Percy."

"Yes," she said, nodding fiercely, biting back tears of frustration. "That was indeed the moment. If only I had possessed a crystal ball to know it!"

He clenched his jaw and dropped his hand.

She felt desperate to be away from him, to be alone, but at the same time, she felt a powerful surge of angry curiosity about him. "It must be easy for you to pass judgment on me. You have never found yourself in a quagmire with no clear way out. You have done everything perfectly in your life, haven't you?"

"What in God's name are you saying?"

"Your marriage, my lord! An impeccable match with a lovely woman by all accounts! You made no mistakes in that regard!"

The prince's expression turned darker; she had clearly struck a nerve. Inexplicably, the knowledge made her feel powerful.

"Yes, Miss Fairchild, I had a wife. I thought you were well acquainted with that fact."

He was angry and strangely restive. In a saner moment, Greer would have stopped there, would have begged his pardon for prying. But none of the old rules seemed to apply any longer, and she said, "I am. But I did not know that you *loved* her so."

He looked as if she had struck him. He suddenly whirled away from her, his hand on his nape, the other hand at his waist. "And what did you expect? Has London jaded you to the possibility?"

"No," she said, although she was uncertain

as to what she thought of the possibility — she'd never loved a man before. Worse — far worse — she had not expected to be so affected by the knowledge that *he* had loved before. It was beyond her comprehension why it should matter to her, why she should even care. But she *did* care, she cared more than she could even admit. "I merely found it fascinating. It is not what one expects to hear about one's captor."

"You are not my *captive*," he said hotly.

"Frankly, I didn't think you were the sort of man to actually love anyone. Not even a poor wife."

He whirled around so quickly that it startled her. He grabbed her by the arm, forcing her back against the wall, and said harshly, "You are young, Greer Fairchild, so young that you cannot possibly begin to comprehend what I have loved and lost. Do you think I do not experience all the mortal desires?" His gaze moved up to the crown of her head. "Do you think I do not feel the anticipation of being with a woman? The arousal? The seduction? The passion that only a man and woman can share in the most intimate of circumstances?"

"I . . . I —" She fumbled for an answer as his gaze raked over the features of her face, lingering on her lips. "What more would you know? If my wife could bear to have our union consummated in our bed? If I lay my hands on her naked breasts? Or my head between her thighs? *What more?*"

He was so angry and forceful that it confounded Greer and, inexplicably, *aroused* her, to the point of danger. She pushed hard against him and whispered, "Do you miss her?"

His gaze pierced hers and he leaned close. "Why such curiosity, Greer? What of *you?*" he breathed angrily. "Have *you* ever loved? Ever felt the anticipation and arousal of it? Ever been seared by a mere look or wholly seduced by the taste of passion and the desire to consummate it?"

His grip of her arm, the intensity of his gaze, those green eyes boring through her, along with the heady mention of arousal, seduction, passion — it was all swirling together inside her, making her feel flushed and light-headed.

The candelabra suddenly felt heavy in her hand; he must have noticed for he took it from her hand and set it on the console beside them, then straddled her skirts with his legs, holding both her arms now. "Tell me, Greer," he whispered hotly, "have you ever experienced love?"

She did not respond, just dropped her

gaze to his lips, dark and moist, and God help her, she wanted to taste them again.

"Was it not *love* you shared with Mr. Percy on my settee?"

"No." She'd never felt with any man, and hardly Percy, anything quite like what she was feeling now.

The prince leaned in so that his mouth was just a hairsbreadth from her cheek, his breath warm on her skin and his gaze burning her everywhere it touched her. "That is because he did not understand a woman like you must be seduced."

Greer had every intention of protesting that she was above seduction, but she could not seem to find the words as he leaned down and kissed her lips. It was not a tender kiss, but one that was blistering with desire. He nipped at her bottom lip, then swept his tongue inside her mouth as he lifted his hand to her face and splayed his fingers along her jaw, tilting her head so that he could kiss her more thoroughly.

The vague whimpering she heard came from her, from the back of her throat as he pressed his body against hers. He let go his grip of her upper arm and slid his palm down to her hand, his fingers tangling with hers, before slipping his hand to her waist and around to her hip, squeezing it, pushing her into his body.

Greer felt the fire stir in her groin, felt it kick up and begin to lick at the doors and windows of feelings she had never experienced — at least not like this, not as *urgently* as this. She felt hot inside her velvet gown, had an insane desire to put both hands to her bodice and rip it open for air. The mere thought alarmed her; yet she did nothing to stop the prince, and if anything, she pressed against his hand at her breast and against his hip bone.

He dropped his hand from her face to the flesh of her bosom, caressing it with his knuckles, then digging his fingers into her cleavage, pushing deeper, until he was able to free her breast from the low décolletage.

He took the tip of her breast in between his thumb and forefinger, rolling it, and Greer gasped, jerked her head away from his kiss, and looked wildly into the foyer. "What —"

He did not allow her to finish, but with one hand around her waist, easily lifted her off her feet, twirled her about, and pushed her into a small alcove, deep in the shadows. He lowered her until her feet touched the ground, and kept moving down her body, brazenly taking her breast into his mouth, nibbling at the peak, lashing it with his tongue. She pressed the back of her head against the cool stone, licked her lips, and opened her eyes. In the large mirror that hung in the foyer, she could see him, his head at her breast, his big hands on her body, and another, stronger surge of wanton desire rifled through her.

Greer's breath turned quick and shallow as he ravaged her breast. She closed her eyes, scarcely realizing that she dug her fingers into his hair to hold his head tightly against her. She could think of nothing but the feel of his body on hers, the damp pressure of his mouth and tongue, the stubble of his beard on her skin, which incredibly, aroused her even more.

Her head lolled against the wall, her eyes closed as an unquenchable thirst began to build inside her. A damp heat pooled between her legs, and Greer pressed harder against him, drawing her leg up and bracing her foot against the wall so that her knee was at his waist.

The prince caught her leg, slid his palm down to her ankle, and grabbed the hem of her gown. Once again she had the weak thought that she ought to protest, to tell him to stop this madness before it was too late, but she couldn't find her voice. His hand moved up her leg, to her knee, and she inadvertently flinched. The prince stilled at her breast, then slowly let it go and rose up, his hand riding up her leg as he sought her mouth again.

He kissed her with all the anticipation and desire she felt at her core as he pushed yards of fabric above her knee, trapping her gown between their bodies and leaving her exposed, and she had no desire to stop him.

He buried his face in her neck, kissing her neck and ear as he moved his fingers along the inside of her thigh, moving so lightly that she could not suppress a tickling shiver. She pressed her hands against his arms, dragged them up, and gripped his shoulders tightly when he slipped one finger into the slit of her drawers.

"Oh," she whispered as her head fell back against the stone wall, her eyes closed as his finger slipped into her damp heat. *This should not be happening.* But it *was* happening, and it was an extraordinary sensation. She turned her head away from his, her body focused intently on his hand and the arresting, heart-stopping burst of sensual pleasure that suddenly erupted within her. When he delved into those folds more deeply, she dug her nails into his shoulders and groaned with ecstasy. *"Oh God,"* she whispered.

The prince increased the pressure and rhythm of his hand while he caressed her skin with his mouth. He moved deep inside her, slipping over wet flesh, moving softly but urgently, touching her in places that sent staggering shocks ripping through her.

He was stroking her beyond the hope of salvaging her virtue, pushing her headfirst into a pool of stunning pleasure and Greer could not — *would* not — stop him. Her body moved hard and imperatively against his hand as she tried to keep from melting.

His fingers danced about the hardened core of her, then slid deep inside her and back again. His mouth moved over her skin, over her cheek, her lips, her eyes, gliding so lightly that her skin simmered to the point she could scarcely endure even the whisper of his kiss. When he dipped his head to her exposed breast again, Greer's pulse beat so hard that she feared her heart could not take the stress. It felt as if she were sliding uncontrollably down a slope toward something warm and utterly explosive.

He lifted up, took the lobe of her ear into his mouth as his hand moved faster. "Let it come," he whispered gruffly.

She suddenly felt the pitch, felt the world turn upside down as she slid off the slope completely. With a gasp, she opened her eyes, her gaze landing on the large mirror in the foyer. And as the world fell away from her, she could see their image — his dark back, his head pressed against hers, his hand between her legs.

The image was stirring, provocative, and with a sob of pleasure, she dropped her head back hard against the wall, and closed her eyes as the life drained from her body, leaving her a limp shell of what she'd been only minutes ago.

The fury of his hand changed then, slowing dramatically, easing the pressure against her flesh, and finally, he removed his hand altogether and helped her lower her leg. Her limbs felt weak; it was a moment before she was able to stand on both feet. It was the prince who smoothed her skirts, straightening them.

Greer had yet to move from the wall, had yet to draw a steady breath. The fog of pleasure was leaving her, and the realization of what she'd just done was rising up like bile in the back of her throat. A thousand questions filled her brain, and she moved awkwardly to return her breast to the confines of her gown.

When she was at last convinced she was put back together, she shakily pushed aside a thick strand of her hair that had worked free of her coif. He watched her, his breathing a bit ragged, too. But in his eyes, she saw something that surprised her.

She had expected to see a look of triumph, of cold, hard reality staring back at her. But what she saw was quite unexpected. His gaze was warm and full of . . . something. Hope?

Whatever she was seeing, it gave the prince an air of vulnerability she would have thought impossible.

Greer would never know what possessed her, but she impulsively touched the scar that ran down his cheek. He flinched as if she had stung him, and instantly covered her hand with his, pulling it away from his face.

She did not speak. Still feeling the extraordinarily ethereal pleasure she had received at his hand, she moved carefully to her left, her gaze never leaving his, moving slowly until she was at the console, where the candelabra provided an eerie light to what had just happened between them.

Greer picked up the candelabra. There were no words to describe the myriad emotions that filled her in that moment. She felt queasy and giddy all at once, and wrapped her arm around her middle. *What had she just done? What madness had invaded her?*

Was it possible that she could be feeling such ragged, unchecked feelings of desire — of *affection,* of *esteem* — for this man?

"*Greer,*" he whispered.

The whisper of her name startled her into the present. Such feelings were insupportable given her situation, and she guiltily dropped her gaze. "I don't understand what has happened between us," she said. "I don't know what is happening to *me.*"

"Neither do I," he said quietly.

Greer lifted her gaze to his eyes, to his scar. "I am determined to hate you . . . but I cannot."

He put a hand to her cheek, and said, "You are beautiful."

His tone was tender, almost reverent, and it confused Greer. "I don't . . . I can't think," she said, to his neckcloth. "I don't know what I am doing," she said again, and slipped away from him, lest she fall into those green eyes.

She could feel his gaze on her as she walked away from the desire that had sprouted and had taken hold of all her senses.

No matter how vulnerable he seemed, or how virile, or how princely, she had just allowed a man who held her here with a power she did not understand do something she had never allowed a man to do in her life.

What had happened to her? When had her senses completely deserted her?

Where in God's name were Ava and Phoebe when she needed them most?

EIGHTEEN

In London, Phoebe was wrapping a swatch of silk around the dress dummy Ava had given her for her birthday. Lucille Pennebacker, Lord Downey's spinster sister, entered the room and held out a folded and sealed vellum. "It would seem your cousin is not dead after all," she announced.

"From Greer?" Phoebe exclaimed happily. They'd not heard from Greer in more than a month now. "*Surely* she writes to tell us she is coming home," she said cheerfully as she took the letter from Lucille and broke the seal.

But her smile quickly faded to an openmouthed expression of dismay as she read. "Oh dear God!" she cried, and in her haste to find vellum on which to write Ava, who was in the country at present and not expected back for at least a fortnight, she stabbed her finger with a pair of scissors and tripped over the bolt of silk, knocking over the dress dummy.

This was precisely the reason why, Phoebe thought furiously as she searched for pen and ink, she had asked Ava not to toddle off to Broderick Abbey, for if something were to happen, it might take *weeks* before she could return to London. But did Ava ever listen to her sage advice? Heavens no!

In Wales, Rhodrick had hardly slept, but when at last he did sleep in the morning hours, he dreamt of being with Greer, of his face unscarred and her deep smile for him. But somehow, Greer changed into Alis Bronwyn, the dark-haired woman who'd haunted him — the same woman he'd believed Greer to be her first night at Llanmair. He dreamt Greer was now beckoning him to Kendrick, but he refused, as he knew where she would lead him.

Yet she was very insistent, and it had alarmed him in his dream.

Rhodrick awoke when the clock struck six, drenched in his own sweat. He eased his legs over the side of the bed and rubbed his knee. He'd thought Alis Bronwyn was gone from his life — he'd not dreamt of her in a year, maybe two. But she had suddenly re-appeared with a vengeance, dredging up old fears that he might very well be bordering on madness.

He dressed to go out, and by half past six he was at the stables. The groomsman on duty was sound asleep, so Rhodrick saddled his horse himself and rode out as the sun was beginning to dawn on a clear day.

"Do you speak English, sir?" Greer asked a groomsman at the stables several hours after Rhodrick had ridden out.

"Aye," the man said, rather unconvincingly.

So Greer resorted to the time-honored method of communication — sketching her request in the air with her hands. "I would like," she said, pointing to herself, "a horse." She simulated riding. "To be saddled," she added, and drew, in the air, a horse with a saddle.

It worked; the groomsman said something in Welsh, then disappeared inside the stable. A quarter of an hour later, he reappeared, pulling a pretty mare sporting a ladies' saddle along behind him.

"Oh!" Greer exclaimed happily, smiling at the groomsman. "Thank you!"

He nodded, tossed the reins over the mare's neck, then cupped his hands to give Greer a leg up. She grabbed hold of the pommel and allowed the man to toss her up like a caber. A moment later, she was trotting out the back gate of the castle walls.

It seemed odd but liberating to be off the castle grounds, alone, after so many days of being confined due to inclement weather and roads mired in mud. Her only problem now was how to find Kendrick. She had seen it from atop the hill behind the castle the day the prince had brought her back in the storm. She reasoned that if she and the mare climbed back up that hill, she should be able to see it.

An hour passed before Greer and the mare managed to make their way to the top of the ridge, primarily because she could not find the trail and the mare had to pick her way up deer trails through dense forest and over rocks. Buzzards and red kites circled overhead, no doubt waiting for her to die so they might feast. But Greer and the mare surprised the buzzards — eventually, they managed to find their way to some part of the narrow path that skimmed the ridge above.

Yet Greer could not see the house. It *had* to be there — she remembered it so clearly from that awful afternoon she'd almost been killed by a falling tree. Was it possible she'd found the wrong trail?

It was another quarter of an hour before

Greer realized that she could not see Llanmair, either, and therefore must be on the wrong side of the ridge looking down at the wrong valley.

With a sigh, she leaned down and stroked the mare's neck. "No doubt you fear you will never see your oat sack again, Molly" — she had named the horse Molly so that she could address her properly, which she'd done several times, assuring her she would eventually find her way — "but on my honor, I remember the way home. Just bear with me a bit longer," she said, and led the horse over the top of the ridge again.

When she crested the ridge, she saw it instantly. Llanmair, big and bold and imposing, rose up on her right, about five miles in the distance, she guessed. To her left was Kendrick, separated from Llanmair by a thick forest, and no more than a mile from where Greer and the horse were standing. With a smile, Greer sent Molly down the hill.

They had to make their way through a thicket and over another rocky deer trail, but at last they emerged on level ground. There was a road — or the remnants of what had once been a road. Greer had to push back the hanging limbs of unpruned trees with her hands as they moved along, losing her bonnet at one point. But then the road opened up, and she could see the stone wall that surrounded Kendrick, and the house's dark slate roof.

The wall itself was intact for the most part — she saw only one place where it was crumbling, but that could be easily repaired.

The thought of *repairing* anything surprised Greer.

Up until this moment, she had only wanted to see the house she'd dreamt of all these years, where her mother had obviously begun her life, to understand where she had come from. But it suddenly occurred to her that with four thousand pounds, she might be able to lease Kendrick and repair it. "*Lease* it?" she said aloud, her voice incredulous in the stillness around her. "For *what,* pray tell? What do you think, Molly, am I so foolish as to think I might *live* at Kendrick, all alone, a ruined spinster?"

The question made her laugh.

But the idea did not.

When she reached the gate, a new dilemma confronted her. The gate was shut. "What a bother," she muttered, and hopped down — swaying into Molly's side until the blood ran in her legs again — but then she straightened her riding habit, and carrying her crop, she marched smartly to the gate and shoved as hard as she might.

The gate did not budge.

"No," Greer said, pushing again. "Oh *no*. I did not come all this way to be *denied* —"

The old gate suddenly gave way, creaking loudly as it moved. It did not open far. The growth behind it was so dense that the gate could not be pushed wide enough to allow Molly entrance, but it was large enough to admit Greer.

She glanced back at Molly, then marched back to the horse, took the reins, forced her away from the grass she was enjoying to a grassier spot beneath the trees, where she could munch to her heart's content, and tethered her to a tree.

With Molly secure, Greer turned and looked at the open gate. Her heart began to beat with anticipation — her desire to see Kendrick was stranger than she could understand. But at the same time, she could not easily dismiss the things she'd heard about it. *Nothing good ever happens there. . . .*

"Ridiculous," she muttered. "The house is quite deserted." Or at least she hoped it was.

She drew a breath to calm her nerves, and valiantly slipped through the gate — a tight squeeze in which she managed to tear her gown — and emerged on the other side in weeds as high as her waist.

The entire lawn was overgrown, but Greer hardly noticed it. The house was in a ruinous state and bore a scant resemblance to the house in her dreams. The stone walls, once white limestone, were now gray. Two large windows were broken and the front door was standing wide open. But it was the house she'd dreamt of, and the only thing missing was her mother standing in the doorway, turning and disappearing inside before Greer could reach her.

All these years she'd believed the house was a figment of her imagination, but it was shockingly real. She stood for several minutes, trying to understand how she could have dreamt it. Had she been here before? Perhaps Mrs. Bowen was right — perhaps her mother had brought her here when she was a young child, and the memory was not clear to her.

Her feet began to move ahead of her mind, and a moment later she was pushing through the weeds, making her way to the open door. She took in all the disrepair as she went — the crumbling chimneys, broken glass, chipped stone, holes in the roof. And she appreciated the irony that like her uncle's house in Bredwardine, this house, another house linked to her past, was empty.

It was almost as if her heritage — or what she'd perceived it to be — had never existed except in her faulty memory.

When she reached the landing, she stood gripping her riding crop so tightly that her hand hurt, leaning to her right, peering into the foyer, afraid of what she might find. She could see nothing within save a few leaves scattered across the tiled entry. So Greer forced herself to put one foot in front of the other, and stepped inside.

She paused just across the threshold and looked around. It had been a grand home once, judging by the marble floor and the silk paper peeling away from the walls. It was faded, but the painting on the ceiling high above her head was still recognizable, that of a blue sky and white fluffy clouds. An enormous crystal chandelier hung over her head, and the crystal drops tinkled together on the breeze through the front door.

It could be cleaned. The chandelier could be cleaned and returned to its previous splendor, she was certain of it. So could the walls and the floor.

Her heart beating rapidly, Greer walked on, into the first room, which also stood empty save the peeling silk paper and moth-eaten drapes. In room after room, she moved past tall marble hearths, paned windows that overlooked a small lake, and chandeliers whose finish had dulled with the passage of time. There was no furniture in any of the rooms and the wooden floors looked dull and marked. She was sure, though, that they could be made new again with a coat or two of beeswax. In the library, empty shelves lined each wall from the floor to the ceiling. The dining room looked large enough to accommodate two dozen. The kitchen and stores were the size that would have supported a large and thriving house.

Upstairs on the first floor were solemn rooms attached to more solemn rooms, the only sign that someone had once lived here the bright squares of paper where portraits had once hung. Remarkably, every room had a vista unlike anything she'd ever seen — mountains, a lake, forests so thick it looked as if they could be cut with a knife.

She found the nursery and tried to imagine her mother there as the child Mrs. Bowen remembered. She found what she believed must have been the master suite, and a sitting room with floral drapery and warmly painted walls.

On the second floor, between a solarium and a drawing room, there was a room whose door was locked. No matter how hard she tried, Greer could not budge it. She resolved to bring something with her the next time she came to break the lock. And oh yes, there would be a next time, and a next — she would see every inch of her heritage, every square inch of the place where her mother had lived. She would clean it with her own hands, restoring her life and her past.

When she had seen the house, she walked out one of six French doors that led onto a terrace overlooking a garden. Rosebushes grew wild, their long, bare limbs dancing in the breeze. The path, like the lawn, was overgrown, but the hour was growing late. The sun was setting a little earlier each day, so Greer did not try to navigate the path, but walked around the terrace, to the side of the house, intent on returning to Molly.

That was when she saw the small cottage at another gate, and the thin ribbon of smoke curling out of the chimney.

Kendrick was not completely abandoned, then — there was still a *bit* of life here.

Greer began striding toward the cottage. She had to climb over a small fence — if there was a gate, it was buried under the overgrowth — and paused on the other side of the fence to free her skirt from a picket when she heard the crack of a twig behind her. Before she could turn, however, she felt something cold and hard and round in the middle of her back.

A gun. God in heaven, she would be murdered.

A man's voice, speaking Welsh, sounded hard and coarse. When she did not respond immediately, he pressed the gun even harder against her back.

"Please, sir, I do not speak Welsh!" she exclaimed fearfully.

The pressure of the gun eased a little. "Why didn't ye say so?" the man said. "Come on, then. Turn round. Turn round, turn round," he urged her.

Greer turned slowly, gripping her riding crop, prepared to use it. The man looked to be about her age. His face, though handsome, was very weathered. His golden hair was a bit matted, his beard two or three days old, and his green eyes reminded her of the prince.

More important, the man was not holding a gun, but a metal rod used to hang kettles over fires.

"Who are ye?" he asked as his eyes raked wolfishly over her body.

"Greer Fairchild," she said as she swiped at a strand of hair that had come loose. "And who might *you* be?"

He grinned, his eyes suddenly shining with amusement. "Ah, ye are a lively one, eh? I am Madoc Jones," he said, bowing at the waist with a flourish of his hand. "Pleased to make your acquaintance, Miss Fairchild — 'tis miss, ain't it?" he asked, his gaze flicking to her hand and back. "Aye, pleased *indeed* — but ye're not to be here," he said sternly.

"Why not?"

Madoc Jones's eyes went wide with surprise. "Because ye're *not*," he said. "The estate has been closed by order of the prince."

"Why would the prince do that?"

"Why does a prince do aught?" he asked rhetorically, then waved his iron rod toward the house. "I don't know where ye came from, but ye must go now. Go on. Fare thee well. Good day."

"Are you the warden?"

He laughed. "I am more the inmate. I live just there," he said cheerfully, pointing with his rod to the cottage. "And in exchange for me neck, I am to keep a watchful eye on the place. No one comes in, and that, miss, means *ye*."

"The prince's orders?" Greer asked.

"Mmm," he said with an adamant nod.

"But my mother was born here," she said,

folding her arms across her middle, the riding crop still in her hand. "She died when I was very young and I never really knew her. This house is all I have left of her."

"Ah, now that brings a tear to me eye, it does," Mr. Jones said with a wink as he firmly took hold of her elbow. "But I suggest ye take it up with the prince."

"Mr. Jones!" she cried as he marched her toward the gate near his cottage. "I've come all this way — surely you can allow me to at least have a look about!"

"All the way from England, from the sound of it, too!" he exclaimed.

"Yes! From London!"

He stopped. "As far as *that?*"

"So you'll let me have a look about?" she asked hopefully, tasting victory.

"No," he said. "I cannot allow it," he added with an easy smile. "Ye must speak with the prince."

"The *prince!*" she said angrily. "Does he keep you captive here as well?" she asked irritably.

"Captive?" Mr. Jones laughed roundly at that. "Quite the contrary, miss — I enjoy living all alone on abandoned land."

"Don't tease me," she responded petulantly. "You've no idea what I have endured!"

"I am sure I cannot begin to imagine, aye," he said congenially. "But ye must endure it elsewhere," he said, and reached for the gate handle.

"All right," Greer conceded with some exasperation. "But do at least allow me to exit the other gate, where my horse is waiting."

"The *other* gate?" He squinted over the top of Greer's head, then whistled low. "I can't remember a time that gate was opened." He glanced at Greer and smiled again. "Ye are a stubborn lass, are ye not?" he asked cheerfully as he wheeled her around and started marching her toward the other gate. "I'm right impressed, I am. Such a delicate thing ye are to have opened that gate!"

She was not delicate, nor was she particularly strong. But she *was* determined. And even though Mr. Jones was making her leave, she was already plotting how she might return without his knowledge.

NINETEEN

The fading sun cast long shadows on what was left of the road, making it difficult to see. Greer could not be certain if she had missed the fauna trail leading up to the top of the ridge or not, but when she reached a stream, she groaned with despair. She had not crossed a stream on the way to Kendrick, which could only mean that she was lost.

She reined Molly up at the stream and jumped down. As Molly drank, Greer looked around at the trees towering above her. There was nothing to mark the path — not a trail, not a cairn — nothing!

She was weary, she was hungry, and she was in something of a snit, for the more she thought of Kendrick, the more she could not fathom how the prince could have let it fall into such disrepair. She grabbed up Molly's reins, and stepped on a rock in the middle of the stream.

But she stepped precariously and instantly slipped off; her boots filled quickly with ice-cold water and the hem of her riding habit soaked it up. "*Blast* it all!" she snapped, and tugged on Molly's reins, dragging them both through the stream and onto the other side, where her lovely boots, purchased at a premium on Bond Street in London, squished with every step.

They walked for what seemed hours, stepping over rocks, picking their way down steep slopes only to struggle up another incline. Greer slipped on one such descent and tried to stop her slide by grabbing onto a tree, and in doing so, tore her glove and put a nasty gash across the palm of her hand.

Beside her, Molly snorted and turned her head, her ears pricked in one direction. Greer paused, heard the sound of someone — or something — coming through the woods. On any other day, she would have been alarmed, but at present, she was so exhausted and hungry and exasperated that she marched around Molly, and with her hands on her hips, she peered into the dark undergrowth. "Who is there?" she demanded, and almost fainted with relief when two large wolfhounds trotted into view.

As the dogs came over to have a look at her, the prince rode into view. He'd been working somewhere — his boots were caked with mud and his buckskins stained with dirt. And Greer had never been so happy to see another living soul as she was to see the prince at that moment. Frankly, it was all she could do to keep from running to him and throwing her arms around his neck.

He reined his horse to a stop and looked down at her, then tipped his hat as if they were meeting in Hyde Park. "Miss Fairchild."

"My lord," she said, bobbing a quick curtsy. "I should like to inquire as to why there are no roads or posted signs in all of Wales!"

One corner of his mouth tipped up in a smile. "The forests around Llanmair are rather large. Our ancestors liked to keep them unmarked for they used the valleys and hollows to hide holy shrines and treasures from the Vikings and, later, the English," he said as he swung gracefully off his mount. "But I assure you, there are many roads and posted signs in Wales."

"Are we very far from Llanmair?" she asked weakly, her bravado gone, replaced by hunger.

He shook his head as he took in her appearance. She hadn't thought of how she might look, and unthinkingly put a hand to her hair, which, until this moment, she had not realized had come loose from her coif. She didn't dare look down — the beautiful riding habit Phoebe had made her was atrociously filthy, if not ruined. And there were at least two tears in the fabric that she knew of.

"A mile or so," he said. He came down off his horse, and with his hand on his hip, he openly assessed her condition.

"Thank *God*," Greer said, flinging her arms outward. She dropped her hands. *"Ouch,"* she muttered, having forgotten the gash in her hand.

The prince glanced at her hand and moved forward so suddenly that Greer instinctively stepped backward, bumping up against Molly, who let Greer know her displeasure by whimpering and butting Greer's head with her snout.

"Molly, stop," she said.

He raised a brow. "Molly?" he asked as he gestured for her hand.

"I . . . I had to call her something," she muttered as she looked again at the gash. Her hand was caked with dried blood, which she had also managed to smear over her palm and wrist. "It's really not as bad as it looks —"

He gave her a look that suggested he thought otherwise, and took her hand in his, turning it over, palm up. *"Hmm,"* was all he said as he reached into his coat pocket and withdrew a kerchief. "If I may inquire," he said as he carefully dabbed at the blood on her hand, "were you attempting to leave Llanmair?"

Greer glanced up at him, but his eyes were hidden behind his lashes as he tended her hand. Her instinct told her that she should not mention Kendrick, so she shrugged. "No," she said defiantly. "I only wanted a bit of air."

"You've come quite a long way for air," he said. "I thought perhaps last night —"

Heat instantly flooded her face and she looked down at her palm. *"No,"* she said softly, quickly, and sucked in a hiss of breath as he touched a part of the gash that had come open. She lifted her gaze — his was dark, but so unflinchingly tender that she was momentarily speechless. She had the distinct impression that he'd worried about her. She had the distinct impression that he did not want her to leave Llanmair.

And it was with no small amount of consternation that she realized that she could not have left Llanmair as easily today as she might have done a week or so ago.

"Greer?" he asked, his voice low and soft. "Am I hurting you?"

God help her, but the way he said her name made her feel weak inside. Fortunately, her ravenous belly grumbled with hunger in response.

He smiled — the sort of lovely, warm, and endearing smile that always surprised her, that seemed so incongruous with his mien. But when her belly rumbled again, his smile broadened into one of amusement, and he wrapped the kerchief around her hand and secured the ends, then reached around her and took Molly's reins. "I think there are two hungry creatures here," he said with a slight wink for Greer. "Shall I take you back to Llanmair?"

"Please," she said gratefully.

He stroked Molly's nose for a moment, then put his hand on Greer's elbow and moved her to the saddle. With his gaze on hers, he put his hands on her waist, preparing to lift her up — but he hesitated, and for a moment, she thought he meant to kiss her.

For a moment, she madly wished he would.

But he pressed his lips together, and lifted her up and put her on the saddle, his gaze never leaving hers. And when he was certain she was seated, his hand drifted to her knee, then slid off, and he turned, silently walked back to his horse, and swung up. With one last look at her, he turned his mount around and headed back for Llanmair.

Molly was no fool. She quickly followed, crashing through the underbrush in an effort to catch up.

When they reached Llanmair, Rhodrick was rather proud of his staff — none of them stared or otherwise indicated they thought anything was amiss with Greer's appearance. And she, being the proud woman that she was, refused to acknowledge that she looked a fright. She lifted her chin and walked into the castle, ignoring the squeak of her boots and the state of her hair and clothing.

In the foyer, she paused. "Thank you," she said. "I am quite certain I would have found my way back eventually, but I fear it might have taken as long as a week."

He smiled.

She did, too. And then she turned and walked up the stairs, that peculiar squeaking marking her progress toward her suite of rooms.

Rhodrick asked Mrs. Bowen to send up a

hot bath to her, as well as some of Mrs. Jernigan's healing herbs for Greer's hand. He could not bear the thought of her losing her ability to play the pianoforte, and while he thought it a shallow wound, he would take no chances.

He retreated to his study with Cain and Abel to work until supper. But with every sound, every creak of the old castle, he lifted his head, half expecting to see her.

Where had she gone today? Had she left with the intention of running away and become lost? Or had she ridden out for air, as she said? Riding for air in a forest with no trails seemed rather odd to him, and it left him with a sour feeling of distrust.

Was it possible she had met Percy?

Ridiculous. Percy was miles from Llanmair now. Or was he? They might have arranged before he left to meet. Rhodrick had not accompanied Percy up to the room where Greer was held the day he'd had the bounder escorted from Wales. He might very well have played on Rhodrick's belief he would take the money and go, while in truth, he and Greer had concocted another scheme.

If they had, it was working beautifully, for he had all but abandoned his distrust of her. Bloody hell, but he really could not abide what was happening to him, this obsession he'd developed for her. Yet, he could no longer deny that he was indeed quite attracted to her, and with an intensity that surprised him.

He harbored no illusions about his chances of ever possessing her.

For one thing, she could very well be a swindler. For another, if she was not a swindler, she could very well be one of London's brightest debutantes, which caused him a different sort of consternation. She talked so happily of society and the events she attended there that it was clear to him that she thrived in the *haute ton.* It was just as clear to him that she would never survive here, in a remote corner of Wales, in a limited and rather stodgy society.

A woman like Greer should be in London. She was witty and beautiful and vivacious. He could not imagine her living here.

For another thing, he was too old for her, by ten years or more, and rather ugly at that. Nor was he particularly suave. He was no match for a woman accustomed to the bright lights and fawning dandies of London.

He hated himself for being so weak — good God, the woman scarcely even realized her power of seduction. It seemed to take nothing more than a smile, or a laugh, and he was succumbing to her charm, taking indefensible liberties with her in the foyer. Such lack of resistance made him feel abominably coarse, particularly when there was no point in it. He didn't expect she could ever come to like him, really, much less *love* him.

Nevertheless, he could feel the dread building in him, the debilitating anticipation of her departure, and the stretch of emptiness that would surely follow. If nothing else, Greer Fairchild brought something fresh to each and every day, and this old castle would feel ancient and musty and dead when she was gone.

He tried to work, but he could not — the debate about what she'd been doing today continued to roar in his mind — and at last he gave in, retreating to his chambers to dress for supper.

He emerged an hour later, washed and dressed, and made his way to the dining room, walking through the portrait gallery and past the conservatory.

He had not expected to see her before supper, but there she was, at her writing desk, her head bent over a piece of vellum, her pen moving violently along, her cleanly bandaged hand holding the vellum.

He paused, wondering if he might interrupt, but then she sighed and paused in her writing and happened to glance up. "My lord!" she said with a start, rising from the table, and quickly hid her letter.

Rhodrick looked at the letter she had shoved behind some books she'd apparently borrowed. She smiled sheepishly. "I was writing my cousins. I write them every day."

That only served to remind him that her cousins should have received her first letter by now. He couldn't bear the thought of receiving affirmation of her identity, that she didn't belong here, and worse, that she would be leaving his life. "How is your hand?" he asked, ignoring the offending letter.

Greer held up the heavily bandaged appendage and grinned. "It is really *quite* all right, although Mrs. Bowen was insistent that she clean and bandage it properly. I assured her it was hardly worth bandaging at all, but she'd gone to the trouble of having Mrs. Jernigan prepare a poultice."

"It will help you heal quickly," he opined. "And for that I am grateful to Mrs. Jernigan. I should not like the world to be deprived of your music for very long."

"The world should not be deprived of very

much," she said with a gracious smile, and walked around the table. The gown she wore skimmed over her figure and looked to be very light, a stark contrast to her black hair and blue eyes. Whatever the color, he thought she looked beautiful, every inch a princess. But for some reason, her regal appearance made him think of her somewhat less regal — and entirely provocative — image last night, in the foyer.

He gripped his hands tightly behind his back. "You seem to have recovered from your journey."

"Yes," she said. "It is astounding what a hot bath will do for one's ill humor."

And now he would add an image of Greer naked in her bath to the many images of her he was constantly trying to banish from his mind's eye. He glanced at the rug at his feet. "Perhaps the next time you go out, you will carry a bit of food for you and Molly."

She snorted, but her eyes were sparkling. "Molly will be much happier, I assure you. But I insist, sir, that as prince of this region, you really *must* install some badly needed roads."

"A road to nowhere is not worth the expense of building it."

"But how can one possibly know if a road leads to nowhere if you don't at least see where it goes?"

He couldn't help but smile at her logic. "Was that your destination today? Nowhere?"

She smiled and folded her arms across her middle. "I was out taking the air. Just as I said."

Rhodrick smiled, too. "There is fresh air to be had in the general vicinity of Llanmair, particularly in the gardens. Or, if you prefer, on the road to Rhayader. But the forest, it would seem, is rather dense for your air taking."

She laughed. "You *still* don't trust me in the least."

"I don't," he said congenially, and held out his arm. "Shall we dine?"

"Please," she said, gliding forward. "I am *famished*."

"What of your letter?" he asked.

She glanced back at the desk. "I'll finish it later."

She was not exaggerating about being famished. In the dining room, Rhodrick watched with some amusement as Greer unabashedly cleaned her plate of each course that was served to her. By the end of the meal, she had forgotten her ladylike posture and was leaning back against the high-backed chair, one arm at her side, the other draped over her middle, smiling with satisfaction. "On my word, I've never dined as well as this," she said with a sated sigh. "What did you call the first dish?"

"*Caws pobi.* Welsh rarebit."

"It was *delicious.* Thank you."

He inclined his head in acknowledgment as the footmen moved to take away their plates and Ifan refreshed her dessert wine.

Greer sat up, sipped the dessert wine, then glanced at him from the corner of her eye. "Will you indulge me, my lord? I should like to make some slight changes to my sitting room."

That surprised him. He had been married long enough to know that a woman intent on changing the décor of a room was not planning on fleeing. "Why?" he asked suspiciously.

"Because. It's rather . . . *cheerless,*" she said apologetically. "Quite a lot of grays and browns. I thought perhaps it might be made cheerier with a bit of color. Mrs. Bowen informed me there were some bolts of cloth in the stores, and as it appears that I shall be here for a time . . ." She glanced at him from the corner of her eye. "That is, until the letter arrives, which I fear is at least a month away, what with all the rain we've had."

The sudden change in her was suspicious. First, her absence all day, and then the letter writing, and now the desire to settle in.

"Mrs. Bowen rather thought you'd not know of the fabric," she continued uncertainly. "She said you rarely go below."

He glanced at the port Ifan put before him. "Perhaps we might have a look."

"How splendid!" she cried with delight. "It is probably time you swept down from your castle perch. I thought the green room could be made into a perfectly serviceable salon with a bit of color and comfortable seating. It's so *warm* with its western light."

He had no idea which was the green room and looked at her blankly. "The *green* room," she said. "As green as your —" She blushed and dropped her gaze. "Your waistcoat," she finished.

"The green room," he said, trying to determine to which room she referred.

She looked up and blinked with surprise. "The *green* room. Dear lord, a master of such a castle with no notion of what he's got! Perhaps we should have a look in there as well."

"All right," he said agreeably. "I shall look."

"Marvelous!" she said, clearly pleased. "Shall I meet you in the green room after you've had your port?"

He nodded.

"Then if you will excuse me," she said, as a footman hurried to remove her chair. With another bone-melting smile, she glided out of the room, her hips swaying alluringly when she walked.

He waited until the door had closed behind her, then looked at Ifan. "Which is the *green* room?" he asked.

"The small receiving nursery across from the mistress's sitting room, my lord."

"Thank you," Rhodrick said, and sipped his port.

TWENTY

A quarter of an hour later, Rhodrick stood with his back to the smooth mahogany door of the green room, brows furrowed in concentration. He would never have believed he might be persuaded to discuss a room's particular furnishings, but here he was, looking at one large settee, a console, and a lamp.

Frankly, he could not imagine what more the room might possibly need, but Greer suddenly gave him a nod and strode into the middle of the room, turned fully about, and said, "Two divans are needed here." She indicated with her hands where they would go. "Facing opposite one another to invite conversation."

"Of course," he said, as if that was a perfectly natural conclusion.

"And I might add that the paint, my lord, is so *dismal.* I hope you won't mind me saying, but it is a rather dreadful shade of green. Far too dark and ominous for a cheerful sitting room. Wouldn't you agree?"

"I —"

"And really, the hearth should be replaced. No one likes to cast their gaze upon *gargoyles* when they are conversing about the latest news from town," she said, pointing to the intricately carved figures in the marble hearth.

"Actually, I think those are hawks," he said, walking forward to stand beside her as they studied the hearth. "I confess to ignorance, Miss Fairchild. What *do* people like to cast their gaze upon when conversing about the latest news from town?" he asked.

She shot him a sidelong look. "Don't tease me. I am perfectly serious."

"So am I."

She laughed. "Anything but gruesome gargoyles."

"Wouldn't one merely look in another direction?"

"Oh dear," she said with a playful smile. "You really aren't very practiced in this, are you?"

"It rather depends on the company."

She folded her arms and studied him. "I wonder . . . if two people share a mutual distrust, what would they speak about were they inclined to converse?"

He looked at her, at her sparkling blue eyes. Of love, he thought. *Of desire. Of how it aches to be away from you.*

"I think I might sit on my divan here," she said, gesturing to a space near the hearth, "while you sit on *your* divan there," she added with a sly smile as she gestured to another invisible divan, "and I would inquire politely about your life. But I would not trust you to be completely forthright, and would have to be particularly artful to drag the least bit of useful information from you."

"While looking at, or away, from the hawks?" he asked.

She smiled bewitchingly. "While looking at *you,* of course."

Rhodrick glanced at the hearth, then at her. He was on dangerous ground, he knew. "Shall we try it?"

"Yes!" she said eagerly. "I shall go first. My dear Lord Radnor, you live in this huge castle all alone! Who is left of your family?"

"That is all you would know? I expected something far more personal or revealing, such as how large is my fortune, or where do I keep the key to my safe."

"That would be impolite," she responded with a coy smile. "I couldn't possibly inquire after your fortune until much later in the conversation. Come then, my lord — I have it on good authority that you *do* have a family — at least a sister, is that not so?"

"It is," he said with a smile. "My parents, as you have undoubtedly uncovered, are deceased. My sister, Lady Wilbarger, lives in Cardiff."

She nodded and looked at him expectantly. "And?"

"And?"

"Do you ever see your sister?"

"Not often. Twice a year, perhaps." Nell enjoyed her life in Cardiff and found Llanmair rather tiresome.

"Have you cousins? Aunts and uncles?"

"One aunt. Two cousins. And my cousin's son, who is, of course, well known to you."

"Is that *all?* No one else?"

He laughed. "I am fairly certain I have named them all."

"Children?" she said, watching him carefully.

"No," he responded, feeling the clench of his gut he always did when he thought of his infant daughter. "Now it is *my* turn. Where did you go today?"

Her smile widened. "For the *third* time, I went out to take the *air.* I tried to find the path along the top of the ridge on which you had led me once before, but I am hopeless with directions and was unable to find it."

He didn't believe her. Greer blinked, put a hand to her throat, and fidgeted with the amulet she wore.

No, he didn't believe her. He did not believe she'd spent an entire day wandering about the forest. She would have eventually come upon a cottage or even Kendrick. And if she had, he couldn't possibly imagine why she would not say so. The suspicion that her long absence today had something to do with Owen Percy continued to swim along the edge of his thoughts.

"My turn," she said. "Mrs. Bowen tells me you allow Mr. and Mrs. Jernigan to live without rent."

He would have to caution Mrs. Bowen from talking so freely. "Mrs. Jernigan is a respected healer and has been all her life. She and Mr. Jernigan were made homeless by an unfortunate investment," he said.

"Yes, but you gave them a cottage on your estate and have allowed them to live freely for several years."

"What of it?" he asked, embarrassed by what he considered a private matter. "They are elderly and well beyond the years of laboring for their bread. Their food and keep is hardly noted in the Llanmair accounts. Why anyone might find that particularly noteworthy, I cannot imagine."

Greer smiled. "I found it noteworthy and extraordinarily kind. It would seem you've been hiding a propensity for kindness."

"I assure you, I have not," he said wryly, and gestured toward the lone settee in the room, where they both took a seat.

"I believe it is my turn," he said, enjoying the feel of her small body so close to his. "Why haven't you married?"

She made a sound of surprise.

"I am direct, Miss Fairchild. I should think a woman as appealing as you, out in high society, should have garnered an offer or two."

She suddenly laughed. "I've had *two* offers, if you must know, but I did not have the sort of feelings I thought one *should* have for a gentleman if one is considering matrimony. Why do you ask?"

"Because I find it peculiar that a handsome woman who is kin to a powerful marquis would come all this way for a mere four thousand pounds."

"That is not a trifling amount," she reminded him.

"But for an unmarried debutante who makes her home in the bosom of Britain's most elite society, I should think that amount too trifling for so much trouble. If you'd married, you would have done far better than four thousand pounds, I should think."

With a devilish smile, she said, "Are you suggesting that I should marry for money, my lord?"

Rhodrick chuckled. "Come now, Miss Fairchild. Isn't that the reason most high-society matches are arranged?"

"Was it the reason *your* marriage was arranged?"

"I beg your pardon," he said playfully. "It is *my* turn."

She groaned heavenward, then turned deep blue eyes to him. "Is it so inconceivable that a woman, unmarried and out, or married, or near death, for that matter, should want to pursue what is rightfully hers? Shouldn't she *want* to live without relying on relatives she scarcely knows for her keep?"

"It is the way of the *ton*."

"And what would you know of the *ton?*"

"I would know as much or more than you, I assure you," he said. "In the years you were running about meadows in a little girl's frock trying to catch butterflies, I attended every Parliamentary session with the hope of doing some good for Wales. I spent four Seasons there, and in the course of two of them, helped to present my sister to society. I think I am well aware of a woman's desires."

Greer snorted. "And I think you do not understand women at all."

That made Rhodrick laugh. He couldn't help it — he laughed deeply, and at Greer's look of surprise, he said, "I beg your pardon, but I would never be so bold as to own that I did."

"Well. If you *did* know a woman's mind, sir, you would understand that she desires to care for herself and in a more tangible way than society and the law will allow. It is abominable that women are left without the ability to inherit or own property unless it falls to them by some twist of fate and the appropriate alignment of deaths in their family."

He realized she was quite serious. "Perhaps if you tell me your trouble, I can help."

"I am merely speaking on behalf of womankind, oppressed by men for *centuries,*" she said dramatically, and glanced down. "Women are treated like these flowers," she said, pointing to the fabric of the settee. "Like tiny little flowers, quite delicate and cultivated to be kept in tiny little vases instead of in the wild, where they would grow to withstand the forces of nature."

Rhodrick looked at the fabric where she pointed. Damn him if he could make out any flowers in the fabric.

"Do you see how delicate they are?"

He stared harder. When he looked up, Greer was staring at him.

"You don't *see* them, do you? You don't see the small white flowers against this beige fabric."

He looked helplessly into her clear blue eyes, which gazed at him suspiciously. "You cannot discern the colors," she said. "Of course not, for why would a man call a red salon red when it is clearly peach?"

She had him there. "All right," he said, and pushed a hand through his hair. "I have an . . . *affliction*," he said, biting out the words. "When it comes to certain hues, I have a devil of a time telling them apart."

"Which hues?" she asked, her expression curious.

"Red and green, primarily. They seem to take on whatever color they are near. Colors in general seem faded, so it is quite difficult at times to tell one from another."

"What colors can you see?"

He looked at Greer, at her shimmering blue eyes, her ink black hair, and the blush of her skin. "Blue," he said quietly, feeling the fire inside him ignite. "I can see the deepest colors of blue."

Her lips parted.

"And black," he said, reaching up to touch the hair at her temple. "I can see the blackest night and the shine of the blackest hair." He lowered his gaze to her lips, soft and full and moist. "I can see the darkness of your lips against the cream of your skin," he muttered, and moved his hand to her face, his broad palm cupping the line of her jaw, his thumb caressing her bottom lip. "But I think I'd never seen real color until you. And now . . . now I can see every color of the rainbow in you and I wonder why the entire world of gentlemen has not seen it."

Greer drew a shallow breath. Her gaze followed a path from the top of his head to his brow, and down the scar to his lips, his chin, and the shadow of the beard he could never seem to tame. And then to his eyes again, to his ailing eyes that could see very little color in the world except for Greer.

But Greer — he'd *seen* her from almost the moment he'd laid eyes on her, standing so defiantly on the road. He had no hope that his desire would ever be returned in the same depth and breadth that he'd come to feel it, but he could not help the desire he felt and was weary of trying to curb it.

When she lifted her slender, bandaged hand and wrapped it around his wrist, he expected her to pull his hand away from her, but she did not.

She gripped his wrist with amazing strength, almost as if she feared he would disappear, and leaned into him, her eyes fluttering shut as she pressed his palm against her cheek.

He put his arm around her and drew her to him and closed his eyes, touching his mouth to her hair, breathing in the rosy scent of her perfume as his hand found her neck and collarbone. "Forgive me," he said hoarsely. "I can no longer pretend that I don't desire you completely."

He felt the release of her breath warm on his skin as she pressed her face into his neck. With her lips and the tip of her tongue, she touched him, tasting him. That small touch sent a deep shiver through him, and he tightened his grip on her as he lifted her face to his, splayed his fingers across her cheek, and looked into her eyes.

"Nor can I," she said softly.

The small promise in her voice forged hope in him. He could not remember ever having felt carnal desire so strongly or urgently. He could not recall a moment of ever having wanted to be inside a woman so desperately as this. "Greer," he said roughly, "I cannot lie — I want you." He cupped her face and lifted it to kiss her. "I don't know what to make of you, I don't know what to believe. But you have bewitched me so completely that I cannot bear to be near you and not touch you. I want to love you."

Greer responded by putting her arms around his neck and kissing him with surprising strength.

He made a guttural sound of desire as he swept her into his arms and fell back, pulling her on top of him. "Stop me," he said hoarsely. "Tell me no, or else I shall ravish you, I —"

She stopped him from speaking with another kiss.

Rhodrick kissed her madly then, leaving scarcely an inch of bare skin untouched. He caressed her body, her neck and the curve of her shoulder, and the swell of her bosom above the bodice of her gown. He moved his hands down her back, her hips, and her legs. Her body was divine, soft and curved in all the right places.

Rhodrick moved abruptly, turning them around so that she was on her back beneath him.

"What have you done to me, sir?" Greer

asked on a wistful sigh as he kissed her throat and her bosom. "How have you persuaded me to ignore all propriety?" She closed her eyes as her hands wandered over his body, caressing his shoulders, his arms, and inside his coat, to his waist and rib cage.

He was driven to a point of unconscionable passion in which he no longer cared for propriety — he cared for nothing but making love to her. "It was never my intention," he said against her skin as every stroke of her hands sent him a little closer to the edge of losing control, every breath she sighed feeding the desire in him. "But it is my body's strongest hunger."

The desire to feel her, touch her, taste her, and oh God, to be inside of her, resurrected the life in him. Not the breath he drew, but the *life*. As his hands and mouth covered her body, she gripped his head, drawing him up, then lifting up to kiss him and fill him with her breath and her tongue.

"I've gone mad, I fear," she said breathlessly.

"Then so have I," he assured her, and kissed her so hungrily that in the back of his mind, he feared he would scare her — yet Greer did not stop him. She moaned deep in her throat and pressed against his aching erection as he dragged his mouth to the fleshy mounds of her breasts.

He slipped his hands behind her back, fumbling with the buttons of her gown until he had unfastened them and could free her breasts from the fabric. He took each peak into his mouth, sucking them, devouring them.

She ran her fingers through his hair and arched her back, pressing against his mouth.

Rhodrick could not name the moment when they had gone from despising one another to feeling a desire unlike any he'd ever known. The gentleman in him — the *prince* in him — demanded that he cease at once before he compromised a young woman's virtue completely beyond repair.

But the man in him knew he wouldn't stop until she asked him to, and even then, he might beg her to reconsider with his hands and his mouth.

At the moment, she seemed to be nearing the point of no return herself, if the little *ohs* and groans were any indication. He abruptly pulled up and looked into her eyes. They were as deep as a well, the look of them seductive, bewitching.

"What is wrong?" she asked innocently.

His gaze still on hers, he stood up, strode to the door of the green room and closed it, turning the key in the lock.

When he turned back, Greer had come up on her elbows, watching him, her hair beginning to slip from its coif, her gown pushed down, revealing her breasts.

He did not hesitate; he strode back to her, pulled her to her feet. He held her gaze, let his hands slide down her arms, touched his fingers to hers, then touched her hips. He did not speak; he couldn't seem to find his tongue, and privately, he feared what he might say.

But Greer, brave Greer — with her gaze locked on his, she hesitantly reached up and pushed her gown off her shoulder. "I suppose this should come off, shouldn't it?"

He swallowed. "Allow me," he said, and caught her hand and pushed it down before lifting his hands to her shoulders and pulling her gown and chemise down. "You are entirely too beautiful," he said as he slowly pulled the clothing farther down, past her waist. "And entirely too bewitching for words," he added, and squatted down, pulling the gown and chemise down her legs as he pressed his lips to her belly.

Greer gasped; she placed her hands on his head for support as he drew a line with his mouth from her belly, down her drawers, to the apex of her thighs. Above him, she swayed, and he glanced up as he put his hands on her drawers and slowly pulled them down over her hips.

"Ah God," he breathed. He openly admired her naked body, greedily taking every bit of her in, from her beautifully flushed face to her swollen breasts to the soft flat of her belly and the springy tuft of black hair at the top of her legs. He was melting inside, the fire had melted him, and he shook his head with wonder that this beautiful woman could, by *any* measure, seem to desire him as he desired her.

"You are beautiful," he breathed. "You are as beautiful as I knew you'd be." He rose to his full height, quickly shrugged out of his coat, and as he worked the buttons of his waistcoat, she undid the knot of his neck-cloth. He tossed the coat and waistcoat aside, as well as his neckcloth. Greer pulled his shirt from his trousers, and he pulled it over his head, tossing it aside, too.

Her eyes filled with wonder as she put her hands flat against his chest, sliding them down to the belt at his trousers, then up, over his nipples, to his shoulders and arms. He feared she would find him repulsive and he quickly unfastened his belt, then gathered her in his arms, burying his face in her neck, and pulled her down to the settee again.

"Don't move. Let me love you," he said,

and kissed her reverently, aware that he'd never know a moment as pure as this again, and he would not squander it. He pulled her onto his lap — she was as light as a feather, her bones small beneath his hands. The warmth of her body seeped into his skin, filling him up, pushing at him again until he thought he could not bear it another moment.

They twisted around, so that Greer was lying beneath him, and he moved his hand down her body, to the softest place of her. "Oh," she gasped. *"Oh my."*

He followed his hand with his mouth, down her chin, to her breasts, and down farther, to her belly, to the crook of her elbow, and inside her wrist, to the side of her hip, and then around, to join his hand.

Greer gasped at his hot breath and drew one leg up. His senses filled with the scent and the taste of her as he moved lower still. When his tongue slipped between the folds of her sex, she cried out, her voice strangled, and her body jerked. But Rhodrick caught her hips, held her still so that he could have her at his leisure. He was deliberately slow, reveling in it, exhilarated by the quickening beat of his heart as she bucked against him. And when he closed his lips around the tiny bud, Greer sobbed with pleasure.

As he drew it between his lips, her body spasmed and she cried out; her hands clutching at his head, her body shimmering against him. She moved wildly, trying to escape the pleasure, but he could not let her go, not yet, not until he'd had his fill. He effortlessly held her steady in his hands and continued to suck that tiny bud until she cried again, sobbing, her legs squeezing him. "I beg of you," she said breathlessly. "No more."

Only then did he rise up and come over her, pushing his trousers down, past an enormous erection. He kissed her roughly, passionately, possessively as he parted her legs with his thigh and lowered his body to hers, pressed the tip of his cock against her wet body, and bit his bottom lip in a supreme effort to keep from taking her like an animal.

Her eyes were closed, her breathing ragged. "I never imagined feeling this way," she moaned.

"Nor I," he averred, and pressed the tip of him inside her.

Greer groaned; he kissed her, continued to stroke her hair, and slid a little deeper, giving her body time to accept him. He slid still deeper, felt the barrier of her virginity, and realized, in the haze of desire and want, that he was grateful for it.

He lowered his forehead to hers. "I want you desperately, Greer . . . but are you certain you want me?"

She opened her eyes. The blue seemed even bluer somehow, and he had the sensation he was looking into a deep pool. She smiled and put her hands to his face. "Yes," she said softly.

He sighed with pleasure and kissed her as he thrust past the barrier and slid deep inside her.

To her credit, the only evidence of pain she expressed was a small whimper. But as her body opened to him, her hands began to move up and down his back. Rhodrick moved fluidly, withdrawing to the tip, then sliding in again, watching her eyes with each stroke. She closed her eyes as he began to stroke her faster; her head rolled to one side, her hair covering her face. But her body moved with his, her hands gripping his shoulders, her hips lifting with each stroke. His breathing grew shallow.

When the raging desire exploded within him, he threw his head back, baring his teeth, letting loose a guttural growl of pleasure as he spilled hot and wet inside her. With a final shudder, he collapsed to her side, his face in her neck, his heart pounding so hard that she could feel it and pressed her hand against it.

"My prince's heart," she whispered.

The endearment was almost his undoing. He closed his eyes and held her tightly, remembering every moment, trying to burn it into his memory so that he would never forget how he felt this night.

They slept, wrapped in one another's arms, until the early morning hours when Rhodrick finally untangled himself from her and quietly dressed. He found a lap rug and placed it over her; in her sleep, Greer moaned and rolled onto her side. Rhodrick smoothed the black hair from her face, stroked her cheek, and squatted down beside her. He took a strand of her hair between his fingers and brushed it across his face before leaning over to kiss her.

When he did, her eyes fluttered open, and she looked up at him with a smile of sleepy satisfaction.

"Sleep," he said, and watched as she closed her eyes and pillowed her hands beneath her head.

Rhodrick stood up, tidied the room as best he could by the light of the single candle that still burned, stoked the dying embers in the hearth, adding another piece of wood to the fire, then quietly let himself out of the room. And as he walked through his cold, dark castle, he wondered if he had just made the greatest mistake of his life, or if he'd just opened a door.

TWENTY-ONE

Greer awoke before dawn, alone, curled into the spot where the prince had lain with her on the settee. She was covered with a lap rug that had been tucked tightly around her. As her eyes focused in the dim light, she rose up on one elbow and looked around the room. Her clothes were neatly folded on a chair, the fire at the hearth had been stoked. But she was alone.

Greer fell onto her back, threw an arm over her eyes, and with a shiver of excitement, she recalled every moment.

She had *never* been so captivated, had never felt quite so alive as she had last night! It wasn't precisely the act itself, which was uncomfortable — but so much more than that.

It was the way he touched her with such reverence, the way he breathed her in and the care that he took in pleasuring her, as if he held something precious and fragile in his hands, and the tender, heartfelt words he'd whispered to her.

It was the way he looked at her, the way his eyes shone from a place so deep that it made her shiver with excitement this morning just recalling it.

Beneath the cover of her arm, Greer smiled contentedly.

Until she remembered that she'd let her usually sound judgment be clouded by curiosity and excitement and . . . *feelings?*

Feelings. Sentiments that felt bottomless, stirred from somewhere so hidden inside her that she could hardly make heads or tails of them now. In the blink of an eye, all the tiny rumblings she'd been feeling came rushing to the surface to overwhelm her, until all she could think or feel was the need to be held by him, to be kissed and caressed by him, to be loved by him. To be loved in the most primal sense of the word.

Love? The notion startled her. Was it love she was feeling? Greer slowly sat up, clutching the lap rug. Was this, what she was feeling, the mysterious thing that had eluded her all these years? When other women talked of loving this or that gentleman, was it *this* that they were feeling? It seemed so much more profound than what made debutantes giggle endlessly.

Was it possible that somewhere in England, Ava had felt these very same stirrings for the Marquis of Middleton? Was it really possible that Greer could be falling in love with a man who was years older than she, who lived in near seclusion in Wales, with so many unanswered questions swirling about him?

It was almost too much to even contemplate.

Greer stood, wrapped the lap rug tightly around her naked body, and gathered her clothes and her shoes. With a glance about to assure herself that nothing was left behind, she retreated to the safety of her bedchamber.

But as she walked into that room, she was reminded that it had once been the bedchamber of a wife he had once loved, and that sobered her. As she put her clothes away and pulled a nightgown over her head, she wondered if the prince still loved Eira? Was it possible for a man to love two women in his lifetime?

"*Stop* it," she chided herself as she climbed into bed. "You have no right to think it." It was true — she was rushing ahead into something she really knew nothing about. In the absence of a formal declaration of esteem from the prince, she was not ascribing any such feelings to him. For all she knew, he'd only done what so many gentlemen in London made a sport of doing — bedding a young woman for the sake of carnal relations. Why should he be any different? After all, she was living under his roof without a chaperone. Not only had she failed to stop what had happened, if anything, she'd been a willing and eager participant.

Her world had turned completely on its head.

When she lay down in her bed, she closed her eyes again, only this time, it was against the ugly image of a ruined debutante, who had let not one, but two men kiss her thoroughly in the space of a few weeks, and had finally succumbed to the unthinkable.

Honestly, where were Ava and Phoebe when she needed them?

Greer finally slept, but in those hours before dawn, she dreamt of her mother. She was standing at the door of Kendrick, beckoning Greer to come inside. As Greer climbed the steps, her mother entered the house, and Greer's steps grew hesitant as a fear of what awaited her began to build in her chest. When she reached the dark threshold and stepped inside, it wasn't her mother she saw at all, but the prince. He was standing in the middle of the foyer, his black cloak moving with the breeze around his ankles, his expression darkly erotic.

Greer awoke in a cold sweat.

Dearest Ava and Phoebe,

I hope this letter finds you in good health. I am feeling very well. I have determined there are some days in Wales that are really rather beautiful, and not as bleak as I had previously thought. Today there is a light dusting of snow on the landscape that makes the forest look pristine and beautiful.

We dined recently with friends of the prince — M & M Awbrey and Lord & Lady Pool. Lady Pool, who was a frequent visitor to London in years past, claims to be acquainted with Lady Purnam. She cannot be entirely certain, but judging from my description of Lady Purnam, she believes they are indeed acquainted. I cannot imagine anyone's having met Lady Purnam and forgetting her easily, not even with the passage of so many years.

I am reminded of someone we knew in years past, Miss Bethany Randall. Do you recall that the poor dear was caught up in a frightful scandal involving a notorious rake? Do you suppose she was careless with her virtue because she fancied herself in love with him? What do you suppose ever happened to Miss Randall?

I hear voices in the corridor, so I should close now. Please give my kindest regards to Lord Middleton, as well as Lucille and Lord Downey. I <u>desperately</u> hope to hear from you soon.

Warmly, G.

She had sealed the letter just as Mrs. Bowen and two footmen entered the conservatory. The footmen were carrying two large arrangements of hothouse hydrangeas, which, at Mrs. Bowen's direction, they deposited on the floor on either side of the writing desk. Greer looked at Mrs. Bowen with surprise; Mrs. Bowen, however, seemed to look everywhere but at Greer.

"What is this?" Greer exclaimed.

"His lordship thought that as it is snowing, you might enjoy some flowers from the hothouse." As she spoke, her gray brows rose nearly to her scalp. "He selected them for you."

Greer exclaimed with delight and stood up to examine the huge vases of colorful hydrangeas. "Oh, they're lovely!"

"I daresay his lordship has not been to the hothouse in two years or more," Mrs. Bowen said, her brows still quite high.

"How gracious of him," Greer murmured, smiling, as the footmen went out. She would have liked nothing better than to question Mrs. Bowen endlessly — What did he say? Was there a message of any sort? How did he look when he asked her to bring down the flowers? Was he smiling? — but she wisely thought the better of it. If there was one thing she had learned in London, it was that servants could spread gossip faster than anyone.

"I trust your hand is healing?" Mrs. Bowen asked, glancing at Greer's unbandaged hand.

"Quite," Greer said, and held up the palm for Mrs. Bowen's inspection, wiggling her fingers. "It is really a very shallow cut. I've hardly noticed it today at all. In fact," she said, lowering her hand and picking up the sealed vellum, "I wrote this letter without giving it a thought. May I have it posted?"

"Of course."

Greer walked across the room to Mrs. Bowen, and handed the letter to her. But when Mrs. Bowen took the letter in hand, Greer did not let go. "If I may, Mrs. Bowen," she said with a bright smile, "I . . . I've been meaning to ask if there is anything more about Alis Bronwyn that you might tell me."

"Miss Alis?" Mrs. Bowen repeated dubiously. "I can't tell you more than what I have already told you, miss —"

"But isn't there anything more about her childhood you remember?" Greer pressed anxiously. "That is to say, what sort of girl was she? Do you recall anything extraordinary about her? My aunt was much younger than my mother and really knew very little about her childhood."

"Well," Mrs. Bowen said thoughtfully as she tugged the letter from Greer's grip, "she was a pretty lass. Long black hair and blue eyes," she said. "Like you, miss. And she was very polite." Her brow furrowed as she thought about it. "I do recall that she was lost once."

"Lost?"

"Mmm," Mrs. Bowen said, nodding. "Got away from her nurse somehow." She shook her head and frowned. "Oh, they looked high and low for the girl. The prince's father and his men were called upon to help them search the river."

"The river?"

"Oh yes," Mrs. Bowen said, nodding vehemently. "She was just a tiny thing. They were quite certain she'd wandered into the

364

water and drowned."

"My heavens! But she didn't drown, obviously."

"No indeed. If I remember correctly, she had followed a pair of rabbits into the woods and had gotten lost. She emerged all on her own several hours later, covered head to toe in dirt and whatnot, and when they asked how she had found her way home, she said something very odd. She said that an old man in a red coat had helped her find her way home."

"An old man in a red coat," Greer repeated. "Who was he, do you suppose?"

"A spirit, Miss Fairchild." Mrs. Bowen said it as if it were obvious. "There was a portrait of her grandfather in his regimentals that hung in the foyer. She said it was him, but the old man had died long before Miss Alis had come along. His spirit led her home."

"A miracle," Greer murmured.

"Indeed it was. I really can't remember aught else," Mrs. Bowen said, smiling a little. "You might inquire of his lordship —"

"Yes," Greer said, wondering if she might broach the subject of Kendrick with him now. She smiled brightly at Mrs. Bowen. "It looks as if the snow has stopped falling."

Mrs. Bowen glanced at the windows and

nodded. "Indeed it does. If there is nothing more, I shall see this is put with the post straightaway. His lordship is to Rhayader on the morrow, and he always takes the post."

"Thank you," Greer said.

Left alone in the conservatory, her letter written, she had nothing to do but either dwell on the prince or read. So she picked up her book on Welsh history and began to read. But as the fire began to die, the room grew cold, and on the settee, Greer shifted below the lap rug she'd brought from the green room as she read about the conversion of the Welsh people to Methodism.

She must have drifted to sleep, for she was awakened by a loud *clop* when the thick tome of history slid off her lap and onto the floor. Greer blinked the sleep from her eyes and pushed herself up to a sitting position, at which point she noticed the prince standing just inside the door of the conservatory, his hands clasped behind his back, watching her. She could feel a delicious smile spread across her lips.

He seemed taken aback by her smile and slowly returned it with one of his own. "I didn't want to disturb you."

"I think the culprit was Methodism," she said sheepishly as she collected her book. "I was reading of Methodism and the Welsh

Bible," she said, before realizing how that sounded. "N-not that I find that the least bit tiresome, for I don't!" she added hastily, looking up at him. "It's inspiring, of course."

"Naturally," he said, his smile deepening. "I didn't realize you were a student of history."

"The history of the Welsh is quite interesting."

"Oh?"

She nodded. "It feels as if it is a part of me in an odd way."

He held her gaze a moment; she could see him swallow.

Greer glanced at the beautiful hydrangeas and smiled again. "Thank you for the flowers, my lord. They are beautiful."

"I thought perhaps they might cheer your writing room. I have no notion what color they are —"

"Pink."

"Ah." He stepped into the room and looked around. "It's rather cold in here."

"I don't mind it," she said, coming to her feet and putting away the lap rug. "It's invigorating."

He nodded, his gaze taking her in. "If you are accustomed to the cold, I should like to show you something."

"Oh?"

He glanced at the window. "It's outside. Nearby, but outside."

She could think of nothing she would like better and nodded. "I shall just get my cloak."

And as Greer walked by him, she glanced up and smiled, and could see that same deep shining in his eyes that she felt inside herself.

TWENTY-TWO

She met him in the foyer, where he was waiting with his dogs and wearing the same long black cloak he'd worn in her dream and a beaver hat. A watch fob glittered at his waist, and he wore a dark blue neck-cloth that matched his gold-embroidered waistcoat. He looked, she thought, regal and handsome and uncommonly virile. He smiled a little as he took her cloak from her hand and held it open for her. She stepped into it, felt a shiver of delight as his hand touched her shoulder, and had to concentrate on fastening the clasp.

He handed her a thick woolen scarf. "For your throat," he said, glancing at the column of her neck. "I would not want you to catch cold."

"Thank you." Smiling, she wrapped the dark brown scarf that smelled of men's cologne around her neck. When he was satisfied she was properly bundled, he handed her a fur-lined bonnet for her head and a fox muff for her hands.

She blinked at the extravagance of the items as she took them from him. "They belong to my sister," he said, and walked to the door, which a footman opened for him. "She wouldn't mind you using them." His commanding frame filled the doorway as he looked out into the courtyard. "Ah," he muttered, "there he is." He turned and held out his hand to Greer.

It was such a simple gesture, nothing more than any gentleman might do, but to Greer it felt as if she'd been waiting for that gesture all her life, for the right man to offer his hand to her. She slipped her hand into his, relished the feel of his fingers closing possessively around hers, and allowed him to lead her out into the courtyard with Cain and Abel trotting alongside.

But in the courtyard, beneath an icy gray sky, there was only one horse — the big black steed she had seen the prince ride. She glanced around, her breath coming out in puffs of frost. "Where is Molly?"

"The trek we will take is short but rather steep. You will ride with me," he said, and glanced at her sidelong. "If you wouldn't mind."

The thought of riding astride that beast

with this man was enough to make a poor ruined debutante swoon, but Greer had moved well past swooning, and nodded happily. She walked with him to stand beside the horse. "Has he a name?" she asked, staring up at the steed's enormous black eyes.

"*Cadfael,*" he said, his voice soft and warm behind her. "It means 'Battle Prince' in Welsh. Shall I hand you up?"

She turned away from the horse's unwavering eye and looked up at the prince. She wanted to speak, to share a private jest. It seemed to her that if two people had shared such extraordinary intimacy, they should at least have leave to call each other by their given names. "What is *your* name?" she asked. "Your full name?"

He put his hands on her waist and lifted her up. "Rhodrick. Rhodrick William Glendower."

Rhodrick. She smiled as he swung up behind her. With his left hand, he gathered the reins, and his right he put around her middle, pulling her back and anchoring her to him. With his head next to hers, he asked, "Ready?"

He could not see the smile with which Greer stared out at the road before them as she nodded.

■ ■ ■ ■

They rode on a narrow forest path that Rhodrick had not traveled in months. It was overgrown, but still passable. Cadfael labored up a steep incline, and then picked his way carefully along a narrow ridge path — which, Rhodrick realized with some chagrin, was blistering cold in the wind. He took the edge of his cloak and wrapped it securely around Greer, who shifted back against him, nestling her slender body against his.

He could scarcely see; the feel of her invited the memory of how she'd looked last night. Her hair inky black against her creamy white skin, her lips dark and moist, and her eyes, always her eyes, tiny seas of blue in a nearly gray world.

As Greer chattered on about Methodists for reasons he had missed altogether, Rhodrick realized that he was breathing a sigh of relief. All morning he had dreaded seeing her, fearing the look of regret in her eyes — or worse. He still could not understand how it had happened. One moment, he was looking at her, wishing that his life had been different, that his face had been different, and the next moment, he was holding her in his arms, kissing her, caressing her. . . .

It was some sort of miracle. Not in his wildest dreams had he believed he might experience the joy of making love to a woman as beautiful and as spirited as Greer Fairchild, to see her brilliant smile in the light of the next day instead of the revulsion he'd feared.

How could it be that she was here with him now, riding through a snow-dusted landscape, chattering about Methodists? How was it possible that she seemed so happy to see him with that deep light shining in her eyes? She had never seemed more beautiful to him than she did at this very moment — not even the day he'd first seen her standing defiantly on the road, wondering aloud if he was as primitive as surely she must have heard.

At the point where the tree had grown partially around a rock, Rhodrick turned Cadfael into the forest.

"What do you suppose they meant to do with them?" Greer asked, piercing his contemplative mood.

"Beg your pardon?"

"The Welsh Bibles," she said. "What did they mean to do with them?"

"Who?" he asked, confused.

373

Greer laughed and turned her head slightly, her face upturned and her eyes shining. "I daresay you haven't heard a word I've said, sir! I was explaining I'd read that when the Bible was first translated into Welsh, several of them disappeared from the churches. Why do you suppose that was?"

"Quite simple, really," he said. "The English were not entirely trusted and the Welsh were afraid of losing something that was very valuable to them. We've one of them at Llanmair. My ancestor took it from the parish church and put it away in a locked box."

She laughed gaily. "You admit to your family's thievery with pride."

"And you," he said, smiling down at her, "have been too long in the bosom of the English, I think. You are far too trusting of them."

She laughed again and faced forward, settling against him as if they had long been lovers. "And you have the sensibilities of a man who lived in another century altogether."

"I beg to differ. I have the sensibilities of a man who has had many dealings with Englishmen. They are not to be trusted."

"Perhaps you — *Oh!*" she exclaimed as

they rode into the clearing. She sat up straighter, looking around at the ancient Viking ruins. "Oh my . . . this is *extraordinary.*"

Rhodrick brought Cadfael to a halt, swung off, then helped Greer down. With her cloak leaving a trail through the snow, she hurried to the first oddly placed stone. "How did you find it?" she exclaimed as she traced a gloved hand over the top of the stone. "What is it?"

"A site of worship for the Norse Druids. Or a Viking burial ground. The scholars who have been here to study it aren't entirely certain." He ran his hand over the rough edge of one stone.

Greer squatted down to look at the markings on one stone, then stood up again. With the dogs following her, their tails high in the air, she walked the circle of the stones, spiraling around to the largest stone in the center, which was larger and cut in a different shape from the other stones. She whirled around to him, her cheeks pink with the cold, her eyes sparkling with pleasure. "It's *wonderful,* Rhodrick."

The sound of his name — so rarely used, and therefore, so rarely heard — filled him with the same sensation of bliss he felt when he heard music. "There is more."

"Where?" she asked eagerly.

He questioned the wisdom of what he was about to do, but he put his hand on her elbow and guided her out of the circle and into the forest. He led her through thick brush into another small clearing, where a small cottage and horse trough stood beneath the boughs of the forest trees.

"What is *this?*" Greer exclaimed with delight.

"I built it years ago for the scholars who came to study the ruins," he said as he took in the thatched roof, the rock walls, and the small lawn. "I let it fall into disuse after they'd gone, but one day, in the middle of a rather fierce storm, I sought refuge within its walls. I found it to be very quiet and, well . . ." He walked forward and opened the door.

Greer looked at him curiously, then suddenly marched forward, brushing past him as she stooped to cross the threshold just behind the dogs, who trotted in as they had, no doubt, a thousand times before.

For a moment, Rhodrick panicked. He'd never brought anyone here. He'd done all the work himself while Cadfael and Cain and Abel looked on. It was his own small place in the world, and if she laughed, if she thought he was mad to find refuge in such a common dwelling on an estate he owned —

He followed her inside. Cain and Abel had already headed to the pallets he'd made for them, plopping themselves down, their long pink tongues hanging identically from their jaws. Greer stood in the middle of the room and looked around, studying the paintings scattered about the room. Paintings he'd made in secrecy and had never shown another living soul.

There was a single chair he had dragged down here behind Cadfael once, the table he had made from wood he had lathed and dragged here, too. There were few appointed comforts — a single rug, discharged from its duty at Llanmair. A tarnished candelabra. A stack of canvases.

Greer turned around fully twice, taking in every detail, then moved to the canvas he'd left on the easel these last few weeks. He had meant to capture the evening light as it descended over the Cambrian Mountains, but he was dissatisfied with it, and had left it. Now Greer was staring at it, wide-eyed, her fingers touching carefully the mountain he'd painted.

He suddenly wished he'd not brought her here. He felt like a fool, like a boy showing off his fort. He could not understand why he'd allowed himself to believe that he was safe, that he could show her the most private part of himself.

He was about to tell her that they must go, to try and erase the mistake he'd made, but she suddenly turned and looked at him with amazement. "Did . . . did *you* paint these?"

He scarcely even nodded.

"They are *beautiful* . . . so very beautiful! But why are they here? You have all of Llanmair to pursue your art."

He glanced around, tried to see this little cottage through her eyes. It was odd to her, as odd as he must seem. "There are times," he said, forcing the words, "that I desire to be away from the trappings of my title and the attendant responsibilities. There are times when I want to be free to paint without servants hovering or strangers calling. And . . ." He paused, glancing at the floor and drawing a breath. "And I don't know if there is . . . *color* in them. Or the right sort of color."

She looked around again, but when she returned her gaze to him, she was smiling brilliantly. "There is color in them. *Brilliant* color, Rhodrick. The mountains are yellow and the sky is blue and the trees are red. But they are *beautiful.*"

In that instant, Rhodrick knew that he adored her, that he'd adored the idea of her for as long as he could remember. He didn't think when he took her in his arms — it suddenly seemed so natural, so right, and so perfect, as if this were the moment for which he'd lived his life thus far.

He put his hand on her jaw and lifted her face to him and studied it — the eyes, of course, the one true bit of color in his world, the straight nose that turned up just a bit at the end, the full lips, the freckles faintly splattered across her nose and cheeks. . . .

"What do you see?" she asked, a smile spreading her full lips.

"I see color," he said honestly, and bent to kiss her cheek. Then one eye, and the other, and then the bridge of her nose.

Greer smiled, lifted her hand, and pressed her palm to his face, smiling as he turned his head and kissed her palm. Her eyes shimmered with a depth of emotion that caused his heart to levitate in his chest. He felt on the brink of something quite deep, something in which he could very well drown were he not careful.

But Greer's warm smile wrapped around his heart and squeezed life into it. He drew her into his arms and kissed her —

crushed her, actually. Her fingers raked through his hair as he unclasped her cloak and pushed it from her shoulders, deepening the kiss.

Greer responded by pressing against him and tangling with his tongue.

Somehow, he managed to push his greatcoat from his shoulders and off his arms, and the two of them fell onto it. Rhodrick's hands eagerly swept her frame, moving up her arm, down the side of her body and belly, then up to her breasts, his fingers fumbling with the buttons of her riding jacket. Greer thrust her hands inside his coat, around to his back, feeling his spine, his rib cage, and the taut muscles in his neck and shoulders.

Rhodrick freed a breast and eagerly brought the rigid peak into his mouth. She rose to him, unabashedly indulging in his ardor for her.

With his mouth and hands, he exulted in her, and she received his caress with pure elation. He paused to remove his coat and waistcoat as she worked the pearl buttons of his shirt. When he had managed to divest himself of that, he put his hand on her ankle and skimmed below her skirt, up her leg. "I think the heavens brought you to me," he said as he unfastened her skirt, surprising himself with having voiced the sentiment aloud.

She smiled seductively and lifted her hips so that he could remove her riding skirt. He pushed the skirt away and began to pull her undergarments down her body. When she was bared to him, he feasted his gaze on her body before kissing the flat hollow of her belly.

Beneath him, Greer sighed with pleasure. The heavens *had* brought her here — nothing else would explain how she was now, against all odds, against everything she had ever learned or known, on fire with a burning hunger for this man's touch. His hardness, straining the fabric of his trousers, pressed against her leg. The soft sensation of his lips against her belly and the flick of his tongue in her navel sent spasms of desire spiraling through her. She gasped with delight, shoved her hands in his thick hair, and smiled lazily as he lifted her leg and kissed her thigh.

As his lips traced a warm, wet path up her leg, pausing to kiss the soft crease behind her knee, she laughed at the dizzying sensation of it. But when his breath brushed against the tops of her legs, she felt that dangerous sensation of being consumed by flames.

When his tongue flicked across the seam of her sex, the pleasure overwhelmed her. Her breathing quickly went from ragged to gasping for air. She helped him as he moved between her legs, shifting to give him access. With a wolfish, purely masculine grin, he lifted her legs, putting them over his broad shoulders, and slowly descended to her flesh.

She was quickly spiraling toward release, writhing beneath him, clutching desperately at his head, moving instinctively to meet the caress of his tongue. His hands held her buttocks roughly, holding her to him as he delved deeper and tormented her in the most intimate way imaginable. The pressure building in her was unbearable; she strained to meet him at the very same time she strained to move away from his ministrations.

But he would not let her go, and the stroke of his tongue quickened, staggering her with the sensation, pushing her higher and higher toward a release. She reached it, plummeting into that release and letting go with a long, low moan of pleasure as a wave of sensual gratification washed over her and carried her out to sea.

Rhodrick rose above her, kicking off his trousers. His gaze was fiercely possessive and full of wanting. Greer put her hand to his solid chest, could feel his heart racing beneath her palm as his swollen cock skimmed her leg. "You make me insane with desire," he said roughly.

Greer's heart fluttered unevenly; she cupped his face with her hands. *"Rhodrick . . ."*

With a groan, he bent to kiss her, the taste of her still on his lips. He grappled for her hand, guiding her to feel the velvet head of his erection, wrapping her fingers around the thick staff, guiding her hand up and down, squeezing her fingers around him until she was doing it alone. Rhodrick moaned low in his throat and kissed her, thrusting his tongue into her mouth as her hand glided over him. He suddenly pulled her hand away and gathered her up in his arms, rolling onto his back and bringing her with him, so that she was on top of him.

She gasped with surprise and delight as he gripped her hips and moved her to straddle him, then moved beneath her, rubbing against her. It was wildly erotic. Her hair, long since fallen from the prim coif she had worn, formed a curtain around her face and brushed his chest. "I cannot resist you," she said wantonly.

She had never seen a man more intent,

had never understood the power of the feminine sex before that moment. His eyes were full of an almost beastly desire that Greer instinctively knew she controlled — with a smile, with her hand, with a soft sigh. It was extraordinarily empowering, and extraordinarily seductive. She smiled with the knowledge of how much he wanted her as he lifted her up, positioned himself beneath her, then led her to slide down his shaft until he was buried deep inside her.

It was hopeless — Greer lost herself in the beauty of it, crying out in ecstasy with the sensation of drawing him deeply into her depths. He taught her how to move, carefully pushing her hair aside so that he could see her face as she glided on him. He rose to meet her each time, eventually putting his hands on his hips and taking over, and then abruptly sitting up, taking her in his arms and rolling her onto her back without missing a stroke.

Lying in his arms, feeling his body surround her and in her, Greer felt beautiful and more feminine than she had ever felt in her life. As his strokes grew more urgent, her body tightened around him, coaxing him to the brink of fulfillment. She watched his face, pressing her palms to his cheeks as his body flowed into hers, as smooth as a river. He reached his hand between their bodies and began to stroke her as he moved faster into her body, stroking her toward another eruption of bliss. As Greer reached another climax, he cried her name with his last powerful surge and convulsed into her, giving his life blood to her womb, then collapsed onto her, breaking his fall with his arms.

He brushed the hair from her face and they silently gazed at one another. Greer could not remember ever feeling quite so alive.

Rhodrick smiled and kissed her, then lay his palm on her breast. "It is cold, isn't it?" he asked, watching her eyes. "You're cold, your skin is cold."

"I'm not cold," she said with a laugh. "I am really rather warm."

He smiled, kissed the curve of her neck and shoulder, and slowly withdrew from her body. "We should return before it grows dark." He covered her with his greatcoat, then stood and dressed, completely immodest, seemingly oblivious to her admiration of his masculine body.

She, however, was not quite so immodest, and by the time he had draped his neckcloth around his collar, Greer had wrapped herself in his coat and had pulled on her undergarments and skirt.

He helped her button the skirt, then turned her around, buttoning her chemise and the bust of her riding habit as if he'd buttoned her up many times before. When he finished, he looked into her eyes. She had the sense that he meant to speak, but that he was struggling to find the right words. "Greer," he said, his gaze moving over her face.

She instinctively knew that he meant to speak of their sin, and she could not bear to hear what he would say, no matter what it was. She had taken leave of her senses, but she had not yet determined what she might *do* about it.

With his hands, he caressed her arms. His gaze fell to her bodice.

"Mrs. Bowen says you are to Rhayader on the morrow," she interjected before he could speak.

He lifted his gaze, his green eyes shrewdly considering her. "I am. Would you care to accompany me?"

"Me?" she exclaimed with a laugh. "No, my lord. I have an entire century of Welsh history to read."

He picked up her cloak and wrapped it around her shoulders. "That is quite a lot of history. Perhaps I can spare you the trouble and tell you what happened."

"No, sir, I will not allow it," she said as she fit the fur bonnet on her head. "How else shall I impress you?" she added with a wink.

He smiled, put his arm around her shoulders, and said softly, "You have impressed me far beyond what I believed was possible," he said. "Shall we?" And he led her out of the cottage, his hand resting possessively on the small of her back, with the two dogs on their heels.

Twenty-Three

Margaret Awbrey noticed something different about Rhodrick the moment he strode into their salon. It was his step, she thought — it seemed lighter somehow. But more than that, her dear old friend was smiling. *Smiling.* Not his usual attempt at a smile, but an ear-to-ear face-splitting smile.

He bowed and kissed the back of her hand fervently, then greeted Thomas with great warmth. Thomas peered at him closely, his gaze raking Rhodi's frame as if he tried to discern the point from which this exuberant spirit was emanating in a man who was normally stoic and dark.

"Rhodi!" Margaret exclaimed, taking him by the hand and leading him to sit beside her on the settee. "What brings you to Rhayader?"

He shrugged, but his eyes were gleaming. "The same that always brings me to Rhayader — business. Ah, but Meg, it is such a glorious day, I could not let it pass without seeing my dearest friends."

"Rhodi, really!" Margaret laughed. "What in heavens has come over you?"

He laughed and shook his head. "Nothing but a natural invigoration that comes with the changing of the seasons."

"Indeed? I've never noticed you to be quite so *invigorated* by the approach of winter."

With a polite laugh, he abruptly stood and strolled to the windows that overlooked the River Wye, his hands clasped behind his back. "The weather has been so mild of late that I'm of a mind to host a small gathering at Llanmair. A soirée, as it were. What do you think?"

Thomas, bless him, almost choked on his tea, and Margaret was so shocked by his declaration that she almost tripped over her hem in her haste to stand up. When neither of them managed to speak, Rhodi turned and glanced uncertainly at them over his shoulder. "You think it unwise?"

"No . . . *no,*" Margaret said instantly, moving forward. Her husband had yet to close his mouth, was still gaping at Rhodi. "I think it is wonderful," she said hastily. "We . . . we are only surprised, my lord. After all these years, and you've not —"

"That is quite right, Meg. After all these years of living the life of a wretched recluse, I, for once, should like to celebrate the Christmas season. It will be upon us before we know it."

"That's wonderful," Margaret said, still watching him, still half expecting him to grin and tell her he was jesting, or that he'd only meant to invite her and Thomas and the Pools, that there really was no sudden change in his demeanor.

"Will you help me?" he asked earnestly. "I admit I'm not entirely certain how to go about such things as the place settings and the flowers, and whatnot."

"Of course, Rhodi. I will help you in any way you'd like."

"Splendid," he said, and looked, Margaret thought, as if he were only a moment from floating out of his boots. "Nothing too large, mind you, Meg. Perhaps two hundred guests?"

Two hundred! She'd have to invite all of Powys to match that number! But she smiled and said, "If you like."

He grinned. "I hoped that I might rely on you, Meg. Thank you." He took up her hand, kissed it again, and with another cheerful smile, he strode to the door.

She realized he meant to leave. "Rhodi,

darling!" Margaret called after him, startled. "Where are you going?"

"I beg your pardon, but it is time I returned to Llanmair. I have quite a lot of work to do yet," he said, and with a nod of his head, he called farewell and walked out, his stride long and determined.

Margaret did not move for several moments after the door shut behind him; neither did Thomas. When at last Margaret did move, it was to her husband's side. She grabbed up his hand and sank onto the chair beside him. "What has happened?" she asked anxiously.

Thomas laughed and tenderly cupped her face. "You do not know, my love?"

"Know what?"

"Your dear friend is in love."

Margaret blinked, then reared back. "In *love?*" she cried, and burst into laughter as she stood and walked to the middle of the room. "That's absurd, Thomas! With whom?" she exclaimed, whirling around to face him.

"Whom do you think?" Thomas asked with a smile. "Miss Fairchild."

Of course she knew whom, but nonetheless, Margaret gasped and sank onto the settee, gaping at her husband. That could not *possibly* be. She could not grasp the wildly improbable, *impossible* actuality that he might have fallen in love with that young, mysterious, *wanton* — she *was* wanton, wasn't she? — woman from London.

But Thomas was smiling at her confusion, and as it began to sink in, as the events Margaret had witnessed with her own eyes began to formulate in her memory into a story, she knew it was true.

She should be happy! She wanted to rejoice for him, for no one deserved to be happy more than Rhodi, not after all he'd been through. For *years* she'd prayed for this. But as she fell back against the settee, she didn't feel happiness — she felt a foreboding like she'd never felt in her life.

Something told her this would not end happily.

That morning, when Rhodrick had ridden out, Greer had watched until she could no longer see his black cape billowing behind him any longer, then hurried to the household stores, where she rooted around until she scrounged up some cleaning rags, some lye, and some oil for wood. She filled a basket with the cleaning supplies, and then another basket with enough food for her and oatcakes and apples for Molly.

Greer carried one basket and pushed the

other with her foot into the foyer, until a horrified Ifan saw her and picked up both baskets, carrying them out to the courtyard and instructing a groomsman to secure them to Molly, who had, at Greer's request, been saddled.

When Ifan returned, she was fitting her gloves onto her hands. The butler paused in the foyer. "Shall I tell his lordship where you have gone, miss?"

Greer smiled at him and fit her bonnet on her head. "No thank you."

Ifan nodded. "And if his lordship should inquire as to your whereabouts, what shall I tell him?"

"Hmm," Greer said, pretending to think about that as she tied the bonnet beneath her chin. When she had finished, she dropped her hands and turned to look at the butler. "I suppose, sir, were I you, that I would say I do not know." With a smile, she walked to the chair where she had draped her cloak, tossed it on her shoulders, then fastened the clasp. When she was satisfied she was properly attired, she turned back to Ifan. "Good day, sir," she said, and sailed out of the foyer.

Fortunately, the snowfall of yesterday had melted enough that Greer and Molly could see the trail. And this time, she knew precisely where she was going. It almost seemed as if Molly did, too, for she reached Kendrick in an hour's time. Greer did not, however, attempt to enter the estate through the back gate as she'd done before, but marched right up to the gate to Madoc Jones's cottage and rapped loudly. When no one answered, she pushed the gate open and looked inside.

The thatch-roofed cottage, just inside the stone wall, was smaller than she recalled — no more than a single room, she'd wager. There was a well-tended kitchen garden to one side, and next to that, a plain dirt area where one rooster and three chickens were pecking.

Greer opened the small wooden gate that surrounded the cottage yard and walked inside, past the garden, kicking a pair of feeding chickens out of her path on her way to the door. She rapped loudly, then paused to listen. Through an open window, she could hear a man groan.

She rapped again.

When he still did not answer, Greer moved to the window. "Mr. Jones!" she called out.

That was met with a bit of harsh muttering in Welsh.

"Mr. Jones, if you please, it is Miss Fair-child calling!"

"Bloody hell," was the mumbled response, followed by a lot of banging about, as if Mr. Jones were slamming into the furniture and walls of the cottage in his haste to reach the door. A moment later, the small door swung open, and Mr. Madoc Jones stepped into the door frame, squinting against the sun and smelling of whiskey. Quite a *lot* of whiskey.

He propped his arm on the doorjamb, hooked the thumb of his other hand in the waist of his dirty buckskins, and glared at her. "Miss Fairchild," he drawled. "I am *certain* we agreed that ye're not allowed here without his lordship's permission."

"I beg your pardon, sir, but *we* did not agree at all. I have returned and I will not be turned away. So will you please lend me a hand?" she asked, gesturing to the gate. "I've brought some things to clean the house."

"*What* house?"

"Kendrick, of course!"

Mr. Jones blinked, then burst into a laugh that sounded as if it had been soaked in whiskey. "Why would a lady of the Quality want to clean that old house?"

"It is filthy," she said primly. "A hand,

please, Mr. Jones?"

"Now, Miss Fairchild, I cannot. Ye *know* that I cannot."

"But you can!" she said with a smile. "Really, what harm is there in cleaning an empty house? His lordship need never know."

"Why do ye want to go and clean that old thing?" he asked, eyeing her curiously.

Because of her life and who she was. Because it was the only real part of her past. "To have the satisfaction of seeing a fine home restored to its grandeur. Come along, please."

His eyes narrowed on her, and Greer was certain he meant to turn her away again. But then he suddenly dropped his arm and closed his eyes with a groan heavenward. "By the saints, ye will cost me my head, ye will," he groused.

But he shut the cottage door behind him and followed her to the gate.

Mr. Jones did more than help her carry her things to the house. He also filled a wooden bucket with water and brought it to her, then wandered around the house with her. The place was so large that it was hard to know where to begin. She decided at last to begin in what she was certain had once been the music room. There was nothing within to tell her that, but in her mind's eye, she could see the pianoforte before the set of floor-to-ceiling windows that overlooked a painfully overgrown garden.

She could see her mother playing it, too, and she wondered if perhaps she *had* seen her mother play here. "Here," she said. "I believe this was a music room."

"Looks like all the rest if ye ask me," Mr. Jones said.

"It's not," Greer assured him. "I just know." As she removed her cloak and bonnet, took off the jacket of her riding habit, and rolled up the sleeves of her shirt, Madoc Jones leaned against a wall and watched her. Greer frowned lightly at him, wishing he would go on, but he showed no sign of leaving, and in fact, as she began to scrub the mantel of the hearth, he perched himself on the windowsill.

"Never thought I'd see the day that a woman of the Quality would bend an elbow in honest work," he remarked idly.

That was because women of the Quality rarely possessed anything like an entire house all on their own. And in light of the last two days — two incredibly bewitching days — she had devised a scheme whereby she would put off her return to London. What was the point in it? Undoubtedly, she was ruined by her own actions. Where there had been hope of marrying well the day she left, now there was none.

But she might convince Rhodrick to let her take Kendrick, and live here — only an hour's ride from him.

She thought, what with winter upon them and the four thousand pounds due her, she might restore it and stay within Rhodrick's reach. Just the thought of him put a smile on her lips. It was almost laughable, she thought, that she had once feared him. She no longer feared him — she craved him.

Her imagination soared as she scrubbed. Perhaps she would marry him. *The Princess of Powys.* It sounded quite nice, really. They would use Kendrick to entertain in the summer months, as it would be more inviting than Llanmair. They would have children, wouldn't they? Children with his startling green eyes and thick black hair.

Or perhaps she would live on her own in this very grand house, just like a man, with the prince as her lover. The very idea reminded her of an illicit novel she and Phoebe had once stolen from Aunt Cassandra. They'd delighted in reading it to each other at night, their eyes growing wide, giggling uncontrollably at the suggestive passages, then rejoicing when the heroine,

Mary Anderson, persevered against all possible odds and earned herself a place in society quite by herself upon her husband's death.

Greer would be that woman. She would be the Mary Anderson of Wales, capable of taking care of herself against all possible odds. Or she would be elegant in her role as princess, known far and wide across Wales for her magnificent assemblies and balls.

"I don't know how ye go about it with such a smile," Mr. Jones said on a yawn as he studied his dirty nails. "The place is uninhabitable."

"No, Mr. Jones, you are mistaken," Greer said with cheerful assurance. "A bit of cleaning and repair, and this house shall be good as new."

Madoc Jones snorted at that.

"What do you suppose is the room upstairs just above us?" she asked him.

"What room?"

"The locked room," she said.

"Ah. That would be where Miss Yates was held, miss."

Greer instantly stopped her scrubbing and looked at him. "Held? What do you mean?"

"Don't ye know how it was that Kendrick came to be closed, then?" Mr. Jones asked, and when she could only blink in response, he grinned with delight. "Aha, no one has told ye, aye? I daresay if ye'd heard of our Miss Yates ye'd not be so keen to restore this old place."

Deep down, something twisted in Greer. "Who is Miss Yates?" she made herself ask.

"The unfortunate lover of the prince or his cousin, depending on who is telling the tale. She was locked in that room until she went mad." He shook his head. "A sad ending, it was."

"W-what happened?"

"She escaped, fell in a ravine — or jumped — and broke her neck. Some say the prince's young cousin was responsible. Some say the prince. Personally, I always thought it right odd that the prince found her as he did. She was at the bottom of a ravine far from here, and he was quite alone when he found her." He leaned in and said low, "Some say he found her only because he put her there to begin with."

"That's preposterous," Greer said, trying to imagine the man she'd made love with having anything to do with it. The same man who had saved her life only just a few short weeks ago. He could certainly have left her in a ravine, and no one ever might have found her. "Your imagination has run amuck, Mr. Jones."

"Perhaps it has, Miss Fairchild," he said. "But ye must admit, it is a bit perplexing."

It *was* perplexing, particularly as it was precisely what Percy had told her. Greer resumed her scrubbing with a vengeance.

Mr. Jones stood and stretched. "She lives here to this day."

"Who?"

"Miss Yates." He smiled when Greer paused in her work to look up at him. "I see her often. She stands in the front door, as if she's looking for someone."

A cold shiver snaked up Greer's spine.

"I don't think the lady will rest until her lover's come for her."

Now Greer frowned irritably. "Had you been drinking whiskey before you saw this apparition, Mr. Jones?" she asked skeptically.

Mr. Jones chuckled low. "Perhaps I had, miss. But when I leave ye alone in this room, ye can't be certain if it was the whiskey or a ghost, can ye now?" With a wink, he stood up and walked across the room to the door. "I'll leave ye to the cleaning, then. I've enough of me own work to do."

Greer pushed a strand of hair from her forehead with the back of her hand as she listened to his footfalls move away from her.

When she could no longer hear him, she glanced around the room. *Ghost indeed.* It was ridiculous. She would find a way to open the locked door, and that would be that. And there was, she was certain, some logical explanation to how the prince had found poor Miss Yates.

"There has to be," Greer muttered irritably. Yet she could not shake the doubts creeping into her mind. And when she heard a strange creaking on the floor above, as if someone were walking above her head, she determined she had cleaned enough for one day and quickly gathered her cloak and her things, and left the house at a rather rapid clip.

By the time she reached Mr. Jones's cottage, she was out of breath.

He was chopping wood. When he saw her, he paused in his work, propped himself up on the ax, and chuckled as she continued to march toward him, her cloak snapping behind her.

"Cleaned it all, have ye?" he asked with a grin.

"Only one room," she said breathlessly.

"Pity, that. I suspect it might have been quite nice to see it clean again."

"I am hardly defeated, Mr. Jones. I shall return on the morrow, weather permitting."

She gave him a pert nod and walked on. But when she reached the gate, she turned and looked at him. He was still standing with his weight propped on the ax, watching her.

"Mr. Jones, if you believe the prince may have had something to do with the poor woman's death, then why are you in his employ?"

"I didn't say I believed it," he said amicably. "And even if I did, I've no choice. I am paying a debt."

She must have looked as confused as she felt, for he chuckled and said, "I'm a drunkard, Miss Fairchild. Caught in the grip of demon drink, as they say. The prince gave me a place to live when most would have seen me hanged. Without him, I've got nowhere to go." He smiled and picked up the ax. "Take a bit of advice from me, miss. Keep your distance from drink." He swung his ax, splitting a log.

Greer turned away. As she walked through the gate, she heard the sound of more wood being split behind her, and felt very unsettled.

When Mr. Morris, the Downey household's butler, brought Phoebe the latest letter from Greer, she didn't bother to open it, but gathered up her cloak and bonnet and all the letters she had received from Greer and hurried across Mayfair to Middleton House, from which Ava had sent word she'd finally arrived.

In the morning room at Middleton House, Ava read them all, ending with the latest, then leaned back with a heavy sigh. "What in God's name has she gone and done, do you suppose?"

"I haven't the slightest notion, Ava, but we *must* go to her!" Phoebe insisted. "Middleton will hire a coach, will he not?"

"Of course he will," Ava said, looking at the letter again. "But the rain is dreadful this year and it will soon turn to snow. It could take some time to reach her."

"Yes, but he must send a coach at *once,* Ava," Phoebe insisted. "She is on the very *brink* of ruin!"

Ava glanced up at her younger sister and smiled weakly. "You must brace yourself, dearest, for I fear that Greer has toppled right off the brink and into the soup of ruin already."

TWENTY-FOUR

It had been years — decades, even — since Rhodrick had felt so light of being, and he could not wait to hold Greer in his arms again.

He conducted his business as if there were a fire raging at Llanmair, then made one last stop before heading out — a jeweler he had used frequently when Eira was alive.

The merchant was happy to see him, of course, as undoubtedly the vision of banknotes and gold coins danced merrily before his eyes. But when he realized Rhodrick was looking for a gift for a woman, he began to eye him curiously, asking questions, the answers to which Rhodrick knew would spread about the region faster than the plague.

"May I inquire as to the purpose of the gift, my lord?" he asked slyly. "A birthday? An anniversary of some sort?"

Rhodrick hardly spared him a glance as

he looked at the dizzying array of jewels before him, all of which seemed the same color to him. "A gift," he said.

"Perhaps if you were to tell me the lady's age —"

"There," Rhodrick said, and pointed to a ring made with a brilliant blue stone, the same color as her eyes. "What is that?"

"A water sapphire, my lord," the jeweler said as he lifted the ring from its case and handed it to him for his inspection.

It was as large as the nail on his index finger, and was encircled by small diamonds. "I'll have it," he said, handing it back to the jeweler. "Wrap it, if you will."

The jeweler put the ring in a small case. As he wrapped it in paper and ribbon, he glanced at Rhodrick from the corner of his eye. "A gift as fine as this would surely commemorate an important event, my lord."

"Mmm," Rhodrick said.

"It will certainly become a family heirloom," he said, and presented the wrapped box to Rhodrick. "How shall I word the bill of sale?"

Rhodrick looked him in the eye. "One sapphire ring," he suggested. "And you may put it to my account." He strode out of the jeweler's shop.

He rode back to Llanmair as quickly as he

could, bent over his mount with his hat pulled low over his eyes, the sapphire ring tucked securely in his pocket.

As he thundered into the courtyard, two groomsmen raced out to meet him. Rhodrick swung down, tossed the reins to one of the boys, and strode into the castle, where Ifan was waiting in the foyer.

Rhodrick swept off his hat and handed it to Ifan. "Send Miss Fairchild to me in my study."

Ifan shifted his glance downward. "Miss Fairchild is not here," he said.

Rhodrick stilled. "What? Where is she?"

"She took the young mare and left shortly after you this morning."

The euphoria that had kept Rhodrick aloft all day began to deflate. He absently pushed a hand through his hair, his mind racing. "Did she say where she was riding?"

"No, my lord; she expressly refused to say."

Refused? The doubts he'd had about her began to snake into his thoughts. He focused his attention on his gloves as he yanked them, finger by finger, from his hand. "When she returns, see to it that she is sent to my study," he said gruffly. "I shall be reviewing the accounts."

"Yes, my lord."

He took his greatcoat from his shoulders and handed it to Ifan, his hand going to the pocket of his day coat and the small package there.

Ifan bowed his response, and with Rhodrick's greatcoat slung over his arm, he quit the foyer.

Rhodrick shook his head to dislodge the doubts that suddenly sprang up in his mind like so many weeds. It was nothing to concern him, he told himself. He had lain with the woman twice, and he was not exactly a novice in the art of reading feminine wiles. He knew from experience that Greer had enjoyed their trysts as much as he.

But when Rhodrick glanced up, his gaze fell on his reflection in the mirror, and he felt a strong, choking twist of doubt.

Greer entered his study with cheeks stained pink from the cool air outside.

"Miss Fairchild," Rhodrick drawled from behind his desk. "Welcome back."

"Thank you," she said as she squatted down to greet Cain and Abel. "It was such a crisp day, I could scarcely bear to sit inside a moment longer." She glanced up at him from the corner of her eye. "I hope you don't mind."

408

"Of course not. You were not lost again, I hope."

"Not at all," she said, turning her attention to the dogs once more. "I think I am beginning to know my way around Llanmair quite well."

He could not possibly imagine how, as Llanmair comprised thousands of acres, and to his knowledge, she'd been out in the acreage only once or twice. "I thought you had a century of Welsh history to read," he said, turning his attention to the papers in front of him.

"Actually, I read quite a lot last night." She stood up and moved to one of the chairs at the hearth, bracing herself against it with her hands. She looked at him strangely, as if she were trying to sort out who he was. "I was rather surprised — the chapter dedicated to the canal building across Wales was rather fascinating."

He knew she didn't find canal building the least bit interesting. "Did you happen upon one of the canals built to bring coal to Powys in the course of your ride?" he asked idly.

"No," she said, looking at him again. "Are there canals in Powys?"

So much for learning her way about Llanmair. Rhodrick abruptly stood, his hands on his hips, and walked to the window. "If you did not see the canals, then where did you ride?"

"Here and there." She joined him at the window, her hands clasped behind her back. "In and out of the forest."

"Did you meet anyone?"

She shot him a dark look. "You do not trust me yet."

He clenched his jaw shut for a moment and thought about it. "Not entirely," he admitted.

"Who do you think I might have seen?"

"Any number of persons, I suppose. Percy, perhaps?"

"Mr. *Percy?*" she exclaimed and laughed bitterly. "I may have been taken for a fool once, but I will not be again."

He was exceedingly glad to hear her say it, yet it did nothing to relieve his anxiety about her.

She sighed. "I did not see anyone I know — how could I possibly? There are miles and miles of forest and fields with not a soul in them."

Rhodrick turned to face her. "Perhaps you encountered someone you *don't* know, then, for I cannot understand why you are so reluctant to tell me what part of my estate you have seen."

She opened her mouth to respond, then shut it, as if she couldn't quite decide what to say. She suddenly lifted her chin. "You may as well end your interrogation, my lord, for I will not answer you. As it happens, I am planning something of a surprise."

"What surprise?" he asked suspiciously.

"If I *told* you, it would no longer be a surprise, would it?" she said, and gave him a defiant smile.

Rhodrick couldn't help himself; he cupped her face and looked at her questioningly. Her lashes fluttered with his touch, but she smiled brilliantly.

Was he a fool? Had he been isolated here at Llanmair for so long that he no longer remembered how to guard his emotions? It was impossible for him to look into those blue eyes and suspect a conspiracy or that she could mean to hurt him in the end.

On the other hand, he could not possibly imagine what she might be doing to *surprise* him. But she'd surprised him once before, by arriving at Llanmair in the manner she had, in the company of Owen Percy.

He was a bloody, lovesick fool, for at that moment, he hardly cared; all he could think of was kissing her and entering her warm, moist body. And as he leaned down, touched his lips to hers, and slid his tongue into her sweet mouth, he knew that he'd lost all hope of reason.

"I have a surprise for you as well," he said.

"I *adore* surprises!" she said happily.

With a chuckle, he dropped his hand from her face and walked back to his desk, where he picked up a bank draft he'd made out earlier. He held it out to her. "Your inheritance."

"What?" Her gaze flicked to the paper, then to him. "Rhodrick!" she exclaimed, and hurled herself at him, wrapping her arms around his neck and kissing him. "But what of the letter?" she asked breathlessly.

"I don't need it," he said, meaning it sincerely. "This is yours to do with what you will."

"Oh my." Greer took the banknote from him and examined it. "I feel as if I have accomplished something quite important."

He laughed and kissed her again. And he was not fool enough to inquire as to her whereabouts again that afternoon lest he risk losing her kisses. Frankly, he quite forgot it and everything else in favor of a game of chess with her. His accounts went untouched, his correspondence lay unopened. He even sent the dogs out with Ifan just so that he might have her all to himself. He forgot the dull ache in his knee that heralded a change in the weather. He forgot everything but Greer.

That night, over supper, she entertained him greatly by reciting the facts she had learned about Wales in her short time here. And he, having pushed his earlier misgivings aside, told her about his desire to host a Christmas soirée.

Greer's smile instantly fell. "A soirée?" she echoed skeptically.

He nodded. "Wouldn't you enjoy it?"

"But . . . but what will your guests think?" she asked quietly.

"That you are my guest. Unless . . . there is a change in our acquaintance."

"You mean when I return to London," she said, frowning thoughtfully.

As if he could possibly let her go. He reached into his pocket for the package and placed it on the table between them. "I have no intention of allowing that," he said quietly, and glanced at his footmen, sending them from the room with a nod.

When the door closed behind the two men, Greer lifted her gaze to Rhodrick. "What is it?" she asked, her voice full of mistrust.

"Why don't you open it?"

She gave him a strange smile and picked it up, pulled the small bow free, and slowly unwrapped it. When she opened the box, her eyes rounded with surprise. "Oh my," she whispered as she removed it from the box. "It is . . . it's *beautiful.*"

"I hoped you would like it."

"*Like* it?" she exclaimed, looking up at him. "It's the most beautiful thing I have ever seen. But Rhodrick . . . I cannot *possibly* accept something so extravagant."

He laughed at her youthful naïveté. "I think you do not understand my intentions, darling. It's entirely my fault, for I did not speak when I ought to have done. I want to marry you, Greer. At once."

Greer recoiled from the ring, pushing it away. *"What?"*

A jolt of fear hit Rhodrick square in the chest. "What is it?" he asked, his voice remarkably calm given the roil in his gut.

"What *is* it?" she echoed with alarm. "This notion of marriage!"

"Greer! Did you truly believe I would bed you and then leave you to fend for yourself?"

"No," she said, shaking her head. "*Yes!* I mean . . . I mean that as I came to Llanmair in a less than respectable fashion, and as I have been *living* here without chaperone —"

"That matters not," he said flippantly.

"It matters quite a *lot,*" she said ada-

414

mantly, and stood up.

"I've long since stopped caring what people might say or think —"

"*I* haven't," she shot back as she began to pace. "And there is London. I *belong* in London, not some desolate castle in the middle of thousands of empty acres!" she cried frantically. "My family — my *life* — is in London!"

"You could have a fine life here," Rhodrick said gruffly.

"Yes, of course, but . . ." She suddenly groaned and covered her face with her hands. "In all honesty, I had not seriously considered marriage a *possibility* before this very moment!"

It disturbed him to know she thought him capable of taking her virtue without considering her future. It disturbed him that she was capable of giving it without considering the same. He stood up, strode to where she was, and put his hands on her arms. "Of *course* it is a possibility, and frankly, after what we have shared, there is no *other* possibility. Do you think me so vile as to compromise you completely and leave you to suffer the consequences?"

She flinched and moved away without answering him. When she refused to meet his eye, Rhodrick realized that he was, indeed, a colossal fool. He'd allowed himself to fall in love with this woman when he should have suspected — he should have *known* — that she would not want to enter into an arrangement for all eternity with a man like him. Why should she? She was young and beautiful and vibrant —

"Please try and understand me," she said, her voice full of distress. "I am touched by your offer, but I am . . . I am wholly unprepared," she said nervously, looking a bit like a caged animal. "I did not think . . ." Whatever she might have said, she thought the better of it, and looked up at him with rueful eyes. "I appreciate your concern for what is left of my virtue, but I am not prepared to make a decision as great as . . . as *this*," she said, gesturing to the ring on the table.

"I beg your pardon," he said tightly, "but what did *you* think to do?"

"I . . . it's rather complicated."

Complicated? *Dear God.* He struggled to maintain his composure. "Please do me the courtesy of telling me the truth, Greer. Is there another man to whom you have pledged your affection?"

With a hiss of breath she glowered at him. "I suppose you mean Mr. Percy?"

He shrugged.

"It seems rather hard for you to believe my truthful declarations, but I shall tell you again, *truthfully,* that there is no gentleman waiting in London for my hand, and I do not now, nor have I ever, held any particular affection for Mr. Percy!"

Her indignation had no effect on him. "Then what could *possibly* be your objection to a match with me? Is my fortune not big enough? My title not lofty enough? My face not handsome enough?"

"You insult me," she said, her voice dangerously low. "I don't know how I can possibly make you understand this, but for these weeks I have been at Llanmair, I have been living a dream, playing at princess, pretending in a fairy tale. But it is not *real.* My life is in London, my *cousins* are in London. Your life is here, and I do not believe our lives were ever meant to intersect."

She had slain him. He surely lay open and bleeding, for it felt no less painful. Rhodrick couldn't say what he'd expected, but certainly it had not been this. He looked at the ring lying on the table, that grand gesture of his esteem for a woman who, not surprisingly, could not return his affections.

"But our lives have intersected, and rather strikingly so," he said simply, but his heart was screaming that this could not be happening, because he *loved* her, he didn't care how they had met, he had fallen headlong in love with her, and now his heart was bleeding with it.

An uncomfortable silence filled the room. "It has been a rather long day," he said, and picked up the box, returned it to his pocket, then bowed. "Good night," he said, his voice damnably soft.

She seemed somewhat taken aback, as if she didn't know what to say or do. She took two steps forward and put her hand on his arm.

It took all the strength Rhodrick had to keep from flinching at the feel of her slender hand on his arm. "Rhodrick, please try to understand." She looked at him with the luminous blue eyes that he adored. He tried to read them, tried to understand what was on her mind, but he realized with a twinge of sorrow that perhaps he really did not know Miss Fairchild at all. "I do understand, very clearly." He removed her hand and quit the room.

Twenty-Five

As Rhodrick disappeared into his study with his hounds, Greer retreated to her suite with many conflicting thoughts whirling in her head and many emotions spinning with sickening speed in her gut.

She'd been shocked by his offer of marriage, astounded, appalled and frightened by it. There had been no understanding between them, no time for her to consider what she was doing, and from the moment she had seen the ring and understood his intentions, she had not been able to collect her thoughts very well at all.

Now, in the quiet of her suite, she tried hopelessly to sort out her thoughts and feelings.

She paced, fingering the charm at her neck. She was moved and rather relieved that he thought to marry her, of *course* she was — and part of her relished the idea of being a princess — but in *London.* Not

Wales. Near her cousins, so that their children could grow up together, near a large and vibrant society. Not here in this lonely part of the world.

Then again, she had become rather attached to the idea of making her own way, of establishing herself as mistress of Kendrick somehow, now that she had the means to do it, and living the life few women dared to even dream. There was a powerful allure to charting her destiny. She understood what a gift the possibility was, particularly after her stepuncle, Lord Downey, had, in the space of one afternoon, knocked her and her cousins quite off their feet by claiming their inheritance and announcing he would see them married as soon as was possible.

On that day, Greer had understood all too keenly that as women they really had nothing on which to stand but the esteem men held for them. It was a precarious place, and as an orphan, with her guardian aunt gone, she existed day to day on the merest shred of kindness extended to her.

When she might live her life as *she* deemed fit, it was impossible to simply turn and walk away, to give herself up to a man she scarcely knew. She would be dishonest if she didn't acknowledge that what Mr. Jones had told her had given her pause.

Yet still, with all her heart, she ached for him. She'd made him believe she didn't love him. She may have been surprised by his offer, but it was clear that he had been equally surprised by her response, and perhaps even a bit unhinged.

She did love him. Whatever her thinking about her future, she loved him.

She glanced at the clock on her mantel. It was half past midnight — the servants had long retired and she could make her way to his study without being detected. She just wanted to talk, to explain her misgivings.

She donned a dressing gown over her nightgown and belted it tightly, then stepped into the slippers Mrs. Bowen had given her. She left her hair hanging down her back.

Having been around the castle long enough to know her way, she crept along in the dark. Her fingers trailed along the stone wall, and at certain intervals, she was aided by a bit of moonlight streaming in through windows.

Unfortunately, the prince was not in his study. The door stood open, the hearth almost cold. Greer debated going to his bedchamber. It was astounding, really, to think of how far and how rapidly she had fallen from virtue. From almost the moment she had stepped foot in that coach with

Mrs. Smithington, she had stepped off some invisible cliff, tumbling past everything she'd been taught about ladies and decency and morals to fall into a pit of degeneracy. But this . . . *this* had to be the worst yet. She was contemplating stealing into a man's room with the full intention of seducing him.

Then again, she reasoned, she had fallen so far that there hardly seemed any point in making a distinction now.

So she continued on, carefully making her way to the other side of the castle, moving slowly in those corridors she didn't know as well, but managing to reach his suite of rooms without the slightest bit of trouble. Nevertheless, she felt a moment of frantic indecision at his threshold.

"Bloody late for this bit of conscience," she whispered beneath her breath, and carefully, slowly, she opened the door and stepped across the threshold into a room that was, fortunately, somewhat dimly illuminated by the embers of a dying fire. The appointments in the room, not surprisingly, were rather austere: one fine leather chair and ottoman, a single table, and scarcely anything else. Greer walked across the thick carpet, pausing to glance at the books on the small table near the chair — a mixture of French and Welsh — on her way to the next door.

That door led to another room that was so dark that she had to feel her way along the wall. She was deadly quiet save for stubbing her toe on the door at the opposite end of the room and letting a tiny mewl of painful surprise escape her. But she quickly recovered, and with both hands, searched until she found the doorknob chest-high. Drawing a breath, she quietly opened it a crack.

She paused there, straining to listen. The fire was still burning, and while she could not see his bed, she realized she could hear his breathing. With a bit more confidence, she stepped inside the room — but was instantly shoved up against the wall, her body pinned by his arms and legs, his hand over her mouth.

She could smell the whiskey, could see it in the way he blinked his eyes, as if trying to clear the apparition before him. His shirt was open at the collar, the sleeves undone at the cuffs. His hair, thick and long, looked as if he'd dragged his hands through it to push it away from his eyes. His face sported the shadow of a beard, and a pained look circled his eyes.

When he at last realized it was her, he

slowly eased up, pushing away from the wall and her, turning his back on her. After a moment, he turned halfway toward her as he tried to tuck his shirt into his breeches. He got the shirt only partially tucked in before he gave up and faced her fully.

Greer was reminded of the first night she'd met him, the night he'd kissed her, and how dark and predatory he had looked then.

He looked that way now, and she could not have been more aroused.

With a strangled cry, she lost her resolve and suddenly flung herself at him, into his arms, groping for him, desperate to feel the strength and comforting warmth of his body.

Rhodrick responded by catching her in his arms and pressing her back against the wall as he pressed his mouth hard against hers. She could taste the whiskey on his breath, could feel the wild pulse of his heart coursing through him as he cradled her jaw. She felt fragile in his arms, felt as if she could shatter at any moment with remorse and euphoria. But desire was sweeping her along on another tide and into his body.

He dragged his mouth across her cheek to her hair, his breath heavy in her ear as he grabbed a fistful of her hair. " 'Rwy'n

dy garu di. Love me, Greer," he whispered
harshly.

The desperate want in his voice made her
heart flail. He didn't have to ask — she *did*
love him, fiercely and deeply, and still it was
not enough, it could never be enough. She
buried her face in his collar, breathing his
scent, as he grabbed her dressing gown and
roughly tore it open.

"Love me," he said again, as he pushed
her against the wall and moved down her
body, lithe and powerful. With a sob, she
threw her head back against the wall as his
mouth closed over the thin fabric of her
nightgown, around the tip of her breast. She
grabbed his shoulders, kneading them as he
continued his trek down, his mouth dragging over her nightgown as he descended to
his knees. His mouth sought her sex through
the fabric of her gown as his hand sought
the hem, pushing up her cotton gown in
thick folds until he could close his mouth
around her flesh.

Greer whimpered with delirious pleasure
as he pushed her legs apart and thrust his
tongue between the folds of her sex, circling
around the hard crest of her need, sucking
and nibbling and swirling around until she
thought she would go mad. She pressed
against him, held aloft by her hands on his

head and shoulders and the strength of his arms.

But just when she felt herself plummeting to release, he rose up, picked her up so that her body hung the length of his, and twirled around with her, depositing her just behind the chair before the hearth. He grabbed her face between his hands and kissed her passionately, then dropped one hand to his trousers. When he had freed himself — she could feel the hot length of him through her gown — he kissed her eyes, her forehead, her mouth, and roughly turned her around, so that she was braced against the back of the chair.

He pulled up her gown, pushed his thigh between her legs, and snaked his hands around her body, one on her breast, one on her sex, his fingers sliding in the place he'd left slick and hot. She could scarcely breathe; she turned her head toward his, grinding her body against his hand.

He kneaded her breast, his fingers squeezing the nipple as his mouth devoured her neck. He pressed his hardness against her, spreading her thighs open with his, and then guiding himself into her from behind, pushing into her with a low cry. As he began to move inside her, he stroked her. Greer instinctively arched against him, shamelessly

426

indulging in the flaming sensation that seeped through her veins and into her groin.

As his strokes grew more frantic, both inside her and on her, her fever turned rabid. She could feel herself moving as wildly against his hand and his body as he moved inside her, allowing herself the freedom to *feel* him, to submerge herself entirely in the pleasure he was giving her.

They moved with such wild abandon that it felt almost animalistic — she burned in every place he touched her, and when he put his hand at her nape and urged her to bend at the waist, she was possessed by unimaginable desire, obsessed with the need to feel him hard and deep within her.

She braced against the chair and met each of his thrusts with a surprising strength of her own. He bent over her, his mouth in her hair and on her neck, his fingers moving magically against her flesh.

"*Bloody hell,* I have wanted you like this," he whispered hoarsely. "I've wanted to take you like this, to have you feel me like this."

Greer panted with pleasure; her body was raging now, wanting the release he sought to give her. This was nothing she'd ever dreamed a joining could be — it hardly mattered what had gone on between them, for it had all been vanquished by his open and unbound passion for her.

"Tell me you want it, too," he said breathlessly. "Tell me you want *me*."

"I want it," she said huskily. "I want *you*, Rhodrick."

He made a low, animal-like sound and the conflagration inside her suddenly erupted. She cried out, soaring and foundering all at once. He cried out, too, his groan dark and deep as he thrust into her once more, his body shuddering with the strength of his release.

With his forehead on her shoulder, he snaked his hand around her waist, anchoring her to him as they both fought to catch their breath. When his body began to slide away from hers, he moved slightly, dislodging himself, then wordlessly turned her around and picked her up in his arms, carrying her with his odd gait to his bed.

He crawled in beside her, spooning her, his hold ironclad, as if he feared she would leave him while he slept.

Greer closed her eyes and dreamily relived every extraordinary moment, her life held at bay for a time, the shadow of reality held at arm's length by the warmth of his body.

She had all but drifted to sleep when she felt his hand on her head, brushing her hair from her temple. "I love you, you know," he said, his voice low and hoarse with emotion. "I have loved you always."

She opened her eyes, staring into dark space as the gravity of those words filtered into the sated fog on her brain.

It was minutes later — almost a half hour later, perhaps, when his breathing had gone deeper with his sleep — that she carefully rolled over, facing him. *"I love you, too,"* she whispered faintly.

TWENTY-SIX

Rhodrick woke Greer well before dawn, bundled her up, and escorted her back to her room. Greer, as beautiful when she was sleepily cross as she was when she'd had a good night's sleep, did not want to go. But Rhodrick insisted — he'd not have the servants gossiping about her any worse than he suspected they already were.

After he watched her stumble into her bedchamber, wrapped in one of his flannel dressing gowns, her hair wild about her shoulders, he shut the door and leaned against the wall for a moment.

They'd made heart-stopping love, and Rhodrick felt as if a shackle around his heart and mind had been broken, as if he had burst through some invisible barrier to freedom.

The minx simply had no idea of the power she held over him — and it was indeed a palpable power. In years past, the sight of a woman's body, the scent of her hair or her sex, or a whispered word of encouragement had always been enough to engage him completely. With Eira, he'd been too fearful of hurting her or alarming her to let himself enjoy her completely. He had not, until now, until Greer, understood how explosive making love could be with a woman he loved. He had not known that it had the power to draw the very essence of him all the way from the curl of his toes and release it into the heavens. He had not begun to fathom how his heart could be as much a part of the act as his body.

And last night, as he had watched her sleeping, he vowed to himself that he would never know lovemaking any other way but this. To engage in sexual intercourse without these extraordinary feelings now seemed to him to be a rather mean substitute for true pleasure.

Rhodrick made his way back to his room and his bed. Lying on the linens that smelled of her and their lovemaking, he closed his eyes, his mind's eye full of the image of their joining. But as he drifted to sleep, Greer's image faded and he was at Kendrick once more.

The house had fallen into disrepair; there were cracks in the mortar and the roof tiles were crumbling. The woman who haunted him stood at the door, beckoning him forward. Rhodrick's blood ran cold — he tried to turn and leave, but the next thing he knew, he was in the woods again, just like he'd been several years ago, following behind a dead woman, just as he had years ago. But this time, when he reached the end of the path, it was Greer he found lying lifeless.

The dream vaulted him awake. He was sweating profusely and it took him several moments to regain his composure. What in God's name would bring that ghost to him again after all this time? He feared now — as he had then — that the recurring dreams of her signaled his descent down a path of madness.

Lulu woke Greer far too early the next morning with a cup of hot chocolate. She looked curiously at Greer's hair, but then bustled off to tend the fire at the hearth.

Greer put her hand to her head, imagining the sight of it after last night. She sat up, feeling a familiar soreness in her body, and glanced sidelong at Lulu, wondering if she, along with all the servants, suspected Greer was now the master's mistress.

If she did, she gave no sign of it as she

tidied up the room.

"Shall I help you dress?" she asked cheerfully as Greer sipped her hot chocolate.

"I, ah . . . I don't know what I shall do today," Greer said uncertainly.

"I'd advise you to dress warmly, miss. Cook feels snow in her bones, and they say she's not been wrong once."

"Oh," Greer said, her brows rising with surprise. "Far be it from me to ignore her bones. The dark gray wool, then, Lulu."

"Shall you breakfast with his lordship?" Lulu asked.

Greer stilled, her cup almost to her mouth. "Did . . . did he ask for my company?"

Did she imagine it or did Lulu give her a look? "No, miss, not that I am aware."

They knew. The entire staff knew how the relationship between her and the prince had changed these last few days. That made a decision imperative. She was silently debating her options when a knock was heard at the door. Lulu went to answer it, and returned a moment later with a note.

"Demetrius, the footman, miss," Lulu said. "He's brought a message from the prince. He asks that you join him and Mrs. Awbrey for luncheon today."

Oh really, *must* she? There was no time for luncheons! If Cook's bones were to be trusted, she needed the day at Kendrick before it became impossible for her to travel the six miles there. But she managed a smile in spite of her disappointment. "Of course," she said.

Margaret Awbrey knew snow was coming the moment she saw Rhodi walk out of the main castle door to greet her — his limp was pronounced and he had trouble hiding it.

"Meg, a lovely surprise," he said as he helped her down from the coach. "I was pleased to receive your note this morning. I had not expected to see you again so soon."

"I know very well you hadn't, but since your visit yesterday, I've been positively frantic about your soirée, sir," she said, linking her arm through his. "Do you realize that in order to do it justice, we must begin planning straightaway?"

"I confess I did not," he said with a brotherly smile.

"It is fortunate you have me about, then, isn't it?" she asked with a wink. "Will Miss Fairchild join us?"

He smiled warmly at the mention of her name. "I believe so," he said, and covered Margaret's hand with his.

Rhodrick escorted her to the main salon,

and as they entered, Margaret was pleased to see Miss Fairchild. She was waiting for them, looking quietly beautiful in a gray wool gown, exquisitely made and simply adorned. Miss Fairchild was the sort of woman, Margaret thought, who did not strike one as a great beauty upon first glance, but upon closer acquaintance, her beauty and grace were undeniable. She could easily picture Miss Fairchild as mistress of this house.

Miss Fairchild smiled and curtsied — as did Margaret — who stole a glimpse of Rhodi.

Thomas was right, of course. To the casual observer, Rhodi looked as commanding and princely as he ever did, quite unfazed by the company of two women. But *she,* his dearest friend, could detect a different energy about him. He reminded her of a cat waiting to pounce, his eyes surreptitiously following Miss Fairchild as she moved in the room.

Even more telling was the way he slowly clenched and unclenched his left hand at his side, giving off the impression that he ached to touch her.

Their talk turned to the soirée. Miss Fairchild mentioned a Christmas soirée she had attended in London that interested

Margaret, and as the two of them began to speak more animatedly about it, Rhodi removed himself with the excuse of having some correspondence that could not wait another day. As he mentioned it, he glanced at Miss Fairchild and exchanged a look so intimate that Margaret felt compelled to look away.

When the door had closed behind Rhodi, Miss Fairchild cast a rather self-conscious smile at Margaret.

"Please do forgive my unexpected call today, Miss Fairchild," Margaret said, "but Rhodi and I have never stood on formality."

"I am pleased to see you, Mrs. Awbrey," she said graciously.

"He's so good, our Rhodi," Margaret continued, watching the younger woman. "Such a dear heart."

She detected a bit of a blush in Miss Fairchild. "He has been very kind," she said. "I fear I would not have been as kind were our situations reversed."

"Oh my," Margaret replied with a laugh. "I daresay there was a time Rhodi might not have been as kind . . . but he has suffered far more than most through the years, and it has softened him."

That certainly gained Miss Fairchild's attention. "What . . . if I may be so bold as to inquire . . . has the prince suffered?"

"Well," Margaret said, settling back, comfortable in her role of Rhodi's confidante. "Certainly the untimely death of his wife, Eira, and their newborn daughter. And that awful riding accident would have left a lesser man lame. I am certain you have noticed his limp?"

"Once or twice," Miss Fairchild admitted.

Margaret nodded and looked at her hands again. "And his looks, of course, which I believe have been hardened by the unkind words of others. Really, some of the things said of him are unconscionable. But I've always believed that if people knew the man beneath the skin, they'd see him very differently," she said with a tinge of bitterness.

"His *looks?*" Miss Fairchild said uncertainly.

Surprised, Margaret looked up and stared at the young woman, trying to detect artifice in her, but she could not. Miss Fairchild seemed genuinely surprised by what Margaret had said.

"He is rather plain in his looks," Margaret said. "His sister is very handsome and she received all the attention when they were children. Rhodi was big and plain and he was teased mercilessly. They used to call him Goliath." At Miss Fairchild's blank look, Margaret frowned. "Surely you have noticed the scar?" she asked, touching her face in the place Rhodi's scar coursed his face.

"Of course," Miss Fairchild said, frowning slightly. "But it is merely a mark. I grant you, he is not handsome in the way men are thought to be handsome in London, but neither is he homely. And he possesses the most arresting pair of green eyes I've ever seen on a man."

Margaret was so taken aback she did not know what to say.

"He seems to me to be comely in a rough sort of way," Miss Fairchild said, her dark brows furrowing in thought. "There is a word," she muttered, tapping the arm of the chair on which she sat. "Ah, yes. *Virile,*" she said, brightening with the thought. "That's it."

Something inside Margaret warmed as if she'd swallowed something hot. It was little wonder Rhodi loved this woman. Yet why could she not seem to shake the feeling of doom?

Nevertheless, she smiled. "Others have not been as generous as you, Miss Fairchild. His mean looks, coupled with a bit of local nastiness, has made him a bit of a recluse in the last five years."

"Nastiness?"

Margaret debated telling her the ugliness Owen Percy had visited on Llanmair but thought the wiser of it. It was too vile to be repeated, certainly, and Rhodi felt so strongly about it. With a smile, she shook her head. "I am sure the prince will tell you in due time."

But Miss Fairchild suddenly sat up and leaned forward, looking at Margaret with intense blue eyes. "Will you confide in me, Mrs. Awbrey? Has it something to do with Kendrick?"

Margaret gasped softly with astonishment. "How do you know that?"

"I don't," Miss Fairchild said quickly, easing back a bit. "I have guessed from the things he has said."

"I pray you, don't mention it to him," Margaret said hastily. "It is not something any of us mentions," she added, and could not entirely suppress a shudder at the memory.

Rhodi had never really overcome his guilt about the girl's death and the length of time it took to find her. When they did at last discover her body, it had been half eaten by animals. Rhodi believed, of course, because he was an honorable man, that he might have prevented it somehow, might have discerned what evil was in Owen's mind.

But if Rhodi was meant to bear some of the guilt, then all of Powys might have shared it with him, for everyone knew the sort of man Owen Percy had turned out to be. And while no one could ever prove what happened to Morwena Yates — whether she'd met her early demise due to madness or maliciousness — the disgruntled sorts on the wrong side of Rhodi's adjudications always cast aspersions on the prince's actions that awful week.

Miss Fairchild was watching her closely. "I don't understand."

"Miss Fairchild, if I may be quite frank," Margaret said carefully, "it is not something that could *ever* be discussed in polite society."

Whether or not Miss Fairchild believed it, she did not question Margaret further. But Margaret noticed that she grew more subdued as their conversation reverted back to the soirée. She nodded and commented politely when it was appropriate, but she no longer seemed particularly engaged, as if her mind had wandered elsewhere.

Once again, Margaret felt the cold shiver of doom sweep over her.

TWENTY-SEVEN

The luncheon seemed interminable to Greer — she could scarcely bear to sit and listen politely as Mrs. Awbrey suggested what Rhodrick might do for the soirée he was determined to host.

She tried to listen, but her mind was occupied elsewhere: Kendrick. It was like an enormous beast sitting quietly in the corner of the room, its secrets swirling about them as they dined.

But indeed it did exist, in a forest clearing not six miles from here, so large that it could not possibly be missed, and too wicked for anyone to acknowledge outright.

Greer was beside herself with curiosity, wanting to know exactly what had happened there, what Rhodrick could not bear to be reminded of. She thought about what she'd been told both by Percy and Mr. Jones, and about the wretched, horrible things that

Mrs. Awbrey's comments had seemed to allude to.

She felt ill with doubt, unable to comprehend how easily she ignored her first chilling instincts about him and then fallen so completely in love with him. But how could she have been so wrong? Could a man who made love as passionately as he have taken the life of another?

Passion. She was suddenly reminded of a remark Aunt Cassandra had made once about the earl of Plymouth, who had, unfortunately and rather publicly, struck his wife. It had surprised many, for the earl was a passionate man and everyone knew of his adoration for his wife.

It had *not* surprised Aunt Cassandra, however, who'd said, "A passionate man is as passionate in his anger as he is in his bed. I don't know why anyone should be surprised."

Perhaps Greer had been blinded by the prince's passion for her, for what did she *truly* know about him other than that he had captured her imagination from the moment she'd laid eyes on him? His presence that day, so fierce and predatory, had stirred fear in her, but it had stirred something else, too, something raw and primal. Their first few meetings had been frightening, but she

442

had been drawn in, seduced by the mystery of him.

And now that she'd come to know him more intimately than any other man she'd ever known, it seemed as if she hardly knew him at all.

She had to go to Kendrick today. She wasn't really sure how Kendrick would answer her questions, but she felt almost as if something were pulling her there. She had to be in that house, to *feel* that house — but first she was forced to suffer an interminable luncheon, throughout which Rhodrick said little more than was absolutely necessary. While Mrs. Awbrey talked, his gaze never seemed to leave Greer for more than a moment.

When, at long last, Mrs. Awbrey had taken her leave, Rhodrick and Greer had retreated wordlessly to the salon. Once inside, when he had dismissed a footman and shut the door behind him, he turned and smiled, his gaze sweeping hungrily over her body.

But before he could speak, before he could take her in his arms, she blurted, "I have a secret."

His expression changed. One brow arched above a slow smile. "I am intrigued. What is your secret?"

Her smile, however, had faded. She extended her hand and said, "Will you walk with me?"

He glanced at her hand, then lifted his gaze to her eyes. His smile had gone, too — he understood something had changed. "I suppose you intend to tell me that you're leaving soon. Or perhaps you mean to tell me where it is you go when you leave this house. Whatever you mean to say, the trepidation in your eyes suggests that you do not expect me to like it."

Greer smiled tremulously. "If you will walk with me, I will show you —"

"Walk where?"

For a moment, she feared she would lose her courage, would succumb to Mrs. Awbrey's warnings. But she could not hide so easily. Something *had* changed inside her. "I've been to Kendrick," she said, surprising herself.

His demeanor changed at once; she had the distinct impression he was struggling to keep from exploding. "And how is it," he said icily, "that you have been to Kendrick?"

"On horseback," she said uncertainly. "I . . . I saw it the day I tried to leave Llanmair, and I remembered where it was."

His reaction could not have been swifter or more volatile. He suddenly turned, swiping angrily at a chair and sending it teetering on two legs before falling to the floor in a loud crash. With his hands on his hips, he let loose a string of Welsh, then glared at the window for a moment, his shoulders lifting with each deep breath. When he had calmed himself enough to speak, he turned to face her.

His eyes were blazing. "Please tell me that I have misunderstood you, Greer, for I do not think I can abide any other answer."

She felt the first crack in her resolve. "You said I might go wherever I pleased, did you not?"

"Anywhere but Kendrick," he snapped. "*That* I expressly forbid. I have forbidden it to everyone in this county!" he thundered. "The gate is *locked,* madam! There is only one possible way you might have gone through a locked gate!"

"You mustn't blame Mr. Jones," Greer said hastily.

"Jones?" he roared.

She instinctively moved behind the chair he had hit, picking it up and putting it between them. "Why are you so angry? It's an empty house!" she said, her voice belying her fear. "Let me show you something, Rhodrick —"

"There is nothing you can show me that will ever induce me to —"

"Please," she interjected. "I give you my word I have legitimate reasons for needing to see it."

He closed his mouth, but his eyes narrowed suspiciously. "A *legitimate* reason?" he said acidly. "All right. Show me your legitimate reason."

"It is not what you think," she insisted, then nodded her head at the door.

"Show me," he said, and gestured for her to precede him through the door. Without a word, Greer turned and walked briskly out of the salon and into the main corridor. Rhodrick was instantly beside her, and for once did not bother to hide his limp. She took him down the servants' stairway into a narrow corridor that twisted and turned its way to another larger corridor. From there, she led him up to the main floor and the portrait gallery.

"In here," she said, and pushed open the oak doors of the gallery. As they crossed the threshold, she half walked, half ran to the painting of the picnic and whirled around to him.

Rhodrick remained at the door, his arms folded over his chest, his expression terribly dark.

Greer pointed at the painting. "This was where my mother was born. That's her in the painting. You can see a resemblance to this hand portrait I have kept," she said, removing it from her pocket and holding it out to him.

He strode forward, taking the small portrait from her.

"And Mrs. Bowen confirmed that she is indeed Alis Bronwyn Vaughan," Greer added.

Whatever she might have expected, she did not expect to see the color drain from his face. He gaped at her, then shook his head. "I grant you, I have been a fool, Greer, but do not make the mistake of thinking me so great a fool as to believe your fraud."

"This is no fraud! It . . . it is too fantastic to believe, I know, but there she is!" she cried, pointing to the tiny portrait and then the painting on the wall.

Rhodrick's entire body convulsed, and he was suddenly moving forward, his eyes on the painting.

"Look," Greer said desperately. "Remember this?" she said, holding up the small charm she wore around her neck. He glanced at her necklace, then at the painting. "You told me it was Welsh, and now I see it here!" she said, pointing wildly to the painting. "My mother is wearing it!"

Rhodrick peered at the painting. "It is a common amulet," he said. "Many women have them."

"My mother left this to me. Aunt Cassandra gave it to me when I turned sixteen."

Rhodrick lowered his gaze, closed his eyes, and braced himself against the wall, as if he'd suddenly been struck by a pain. He muttered something in Welsh, then looked at Greer, his expression gone from angry to ill. He stared at her, myriad emotions flashing through his eyes. He looked horrified by her.

"Who *are* you?" he demanded at last. "What sort of bloody game are you playing?"

"I think a better question is who are *you?*" she retorted, her voice trembling with rage and *such* regret. "Why do you forbid everyone from Kendrick? What secret do you hide there?"

"You don't understand," he said, his tone deadly.

"I do! I know what happened, what you seek to hide!"

"What in God's name are you talking about?" he roared, his expression turning black. "Is this another of Percy's lies?" He suddenly surged forward and caught her by the arm. Greer shrieked with fear, but he yanked her against his body before she could react. "Are you capable of understanding the truth when you hear it? For if you are, then you will see Kendrick as *I* have seen it. But be forewarned, madam — if you want the truth, you will have *all* of it."

Greer felt as if she were choking — she could not seem to find her breath, much less her voice. Fear had taken its place — wild, consuming fear.

But he gave her no quarter. With his hand gripping her arm tightly, he dragged her from the gallery, marching her along with surprising strength and speed for a man limping as badly as he was.

In the foyer, he shouted for the horses to be saddled at once, sent a frightened chambermaid running for Greer's cloak, and ignored Ifan when he asked, in a voice full of alarm, if he could be of any service.

It seemed forever before the horses were brought around, and during that time, the prince did not soften a moment. His jaw bulged with the force with which he clenched his teeth, and his breathing was hard. The moment the horses were brought into the courtyard, he jerked Greer along with him. He ignored the young stable boy who had placed a mounting block alongside Molly, and lifted Greer to the saddle himself, tossing her up in spite of her protests.

He mounted his horse with the same speed, then barked an order in Welsh. A stable boy with eyes as wide as moons grabbed the reins of her mount and handed them to him.

Without a word, without so much as a glance at Greer, he spurred his horse on. Molly neighed her displeasure, but she broke into a gallop behind Cadfael.

Greer fought to stay in the saddle; Rhodrick rode recklessly through the forest without a care for her safety or his. He led her down an overgrown trail she had missed previously, but he was not deterred in the least — he was merciless in his desire to reach Kendrick.

At Kendrick, he dismounted in one fluid movement and was striding toward her in his strange gait before Greer could peel her fingers from the pommel. He brought her down in such a manner that her body scraped against his, then took her elbow in his iron grip and pushed her toward the gate, which he kicked open with such force that it banged back against the stone wall.

After he pushed Greer through it, he let go of her and strode on to Mr. Jones's cottage.

"Rhodrick, do not harm him!" Greer

shouted, running after him.

But Rhodrick scarcely heard her — he scarcely heard anything but the roaring in his head, the events of that ignoble week so long ago crowding his thoughts and dredging up memories of sights and sounds and smells he'd long since buried, not to be resurrected. *Alis Bronwyn.* How could he have missed the resemblance? He'd seen Alis Bronwyn only twice after she'd grown, when she'd come back to Kendrick to visit her uncle. She had grown into a dark-haired beauty like her daughter, and while Rhodrick knew she'd married, he hadn't remembered she'd married a Vaughan until that moment in the gallery.

He feared he might kill Jones. He had saved him from jail, had given him refuge and a simple job instead of hanging him as most had wanted. Rhodrick had seen something good in him, something that his terrifying attachment to drink had almost drowned.

This was his thanks for having saved him? He couldn't stop one woman from entering that wretched house?

Jones was dead asleep, of course, lying on a dirty mattress next to a jug tipped over on its side. The place reeked of cheap whiskey. Rhodrick kicked the bottom of Jones's feet

— three times before the man was roused — then grabbed him by his dirty collar and hauled him up. "I told you no one was to enter the house," he said in Welsh.

Jones's eyes went wide. "I did not, milord! On me life, I did not!"

"Then Miss Fairchild is a liar, is that it?" He could see from the expression of fear that passed over Jones's eyes that the man was lying, and it was all the excuse Rhodrick needed to haul him out of the cottage, tossing him onto the ground in the midst of his chickens, sending the lot of them flapping around and squawking. Jones rolled onto his knees, managed to push himself up. "Hear me out, milord," he begged in Welsh.

"There is nothing to hear!" Rhodrick roared. "The one thing I asked you is to keep this house closed! Is it so much to ask that she be allowed to rest in peace?"

Jones scrambled to his feet and shifted his gaze to Greer. "I beg ye, miss," he cried imploringly in English. "Tell his lordship ye gave me no choice!"

"I didn't," Greer said frantically, the abject fear in her eyes piercing Rhodrick's heart clean through. "He told me I was forbidden to enter Kendrick, but I went on. There was nothing the poor man could do to stop me short of physical force."

452

"Why?" Rhodrick bellowed heavenward in an explosion of frustration as the bleary-eyed Mr. Jones stepped out from between them, watching them both warily. "Why are you so determined in this? It is time for the truth, Greer. Is this another of Percy's schemes? Does he seek to defile this house again?"

Her expression turned furious. "For God's sake, it has nothing to do with Mr. Percy!" she cried angrily. "I *told* you! This," she said, gesturing wildly to the house, "is where my mother was born. Where she *lived!* I have nothing of her, nothing but a few trinkets, save this house!"

If by hook or by crook Percy had put her up to this, the wench was about to discover the extent of Percy's depravity. Rhodrick closed the distance between them and grabbed her arm. "I will show you the house you hold so dear," he said, yanking her along at a clip. "And I will tell you how Mr. Percy has ruined it for all time. You should steel yourself, madam, for I assure you, you will not like the tale."

"I think it is *you* who does not like the tale, sir," she said angrily, trying to pull her arm from his grip. "You cannot *bear* that the truth be known. You cannot bear that *I* know the truth!"

453

"You are naïve," he said heatedly. "You know *nothing* of the truth."

"I don't know how you can face it," she said breathlessly as they reached the steps leading up to the entry.

"Hush," he said harshly, and pushed her up the steps. "Do you honestly believe that Owen Percy would tell you the truth? How can you possibly believe he is anything but a liar and a profligate after what he has done to *you?*"

Greer recoiled at the vehement way he said it; but he pulled her into the house, thankful that no ghosts, no Alis Bronwyn, had come to meet him. The realization emboldened him, and he marched her to the stairs that led up to the room that had remained locked for eight years.

"Pray tell, what incredible fiction has Percy told you, precisely?" he asked as Greer struggled to keep up. When she did not answer right away he whipped around. *"What did he tell you?"* he roared.

Greer yanked her arm free of his grip. "That you compromised the daughter of a solicitor from Rhayader," she said coldly, rubbing her arm. "And when you had ruined her completely, you tossed her aside like so much garbage."

"He is a master at creating tales," Rhodrick said with a snort of disgust. "What else?"

"That soon after you refused her, the poor girl went missing."

"The bloody bastard," Rhodrick muttered as they reached the room. He'd never known a blacker soul than Percy's. There had been something quite unpleasant about him even as a young boy. "Go on," he said roughly.

"He said . . ." Her voice was breaking. "He said that she was never seen alive again."

"And how does he implicate me in her disappearance, other than to *say* I caused it?"

"When she was nowhere to be found," she said, her voice trembling, "he said that only you knew where to find her. In all the acres at Llanmair, only *you* knew."

He paused at the locked door and turned to look at Greer, the woman with whom he had fallen desperately in love, and cringed inwardly at the look in her eyes. He despised her for it. He abhorred that she had given herself to him if she could believe this of him.

"Is that all?" he asked calmly, his heart having shut down, his emotions having disintegrated into blackness.

She swallowed. "He said that all of Powys

believes you killed her, and he supposed that the only way you might have found her was if you had put her there to begin with."

Rhodrick chuckled. "Did he indeed?" he asked coldly. He reached into his pocket and withdrew a set of keys, then fit a key into the lock and opened it.

The door did not open easily. The wood had swollen, and Rhodrick had to force it open with his shoulder. As the door swung open, the musty smell that emanated from the room nauseated him.

But he forced himself to stride inside, his hand groping along the shelf for the stack of candles he knew was there, guided by the light filtered through a dirty window. He found the tinderbox, and with some doing, managed to light the flint.

Greer was standing across the threshold, looking ill.

"Come in, then, and have a look about," he said angrily. "You wanted this."

She hesitated before taking a single tentative step across the threshold.

The room had obviously been untouched for years, just as Miss Yates had left it the night she escaped. The evidence of her increasing madness lay all around them. In the corner, a table had been overturned and the oil from the lamp had spilled, leaving a dark, indelible stain. A garment on the bed had been ripped in several places, as if someone had taken a dagger to it. A tea service lay in fragments of china on the floor beneath the wall where it had been hurled, judging by the splatters of tea on the silk paper and the bits crushed under the weight of a man's boot.

As Greer stepped deeper into the room, she put her hand to her mouth.

"You have given me Percy's version of events," Rhodrick said. "Now I shall give you mine. It was Percy who compromised Miss Morwena Yates, Greer — not I. He seduced a naïve, innocent young woman much like you, took her virtue when he was not, as was his habit, in the bed of a married woman in Powys, and pledged a love for Miss Yates that he did not possess in his black heart."

Greer picked up a piece of needlework, still in the circular frame, the canvas yellowed with age.

"When Miss Yates discovered she was carrying his child, instead of doing the honorable thing — for the honorable thing was never Percy's concern — he dismissed her and left her to fend for herself. As you might imagine, the shame she had brought on her family was so great that they could scarcely bear it."

Greer shifted her gaze to the bed.

"I accepted the responsibility that Percy would not and had sent the young woman to a safe place to bear her child. She bore Percy a daughter — but she did not take the position of governess I had secured for her in Cornwall, as I believed. She had, in her grief, convinced herself she was quite in love with Percy. Unbeknownst to me, she returned to Rhayader with the hope of gaining his affection and support."

Greer turned slightly, so that he could not see her face; but he saw the rise and fall of her shoulders as she took a steadying breath.

"In the meantime, I had let Kendrick to Percy with the vain hope that he would settle in and refrain from his scandalous behavior. Miss Yates came to Kendrick, no doubt desperate for him to right the terrible wrong he'd done her. He would not see her, of course, or acknowledge her in any way. In fact, he sent her away, for she had, to all intents and purposes, ceased to exist for him. But in her desperation, Miss Yates returned to Kendrick once more to see Percy. Unfortunately, on the night she appeared, my wretched nephew had gathered some influential men of Powys with the hope of securing a loan for some ridiculous venture or another."

He shifted his gaze to Greer. "Miss Yates embarrassed him — Percy has always been far more concerned about himself than anyone else, and, I think, feared what his potential investors might think more than he cared about the woeful condition he had put on Miss Yates. So he escorted her here, to this room, where they argued. When it became apparent she would not leave, he locked her inside rather than have her embarrass him again. And here is where he kept her, in this seldom-used wing of the house, locked away for almost a fortnight."

"If that is so, then why was Mr. Percy not brought to the proper authorities when it was discovered?" Greer asked.

Rhodrick smiled coldly. "Because Miss Yates was nowhere to be found."

He held the candle high and walked across the room to stand before her. "It was days after her initial disappearance that her father faced what he thought was true — that she'd fled her shame. Percy confirmed it. He said she'd come to Kendrick, and they had argued. He even confessed to having put her away until his guests had departed. But he swore to me that he'd then advised her to go home to her mother and seek her solace there. He claimed to have never seen her again after that night. But in reality, he'd held her prisoner here as he considered what to do," he said, gesturing to the room. "Lord knows how long he might have left her when she turned mad. Look at her clothing, cut to ribbons. Look at the furniture overturned, the tea service hurled against the wall. See the scratching here?" he asked, pointing to words that were impossible to make out beneath the window sash. "She scratched those with her fingernails."

"But . . . what happened then?" Greer asked breathlessly.

"She surprised the old crone Percy had hired to tend her one day, knocking her to the floor and then fleeing into the wilderness, mad with despair."

"Oh dear God," Greer whispered.

Rhodrick glanced around. "I have left this room exactly as it was found with the fruitless hope that one day, justice would be served." He turned back to Greer.

The look of loathing in her eyes had been replaced by sadness. "How do you know what happened? Did Percy tell you?"

He could feel the color bleed from his face as he remembered the morning he had confronted Percy with his suspicions. "Not exactly. Percy panicked when he could not

460

find her, I suppose. He fabricated a tale in which he said that a mad Miss Yates had come back to Kendrick and then fled into the forest. Every able-bodied man in Powys searched for Miss Yates. We began at sunup and searched until dusk, but it wasn't until the fifth day that she was found. By then, Percy had failed to pay the crone for her trouble, so she confessed her part in it to me and accused Percy of locking Miss Yates away."

"But . . . but why didn't Miss Yates seek her family when she escaped?"

Rhodrick sighed, regretting that he must tell her such a wretched tale. "Unfortunately we will never know what truly happened. By the time Miss Yates was found, most of her body was gone, scavenged by animals. From what was left of her, we know that her neck had been broken. I think as she fled, she became disoriented and ran deep into the forest. She was probably unaware of the ravine and fell to her death."

Greer made a sound of distress and turned away, lurching unsteadily for the door and grabbing the frame. "I don't understand! If this is true, then why hasn't Mr. Percy been brought to justice?"

Rhodrick shrugged and glanced at the embroidery. "Because it was a gentleman's word against that of an old woman who had a fondness for drink."

"How did you find her?" Greer demanded. "He said you found her. He said that in all these acres, only *you* could find her. *How?*"

Rhodrick debated telling her. At the moment, he hardly cared if she thought him mad. But he'd never told a soul that extraordinary tale, had never voiced it aloud, and he could not bring himself to start now. "Luck," he said.

"*Luck?* You would have me believe it was *luck* that led you through thousands of acres to find her?"

His hand curled around the candle, gripping it tightly. "What other explanation is there? Perhaps you still believe Percy."

"I find it extraordinary," she said, with far less calm than he, "that you continue to distrust me. I only wonder aloud how you might possibly have found a woman's devoured corpse in so many empty acres. Did a bird tell you? Did you remain silent to protect someone? Do you not find it remarkable that you alone knew where to find that poor creature?"

"I have answered you plainly. What else could you possibly need to hear?"

She turned toward the door. "I cannot bear to be in this room at all . . . much less with you."

"The feeling is entirely mutual," he said, and blew out the candle, sending the room and his heart into blackness.

They hardly spoke at all as they made their way back to the horses. When they reached them, Rhodrick came behind Greer, putting his hands to her waist to lift her up, but Greer pushed them away. "I can do it," she said, and struggled to lift herself up.

An old, familiar feeling of unworthiness rushed up within him and he turned away, mounted Cadfael, and spurred him forward. He did not look to see if she followed — he scarcely cared if she did.

As they rode to Llanmair, his knee ached fiercely and he noticed the air turning colder and damper. They were in for quite a storm, he reckoned, and wished to be in the privacy of his study so that he might massage his knee.

Alone.

By the time they arrived at Llanmair, the first few snowflakes had begun to fall. Greer hardly seemed to notice; she marched past him, disappearing inside. When he entered behind her, she had yanked the hood of her cloak off her head and was struggling to undo the clasp. Rhodrick meant to walk by, to leave her, but he caught sight of the man standing in the shadows, still wearing a cloak.

Greer must have seen him at the same time for she made a sound of surprise. "My lord Harrison!" she exclaimed.

"Miss Fairchild," he said, bowing low. "I have brought you a letter from the marquis of Middleton."

"Ava!" Greer cried with apparent relief, and took the vellum from the man.

He, in turn, shifted a cold gray gaze to Rhodrick. "Geoffrey Godwin, Viscount Harrison, at your service, my lord. I have come on behalf of the marquis of Middleton to bring his sister-in-law safely home. At *once.*"

TWENTY-EIGHT

Dearest Greer,
We are <u>desperately</u> worried and hope that this letter finds you well and unharmed! The situation seems absolutely dreadful and you really must come home at once, darling! We have enclosed a letter from the marquis of Middleton in which he vouches for your true identity and character, and naturally, Lord Harrison has the funds necessary to see you home posthaste!

"You needn't worry about that, Phoebe," Greer muttered as she paced her room. "I shall leave at first light!"

You must believe that I take no satisfaction in being proven completely right about this journey — I knew it was a ghastly idea from the start! You are lucky you haven't gotten yourself killed if you haven't already. Ava stands nearby and she asks that I remind you that you said you'd not be gone for more than <u>one</u> month, <u>two</u> at the most, and now it is almost <u>nine!</u> We had all but given you up for lost!

"If only I had listened to you then!" Greer cried, shaking the vellum at the painted ceiling.

I regret to inform you that your Mr. Percy has not called on the marquis on your behalf. Ava said that is because it has been an unusually rainy autumn, that he is surely and unavoidably detained. I rather think that he might have traveled at least faster than the post. Ava and I had quite a row about it, but it is really of no consequence now, for we have received word that you are alive, thank heavens!

Now you must come home, Greer, for all is restored to us. Not our mother's fortune, of course, for Lord Downey is, according to Mr. Laramie, the solicitor, quite within his right to keep it and shows no indication of wishing to share even a portion of it. But the marquis is a very generous man, particularly to me, for he understands now what I have endured living with Ava all these years. He has made available enough funds to see us both properly married, so please do come home. Lord Harrison will see that you do.

I must close now. Ava is feeling poorly and needs me, although she is very stubborn and will not admit it. She has not endured her delicate situation very delicately at all, and really she has always been rather cross with even the slightest headache.

"Her delicate condition? Ava?" Greer whimpered, sinking on to the settee.

We did tell you she is with child, did we not?

"No, Phoebe, you did not! But when?"

We anxiously await your return! All our love, P.F.

"Oh, Phoebe!" Greer cried, closing her eyes. "Couldn't you at least have told me how long she's been carrying the child?"

She read the letter again, then the letter attached to it from the marquis, in which he greeted the earl of Radnor as if they were acquaintances, vouching for Greer and her identity and informing him she'd be leaving in Lord Harrison's company at the first opportunity.

She was leaving.

She had her inheritance and would leave this awful place once and for all.

And she did find it awful, didn't she? Not a single modern convenience to be had, not like in London. And really, all the peace and solitude could drive a person quite mad. Not a bit of society, and one had to travel *miles* just to have tea with someone other than the staff.

Granted, she couldn't bear the thought of leaving Kendrick — but given the horrific events at that house, she could hardly see how she might stay. She shuddered at the memory of Rhodrick's tale and the question raised itself again: How had he found Miss Yates? A forgotten trail? Someone whose identity he needed to protect?

However he'd found her, the tale was too gruesome, and Kendrick would always be tainted with it. Had she been the prince, she would have endeavored to wash away all memory of that tragedy. She would have cleaned the room and painted it a bright and cheerful color. She would have brought that grand house to life again.

But she was not the prince. She was scarcely even Welsh any longer. Seeing Harrison again — dressed in finery found only in London and Paris, his demeanor impeccable — had reminded her of all that London had to offer. That was where she truly belonged.

She had simply passed the weeks playing at a fantasy here, but now that Harrison had come, she could plainly see that she did not belong here. Ava and Phoebe were waiting for her, and she was desperate to see them.

It was settled. She had to leave. She had to take her inheritance and leave this place with all its secrets. And Kendrick. *And she had to leave him.*

Greer fell back against the settee, one arm draped over her belly, the letters lying listlessly in her hand.

She really had no choice.

But oh, how she dreaded it! And for so many conflicting reasons that it gave her a stifling headache.

That night she dreamt of her mother, standing, as always, in the door of Kendrick, beckoning Greer into a grand mansion. Greer entered as she always did, trying to reach her mother before she disappeared, trying to catch her, to put her hand on her before she faded away, and as always, she could not reach her.

But she did reach Rhodrick. Somehow, she went from following her mother to being in his arms again, in the grand salon at Kendrick. Only it was no longer an empty shell, but a palace, with crystal chandeliers and beeswax candles and thick wool rugs at her feet. She was dressed in a resplendent ball gown of pale blue silk, and somewhere, an orchestra played a waltz.

She danced a waltz with Rhodrick, moving sure-footedly across a highly polished dance floor, twirling beneath the glittering crystals.

He moved her with grace and ease, and she seemed to float securely in his arms, basking in his brilliant gaze, the feel of his hard body surrounding hers. She did not fear him. She *loved* him.

When Lulu arrived the next morning, Greer had already dressed in a somber brown and black traveling gown, for she had every intention of leaving as soon as a coach could be summoned from Rhayader. Lulu looked surprised, but did not question Greer's request that she pack her trunk. She did, however, tell her that Lord Harrison awaited her in the red salon.

"Please tell him I shall attend him very soon, but that I must first have a word with the prince."

Greer found the prince in his study, a fire blazing at the hearth, his head bent over some papers. He scarcely glanced up when she entered. Cain and Abel, as usual, greeted her enthusiastically. "Yes?" he asked dismissively, as he might inquire of a servant.

"I have a letter from the marquis," she said, walking across the room to hand it to him. "It should answer all your questions."

"I have no questions," he said briskly.

Greer's eyes narrowed. "It is directed to you."

With a sigh, he held out his hand. Greer put it in his open palm, and noticed the haggard look around his eyes, the edge of pain in them. By his elbow sat a tot of whiskey at this early hour. His knee was paining him, she knew.

He quickly opened the letter, scanning the contents, expressionless. When he had finished, he folded the vellum and handed it back to her.

"Well, then, there we have it. You are indeed Miss Greer Fairchild of Mayfair." He glanced down at his desk. "Congratulations. I will send you from Llanmair at the first opportunity."

"I think it is best," Greer said softly.

"Then we are in agreement," he responded without rancor. "Unfortunately for us both, the weather is not in agreement."

"The weather," she repeated, trying desperately to gauge his reaction, to detect any hint of regret, any sadness.

"I don't think you will be leaving today or tomorrow," he said, turning his attention back to his work. "You must endeavor to abide Llanmair a bit longer."

Greer jerked her gaze to the window and hurried to it, pushing aside the heavy drapes and bracing her hands against the stone sill as she leaned over to see out. Llanmair was an island in a sea of snow.

And it was still falling.

"But . . . but I cannot wait! I am ready to leave now!" she exclaimed. "There must be *some* way out!"

"You might walk out, if you think you are capable. But I will not risk man or animal to take you."

Now that her decision was made, the thought of staying was excruciating. She couldn't see him and not feel his pain — or hers, for that matter. "I cannot bear a delay," she said with some desperation. "It is not to be borne!"

He moved before she even saw him, was at her back before she could turn from the window, his arm like a vise around her waist, holding her tightly to him, to his broad chest, his powerful legs. "You think you are alone in that?" he breathed into her ear. "Do you think it easy for me? One moment you want my arms around you and the next you cannot bear to look at me."

"That's not *true* —"

He abruptly forced her around to look at him. "Do you find me so hideous?" he demanded, his gaze raking over her. "You did not find me so hideous when I was making love to you." He bent his head, his mouth in her hair. "You *enjoyed* my touch."

She felt the heat of the truth in that statement flow through her body and with both hands she pushed hard against his chest. "Rhodrick, *stop.*"

To her horror, he kissed her neck, sending a red-hot jolt of desire through her. "Are you as callous as that, Greer?" he murmured in her ear, his breath hot on her skin. "Can you lie with a man without the slightest care for what is in his heart?"

She turned her head away, squeezing her eyes tightly shut against a tide of tears that had erupted from nowhere. "God in heaven,

Rhodrick, I care more than you know!" she cried angrily. "But I cannot make you happy, nor you me. I don't belong here, I don't want to *be* here! This is the *only* way."

He did not speak at first; she opened her eyes, saw something hard in him had risen up. He dropped his gaze to her mouth and looked at her in a way that made her body erupt with furious longing.

"So do I care, Greer. So do I," he said gruffly. "No, you do not belong here, and nor do I want you here. That is why I will send you away as soon as possible."

His words were what she had wanted to hear, but instead of relief, they only brought her pain, striking her with such force that tears suddenly began to fall. She could not speak. There was nothing in her throat but sobs.

He pulled her into his embrace and bowed his head over hers for a moment. "Trust your instincts," he said, and caught her mouth in a kiss so full of longing that had he not held her up, she would have fallen to her knees.

She felt helpless with desire, weak in her resolve, and worse still, she felt an almost preternatural feeling of love for him.

But then he suddenly released her, stumbling back, dragging the back of his hand across his mouth, his eyes blazing with heat and sorrow.

"Please leave me now, for I am done with our brief acquaintance."

She suppressed a sob of grief, gathered her skirt in one hand, and walked out of his study and into the corridor without looking back. It wasn't until she had turned the corner that she began to run for the privacy of her suite so that she might weep.

Twenty-Nine

The snow stopped that afternoon but the wind raged into the night, making the old castle groan like a chorus of old souls. Greer remained in her suite of rooms and did not emerge again until supper that night, looking worn and pale. Lord Harrison joined them, and spent most of his meal making polite conversation while observing Rhodrick with suspicion.

Rhodrick was grateful when the interminable meal was over for he could not bear to see her face.

He was feeling absurdly directionless, almost as if he were walking in the blizzard with no sense of up or down. He could not begin to guess how everything had changed so, how he had gone from being euphoric with love to wishing Greer had never come to Llanmair. If he had the power, he would rip the clouds from the sky with his bare hands and drag the sun to beat down on

Llanmair, just so that the snow would melt and she could *leave* here and his torment would end.

When she was gone, he would return to his life, his simple life, and think no more of her.

Unfortunately, his mind was refusing to cooperate. He was tortured with dreams of her, of her body on his as she rode him, of her smile, and her blue eyes standing out in a sea of so many faded colors. And when he thought of kissing her, he knew nothing but the memory of her in his arms, the sublime feel of her body against his.

How could he, a wise man, have been made so desperate for love? Moreover, why had *she,* his ghost, brought Greer here?

There was only one possible explanation — just as Alis Bronwyn had come to show him the way to Miss Yates, she had brought Greer here. Nothing else could explain how a dead woman who had been haunting his dreams could be Greer's mother. When he'd seen the hand portrait Greer carried, he'd been stunned, and he'd known in that instant that there was only one possible way that Greer could have found her way to Llanmair. The knowledge that Alis had reached beyond the grave again was enough to drive him to the brink of madness.

He slept mostly on the settee in his study, beset by the pain in his knee and the images he could not banish from his mind's eye. When morning inevitably came, he felt half crazed with his thoughts. He and his dogs wandered the empty corridors of the castle, their breath freezing the moment it left their bodies. At least the sun was shining and the snow was melting.

His restless wandering took him to the library, where he found Harrison seated at the hearth, quietly reading. The man stood when Rhodrick entered, bowing. "Radnor," he said.

"Good afternoon, my lord," Rhodrick said as he crossed to the sideboard and poured a whiskey. "I trust you find your accommodations suitable?" he asked, motioning to the decanter of whiskey in silent question.

Harrison nodded. "I do indeed, thank you. I regret that we must impose on your hospitality a little longer."

Rhodrick shrugged as he poured another whiskey. "It is no imposition," he said truthfully, and handed the whiskey to Harrison. "Here. It will chase the chill away."

Harrison took the tot and drank.

"I rather supposed Miss Fairchild would be with you," Rhodrick remarked, taking a seat across from where Harrison had been sitting.

"She is in her rooms," he said, resuming his seat. He took another sip, then held the tot up to examine the color of the whiskey. "In truth, my lord, she seems to be rather conflicted."

That brought Rhodrick's head up. "Did she say so?" he asked, despising himself for sounding so eager.

Harrison calmly returned his gaze to Rhodrick. "She said quite a lot, actually. Miss Fairchild has developed a rather strong affection for Llanmair and its inhabitants. She talked at length about her visit here."

Rhodrick couldn't help but smile — no one knew better than he how the woman could talk when she was of a mind.

"She told me about the inheritance," Harrison added. "That was very kind of you."

"Kind?" Rhodrick smiled a little and shook his head. "It is rightfully hers. Frankly, I'd hoped that the sooner she had it, the sooner she'd be gone from my house."

The remark seemed to give Harrison pause. "I beg your pardon, but I am certain she did not mean to impose."

"Oh," Rhodrick said with a flick of his wrist, "I think you mistake my meaning. I mean only that this is no place for a young woman such as Miss Fairchild. It is time she returned to her family and her life."

"Yes," Harrison said, and drained the tot of whiskey in one gulp. "I will happily see that she is safely returned." He smiled as he put the tot aside. "Thank you for the whiskey. If you will excuse me, I shall go and see her."

"Of course," Rhodrick said, and looked broodingly at the fire as he listened to Harrison's footfall moving away from him.

When supper was announced, Lulu asked Greer if she would dine with Lord Harrison, as his lordship had retired.

"Retired?" Greer asked. "As early as this?"

"His leg, miss. I think it bothers him greatly today."

"Oh," she said weakly, feeling a sharp pain of empathy for him.

She and Harrison dined alone, seated side by side before the hearth, the better to keep warm.

"You haven't much of an appetite tonight," Harrison remarked.

Greer smiled miserably. "It's too cold, I think."

Lord Harrison nodded and took another bite of beef stew. "The cold makes me ravenous," he said. "It's nature's way of fattening us up for the long winter months."

"Ah," Greer said, and speared a bite of potato. But she couldn't eat it — her nerves had her stomach in knots. "I beg your pardon, Lord Harrison, but would you think ill of me if I excused myself? I am feeling a headache coming on."

"Again?" he asked, looking at the stew.

"The cold," she said weakly.

"Of course," he said, and stood instantly, helping her out of her chair. But as Greer walked away, he stopped her. "Miss Fairchild?"

She paused and looked back at him. "Do you think your headaches will diminish once you reach London, or do you think they will worsen?"

She could feel herself color. "I . . . I don't rightly know, my lord," she said truthfully.

"Perhaps you should consider which place better suits your health," he said, and smiled, then resumed his seat and his meal.

Greer walked out of the dining room, feeling weaker with every step she took. It was a fair question, she supposed, for she could scarcely bear the thought that she'd never see the prince again, that the next time she left the castle, it would be for good.

There were so many things tumbling about in her mind these days, so many conflicting emotions and questions about what was important in one's life.

Yet there was one question that she could not explain away, one question that kept everything at sixes and sevens. How had the prince known where to find the body of Miss Yates?

THIRTY

Harrison sent his driver to Rhayader the next morning to check the conditions of the roads. The man returned shortly after noon and declared the roads muddy but passable.

"I should return her to her family," Harrison said as he stood in Rhodrick's study. "Unless, of course, you think it is unsafe to travel," he said, looking at Rhodrick pointedly.

"No," Rhodrick said, averting his gaze. "If your man says the roads are passable, then by all means, you should go."

Harrison looked at him a moment longer, than nodded curtly. "We'll leave today," he said, and walked out of the study.

Rhodrick swallowed down another bitter swell of disappointment and limped to the bellpull. When Ifan appeared, he said, "Have Miss Fairchild's things readied. She is to London today."

As Ifan quit the study, Rhodrick stroked

Cain's large head and stared at the clear blue sky visible through his window. It was time, he told himself, to put this dream aside and move on with the business of his day. It was time to forget.

His only fear was that he'd spend every single day of the rest of his life forgetting.

Lord Harrison found Greer in the library, reading. "The coach is ready, Miss Fairchild. We can leave for London today."

"Today?" Greer exclaimed, startled.

"Today," Harrison reiterated. "Have you packed your things?"

Stunned, Greer shook her head. She had known this moment would come, but had thought there might be a bit more warning than this. "Are you certain a coach can leave today?"

He smiled almost sadly. "I am."

"Perhaps we should wait for better weather," she suggested anxiously.

"Greer," he said quietly, "your family is waiting for you. I don't think I need to tell you that to stay a moment longer than is absolutely necessary is unwise, for a variety of unpleasant reasons."

He referred to her reputation, of course.

"And besides," he continued gingerly, "your family wants you home where you belong."

Blast it, she could feel the salty sting of tears welling in her eyes. "Yes, of course you are quite right, my lord," she said. "I must return to my cousins." And how frightfully tedious *that* sounded. Now that Ava was married, Phoebe could not be far behind, and Greer — well, even if her reputation wasn't in tatters, she had no real prospects. She'd be a burden to them both.

She glanced up at Harrison. "All right," she said, and stood. "I've got quite a lot to do."

With the hour now upon her, she felt a jumbled mess of raw nerves. Out of habit, she put her hand to the necklace she always wore, the one the prince had said was a Welsh amulet.

She certainly didn't feel any magical force.

Two hours later, Greer was dressed, her trunk had been taken from her suite, and all that was left was to seat herself in the coach and go. Mrs. Bowen and Lulu were waiting for her in the small foyer, and as Lulu helped her on with her cloak under Harrison's watchful eye, Rhodrick appeared, his shoulder propped against the wooden door, his arms crossed over his chest.

Greer pulled the hood of her cloak over

her head so that she could not see his face, and said good-bye to Lulu and Mrs. Bowen.

"The address of my cousin's house is on my vanity," she said to Lulu. "Will you write me?"

"Of course, miss," Lulu said.

Greer smiled and squeezed her hand, then looked at Mrs. Bowen. "Thank you . . . for everything," she said, fighting to keep back the tears. "You have been too kind."

"We shall miss you, Miss Fairchild," Mrs. Bowen said warmly.

With a nod, Greer forced herself to turn and face the prince.

She had no idea what to say or do — it seemed absurd to curtsy to him after what they'd been to one another, but she did so without thinking. He watched her closely, his expression void of emotion. It seemed cruel that she should be the only one to feel this painful parting so deeply.

He pushed away from the wall, reached into his breast pocket, and withdrew a folded vellum tied with ribbon. "I took the liberty of writing to your brother-in-law to vouch for your conduct and the watchful eye of Mrs. Bowen during your stay at Llan-mair."

The act of kindness astounded her. His letter would go a long way toward protecting her reputation. "I . . . thank you," she said.

He gave her a short nod, then pressed his lips together as his gaze roamed her face. "Very well, then," he said quietly. "I wish you Godspeed in your journey home." His eyes drifted over her body, lingering on her eyes.

"Miss Fairchild," Lord Harrison said from somewhere near the door.

The prince turned and began to walk away, his gait slightly uneven, his hand clenching and unclenching at his side.

"Wait!" Greer said, and hurried after him. She reached up, unclasped the charm she wore around her neck. "I want you to have this," she said, holding it out to him. "It . . . it belongs here."

He glanced at the necklace, then at her.

"Please," she whispered, and took his hand and dropped the necklace in his palm. He closed his hand tightly around it, then put it in his pocket.

"Thank you," she said.

He nodded, and walked on. She watched him go, then turned uncertainly to Mrs. Bowen and Lulu.

"Cook prepared a basket for you, miss," Mrs. Bowen said. "It's filled with cheese and bread."

"How kind," Greer said absently, thinking about Rhodrick's walking away from her. "You must thank her for me."

"I put in the book of Wales you read," Lulu added. "His lordship said that I might."

"Oh," Greer said, feeling suddenly overwhelmed, once again seeing Rhodrick walking away, walking out of her life. "Thank you. That is . . . *really,* that is too kind." She forced a small smile, adjusted her hood once more, and glanced at the door Ifan had opened. A wintry blast of cold air filled the small foyer, and just beyond the door, in the courtyard, she could see the coach, the breath of the horses coming out in great plumes of white.

"I shall await you at the coach," Harrison said, clearly eager to be gone.

Mrs. Bowen folded her arms about her to warm herself. Lulu visibly shivered.

"Well then," Greer said, hesitating. "I suppose I must go now," she said. "I shall miss you dearly."

"And we you, Miss Fairchild," Mrs. Bowen said, who was now shivering alongside Lulu.

"I will be on my way then," she said, and glanced again at the door. Ifan looked at her expectantly; Mrs. Bowen and Lulu shivered more. Yet Greer could not seem to make her feet move.

"Miss?" Ifan said.

"Yes," she said, and moved stiffly to the door, managing to put one foot and then the other across the threshold. Behind her, Ifan quickly pulled the door closed and gestured for her to accompany him. He walked quickly to the coach, where Harrison stood by the open door, his gloved hand held out to her.

She reluctantly allowed him to hand her up. Harrison followed, taking the bench across from her.

"Godspeed, Miss Fairchild," Ifan said, and shut the door to the coach. She heard him shout up to the driver, saw him hurry back to the castle door to get out of the cold.

"Take heart," Harrison said kindly.

The coach lurched forward, and the gray walls of the castle with the birds' nests and the nicks and marks of ancient battles began to roll by. The big gates swung open; the coach lumbered through.

Greer turned as the coach passed through the gates and saw a pair of red kite hawks fly out of some crevice and soar into the blue sky.

She had no idea why, but seeing the red kites fly made her realize she could not leave, not without knowing how he had found Miss Yates, and she suddenly felt desperate to know. *She had to know.*

Greer suddenly pounded on the ceiling. "Stop!" she shouted. *"Stop!"*

"What are you doing?" Harrison exclaimed.

"I forgot something," she said breathlessly as the coach pitched to an abrupt halt. Greer was already out of the coach before anyone could climb down to help her. She was running as fast as she could on the tracks the coach had made in mud and slush, oblivious to Harrison's shouts. The hood of her cloak slipped off her head as she picked up the garment and struggled to reach the courtyard before the gates swung shut and Llanmair was forever gone.

Rhodrick was standing beside the window. As the coach rolled away, he clenched his jaw and pressed his palm to the cold glass. "It is for the best," he muttered. "It is best."

As he was about to turn away — he could not bear to see the coach disappear altogether — he saw it come to a sudden stop.

He paused; the door swung open and Greer all but fell out, righting herself at the last moment. She gathered her cloak in one hand and ran as Lord Harrison vaulted out

490

after her. But Greer ran in the mire as best she could, almost as if she fled from someone or something, and quickly disappeared from his view as she neared the castle.

Confused, Rhodrick turned and looked at the hearth, his mind and heart racing.

Several minutes later, one of the dogs lifted its head, and he heard a commotion down the corridor. In another moment, she was at his door, her chest rising and falling with her panting, her cheeks flushed. She braced herself with both hands against the door frame and looked at him with eyes as wide as saucers.

He self-consciously shoved a hand through his hair. "Have you forgotten something?"

"How did you find her?" she rasped. "Please! I must know the answer, Rhodrick."

The question made his heart sink, and he abruptly turned away. "There is no point in treading over old ground —"

"There is *every* point," she insisted, coming into the room. "I have been wrong about *everything* else, and it is the only question remaining."

That earned his attention; he jerked his gaze to her and noticed that her eyes were glistening. "You've been wrong?"

"*Astoundingly* wrong," she said, flinging

her arms wide in an effort to show him just how wrong as she struggled for breath.

He turned fully toward her. His heart had begun to skip and drum erratically in his chest on a wild, ridiculous hope.

"I thought the house . . ." She sighed, pressed her fists to her temple a moment. "I cannot seem to put aside the question of how you found her."

She looked up to him and clasped her hands together at her breast. Her blue eyes implored him as she moved deeper into the room, closer to him. "I am pleading with you now — tell me how you found her, I beg of you. Tell me how you found Miss Yates so that I might go back to London secure in the knowledge that I was right to deny myself the best and happiest thing I have ever known in my life!"

"I cannot, Greer," he said quietly, his heart and mind racing frantically. "I cannot."

"But *why?*" she cried. "What more can there be than what I have already made of it?"

He wanted nothing more than to take her in his arms and confess all to her. "Because I could not bear to see the look in your eyes when you believe that I am mad."

"How can I think you mad?" she asked

earnestly, her eyes glistening. "How can I think anything but that I love you?"

The admission stunned him — Rhodrick suddenly understood that if he was to make her his as he desperately wanted to do, he had to tell her the truth. And there was nothing more to lose at this point. He summoned his courage and said simply, "Your mother showed me."

Greer paled. She seemed incapable of speech and sank heavily onto the chair at the hearth. It was as if she'd been wounded, was in some sort of pain. "M-my mother died almost fourteen years ago."

"Yes," he said, nodding. "I am well aware." He shoved both hands through his hair, trying to think how he might explain this madness. "I never even knew her. She was gone from Kendrick when I was just a lad."

Greer's hand fluttered to her throat, to the place the amulet had hung. "Is this some sort of jest?" she asked weakly.

"No," he said with a firm shake of his head. "Would that it were." He winced at Greer's expression of horror. "Just . . . just hear me, Greer. Just listen, will you?"

Her stunned expression was his reply.

"There are many in Powys who believe in Welsh lore and magic, but I've never been among them. I've always rather thought that

493

the belief in spirits was for the uneducated."

Greer blinked; she was unmoving, her gaze riveted on him.

He looked helplessly at his hands. "As I told you, Morwena Yates was quite in love with Percy. She believed his wretched lies and held on to the absurd hope that he would make an honest woman of her. I know, for she told me as much. Of course I tried to dissuade her, but there was nothing I or her parents could do to convince her, and inevitably, Percy ruined her. It is as I told you — I sent her to Cornwall to bear her child and to take up a position as governess. But she returned, desperate to win his affection, and that night she appeared uninvited at Kendrick." He glanced up at Greer and said bitterly, "I so foolishly let Kendrick to him."

Greer said nothing, but swallowed hard.

"How shall I tell you this?" he asked, more of himself than of her. "How shall I relate what happened? You will think it madness, Greer, but when Miss Yates went missing, I knew she'd met with her death because I had *dreamt* it."

Greer's sharp intake of breath was a knife to his heart. "Steel yourself, for I must tell you furthermore that . . . Alis Bronwyn, whom I knew as an older child when I was but a lad, and had met only once or twice when I came of age, came to me in a dream. She was standing at the door of Kendrick, beckoning me forward."

With a sound of great despair, Greer covered her mouth with her hand.

He would lose her with the truth, Rhodrick thought, and turned away from her, finding the look on her face unbearable. "When in my dream I followed the . . . the *apparition,* I suppose you might call her, I saw the room where Miss Yates had been kept. I *saw* her there, going mad in that room."

He dared not glance at Greer, dared not see the denunciation of his admittedly bizarre dream in her eyes. But he'd said too much to stop now, so he continued, "Naturally, I thought it only a dream." The horror of it all began to rise up in him again.

"A week or so later, my fears were confirmed when Mr. and Mrs. Yates called on me to relate that their daughter had gone missing. I confronted Percy, and he denied it. But I took myself to that room and found it, just as you saw it. That was when Mrs. Evans, who'd tended to Miss Yates, confessed that Miss Yates had escaped.

"I organized search parties at once, of course. I rode every day, all day, to the point of exhaustion, looking for her and finding nothing. As you said, there are thousands of empty acres here."

He paused; it was difficult recounting this aloud. He'd refused to even think of it these last few years. "When . . . when I had given up all hope of finding her," he said haltingly, "I had another dream. Your mother came to me again, standing at the door of Kendrick. This time, she whispered where I should look for Miss Yates. 'The old canal bridge,' she said."

He glanced at Greer from the corner of his eye. She was staring blankly at him, her eyes rimmed with an emotion he could not and dared not fathom.

"I left before dawn the next morning, and I searched around the old canal bridge for the better part of the day. I found nothing, and naturally, I thought I was losing my mind. But she came to me again that night, and once again urged me to look at the old canal bridge." He chuckled derisively at his own tale. "One might think with all the preternatural assistance I was receiving, I might have found Miss Yates. Yet I searched another day to no avail. On the third night, your mother showed me the precise place. She *took* me there in a dream. I could see Miss Yates plainly, lying at the bottom of the ravine."

He stopped and glanced heavenward. He had seen her lying there in the exact manner in which he later found her. "The next morning, I remembered the path and a peculiar fork. I rode again, and this time, I crawled down the steep embankment and I found her. She had fallen — or jumped — who can know considering her state of mind? But her neck was broken."

He dragged his gaze to Greer. Tears were glistening in her eyes, but she remained silent. "I should never have found her," he said, his voice low. "*No* one should have found her, not as remote as her body was. I told the authorities that my dogs had found her. No one questioned it — I rather believe they all think that in the course of searching thousands of empty acres, the dogs and I stumbled upon her."

Greer said nothing. He waited, silently begging her to say *something.* But she didn't speak; she covered her face with her hands and sobbed.

Rhodrick could not possibly have felt worse. She was no doubt lamenting the surrender of her virtue to a madman, and an ugly one at that. He turned to the window and stared out at the crystal blue sky.

He had no idea why, after all these years,

he had voiced aloud the very thoughts he'd struggled to put away. The price of it was too great to pay, the pain of it unbearable.

"I closed Kendrick, of course," he said, wondering vaguely why he continued to talk. "Because such a heinous crime occurred there, and because of the ghost that had long been rumored to roam those halls — well before your mother was born — I was convinced it was prudent. And I did not dream of your mother again until you appeared on my doorstep in the company of Mr. Percy."

He glanced at her from the corner of his eye and felt a dangerous swell of sorrow and longing. "Admittedly, that night, I had been drinking quite a lot to dull the pain in my leg — but when I saw the amulet around your neck, and your . . . lovely blue eyes," he said, almost choking on the words, "the only *true* color in this grayish world of mine, I mistakenly thought you were her. I did not realize the connection until you showed me the hand portrait. I recalled that she'd married, but I had quite forgotten the name of Vaughan. It is a rather common name in these parts. Since you have come, I have dreamed of her thrice more . . . always at the door of Kendrick, always beckoning me inside."

Greer continued sobbing quietly.

"Please do stop," he said. She did not move. He drew a deep breath and walked to her side. He withdrew the handkerchief from his pocket that he had carried with him every day since she'd come and went down on one knee before her. He touched her leg; Greer uncovered her face and looked at the handkerchief as he unfolded it, removing her amulet, which he'd put there for safekeeping and the ring he'd foolishly given her, and handed her the cloth.

She looked at the amulet and ring in his hand, and the handkerchief she thought she'd lost, and understanding dawned in her eyes. More tears fell as she carefully took it from his hand.

"Please stop," he begged softly. "Your tears are unbearable for me, for I have loved you, Greer. I have loved you from the beginning of time, long before I ever met you. And now I have dashed all hope of loving you with my mad ramblings. There now," he said, with a tender caress of her knee. "You have the answer you sought and Lord Harrison is waiting to take you home. There is no need to burden yourself further."

Greer did not get up and run from him as he'd hoped; she caught a sob in her throat and flung herself at him so suddenly that he scarcely caught her. She fell down on her knees before him and buried her face in his shoulder. Rhodrick tried to sit her up, but she clutched desperately at him, and he stilled, lifting his hands in the air, afraid to touch her.

"Can you ever forgive me?" she sobbed. "Please forgive me, Rhodrick! I love you, I *have* loved you, too! To think that all this time, she was leading me to *you* and bringing me home where I belonged!"

He grabbed her shoulders and forced her to look up. "What are you saying?"

Greer dragged the back of her hand beneath her nose. "You are not mad! I know what you are telling me is true, because *I* have had those very dreams of her! Always standing at the door at Kendrick, smiling and beckoning me within! But the last times I have followed her inside, *you* have been waiting there!"

She abruptly grabbed Rhodrick by the arms. "Don't you see?" she demanded frantically, shaking him. "I have had a single dream of my mother for years. From the time I was a girl, after she died, I dreamt of her standing at the door of a big white house — a house I didn't even know existed until I saw Kendrick. Rhodrick, I *dreamt* of Kendrick before I ever thought to come to

Wales! She brought me to you," she said wildly, taking his face in her hands. "She brought me to *you*." She flung her arms around his neck and cried.

Somewhere in the space of that moment, his heart began to pound so hard that he feared it would push through his skin. "But how —"

"I don't know!" Greer cried. "I scarcely care! But I know it is true, I know that she has given you to me. She has watched over me when I despaired what would become of me, and she led me to you."

Rhodrick pulled her arms from his neck, took her hand, and pressed it against his chest. "Do you feel it? It has not beat so wildly as this in thirty-eight years of living. It only began to beat when you came to Llanmair, Greer. You can't leave me." He grabbed her face between his hands, kissed her forehead, her nose, her lips. "Promise me you will never leave me."

"I can promise you no less," she said. "I love you, Rhodi. Above all others, I love you."

For the first time in his life, Rhodrick felt his heart truly soar.

Forty minutes later, Ifan led Lord Harrison to the portrait gallery, of all places, where the prince and Miss Fairchild stood. The prince's hair was mussed, his neckcloth quite undone, and he was smiling like the village idiot.

"Miss Fairchild," Harrison said sternly, "the carriage is waiting. Are you coming?"

"Carriage?" the prince casually repeated, then, as memory served, he nodded. "Yes, of course. You are no doubt in a hurry to be on your way, my lord, but I should hope you would stay until a special license is obtained and the vicar can join us." He looked at Ifan. "Send for him, Ifan, will you, and a special license. No, no, never mind. I shall fetch the license myself."

Next to him, Miss Fairchild giggled, and the prince smiled at Harrison. "You will stay, won't you, Harrison?"

And Rhodrick smiled broadly, as broadly as Ifan had ever seen him smile in his thirty-odd years of service at Llanmair. He blinked at his smiling lord, then bowed sharply and turned, walking briskly from the gallery. As he went, however, he was certain that he heard the prince laugh.

He arrived in the foyer, where Mrs. Bowen and Lulu, freezing to death, waited for Miss Fairchild.

"Well?" Mrs. Bowen asked.

"Have her trunk brought in," Ifan said,

and rolled his eyes when the two women squealed with delight.

THIRTY-ONE

Down on her knees, pinning the last folds of the gown she was making for Ava, who could scarcely fit into anything now that she was carrying a child, Phoebe had a mouthful of straight pins. She almost inhaled the lot of them when Lucille burst into the room, holding vellum aloft. "Lord Harrison has returned!" she cried.

Phoebe quickly spit out the pins and sat back on her heels. "I swear it, Lucy, one day you will find me sprawled in a fit of apoplexy, you do startle me so. Has Greer come with him?"

"However should I know?" Lucy asked. "Your sister Ava sent a messenger to say that you are to come soon, for Harrison will call on Middleton this afternoon."

"Oh!" Phoebe cried. "That can only mean she's come home!"

But when Phoebe arrived at Ava's later that day, breathless and smiling, she found no one about but Ava, who paced restlessly in the salon, one hand on her growing belly, the other on the small of her back.

"Has she come?" Phoebe asked, her smile fading.

"I don't know!" Ava said irritably. "I can't understand *why* Harrison is being so coy, so I've sent Middleton over to have a look. It is just as I told Middleton —"

The door swung open at that moment, and Middleton himself strolled in. "What did you tell me, darling?" he asked calmly. "Or perhaps a more appropriate question is, what have you *not* told me?" he asked, and chuckled with amusement at his own jest.

"Jared!" Ava cried. "Where is she? Has she come?"

He extended his hand, holding a vellum between two fingers.

"Not another letter!" Ava exclaimed as Phoebe snatched it from her brother-in-law's hand and broke the seal.

"Well? Is it from Greer?" Ava demanded.

"It is," Phoebe said, and unfolded the vellum. *"Dearest Phoebe and Ava,"* she read aloud. *"I have the most extraordinary news! I was quite wrong about the prince, and now we are to be married!"*

"Oh my *God!*" Phoebe cried, sinking onto

a settee.

"What?" Ava shrieked, taking a seat next to Phoebe. "What else does it say? Give it over," she insisted, and reached for it, but Phoebe batted her hand away as the marquis strolled to the window and stared out as she read.

"I shall be married when this letter reaches you. Please do not be cross, for the prince and I agreed that it was improper for me to remain here another moment without the benefit of marriage, and Lord Harrison agreed, so there was really no time to invite you all to Wales for the ceremony. I know you must have many questions, and I shall answer them all when we return to London in the spring. I could not bear to be away for Ava's lying-in.

"Oh darlings, I cannot wait for you to meet him, for he is a most extraordinary man —"

"Is she referring to the same man she previously called an ogre and a beast?" Ava demanded.

"Apparently," Phoebe said, frowning, and continued to read. *"He is kind and wise and quite well traveled and very tolerant of my views of Parliament. I hope you will come to love my husband as I do. Please thank the marquis for his generous letter and Lord Harrison to see me home. It seems neither is needed any longer. Lord Harrison is a bit* cross, for another snow makes it impossible for him to travel, and he claims to be stranded here. I must close now, for we are to host a Christmas soirée. With love, G."

"Oh dear *God!*" Ava exclaimed, and snatched the letter from Phoebe's hand. "And I had *so* hoped to present her to our guests at our gathering this evening. Now it shall be dreadfully tiresome."

"Oh, I think not," Middleton said easily. "You have yet to host a tiresome event, darling."

Ava looked at Phoebe and rolled her eyes, then slumped back against the chair, one hand resting listlessly on her belly. Phoebe joined her, staring morosely at the carpet, wondering if they would ever see Greer again.

In a posh hotel in London that very afternoon, Greer straightened Rhodrick's neckcloth. "A gathering," he said, the distaste evident in his voice. "A lot of sitting about and wishing to be somewhere else, isn't it?"

"Speak for yourself, Radnor," Lord Harrison said gruffly. "Some of us have been put away in Wales too long without the company of beautiful women."

Rhodrick grinned at that.

"I don't know if it is wise to surprise Ava and Phoebe," Greer said uncertainly. "They can be rather cross at times."

"They will be delighted," Harrison said. "I can't think of another pair who could possibly be more delighted with a surprise such as this. But now, if the prince and princess will excuse me, I believe my business here is complete. I shall see you tonight."

They said good-bye, and Rhodrick saw him out, thanking him for his help. When he returned to the dressing room, Greer was seated at her vanity. As he watched her don sparkling earbobs, he thought again that he was perhaps the luckiest man in all the world. The beautiful woman sitting here was his *wife*. It seemed almost a dream to him yet.

As for dreams, neither of them had dreamed of Alis since marrying. Having brought them together, she seemed to have left them to their happiness. But Rhodrick had dreamed of something else, and now he walked and stood behind Greer, and put his hand on her shoulder.

She smiled at him in the reflection of the glass.

"I should like to take a turn about town before we meet your cousins," he said.

"A turn?" She twisted about on the bench, caught his hand, and kissed it. "Surely you are not frightened of them?"

"Frightened of two young women who, by all accounts, are just like you?" He leaned over and kissed the top of her head. "I am trembling at the prospect."

Greer laughed and stood up, put her arms around him, and kissed him heartily. "Then a turn about town to help settle your nerves," she said. "But you mustn't fret. I won't let them eat you."

An hour later, Rhodrick directed his driver to proceed to Audley Street, near Hyde Park.

"Audley Street," Greer said, raising her brows with surprise. "One might mistake you for an English duke, my lord."

He smiled, took her hand in his. When they reached Audley Street, he directed the driver to stop. "Let's walk, shall we?"

"Walk?" Greer asked, peeking out the window. "But we are expected at Ava's."

"We will be at your cousins' soon enough," he said, opening the door. "Let us walk."

Greer sighed, but was smiling as he helped her down from the carriage. They walked past the first large town house, but at the second, Rhodrick paused and glanced up the steps to the double doors. Greer looked up, too, her face full of curiosity. "Who lives here?"

He smiled mysteriously, took her hand, and started up the steps.

"Rhodrick!" she said, tugging at his hand. "It is too late to call unannounced!"

"It is never too late," he said, and with a yank, pulled her up beside him. At the door, he knocked.

"You see? There is no one about," Greer said, and turned to go.

"Not so quickly, madam," he said, and withdrew a key from his pocket. As Greer watched, wide-eyed, he opened the door and held it open for her.

She leaned to her right, looked inside, and saw that it was vacant. "I don't understand."

"Sometimes I wonder what is in that head of yours," he said fondly, and gave her a gentle push over the threshold.

She twirled around in the foyer. "Whose place is this?" she asked again.

"Yours."

It took a moment for his response to register. But when it did, Greer turned slowly from where she stood, peering into an empty salon. "What did you say?"

"Tell me what you think of this, Lady Radnor. Suppose we were to spend the winter and spring in London so that you might dance and dazzle the masses with the art of your conversation during the Season, and then return to Llanmair in the summer and fall?"

She gasped, her eyes full of hope as she clasped her hands together at her throat. "Do you mean it, Rhodi?"

He smiled at his beautiful young wife. "Of course I mean it. You must know by now that I would do anything to make you happy, including spending the interminable social Seasons in London."

With a squeal of happiness, she rushed across the tiled entry to him, flinging her arms around him and kissing his face.

"But I won't like it in the least," he said, as she smothered him with kisses. "I will think it all a lot of flummery and nonsense. Harrison has assured me that I may join him at a gentlemen's club —"

"I love you," she said breathlessly, and kissed him on the mouth.

"I love *you*," he said, meaning it with every fiber of his being. "And it is alarmingly true that I would do anything for you."

"Anything?" she asked softly, and slid one hand down to the juncture of his legs, cupping him.

Rhodrick raised a brow. "What are you about, Mrs. Glendower?" he asked.

"I want to say thank you properly," she said, and with a mischievous smile, she slid down his body and to her knees to show him just how much she adored him.

A half hour later, Ava was sitting listlessly on the settee in her pristine grand salon, moping.

"You look piqued, my love," Middleton remarked.

Ava exchanged a look with Phoebe. "My good humor is dashed along with my hopes of ever seeing Greer again, if you must know."

"I do think she has abandoned us," Phoebe added, her good humor likewise gone.

"Good Lord," Middleton muttered. "Excuse me, ladies, but I think I hear someone at the door."

"Send them home, Jared. I can't possibly entertain," Ava said dramatically, and as her husband went out, she said to Phoebe, "I wanted him to send messengers around and cancel, but he wouldn't hear of it. He can be so beastly at times."

"You would think she would at least come to London to be married," Phoebe said, ignoring Ava's remarks about her husband, whom Phoebe knew she adored completely.

But she was still hurt that she'd not had the opportunity to make Greer's wedding dress. "Why did they have to marry in *Wales* of all places?"

"Didn't you read my letter?" Greer asked. "I was very clear why I married in Wales."

With twin shrieks of surprise, Ava and Phoebe scrambled to the door where Greer stood, grinning broadly. The three of them hugged one another tightly, their voices rising as they all chattered and laughed and squealed happily at once.

At the threshold, the marquis of Middleton stood beside the prince of Powys, earl of Radnor, watching them. "I don't believe I extended you a formal welcome to the family," Middleton said.

"Thank you," Radnor responded.

"I think it only fair to warn you that you should expect a lot of this sort of behavior."

"Indeed?"

"Oh yes," Middleton said, clasping his hands behind his back and nodding sagely. "And sometimes, they are angry with one another. On those occasions, it is much louder."

"That seems impossible," Radnor muttered.

Both men were startled when Ava's head

popped up and her eyes narrowed on Radnor. "He doesn't look the least like an ogre!" she declared as she suddenly started marching toward him.

"Gird your loins," Middleton muttered, and stepped away just as Ava reached him, staring up at him. Like her cousin, she was beautiful, but blond. And behind her was Phoebe, who was, Rhodrick thought, uncommonly beautiful. And behind her, his Greer, dark where they were light, beautiful and absolutely glowing with joy. She winked at him as Ava studied him.

"You are a wretched man," Phoebe said. "Tell him he is, Ava."

"You are," Ava agreed.

"I beg your pardon?"

"Really, sir, could you not have married in London? How could you have married without us?" Ava demanded.

"Don't answer her, Rhodrick, for you will only agitate her further," Greer warned cheerfully.

"Oh blast it," Ava said, and suddenly threw her arms around his neck, kissing his cheek. "How very wonderful it is to meet you, my lord. Anyone who can bear Greer for more than an hour without being *completely* exasperated is very welcome in this house and in this family," she said with a warm smile.

"Thank you."

"I am Phoebe, my lord," Phoebe said, curtsying politely, and then she, too, kissed his cheek. "Thank you for bringing our Greer safely home. I mean, to London, as I imagine she will live in Wales now."

"It is my great pleasure," he said, smiling at Greer.

"Come in, sir! You must sit and tell us all about Wales," Ava said, linking her arm through his.

But Phoebe stood back as she often did, watching as Ava seated herself beside the prince and Greer — a shining, glowing Greer — who sat across from her husband. It was clear that Greer loved him as much as Ava loved the marquis. And she was a princess now!

Blast it all, but it was precisely as Phoebe had feared. She was the last of the three to be married, and as she had no suitors clamoring for her hand, she undoubtedly would become the batty old spinster at whom the neighboring children would one day throw rocks.

At least she would be a finely dressed spinster, she thought in an effort to console herself, and glanced down, admiring her handiwork on a stunning green silk. She really was *quite* talented, if she did say so herself.

"Phoebe! Stop admiring yourself and come here," Ava called out to her. "He's telling us what awful things Greer did while she was in Wales."

"I was not awful!" Greer protested with mock indignation, but took Ava's hand and squeezed it fondly.

The prince caught Phoebe's eye and smiled so warmly that she was instantly drawn to him. Oh yes, she could see why Greer had married him, and she felt a ridiculously unbridled surge of happiness for her.

"Phoebe!" Ava insisted.

"Really, Ava, must you always command us to and fro?" Phoebe responded, but she was already moving forward to join her family.

ABOUT THE AUTHOR

Julia London is the *New York Times* and *USA Today* bestselling author of *The Hazards of Hunting a Duke* (the first novel in her Desperate Debutantes trilogy), *Highlander Unbound* (a finalist for the Romance Writers of America's RITA Award for Best Historical Romance), *Highlander in Disguise,* and *Highlander in Love* (also a finalist for the RITA Award) — all published by Pocket Star Books. She also contributed a short story, "The Merchant's Gift," to the anthology *The School for Heiresses.* Her other romantic novels include the Rogues of Regent Street trilogy. She lives in Austin, Texas. You can write to Julia at P.O. Box 228, Georgetown, Texas 78627, or email her at julia@julialondon.com.

The employees of Thorndike Press hope you have enjoyed this Large Print book. All our Thorndike and Wheeler Large Print titles are designed for easy reading, and all our books are made to last. Other Thorndike Press Large Print books are available at your library, through selected bookstores, or directly from us.

For information about titles, please call:
    (800) 223-1244

or visit our Web site at:
    www.gale.com/thorndike
    www.gale.com/wheeler

To share your comments, please write:
    Publisher
    Thorndike Press
    295 Kennedy Memorial Drive
    Waterville, ME 04901